Includes Bonus Story of
Strong as the Redwood
by Kristin Billerbeck

Love's Story

DIANNE
CHRISTNER

BARBOUR BOOKS
An Imprint of Barbour Publishing, Inc.

Love's Story (previously titled *Storm*) ©2000 by Dianne Christner
Strong as the Redwood ©1997 by Kristin Billerbeck

Print ISBN 978-1-63409-901-1

eBook Editions:
Adobe Digital Edition (.epub) 978-1-68322-036-7
Kindle and MobiPocket Edition (.prc) 978-1-68322-037-4

All scripture quotations are taken from the King James Version of the Bible.

This book is a work of fiction. Names, characters, places, and incidents are either products of the author's imagination or used fictitiously. Any similarity to actual people, organizations, and/or events is purely coincidental.

Published by Barbour Books, an imprint of Barbour Publishing, Inc., P.O. Box 719, Uhrichsville, OH 44683, www.barbourbooks.com

Our mission is to publish and distribute inspirational products offering exceptional value and biblical encouragement to the masses.

 Member of the
Evangelical Christian
Publishers Association

Printed in the United States of America.

Prologue

The storm that blew through the offices of *McClure's* magazine was five-foot-four and brunette. Meredith S. Mears's middle initial stood for Storm. Whether her parents named Storm after her personality or whether her personality took shape around her name, the other reporters knew not, but one thing stood certain, the name accurately described her as she strode past.

Several pairs of male eyes followed the green skirt that swayed around tiny black-heeled lace-up boots. She marched to a door with a nameplate that read ASA SMYTHE, EDITOR, and her small hand shot up and knocked. They watched her hesitate, then turn the knob. The door opened and closed. One reporter cocked an eyebrow, another frowned, and the men returned to their work.

Meredith straightened to her full height and cleared her throat.

The comb-slicked top of a gray head whipped back, a deep voice broke the silence of the room. "What can I do for you, Storm?"

She slapped down her latest article on his desk. "I want a real assignment."

The editor did not flinch, only nodded his head toward the chair that faced his desk. "Why don't you sit down, and let's discuss this matter like two civilized people."

Meredith seated herself, planted both feet firmly on the floor and clasped her hands in her lap to keep them from trembling. The man across the desk, with nerves like steel, was not only her editor, he was the one person who knew how to help her keep her goals in perspective and meet them. To be a journalist—in a man's world in the year 1899—was not an easy thing. Asa Smythe made it easier.

"Now then, what determines a real assignment, Storm?"

"Covering a subject that makes a difference in the world, writing something other than the society column, fashion reviews, or advertisements."

"Did you ever stop to think that your position at *McClure's*, in and of itself, is doing just that for the advancement of women?"

"That's not my purpose here, and you know it."

"It may not be your purpose, but it is the issue."

"This is not about women. It is about me doing something worthwhile."

Asa straightened the paperwork on his desk. "And what are these pressing concerns that you harbor?"

She leaned forward. "You know how I hate it when people or animals get mistreated or hurt." The fine lines on Asa's face deepened. It was true, she could not stand seeing any living thing hurt.

"I've read some of John Muir's writings," she continued. "Last week I had the chance to hear him speak on the issue of conservation of the western forests. He portrays the tree as a living thing. His speech has been nagging at me all week. Something needs to be done before the loggers use up all the good timber out West, as they have in the East."

"Oh no." Asa shook his head. "You cannot even think that I would send you on such an assignment."

"It is exactly what I'm thinking. It would be perfect for me." She stood and paced the room. "Think about this angle, a woman's view of the backwoods, the Wild West. It would be romantic."

"Romantic! What are you thinking?"

"It would make a great series! I could get inside the heads that fell the trees, the minds that make the money. From a female perspective, I could. . ."

"Stop right there. Do you have any idea what a loggers' camp is like?"

"Well, no. That's just it. Neither does the average person. I could make this story come alive. I know I could."

"It is impossible. Why, once a man becomes a logger, his life expectancy is only seven years."

She shook her head, and a dark strand worked loose from her upswept hairdo. Her slender fingers hastily tucked it back into place. "What has that got to do with anything?"

"It means, young lady, that your life expectancy in such a place would probably be about seven days."

"Exaggerating a wee bit, aren't we?"

"How would a woman with your good looks survive in such an uncivilized place? Where would you stay?"

Her chin rose. "I've done a bit of research myself. I'll choose a camp that's close to civilization, and I'll take along a male photographer."

Asa groaned something incoherent, then said, "No. It is out of the question. I am sure we can find something safer that would suit you."

Meredith placed both palms on the desk across from him, her face close to his. "I can do it. Please, Asa. It is something that I need to do, either for *McClure's* or on my own, but I'd rather do it for you."

"Go away. Let me think."

"Yes sir." Before she reached the door, she turned back. "One more thing. I have in mind the California logging camps. I could take the Overland Limited all the way to San Francisco. It's only a three-day trip from Chicago, and going by rail is ever so safe these days."

"Storm."

"Yes?"

"Please, go away."

Another nod, and Meredith was out of the editor's office. She whisked past the other reporters with a smug smile, her thoughts already far away. *Hmm, what clothes will I need in San Francisco?* Before Meredith packed any clothes, however, she had an unpleasant chore to attend to, another call to make.

❧

She knocked at the door of the house where she was raised. The door creaked open, and her father's hazel eyes rested on her, then closed like iron gates. The lines around his eyes and mouth sagged. He shrugged stiff shoulders and left her standing on the stoop. Because she was expected to follow him, she did. The way he hunkered down at the paperwork strewn on the kitchen table, it was obvious he didn't want to be bothered. But Meredith tried. She placed the latest edition of the *McClure's* on the table beside him. He merely glanced at the printed intrusion and left it lay.

A pot of coffee warmed on the stove, so she poured them each a cup. "I have an assignment." Instead of giving her a reply, her father took a swig of his drink. "I'm going to California to do a story on forest conservation."

He eyed her over the rim of his cup, and Storm took a gulp of the bitter liquid while she waited. Her father picked up the *McClure's* issue and squashed a fly with it, then tossed the magazine on the floor by his feet. "If you go west, then you're a bigger fool than I thought."

Meredith slammed the cup down with a rattle; coffee splattered her father's paperwork.

"I need to get far away from you. You never have loved me." With tears welling up, she strode past him and slammed the door on her way out.

Inside the house, her father's arm lashed out and swept across the table. Papers scattered and floated down to the floor over shattered glass. His head dropped into his hands, and he combed his fingers through his hair, wondering how his life had gotten to such a low point. *She's right.* He leaned his old bones over the side of his chair and groped for the magazine that mattered so much to Meredith.

Chapter 1

The train screeched, iron scraping against iron, and lurched forward to start Meredith on her westward journey. Without a bit of regret, she watched the depot disappear from view. After coughing up cinders, the locomotive clacked up momentum, eventually settling into a comfortable rhythm of motion. Beside her, Jonah Shaw thumbed open a red-and-white cloth-covered book entitled *An Adventure in Photography*.

"Have you been west before?" she asked her traveling escort.

"Mm-hmm. Once."

The fifty-year-old photographer had an attitude that reminded Meredith of a crusty old schoolmaster she'd once had, who rapped his students across the knuckles with a stick when they became too rambunctious.

She hunched close. "Did you like it?"

He slowly lowered his book to his lap. "I never decided."

"I think I shall like it."

"Why?"

"I hear it's a vast land with plenty of room to prove some things."

He did not reply, but raised his book until the only part of his face visible was his smooth bald forehead.

She patted his arm. "Don't be so stuffy, Jonah." He flinched, and when she saw that she would not get any more out of him, she set her mind to work. Within moments, she had come up with a way to pass the time. She reached down by her feet for her brown leather portfolio. It was full of writing materials, and while most women carried parasols, this portfolio accompanied Meredith wherever she went.

"Excuse me, please."

"Where are you going?" Small, stern eyes peered over his book.

"I've come up with an idea for a great story. Asa will love it."

"But where are you going?"

She stepped over him. "To interview the passengers." Meredith kept her back to Jonah, sensing his wary eyes upon her. *He'll soon get tired of doing that.* She worked her way to a vacant seat and fine prospect. "May

I join you a moment?"

A woman with a tiny baby in her arms and another child playing at her ankles considered her peculiar request.

"Of course. It's my son's seat, but he's inclined to play right now."

Meredith looked at the fuzzy-haired boy whose pudgy hands were exploring the fabric seams of the train's seat.

"He seems an intelligent, inquisitive lad to say the least. My name is Meredith S. Mears. I'm a reporter. I'm doing a story on the people who take the Overland Limited. Would you mind telling me about your travels?"

"Going to Chicago to visit some relatives."

"Traveling alone with children. What a brave soul you are."

"Thank you."

Meredith caressed the baby's dimpled cheek. "Have a good trip."

Next she worked her way toward an interesting subject, a square-faced woman who wore a diamond brooch and traveled with a servant. There were no empty seats, so Meredith merely hovered over the woman as she introduced herself and her intentions.

"I think not." The woman placed her hand over her ample bosom and turned her angular face toward the passing landscape.

Meredith straightened her torso. A reporter never gives up, so she cast a quick look about the train to see whom she should interview next. But the tracks made a sharp curve, and the sudden sway of the train sent her reeling across the aisle in utter helplessness.

Some hands reached out to steady her. She bumped her elbow hard on one of the seats. Her paper flew up and her pen rolled away, down the aisle. It took several helpful gentlemen to get everything straightened out. With a gush of apologies, she stumbled back down the aisle, across Jonah's legs, and collapsed into her seat. She did not look at him as she rubbed her throbbing elbow.

"Have you proven anything yet?" Jonah asked from behind his book.

Meredith did not reply. Before long, the pain in her arm subsided, and she eased back into the corner of her seat and closed her eyes.

⌘

Meredith awoke to the sound of the train's shrill whistle and the conductor's call, "Chicago Station."

It took about an hour to detrain, check on their luggage, find something to eat, and board their next train. This one would take them to their destination. It was long and full of Pullman sleeping cars, dining cars, smoking cars, plush seats, and every convenience known to travelers.

"Perhaps you'd like the aisle this time?" Jonah asked.

"Yes, please." Meredith set down her portfolio and straightened the pins in her hair.

At last the train wheels turned; the floor rumbled at Meredith's feet. City buildings passed in and out of view, making Meredith dizzy until they had picked up speed and entered the greener countryside. When the slight discomfort of head and stomach subsided, Meredith reverted to scrutinizing the other passengers, still intent on continuing her interviews.

One man, in particular, who occupied a window seat just across the aisle, caught her interest. His melancholy gaze was fixed on the passing scenery. Meredith sensed a hurt or regret of some sort in those soft brown eyes and wondered about his life. It only seemed natural to ease into the seat next to him.

"Hello."

ℰ

Thatcher Talbot jerked his gaze from the window and stared in disbelief at the forward woman, her autumn-colored eyes sympathetic yet gently probing. There was a dusting of ginger across her nose and cheeks. A multitude of thoughts rushed through his mind. *I noticed her when she boarded the train.* He remembered feeling a bit envious of the balding man that accompanied her.

"I'm Meredith S. Mears, New York reporter. Doing a story on the people who travel the Overland Limited."

He stared at her extended hand, and the urge to press it to his lips left him with a voice of warning. *Reporter. She'll expose you.*

After a considerable pause, the woman dropped her hand. Her voice took on a professional tone. "May I ask you a few questions?"

See! The warning voice gloated. He frowned. "No, I was about to get some much-needed rest." Then he stretched his legs, cocked his hat to block out the world with its nosey reporters, and slouched in his seat.

From beneath his hidey-hole, his face burned when he heard the passenger one seat behind him offer, "You can interview me."

ℰ

Meredith felt a prick of hurt and turned from the uncooperative passenger to the voice beckoning her. Once Meredith accumulated enough material for her story, she started back toward her seat, careful to watch for the quirks of the train. A keen desire to steal another glance across the aisle at the man with the melancholy expression could not be suppressed.

He was gone.

⚜

Three days later, a wilted and wrinkled Meredith stepped down from the train that had whisked her across a continent. She raised her arm to shade her eyes from the sun, gave a small cough to expel the dust from her lungs, and gazed at the new world that received her, San Francisco.

"I'll go get our baggage and be right back," Jonah said. He removed his hat to wipe his brow, then replaced it on his smooth head.

"Thank you." Meredith pointed with a gloved hand. "I'll wait over there, out of the way."

"Good."

Meredith had learned from experience that one of the best ways to encounter a new situation was to stand back and study how things were done. A welcome summer breeze ruffled her skirt, and she reached up to straighten her hat with one hand while the other clutched her brown leather portfolio.

Tall buildings on streets that ran straight toward the sky surrounded the depot. The tang of sea air and the aroma of food from nearby vendors mixed with the sooty foul smells from the trains. Soon her attention settled onto some familiar faces from the trip. "Good luck to you," she called out to a fellow passenger, giving him a wave.

The woman with the large diamond brooch strutted by with a small group of people. Meredith caught the words "new woman." The accusation hurt. That was the name going around for the progressive women who were stepping out of social boundaries with the turn of the new century. Meredith, however, did not consider herself a part of that radical group. She had nothing to prove to the world about being a woman. She only needed to prove to her father. . .well, she certainly would not think about that today.

A trickle of sweat ran down her brow, and an unfeminine wetness beneath her arms caused discomfort. She noticed a line of horse-drawn hackneys and wondered if she should secure one, when Jonah's thin but sturdy figure appeared with a porter. She fell into step with them as they made their way to a hackney. The driver stood by his rig.

"We need a hotel close to a cable car and a post office, and we'll be needing to get some supplies. We're heading north into the wilderness," Meredith said.

The driver glanced at Jonah, saw his nod, then replied, "I know just the place, ma'am."

Meredith smiled and stepped up into the hackney with Jonah close behind her.

"Was your equipment all right?"

Her traveling partner smiled. "All intact."

"My typewriter?"

"Fine."

"Good." When the coach took off, her head snapped back, and she reached up to secure her hat.

*

The Old Mission Hotel, a low adobe structure with a wide veranda across the front, hugged a small hill and provided a contrast to the more common Victorian inns they had passed. Two rooms were secured. After they inspected their rooms and tucked away their belongings, Meredith met Jonah in the hotel lobby to discuss their plans.

"I thought we might find the closest land office and do some inquiring," she said.

He raised an eyebrow. "You mean you haven't chosen a camp yet?"

Her eyes lit. "That, Jonah, is our objective."

"But Asa said that you—"

"What Asa doesn't know won't hurt him, will it?" She patted his hand. "Don't worry so. We'll see what's available and decide tonight over supper."

Jonah stood. "Perhaps I was too hasty to jump on this assignment...." His voice trailed off, but Meredith didn't wait around to hear his next complaint.

*

The land office wasn't far. When their business was concluded, she took Jonah's arm and chatted all the way back to the hotel. Inside the lobby, she patted her portfolio.

"I'm going to my room to look over this information. Shall we meet

11

at dinner to discuss our plans?"

"I suppose so," Jonah said.

"Look, Jonah. This assignment is not a contest between us. We need to work as a team. Sometimes it feels as if you have a problem with me."

"A man likes to take the lead once in a while."

"Whenever you feel the urge to do so, go right ahead."

He stroked the downward tips of his mustache. "We'll see, Storm."

Still, she hesitated to leave. "There's one other thing."

"What's that?"

"Once we get to the logging camp, I'd rather you didn't call me that name in front of other people."

"It's your name."

"I know, but I have a feeling this isn't going to be an easy assignment, and I don't want to give a wrong impression to any of those loggers. Know what I mean?"

"Yeah. I guess I do."

⁂

At dinner, they agreed that Bucker's Stand would be the most convenient logging camp to investigate. Its location was north of San Francisco in the redwood country. The closest town, called Buckman's Pride, was situated on the coast.

"The way I look at it," Meredith said, "we have two choices. Either we can go by ship, or we can find us an overland guide."

"Any ideas where we would find such a person?" Jonah asked.

"I've been thinking about that. Most loggers coming from the East pass through San Francisco. I'd wager that some of them pick up supplies while they're in the big city. We just have to figure out where they purchase them."

Jonah's blue eyes sparkled. "That just might work." He leaned close across the table. "If we could find such a place, we could hold off making our decision until we talked to a few of them, get their advice on the best method of travel."

"Good idea." Meredith beamed, then stifled a yawn. "Well, now that we have that settled, I think I'll go to my room. I need to finish up my Overland Limited story so we can get it posted tomorrow."

"Go ahead. I'll just mingle down here a bit and see if I can glean any information about where your loggers buy their supplies."

"Good idea." She patted his hand. "Good night, then."

"Good night, Storm."

⟡

The next morning Jonah greeted Meredith with news that he knew where the loggers purchased their supplies.

"Wonderful! Is the postal office on the way?"

"I believe so. We'll need to take the cable car."

They ate breakfast at the hotel, walked to the post office to mail Meredith's story, then rode the cable car to a shop called the Outfitters. With Meredith's first step inside, the heel of her shoe caught in a gaping hole.

Jonah's hand shot out to steady her. "Watch your step." He nodded at a nearby man. She followed Jonah's gaze to the man's boots. They had spikes in them. "Loggers' boots," he whispered. "That's what's tearing up the floor. I guess we're in the right place."

Meredith smelled the masculine scents of leather and tobacco. Her eyes roamed over the displays of tools, leather goods, clothing, bedrolls, rolls of canvas, coils of rope, liniments, and books. Along the wall lined with tools such as picks, shovels, axes, and handsaws, she caught a snatch of conversation between two men. She heard them mention Bucker's Stand, and that was all she needed.

She walked up behind them. "Excuse me, sir." The men did not turn around to acknowledge her. She glanced at Jonah. He hesitated, then cleared his throat. The men quit talking.

"Pardon me, may I have a word with you, sir?" Meredith asked.

The closest man turned to face her, while the other tipped his hat at Jonah and went back to his shopping. The well-cut tan suede vest enhanced the man's masculine form. She looked up expectantly, and to her ill fate, into familiar brown eyes. The melancholy man from the train. She hadn't realized he was so handsome.

He smiled and stared at her for an uncomfortably long period of time before asking, "Did you want something?"

Her face heated. "Yes. In passing, I overheard you mention Bucker's Stand. May I ask, are you headed there?"

The man removed his hat and smirked. "I am."

"The reason I ask is, my friend and I are looking for someone to guide us, accompany us, to Buckman's Pride."

"I'm sorry, I can't be of help." He replaced his hat and turned to go.

"Wait." She grabbed his sleeve. "We can pay." He stopped, looked at her, then at his arm. Instantly, she released him. "I. . .I'm sorry."

"So am I." Then he was gone.

Jonah had observed the entire scene. "I thought we were going to find out what the overland trip was like before we offered to pay someone to guide us."

She leaned against a shelf filled with boxes of nails. "We were. I don't know what's gotten into me. I've never acted so unprofessionally. It's that. . .that man. When I saw him, I couldn't think clearly. Why, he makes my blood boil!"

Jonah lifted a wooly eyebrow that matched his brown mustache in color. "Well, I hope we don't meet up with him again. He seems to bring out some mighty strange behavior in you. If I didn't know better, I'd think you were smitten with him."

"What!" She jerked away from the wall, and her hand struck a shovel that clattered to the floor. "That is utterly ridiculous. You know me better than that." A clerk appeared to pick up the shovel and straighten tools. She stepped away, then had to jerk her foot loose from where it had sunk deep into a groove in the wooden plank. "Let's just get back to work, shall we?"

✑

By midafternoon, Meredith and Jonah had nearly concluded their business. They would travel by land, and they had secured a guide. They stayed in the Outfitters long enough to make several purchases. Meredith did not miss how Jonah's eyes widened when she examined the men's clothing, cut in a very small size.

"Get yourself some loggers' clothing, Jonah. We'll fit in better when we reach the camp."

"I don't see anything here that appeals to my sense of. . ."

"Nonsense!" she interrupted, grabbing his sleeve. "Here." She placed a set of trousers in his arms. "And you'll probably need this." Another article slapped him across the shoulder.

"If you insist that I wear these duds, then move out of the way, Storm. I'll do my own choosing."

"You don't need to get in a huff about it. I'll work on the rest of our list. It was so good of our guide to make it for us."

Jonah pointed. "Better get some different shoes while you're at it."

"You're absolutely correct," she said, and noticed the glitter of surprise in his eyes.

After that, they each purchased a set of saddlebags, and Jonah bargained with the store owner to trade their travelling trunks for several leather bags. When all the arrangements for their trip were in order, Meredith and Jonah returned to their hotel to dine and retire early. They would leave in the morning.

Chapter 2

Meredith rose early and dressed in her newly purchased male attire. She hesitated outside the hotel lobby. The clothes she could get used to, but not the abominable hat. She owned a multitude, all colorful and elaborately embellished with feathers and bows and birds and whatever attracted her attention and her delight. But this one was plain brown and round like a soup bowl with a large brim, which she supposed was to shield her face from the sun. It also hid her long brown hair, secured beneath in a tidy knot. Her hand crept up to examine. . .

"Storm! You're up."

Meredith jerked her hand down. "Don't do that!"

"Sorry," Jonah said with a grin. "I didn't mean to frighten you." He studied her. "Sensible clothes. Let's have breakfast."

She felt relieved that her travelling companion awoke on the congenial side, yet she regretted his catching her in a vain moment.

❧

Breakfast was hot and filling. Soon they were outside the hotel. Their guide, Silas Cooke, appeared right on time.

Meredith strode toward him. "Good morning, Mr. Cooke."

Silas Cooke watched her with skepticism; his eyes flitted across Jonah, then returned to her with a new brightness. "Good morning to you, Miss Mears." His blue gaze ran over her appraisingly, and his beard gave an odd twitch. "Didn't recognize you right off. See you're a sensible woman."

Jonah chuckled. "I've heard her called a 'new woman' repeatedly, but never 'sensible.'"

Meredith gave Jonah a cutting look. "You said so just this morning."

Jonah stared at her feet. "I said your clothes were sensible. By the way, those boots look comfortable."

"We're wasting time," Meredith said.

Silas brought around the horses and two pack mules. Meredith needed assistance mounting the smallest horse. She imagined her riding would improve on this assignment. For some reason this small challenge gave her great satisfaction, and poised straight in the saddle, she felt eager to start the assignment of a lifetime.

Meredith soon shed her self-consciousness where her clothing was concerned. No one gave her a second look. Loggers and miners passing through San Francisco were a commonplace event. The morning passed pleasantly without incident. Jonah pointed out the tall Call Building, which housed the San Francisco newspaper.

They boarded a ferry once, where Meredith marveled over the flocks of pelicans and caught a wonderful view of the Cliff House, a mansion turned into a famous eating establishment. After that, they mounted up again and turned their back to the hills and harbors of San Francisco with all its bustling civilization.

The trail meandered along the coastline, providing a fearsome sight. The edge of the earth broke off hundreds of feet above rock and water. At times the narrow path hugged so close to the cliffs that Meredith's heart would pound with fright, and she would force herself to think of something other than toppling over the bluff and into the slapping white foam so far below.

Her legs and shoulders ached, not only from the long hours of riding but from tensing her muscles in fear. Meredith welcomed every opportunity to dismount and stretch her miserable legs. *I might learn to ride better, if I live that long.*

That night at camp, Meredith went for a short walk along the cliffs. A ship bobbed at sea, birds shrieked overhead, and the feel of the moist, salty air was cold against her face.

"Water as far as the eye can see."

She jerked her head around. Silas gazed out over the scenic panorama. "It's incredible. Makes me feel like a tiny dot in the universe," she said.

"Take a good look. Tomorrow, we're going to move inland."

Their camp nestled securely within the shelter of some large rocks. Silas unloaded some supplies from one of the pack mules. He cooked their supper over an open fire. Meredith inhaled the food, then felt her eyes droop.

Silas nudged her. "Smooth out a spot, like this, for your bedroll."

She followed his instructions, and before she knew what had happened, the light of day shone again, and it was time to climb back up into the saddle.

The trail turned rugged and hilly and wound through dense forest with trees huge and plentiful enough to stretch the imagination of any easterner, and Meredith wondered if conservation was even an issue here, in the West. That evening she felt sore and stiff, but able to do her part in setting up camp.

After their meal of smoked ham, beans, and biscuits, Silas pulled out a chunk of wood he carried with him and started to whittle. "I worried about this part of the trip. But you're an excellent outdoorsman," Meredith said.

"I agree. I don't know how you do it, but you make us quite comfortable with our scanty provisions," Jonah said.

"Just natural. I've lived my life in the wilds." Silas laid the wood on his thigh, reached into his trousers for a pint of whiskey, and took a swig.

"How long have you been in logging?" Meredith asked.

"Most my life. I only regret I missed the gold rush. Course it didn't make my grandpap rich. The gold brought him, but he fell in love with the land."

"Mm," Meredith said.

"It does grow on you," Jonah said.

"Wait until tomorrow."

Meredith wondered if Silas would even be able to ride the next day, with all the whiskey he consumed. She fell asleep to tales about Silas's grandpap's gold-digging days.

But Silas rose sharp as the sole on a logger's boot. Meredith need not have worried. About midday, she found out what Silas meant the night before when he said, *"Wait until tomorrow."*

❧

First, she heard it, a roaring sound coming from the hills, which grew louder as they rode farther up the trail. Silas stopped his mount, and then she saw the most beautiful waterfalls in the world.

They ate at the majestic spot. Jonah unloaded enough equipment to take photographs while Silas watered the horses. Meredith found a secluded place to sponge bathe. Afterwards, they followed the river west until they came to a shallow place, calm enough to ford.

On the far side, Meredith twisted in her saddle for a final look. "Must we leave it behind?"

"I reckon you want us to build you a castle here," Silas said.

"No, I expect not. I enjoy civilization too much. But it is something to remember."

They rode harder after that to reach the location where Silas wanted to camp that night.

✍

The next day a different sight tugged Meredith's heartstrings, acres and acres of destroyed forests. The damage gouged deep into the woods and stretched a couple miles along the trail.

"What caused this, Silas? Fire?"

"It's just stripped from logging."

"But it's horrible."

"There's plenty more trees, ma'am. Don't worry about it none." She cast Jonah a look of concern. "We'll have to take some pictures, Silas."

It was time for the West to think about conservation.

Chapter 3

After several long days of travel, nights camping under the stars, innumerable saddle blisters, and unmentionable aches and pains, Meredith's horse trotted back into civilization. It was not New York, Chicago, or San Francisco, but a form of civilization. Meredith tipped her head back to peer out from under the abominable hat.

There was a hotel, a saloon, and several stores farther uphill, yapping dogs, barefoot children, but mostly there were men. She strained her eyes to catch a glimpse of skirt, or lace, or a pretty hat or two. A large sawmill prevailed over all of the other establishments, usurping more than its share of property, people, and town noise. It would be a good place to begin her investigation of the lumber world. The town was perfect, better than she had expected.

Silas delivered them to the front stoop of the only hotel in Buckman's Pride and bade them farewell. Meredith assured him they would meet again, and something in the twinkling of his eyes gave Meredith to believe that the lumberjacks would probably hear of her presence long before she stepped foot into their camp.

The elderly hotel clerk was courteous and kind enough to head them in the direction of permanent lodging. They had two options, get a discount price at the hotel or inquire with a Mrs. Amelia Cooper who oftentimes took in boarders. Meredith and Jonah made plans to bathe, change into proper clothing, and immediately search out the woman.

❧

"My name is Meredith S. Mears, and this is my business associate, Jonah Shaw. We heard you might take us as boarders."

"Glad to meet you. I'm Mrs. Cooper. You two married?"

"No ma'am," Jonah said, hat in his hand.

"I don't allow any unlawful male-female goings-on. . . ."

"Oh no." Meredith shook her head. "I am a reporter from New York City, and Jonah is a photographer. We've come to do a story for *McClure's* magazine. We would need two rooms, and I can assure you that all that will be taking place between us is strictly," she paused to smile, "journalism at its best."

The woman, tall, large-boned, with a plain but pleasant face, studied them, hat to boot. Meredith made her own observations. The woman dressed and handled herself with social grace. Meredith could read Mrs. Cooper's mind. *One of those Eastern reporters.*

"What kind of story are you doing?"

"One on Bucker's Stand logging camp."

"Nothing harmful, I hope."

Meredith flashed the woman a smile. "I hope not, too."

"I see." Mrs. Cooper took several moments to digest this. "I do have two rooms that I could let to you. Would you like to see them now?"

"Oh please," Meredith said. She cast Jonah a hopeful smile, and they followed the landlady's swishing yellow gown, which was to Meredith an unexpected article in such a backwoodsy place. Mrs. Cooper paused for them to look into a formal but cozy parlor. It consisted of mahogany furniture with comfortable-looking quilted backs, a rosewood shelf clock, Victorian lamps with tassels and butterflies, a well-worn floral rug, and a fireplace.

Must be a wealthy widow stuck here for some reason.

They passed down a short hall and up a flight of stairs. At the far end of the upstairs hall, two vacant rooms were located across from each other.

"I only have these two rooms available, no other boarders right now."

The first was small but furnished with a desk. "Perfect," Meredith said.

"Would you have a small room where I could develop photographs?" Jonah asked.

"Hmm." Mrs. Cooper rubbed her chin. "Let me think a moment."

Meanwhile, Jonah inspected the other room.

"There's the shed out back." Mrs. Cooper pointed toward the window. "Since my husband died, I only use it for storage. Things would have to be rearranged."

"I'd have to hang my photographs."

"Yes," she nodded. "I think we could work out something."

"Good," Jonah said. "When can we move in?"

"Tomorrow."

Reporter and photographer waltzed back toward the hotel, exuberant over their good fortune.

"The lodgings couldn't be more perfect," Meredith said.

"I agree. This is going to be a pleasant assignment. Buckman's Pride," Jonah said with satisfaction, "a civilized place."

Even though Meredith was just as pleased with their new accommodations and also excited about the assignment, she said, "I'll hold my judgment for a later time, on the West, be it wild or tame. But I do believe. . . Look! Look there. A dress shop. And there are hats in the window."

Jonah peered through the glass at the display. "What do you think of the West now?"

"Well, the styles are certainly not the latest thing," she said, "but they're fine enough." She pointed. "Look at that yellow number with the green ostrich feather. It is most delightful."

"It would go nicely with your brown riding skirt, better yet your men's trousers."

"Scoundrel."

He took her elbow. "Come along, Storm. We didn't come here to shop."

As they started off, someone caught Meredith's attention. She didn't mean to stare, but the back of the man's head looked familiar. His shirt-sleeves were rolled up, and large arms bulged as they heaved supplies into the back of a wagon. Then he turned, and his face came into view. It was that man again! She swallowed and tightened her grip upon Jonah's arm. What was wrong with her? Just because he was the most handsome man she'd ever seen was no reason to ogle. She tore her eyes away and straightened her stance. He had been rude to her on the train and at the Outfitters. He was nothing to her. She would think about something else.

"Jonah. As soon as we're settled in, I want to visit the sawmill."

"That mill will provide some great photographs. I can't wait to get started."

They discussed plans for their assignment, and Meredith puffed under the steep incline of the street. "Not so fast, Jonah. This climb is taxing."

"Forgive me, Storm." He slowed his pace.

A team of horses clattered past, pulling a wagon. "Eek!" Mud splattered Meredith from hat to boot. "Of all the. . ." She wiped her face with her sleeve and peered, unbelieving, at the back of the driver of the wagon that had just plastered them with grime. "It's him!" she spat.

"Who?" Jonah asked. He, too, brushed off specks of mud, though Meredith had received the brunt of the avalanche. "Do you know him?"

"Of course! The man from Outfitters! That rude, horrible man!"

Jonah squinted at the wagon in disbelief just as it topped the hill. The man didn't even realize what he'd done.

Meredith's hands fluttered up. "And he's ruined my hat."

"Come along, missy. Let's get you back to the hotel."

She hiked up her skirt a few inches and stomped up the hill, now oblivious to the steep incline.

Chapter 4

The hotel manager arranged for a hired wagon so Meredith and Jonah could move their belongings and equipment to Mrs. Cooper's. Once they arrived, she gave them keys to their rooms.

Meredith circled the pile of leather bags, which had been plunked down in the center of her room, wondering where to start. Mrs. Cooper gave a soft rap on her door.

"Come in."

The landlady smoothed back several gray-streaked blond hairs. "I hope everything is satisfactory. If there is anything else I can do to make your stay more comfortable, please let me know."

"Everything is perfect." Meredith's eyes ran across the small window above the desk. "It seems you've thought of everything and arranged the room just as I would have."

"After so many boarders, it gets a little easier. Dinner is at six. I only do breakfast and dinner." Meredith nodded. "I'll just check in on Mr. Shaw, now. I need to show him the shed he'll be using."

"Please, tell Jonah that I'll help him as soon as I'm finished here."

"I will." Mrs. Cooper nodded and the stray hairs worked free again.

Once the door had closed, Meredith unclasped the leather bags. Her clothing went into a wardrobe in hopes the wrinkles would not need to be steamed. Her hats she arranged and rearranged about the room, some on hooks by the door. *That looks cheery.* When her personal belongings were in place, she dove into the writing supplies and organized those on the desk by the window.

She retrieved her typewriter, handling it like a piece of fine china, and positioned it in its place of honor, center front of her desk. She traced the gold ornate lettering, *The Chicago*, across the front of its black cover and inspected all of the keys and parts.

Satisfied, she took a final inventory of the room. Her gaze lingered upon the mud-splattered green velvet and black-rimmed hat, and she crossed the room to it, plucked it off its peg, and dropped it into an empty bag. Next, she rearranged her desk. With a satisfactory nod, she pulled open the curtains above the desk. Jonah was in the backyard by the shed.

Perfect. I can see when he's in his studio. With a song on her lips, she closed the curtains and changed into an old gown.

☙

Just as she arrived at the shed's open door, a cloud of dust accosted her. With a cough, she jumped back.

"Is that you, Storm?"

Another cough. "Yes, it is."

Jonah's head peeked out, then the rest of him appeared, his hands gripping a broom handle. "Sorry about that. I didn't know anyone was about."

"So I see. Looks like you're doing serious housecleaning."

"Come look," Jonah said. "This place is going to be great."

He stepped back inside, and Meredith tiptoed in behind him. Cobwebs scalloped the cluttered room. "I'm glad you're so excited. It looks like a lot of work to me."

"Oh, you're right there. Mrs. Cooper said that most of this stuff can go down to the mill. I'm going to move everything outside and let her tell me what goes and what stays. The rest she'll take inside the house."

"Why the mill?" Meredith asked.

"Didn't she tell you? Her late husband was a partner of Cooper's Mill. She figures the mill's owner can use some of this."

"Really. What can I do to help?"

"Hmm. Maybe you should sweep down cobwebs," Jonah said, offering her the broom. "And I'll start dragging these crates outside."

"Done," Meredith said.

By the time they had emptied the old building of every tool, bucket, boot, and fishing pole, Mrs. Cooper poked her head inside. "You've been working so hard out here. I thought you might welcome a snack."

"Thank you, Mrs. Cooper. How thoughtful," Jonah said.

Mrs. Cooper pushed the tray of milk and cookies at him.

Meredith and Jonah perched on crates to enjoy the snack while Mrs. Cooper shuffled through boxes and rattled off instructions.

"This must be hard for you," Jonah said.

"It is. James was as good of a man as they come. But this needed to be done sometime, so don't worry about it."

Jonah nodded.

By early afternoon, the mopped-down shed was as clean as it would

25

get. Meredith rubbed her palms on the skirt of her gown. "It looks real good, Jonah."

"Did you want to go to the mill with me?"

"Now?"

"After I locate that hired wagon. That'll give you time to change clothes and freshen up." He brushed a cobweb from her hair.

"Think I need it?"

Jonah gestured with a small wave. "I won't venture a reply to that. But if you wish, meet me here after I get things loaded, and we'll go to the mill together."

Meredith sneezed. "Oops. I'll be here."

Cooper's sawmill backed up against the Mad River a mile from where it spilled into the ocean. Buckman's Pride situated itself with its right arm resting along the river and its left arm embracing the ocean. The river produced the power to run the giant circular saws. They cut the large logs that came downriver from the logging camp. Because these redwood logs dwarfed any trees on the East Coast, the saws loomed bigger than any Jonah had ever seen.

"Look at those," Jonah pointed. "I've never seen anything so huge."

"I've never seen anything so fearful," Meredith said. "It all looks so dangerous."

The operation mesmerized them until a mill worker passed nearby, shouldering a bundle of leather straps. He shouted out, "Need some help?"

"Yes sir," Jonah answered. "Have some business with the owner."

"You'll find him in there." The man nodded toward a nearby building, then continued on.

Jonah took Meredith's elbow and directed her toward the place the worker had indicated. Inside the warehouse, shingles were stacked in pallets along the wall. Beyond that was another door. They went to it, and Jonah knocked. Meredith straightened her hat.

"Come in," a deep voice drawled.

They entered. Two men occupied the room; one sat behind a desk and the other stood in the middle of the room.

Jonah strode to the desk. "I'm Jonah Shaw, New York photographer." The gray-haired man leaned over his desk and shook Jonah's offered hand. Meredith rushed forward. "Meredith S. Mears, journalist with *McClure's* magazine."

"Clement Washington," The owner said, also taking Meredith's hand. He settled back in his chair. "Seems to be my lucky day. You reporters know something I don't?" His question lumped them together like so much dead wood. "As if I don't have a business to run around here. Why don't you just talk to Ralston, here, so I don't need to repeat myself."

Deep furrows edged Frederick Ralston's frown. He introduced himself as a reporter for the Buckman's Pride newspaper.

"I don't mind people nosing about my business, exactly," Clement Washington said in his southern accent, "but I'm a busy man." He rose as if the matter was settled, and they were all dismissed. "Maybe some other time."

"Mrs. Cooper sent us," Jonah said. Clement jerked up his head and listened. "I've set up a studio in her shed, and in the process, we've cleaned out some of Mr. Cooper's belongings. She asked me to bring his things to you. They're crated up," he motioned, "outside in a wagon."

"Oh? Well, that's a different story." The mill's owner took a step toward Jonah and slapped his arm. "Let's go see what you've got."

They followed him outside, Jonah matching stride with the southerner.

Meredith lagged behind with the newspaperman. "I'm excited to learn that there is a newspaper in Buckman's Pride."

"Why is that?" The reporter's tone was frigid.

She shrugged her shoulders. "Just love the business."

"There isn't any room here for another reporter. It's a small operation."

"Is that so?"

Meredith pranced off and caught up with Clement Washington and Jonah. "I've never seen anything as excellent as these redwoods." Her breath came in heavy spurts. "How far do you ship your lumber? It must be in great demand."

"It is." Pride laced his voice. "We ship timber all over the West Coast. San Francisco and farther."

"How is the harbor here?" She cast a glance at the newspaper reporter, who had tagged after them. His eyes turned to dark narrow slits. Meredith knew he resented her conversation with the mill owner and wondered what made him so disagreeable.

"Too shallow with sandbars. There's no harbor to speak of along this

27

coast. Mostly use steam-powered schooners now. They get around good, as long as they don't get caught in a storm of course. You might want to take a look at the wharf where the timber gets loaded onto the schooners. It's something to see."

"I would like that."

"Just a fortnight ago, we lost a couple schooners. Nearly their whole crews went down with the ships. Horrible." He shook his head, his eyes reliving the scene.

"I'm sorry," Meredith said.

By this time, they had reached the wagon. The man, who looked as if he'd be more at home on a cotton plantation than a sawmill, grazed his eyes over the bittersweet belongings of his old partner. "James always did take care of his tools. I'll get someone to come unload this stuff. Thanks for your trouble. Give Mrs. Cooper my regards and enjoy your stay."

As Washington shuffled away, the newspaperman gave Meredith a smirk. "We did an article on that storm. Good day, Miss Mears."

"I'll drop by to see it," Meredith called over the man's shoulder. She saw his back flinch, though he did not give a reply. Perhaps it was old news, but it would make good material for her magazine articles.

Once they were alone, Jonah said, "You shouldn't have set his teeth on edge like that. I might like to work with him sometime."

"Me? What did I do?"

"Just born a woman, I suppose."

"Humph!" She squared her shoulders. She was well aware of that, having heard it enough times in her past. Her father's words surfaced. *"You should've been born a boy. If your ma had to die birthing you, it was the least you could have done for me."*

Chapter 5

The coffee sloshed over the rim of the china cup and caused a puddle on the white tablecloth. Meredith rushed forward. "Here, let me help."

"What? Oh! How clumsy of me." Mrs. Cooper hurried to get a rag, but when she returned to the table, her eyes swept over her guest.

The reporter's face burned. "I should have forewarned you. I plan to dress like this when I ride out to Bucker's Stand, and that's where I'm headed this morning."

"Why?" Mrs. Cooper asked.

"Because it's a man's world out there," Meredith said. She seated herself at the table, Mrs. Cooper's chilly gaze fastened upon her. "I'll fit in better."

"Well, I never."

Concern shown in Jonah's eyes as he watched the women spar.

"I don't know how New York City behaves these days, but the folks in Buckman's Pride won't take kindly to a woman dudded up like you are, no matter what the reason."

"I guess they'll have to adjust." Meredith's appetite left, and she pushed her plate away. "I'll meet you at the stables, Jonah."

"Yes ma'am. After I've had my breakfast." He was careful to avert his eyes from both women.

⌘

"That woman runs hot and cold," Meredith said when she and Jonah left the stables toward Bucker's Stand.

"I hadn't noticed."

Meredith cocked an eyebrow at Jonah. "Perhaps that's because she's mostly hot when you're around."

"You think so?"

She grinned and let the matter drop.

"These trees," motioned Jonah, "stretch on forever. I think there's about as much chance using up all this timber as there is using up the very air we breathe."

"I'll keep your opinion in mind, old man, when I write my story."

"I think I could stay in these woods forever."

"Where's your camera equipment, Jonah?"

"I won't be taking any photographs today. First I need to set up scaffolds that will get my camera high enough to scope the trees."

"Oh? Something permanent?"

"Perhaps. When I'm working I'll stay at the camp for several days on end."

"So today's a scouting trip?"

"More or less. I didn't want you to have to ride out alone the first time."

"That's kind of you. I have to admit my stomach is a bit jittery."

Jonah shot her a look. "Is that a fact?"

A good two hours passed until they finally rode into Bucker's Stand. "Whew!" Meredith said. "I was beginning to think we'd gotten lost."

"Me, too," Jonah said, reining in his horse. "But, this is it. How do you feel?"

"Ask me that again tonight."

Jonah chuckled beneath his thin walrus mustache.

The camp appeared to be nearly deserted. The few men they saw froze and stared at Meredith with hungry expressions. "Guess the clothes aren't working," Jonah whispered.

"Hush. Where is everybody?"

"Probably in the woods."

They dismounted and asked the first man they came across where they could find the camp foreman.

"Bull of the woods? Thar, in that tent." The burly man pointed toward a rectangular gray structure.

Jonah nudged Meredith toward the tent indicated, while she took stock of the place.

One man, whose wrinkled face looked like leather, made a smacking noise with his lips, and Jonah gave her a light tug. "Hurry up."

She felt a surge of disgust. "They'll just have to get used to seeing me around."

Jonah peeked inside the tent's open flap, and a black bear of a man motioned them inside.

"If you're looking for a job, I don't think you'll do," he said. His black eyes glanced over Meredith. "Especially that one."

She strode forward. "We're not looking for a job. We have one. Meredith S. Mears, New York journalist." She stuck out her hand.

"Jonah Shaw, photographer. You had any photographs taken of your camp yet?"

"Mm, nope."

"Well, I'm your man then."

The black-bearded bull of the woods did the formality of shaking their hands. "Josiah Jones. I can appreciate that you've come a long way. But I don't think you'll want to be sticking around. This is no place for city folks. It's rough, and it's dangerous. You'll likely get in the way of my men and get yourself killed." His eyes raked over Meredith. "The only women here are ones who serve the meals, and they're loggers' wives."

"Mr. Jones, we have come a very long way, and I have no intention of leaving Buckman's Pride without my story."

"Staying in town then?" The bull asked.

"And I've set up a studio. We'll be around for a bit," Jonah announced.

The bull shrugged his shoulders. "Don't say you haven't been warned. I'll not be responsible for any harm that comes your way. And I'll be mighty displeased should one of my men come to harm because of you. Accidents happen around here too easily as it is. The men don't need distractions."

"Understood," Meredith said.

Just then, a shadow indicated someone had entered the tent's doorway.

"Talbot," The bull said with a sudden smirk on his face. "Got a job for you. See that these folks get shown around, and answer whatever questions they have, best you can."

"But I was on my way back to the field, sir. One of the peelers sent me with this message."

"I'll take it." Josiah Jones reached out and took the piece of bark that served as paper. "And you'll take these folks. Try to keep them out of harm's way, if you can."

"Yes sir." The man's voice was both reluctant and familiar.

A dread fell over Meredith. She sensed that this was the one man she most wanted to avoid. Afraid to discover the truth, she turned very slowly.

☙

Even though the slight person dressed like a man, Thatcher Talbot instantly recognized the reporter from the train and her photographer. The last thing Thatcher needed was her following him around, ready to delve into his personal life. His signing on with this outfit, however, was too recent for him to raise any objections to the boss's orders. When her eyes met his, he smelled trouble.

"No," Meredith said. The bull of the wood's black brows furrowed. "Is Silas Cooke available? We're friends, and I'd really appreciate it if. . ."

"Does he look like he's available?" The bull of the woods asked.

"Come on." Jonah took Meredith by the arm. "Mr. Talbot will do just fine."

Beyond the tent, out of the bull's sight, Meredith dug in her feet. "No! He will not do just fine. He's the horrible man who ruined my hat."

"I what? I don't know what your problem is, woman," Talbot backed up a few paces, his hands fending her off, "and I don't think I want to know. I don't like this any better than you do."

"In Buckman's Pride, the day I arrived, you splattered my gown and hat with mud. You are a. . .a beast!"

He shook his head. "I think I'd remember such a thing."

"It was you," Jonah said. "But you didn't realize you did it."

"Well, that explains it then. I'm sorry, ma'am. I'd never do something like that intentionally."

Meredith gritted her teeth and thrust herself in front of him, the top of her head at his chin. She tilted her head back. "You, sir, are a rude man. I'd rather be hung from a rope and dragged by my heels through these woods," she gestured to the surrounding trees, "than be escorted by the likes of you. But this assignment is important to me, and since you're all we have, you'll have to do."

Thatcher wanted to take the woman over his knee. "And you, ma'am, are a spoiled brat. But since my boss has given me this duty, and for your friend's sake, you'll have to do."

"Well!" Meredith jerked her head so hard her hat slipped.

32

Jonah gripped Meredith's shoulder and stepped between them like a referee at a prizefight. "If I were to set up camp for a week or so to take some photographs, where would I stay?"

Talbot eased back. "This way." He tramped off with Jonah and Meredith jogging after him. "I suppose the bull would put you in the bunkhouse with the rest of us." He stopped in front of a long building with rows of bunks so close together that they had to be accessed from the foot end. "And if you didn't like this, you could just pitch a bedroll outside. Course, with the wild animals, I'd recommend the bunkhouse over the woods."

"Are the animals here as ferocious as the men?" Meredith asked.

"Most are." Talbot met her glare, hoping to frighten her.

Meredith raised her hands in surrender. "Look. We're wasting time. Why don't you let us follow you back to whatever it was you were doing. I'd like to see the loggers in action. Wouldn't you, Jonah?"

"Yes. That's a good idea."

"It's not safe out there," Mr. Talbot said.

"We've been through all that with the bull," Meredith said. "We promise to stay out of your way, and we'll even find our own way back to camp when we're done."

Talbot shrugged. "Have it your way." He charged into the woods, not really caring if they kept up with him. They did. About twenty minutes later, they entered a tiny clearing where men were working together.

"By the way," Meredith said. "What's a peeler?"

Talbot rolled his eyes. "A man who peels bark off a log." He looked over the logging site. "You two can stand over there." He pointed.

The loggers gave Meredith and Jonah several sidelong glances. Meredith didn't care; she was too intrigued with the logging operation. Questions popped into her head as quickly as the axes dropped wood chips onto the forest floor.

❧

Talbot looked up once to see Meredith and Jonah tramping off alone. He figured they were heading back to the camp. The bull had put them in his care, so he took off after them. The crackling twigs made Meredith jump. Talbot stifled a grin.

That evening, Talbot lounged on his cot, his arms folded under his head, his eyes staring up at the ceiling.

"She sure is a pretty one."

Talbot's head shot up, but when he saw it was Silas Cooke, he grinned. "Too pretty for her own good."

"Hers or yours?"

Talbot sat up and motioned. "Sit a spell."

Silas parked himself on the foot of Talbot's cot. "She doesn't like you much, does she?"

Talbot laughed. "Why don't you tell me about your trip together?"

The other man's eyes lit up.

Chapter 6

Good morning." Meredith smiled at two women crossing Main Street. One returned the smile until her black-haired companion elbowed her, then quickly tore her eyes away. Meredith felt the heat rush to her cheeks. Unlike New York City, Buckman's Pride was a small town. Had Mrs. Cooper spread some gossip? Her writing experiences trained her not to make assumptions, so she squared her shoulders and sought to dismiss the incident.

At her destination, a wooden sign swung from two ropes. It read: BUCKMAN NEWS. A bell jingled as she pushed open the door. Inside, the familiar smells of ink and paper filled the room. Frederick Ralston, the blond-haired, fragile-looking newspaper reporter, looked up from his work.

"Hello," Meredith said.

"Expected you sooner or later." His voice reminded her of a New York winter day.

"Is there a reason you dislike me?"

His fingers poked at printing blocks. "Just don't like women nosing around in men's business."

An older man with an apron draped over his thick belly entered from a back room. He wiped his hands when he saw Meredith in her feathered hat and flowing gown. "Well, there, what can I do for you, miss?"

Meredith stepped forward. "Meredith S. Mears, journalist."

"My hands are dirty."

"No matter." Meredith warmed beneath the short man's smile.

"Charlie Dutton."

"Are you the owner?"

"Yes ma'am."

"You have a delightful shop." She made a slow circle of the room. "Mr. Ralston invited me to come and look at an article he wrote about the schooners lost in the harbor."

"He mentioned it. Let's see what we can find."

Frederick Ralston's resentful eyes followed her. She flitted about the room to examine the presses until Charlie Dutton returned with the discussed issue.

"Here we are, Miss Mears. You can sit at that table if you like. Take your time."

"Thank you." Meredith took the paper and went to the designated table. The article detailing the helpless sailors' plight against the forces of nature moved and saddened her. The coast had abundant resources, which, when harvested, would pile money in some men's pockets. Her fingers traced the printed lines, marking her spot. But how many men would die taming the wild land? The ocean's treacherous rocks, sandbars, and storms could easily splinter the latest design of shipping vessel. They snuffed out men's lives in their prime and left families bereft. Her finger tapped her cheek. Dead men didn't make fortunes. Their risks were another man's gain.

Was it the same in the woods? Instinctively, she knew it was. Asa had said a logger's life span was only seven years. The bull warned about accidents. All of a sudden, it seemed important to ride to Bucker's Stand again. She knew the topic of her first story.

"I'm done here. Thank you for letting me read this."

"You're welcome," Charlie Dutton said.

"Are you hiring?" she asked.

"Sorry. It's a small paper, and I have to keep our staff small as well."

She glanced at the younger, brooding man across the room. "I understand. Thank you again, and good day."

"Good day, Miss Mears."

To finish out the day, Meredith compiled her completed articles and sent them off to Asa. Once this was done, she returned to her room and typed far into the night.

☙

The next day she rode out to Bucker's Stand. Jonah had gone a day earlier to set up his equipment at the logging camp. Once she arrived, she stabled her horse. A mass exodus of brawn and boot erupted from the mess hall. Meredith slunk behind a tree to observe. Two men passed nearby, engaged in a shoving contest and shouting loud oaths at one another. Meredith shrank further around the tree.

A moment later she saw Jonah, walking with Silas Cooke.

"Jonah!" Meredith stepped out with her portfolio in hand. "Wait!"

The two men turned back. "I didn't know you were here," Jonah said.

"I just got here. Hello, Mr. Cooke. On your way to the field?"

"Sure enough," Silas said.

"I'll just tag along then."

She chatted with the men until they reached Jonah's equipment. Meredith's eyes widened. Before them spread what looked like a giant spider web, the loggers being the spiders. Her journalistic mind allegorized even as she tried to grasp the operation.

Huge cables strung through pulleys and fastened to the tops of trees sloped downward to the earth. Several loggers worked to fasten these cables to logs. Before Meredith had it all figured out, there was, all of a sudden, a great creaking, then a terrible crashing noise, and one of the huge logs in the midst of them jerked violently and lurched straight up into the sky. Meredith scrambled backwards in terror, letting out a shriek.

Jonah shouted, "Shocked me, too, the first time I saw it."

Meredith's hands flew to her heaving bosom. Once Jonah's comment sank in, her pulse calmed. She scrambled for a safe spot, somewhere she could observe and stay out from underfoot. A rotting stump looked inviting and removed from the action, and she backed onto it. Her gaze returned to the steam engine yanking giant logs and hurling them up into the air, crashing through any obstacle.

There was a system to the madness. Logs were yanked toward the river, where they would be floated to the mill. Even the ground beneath her shook when the mighty logs rolled or moved. She watched the process with riveted interest and imagined the sorts of accidents that could occur, until a distant physique caught her eye.

Thatcher Talbot helped to fasten the cables. She observed him from her perch and jotted down notes. Hours sped by while she quietly penned words. Once when her concentration broke, she looked up to see Talbot striding toward her. No, not toward her. Jonah seemed to be the object of his wrath.

"Can't use that photograph," Talbot yelled up at Jonah.

"What?" Jonah called down from his perch.

Instead of answering, Talbot climbed up the scaffolding like a monkey Meredith had once seen at a zoo, until he was nose to nose with Jonah.

Another log lifted and slammed down, drowning out the two men's conversation, but Meredith saw Talbot thumping his finger on Jonah's camera. They argued about a photograph.

She scrambled off the stump and to the bottom of the scaffolding, where she crooked her neck to follow their conversation.

"I do have a say, and I say no!"

"Why don't you wait until they're developed and have a look at them. Then you can decide."

"I want that plate." Talbot fumbled for the glass.

Jonah jerked it out of the camera, and Thatcher smacked it against the tree trunk. A large crack zigzagged across the plate. He handed it back to Jonah.

"You can't do that," Meredith yelled.

Talbot glanced down at her as if she were an insignificant wood tick, then climbed down and brushed past her. The touch of his arm upon hers sent fire shooting up her shoulder. She jerked away.

He halted, as if he felt it, too, cast her a dark look, and strutted away.

She leaned on the bottom of the scaffolding, trembling. "Jonah! I need to speak with you."

The cameraman's face was flushed. He climbed down and brushed himself off.

"I need to get back to town," Meredith said.

Jonah nodded. "I'll see you back to camp."

The two hiked toward the camp in silence until Meredith thought she would explode. "Why did you let him bully you that way? He had no right."

"He does have a right to say if he doesn't want his photograph published."

"He did this just to spite me."

"I don't think so," Jonah said.

Meredith mulled it over until they reached the camp. "I'm taking this to the bull."

Jonah snatched at her arm. "Don't. I've plenty of good photographs. We don't need it."

"You looking for me?" a voice from behind caused Meredith to jump.

"Yes," she said when she had caught her breath. "One of your men threatened Jonah."

"How's that?"

"Meredith," Jonah's voice warned.

"He purposely broke one of Jonah's plates."

The bull scowled at Meredith with his black eyes. "Some stories are better left untold. Men's lives can be like that." He tipped his hat and walked off toward his tent.

Her mouth gaped.

"It's not your problem, Storm."

"I'm a reporter. If. . ."

"You better leave so you can get to town before dark."

Jonah's change of topic was like a dousing of cold water, and Meredith's fire sputtered. She backed off. "What about you? Will you be all right here?"

"I'll be fine. I like it here, Storm. Don't ruin it for me."

Meredith's cheeks burned. "You're right, then. I'd better go."

That evening Meredith soaked off her trail dust. It was worth the extra effort to use Mrs. Cooper's rustic indoor plumbing. Water first had to be pumped, then emptied by hand. Meredith did her own pumping, but Mrs. Cooper hired a boy to empty the tub for her guests. Meredith rubbed the kinks in her neck and stretched her sore legs out over the edge of the tub. She hoped her articles for *McClure's* magazine would please Asa, her editor. The soft nightgown draped over a nearby chair looked inviting. It wasn't easy to make the long ride out to the camp.

As she bathed, she recited a favorite verse, one that usually uplifted her in weary times. "'I can do all things through Christ which strengtheneth me.'" The Spirit of God nudged her spirit. *Why were you so mad at Mr. Talbot? Because he's rude and. . . and. . .he's hiding something.* She disregarded God's question in lieu of her own. *Why didn't Talbot want his photograph taken? What is Thatcher Talbot's story?* Meredith reached for her towel.

Chapter 7

Meredith awoke to the familiar saying of her editor. *"If you fall off the horse, Storm, you've got to get right back on."* The horse, in this instance, was her story. And her instincts told her that her story somehow included Thatcher Talbot. Otherwise, why would her thoughts be consumed by him?

She donned her brown riding skirt and rehearsed her plans to ride to Bucker's Stand and get Thatcher Talbot's story.

On her way out of town, Meredith reined in her horse outside the newspaper office and dismounted. In her haste, however, her foot slipped through a crack, undoubtedly carved by some logger's boot, and sent her flailing. She gave a gasp of exasperation and caught her balance. *Take it easy. You know the hazards.* Then at a more dignified pace, she started off again.

The bell rigged on the door of the newspaper office announced her arrival. After a few polite words, Meredith slapped her story down on Charlie Dutton's desk.

"Read this. You can tell me later what you think of it. Good day, gentlemen."

She strode back to her horse, confident that the newspaper editor would find her article about logging hazards of interest.

Two hours later, at Bucker's Stand, the noises of the steam donkey, falling trees, and singing men led her to the center of activity. Jonah waved from his treehouse studio. She waved back, amazed at the way the city man had adapted himself to the rugged environment and rough-edged lumberjacks.

As usual, Meredith drew some open stares and stolen glances, but she turned a blind eye to all that and put the first phase of her plan into work. Mr. Talbot was peeling the bark off logs. She nestled into the comfortable crook of a low tree branch and reached into her portfolio, aware that Talbot gave her a curious glance. Her back braced against the tree's trunk, she leisurely swung her legs and began to write, ever watchful of Talbot—her tactic to unnerve him enough that he might approach her and begin a conversation.

An hour passed. At one point, Meredith became so engrossed in her writing that she unconsciously shifted her seat and caught a splinter in her upper thigh.

"Ouch." She winced, then cast a quick glance to see if anyone noticed.

To her knowledge, no one had. She scooted off the limb and took stilted, painful steps toward a large redwood. She ducked behind it and twisted to inspect the damage. Her skirt was skewered to her hip with a splinter about the size of a sewing needle.

"Ah," she groaned.

To see the sharp piece that punctured flesh to clothing intensified the stabbing pain. She twisted again, took ahold of the sliver, held her breath, and yanked.

"Ah." The barb pulled her skin and remained skewered.

"Miss Mears?" It was Talbot's voice.

"Go away," she called from her hideaway.

"Do you need help?" His voice now came from just around the other side of the tree's large round trunk.

"No."

"Listen. I saw what happened."

Her heart raced. This wasn't going as she had planned. She felt helpless, trapped, foolish. She twisted around and took another look. Now the puncture wound was bleeding and seeping through her skirt.

"I'm coming around the tree."

She closed her eyes to wait for the inevitable and leaned her shoulder against the tree trunk.

⌇

When Thatcher rounded the redwood, his first glimpse of her, pale and frightened as a rabbit, plucked his heart. The woman had been watching him for the past hour and writing in that notepad of hers. It was most unsettling, and he had been ready to go over and suggest she run along and distract someone else. But when he had looked over and seen her predicament, he knew he needed to help. He stole a quick look at the problem.

"That looks painful. Did you try to pull it out?"

She nodded, her autumn eyes cloudy, her lips pursed.

"Mind if I have a try?"

She shrugged and turned just a bit.

41

Thatcher cleared his throat, concentrated on the splinter, and gently took hold of it. "This might sting."

"I know."

"Why don't you put both hands on that tree trunk? You know, brace yourself a bit."

She cast him a frightened look, then placed her palms on the rough bark.

"Tell me when you're ready," Talbot said.

"Ready."

At the sound of her faint voice, he pulled, felt her flinch, felt the splinter release and slide out, and then waved the offensive thing like a banner. "Got it."

She took several gasping breaths. "Let me see."

He handed it to her.

"No wonder it hurt, look how jagged it is."

"You might have a deep puncture wound there." He handed her a folded handkerchief. "Better press that against the spot to stop the bleeding."

She nodded. "Thank you."

Thatcher wanted to get her mind off her wound and make sure the bleeding stopped. He searched his mind for small talk. "Who do you write for?"

"*McClure's* magazine."

"Mm. New York."

"You've heard of it?"

He smiled at her assumption that he was uneducated. "I've read it."

"I'd like to do some articles for the local newspaper while I'm here."

"Don't know much about that. Haven't been here long myself."

"That's right. The bull did say you were new man on board."

"What does *McClure's* find so interesting about logging?"

"Whatever I write will be interesting, Mr. Talbot."

He chuckled. "And what will you write about?"

"About danger, conservation, the spell these huge trees weave over people, about the loggers themselves."

He leaned against the tree, just inches away from her, and crossed his ankles. "Just hardworking men."

"What compels you to work here?"

"Always wanted to see the West."

"Is it what you expected?"

"Haven't seen enough of it yet to tell."

"You going to move from camp to camp?"

"Maybe."

"Do you worry about the dangers, accidents? Maybe there won't be a tomorrow."

"Men need to set their minds on their work, not the dangers, Miss Mears."

"May I quote you?"

"Hmm?"

"What you said just now, may I quote that?"

"I didn't know I was being interviewed. I thought I was just making conversation with a pretty lady."

"I won't use your name," she said.

He shrugged and changed the subject. "Did the bleeding stop?"

Meredith removed the pad and checked it. "I think so."

"Why don't I go get your things and help you back to camp?"

The pretty reporter accepted his help, though he could tell it pained her to do so. He collected her things, resisting the urge to rifle through her notes, and carried them back to the tree.

She placed everything inside her portfolio with swift movements of her petite hands. "Ready."

"We'll go slow. Tell me if it hurts too much."

"And what will you do if it does?"

Thatcher shrugged. "Throw you over my shoulder."

"It feels just fine."

When they reached camp, he asked, "You plan to ride back to town?"

"I don't have much choice."

"All that bumping around in the saddle might start the bleeding again."

"I think I'll be fine. Once a puncture wound swells and closes, the bleeding stops."

"How'd you learn that?"

"My older stepbrother, Charles, is a doctor."

He shrugged. "If you're sure."

"I'm sure."

"I'll go get your horse then."

❧

When Meredith arrived home, Mrs. Cooper took one look at her, limping into the parlor, and rushed forward. "My dear. What's wrong?"

"My leg," Meredith moaned. "I got this horrible splinter in it."

"Why, it's bleeding, you poor thing. Let's get you into a tub and see what it looks like."

"Mm. That sounds wonderful. It's so sore."

The rest of the evening, Mrs. Cooper clucked over Meredith like a mother hen, and Meredith let her.

❧

The next morning Meredith's wound, covered with Mrs. Cooper's special drawing liniment and a bandage, felt so improved that she only remembered it at times when she bumped it against something. Meredith supposed it had served a purpose. She'd gotten her interview with Talbot, though it had not revealed much. In fact, it was more as if he had interviewed her. Somewhere she had lost control.

After breakfast and reassuring Mrs. Cooper for the third time that she really felt fine, she walked to the newspaper office. She opened the door in one breath and asked the editor in the next, "Did you read it?"

"It's very good. Can I print it?"

A glow of pleasure crept over Meredith. "Yes."

"You've made them into heroes. The loggers will love it. Everyone will. It's the female perspective of courage that makes the story. It's. . ."

"Romantic?"

"Yes, that's it. Romantic. Can you do more of these?"

"I was hoping you would ask."

Enthusiasm laced his voice. "We could do a weekly column. Or whatever you can get me, if that's too much."

"You've got a deal, Mr. Dutton."

Even the memory of Frederick Ralston's glare didn't keep Meredith from humming a tune. Now if only Asa thought her articles were romantic, newsworthy. He had scoffed at her. Or was that because he was protective? Asa had not replied to the articles she'd sent him. But she was pleased with her efforts so far. She was getting a story in a man's world, a good story.

❧

Mrs. Cooper saw Meredith enter the house. "That gown is so much more appealing, dear. Doesn't it do as well as trousers?"

Meredith answered her landlady in her most patient tone, after all, she had been so kind to her the evening before, almost motherly.

"I don't enjoy wearing men's clothing. A journalist has to do things that aren't always pleasant just to get a story. The readers will remember the story long after they forget what I wore. They'll remember where Buckman's Pride is. They'll recall what happens at Bucker's Stand."

"I understand your point. It's just hard to see you bring the town's scorn upon yourself. I wish folks could see you for the nice girl you are, as I do."

Meredith eased down at the kitchen table, sitting on her good hip. She set her portfolio on the floor, propped her elbows on the table, and cupped her chin in her hands. Her voice took a faraway tone. "I confess, I do care what they think. Two ladies snubbed me the other day, wouldn't even return a greeting. Why? I'm sure they never saw me in trousers. I don't parade around town in them."

Mrs. Cooper's high cheekbones blushed even more than their usual peachy color. "It is a small town."

"Perhaps you could pass on a few good words for me."

"I could do better than that." Mrs. Cooper perked up at her own sudden idea. "I could have a dinner and invite a few choice people. They can see for themselves what a delightful creature you are."

Meredith brightened. "You would do that?"

"Yes. And we could invite your partner, Mr. Shaw."

"He's coming back to town tomorrow to work in his studio for a few days."

"Splendid! I'll get to work on it."

"Thank you, Mrs. Cooper. I do appreciate your concern."

"Save your thanks, dear. We'll have to wait and see what happens."

Mrs. Cooper leaned across the table and patted her hand. "I didn't mean that the way it sounded. It'll be fine. You'll see."

Meredith nodded and reached down for her portfolio. It was important to her to make a favorable impression. In New York, the ladies had loved her. There she was the height of fashion, the epitome of what women hoped to be. Maybe she was a bit of a "new woman." Perhaps this small town wasn't ready for her. Could she fit in?

Chapter 8

The town stableboy handed Meredith a note.

She cast a glance around her, then unfolded it and read:

Miss Mears,

I hope you don't think me presumptuous, but I knew your intentions of going to Bucker's Stand today to work on the column. I have a bigger story that really needs a woman's perspective, this edition's big news. Come see me.

Charlie Dutton

Presumptuous, indeed. She stuffed the note into her pocket, took leave of the stableboy, and headed straight for the *Buckman News*. That contrary, pale-faced reporter was probably behind this. It better be some big story, if, indeed, there was a story.

The newsroom door banged and its bell clanged behind Meredith. "Mr. Dutton!"

The elderly editor offered a sheepish smile. Ralston wasn't in the room. "I was expecting you."

Meredith wrenched the piece of paper from her pocket and waved it. "What is the meaning of this? Is there really a big story?"

"It's as big as twins."

It took a moment for the meaning of his words to settle in. "Someone had twins?"

Dutton nodded. "Last night Francine Wiley delivered a set of twin boys, and as far as I know they both lived. It's a miracle."

Meredith tried her hardest not to smile. She knew the survival of twins was a momentous occasion. In a town this size it would be the big story. "You're right. This is today's story." She set her portfolio upon the closest desk and withdrew a pencil. "Give me directions."

On her way out the door, she turned back to the newsman. "You do understand this wasn't fair? I am capable of handling both stories and should have been allowed to do so."

"Perhaps. Time will tell. Now hurry up and get your story before the whole town gets it on their own, firsthand."

"Humph!" The door banged again, and Dutton chuckled.

⟡

Meanwhile at Bucker's Stand, an amazing thing took place. None of the loggers, including the bull, could hear often enough the marvelous things that had been written about themselves.

From the groaning tree to the whining sawmill, to list the ways a logger can be maimed, crushed, or killed is a countless task. Yet by use of their brawn, ingenuity, and courage, they persevere. Just as no axe can reach the center of a giant redwood, no words can describe the courage of the lumberjack. These noble men—whose boots tread the carpets of the deep woods and whose dreams soar just as high as any other man's—are out to tame the untamable by raw muscle power and tough determination. Every lonely bucker, every axman, faller, climber, peeler, and bull is somebody's son or brother or husband with a life expectancy of only seven years, so dangerous is the job. I stand beneath the canopied trees, whose roots entangle the logger's heart—wooing dreams and sapping life's blood—and ask, "Don't you worry about the dangers?"

"Men need to set their minds on their work, not the dangers," I was told. And not only are these men's minds on their work, but their hearts. . . .

Thatcher Talbot refolded the worn, now fragile, newspaper in a reverent gesture and laid it back on the mess hall table. When he read his quote, his heart swelled with appreciation. The reporter would not praise without merit. She had seen into their souls. She understood.

Ever since he had laid eyes on her on the train, she had intrigued him, her beauty and spirit slinking their way into his inner being. If she was this perceptive, this deeply moved, perhaps she was worth knowing.

But his life held so many uncertainties right now that it wouldn't be wise to form any kind of an attachment. He shook his head. The eastern reporter had wormed her contrary self into his every thought and emotion, and he didn't know what to do about it. And now, her name was praise on every man's lips in the camp.

Someone entered the tent, and Thatcher looked up. "Silas," he motioned. "What do you think of this article?"

✍

Mrs. Cooper was as pleased as a woodpecker in a dead tree, doing what she liked to do best, entertain.

"Pass the meat, dear," Mrs. Cooper said. "Miss Mears used to write the society column in New York City."

"How very interesting," Beatrice Bloomfield, the banker's wife, said. "You must find it very dull in Buckman's Pride."

"Indeed not." Meredith smiled at the woman, so near her own age, the one who had snubbed her in town. "Just the other day, the Wiley twins were born. Did you read my article?"

"Well yes, I did. But we both know that's a rare occasion."

"Nonsense. This town is a writer's dream come true."

"And how is that?" The dark-haired beauty asked.

"Buckman's Pride oozes with adventure, Wild West, romance, interesting people, and determination. I like the spirit of this town."

"As do I," Jonah said as he stabbed a piece of meat with his fork. "I'll find it very hard to leave."

"Must you leave?" Mrs. Cooper asked.

"I'll give that question some serious thought." His intense gaze made Mrs. Cooper's blue eyes sparkle in the same cornflower blue as the floral-patterned coffee cup poised next to her cheek.

"We would consider you a valuable addition to our community," The banker replied.

"And you?" Beatrice Bloomfield asked, her brown-eyed gaze fixed on Meredith.

"I plan to return. My father lives in New York."

"Oh? Does he greatly influence your life, my dear?" Mrs. Cooper asked.

"Yes, I suppose he does," Meredith said. There was a general silence around the table, and Mrs. Cooper passed the food again. Finally, Meredith asked, "Is there a women's auxiliary in Buckman's Pride?"

"Why, yes. We have the Women's Circle, which does charitable deeds," Beatrice Bloomfield said. Her thin lips formed a smug smile.

"May I come to one of your meetings?" Meredith asked. "I could do an article on your work."

"Well, I couldn't say without discussing it first with the other ladies."

"We have a meeting next Monday night, don't we, Beatrice?" Mrs. Cooper asked. "I'll remind you to bring it up."

"But it might interfere with Miss Mears's more important projects, traipsing off to Bucker's Stand and all."

"Traipsing?" Meredith repeated in an insulted tone.

"You do ride unaccompanied to the men's camp."

"I escort her or meet her at the camp," Jonah said.

Meredith cleared her throat. "I would not traipse in New York. But," she shrugged, "here in the wild..."

"You assume incorrectly," Mrs. Bloomfield said. "I also am from a city, Chicago. And I find your conduct here..."

"It is Miss Mears's story that is important." Mrs. Cooper gave Meredith a look of censure, yet flew into a long-winded exoneration on her part. "You see, long after Miss Mears has gone back to New York City, the things remembered will be her stories about Buckman's Pride and Bucker's Stand. Folks who read her articles back in the East won't know that Miss Mears got her story traipsing across the country in men's clothing." Amelia Cooper gasped and put her hand over her mouth.

Beatrice Bloomfield's eyebrows arched.

Amelia recovered and said, "But the things she writes are what they'll remember."

Meredith cast Mrs. Cooper a grateful glance. The woman had tried to defend her, even if she did have a slip of the tongue.

"We shall see," Mrs. Bloomfield said. "What a delightful dinner this has been." She pushed back her chair.

The men at the table bumbled to their feet when Mrs. Bloomfield stood.

"Mrs. Bloomfield, would you like to see my studio?"

"Perhaps some other time, sir."

"I would like to see it," The quiet-mannered banker said.

"It really is something to see, Beatrice," Amelia Cooper urged.

As the group of dinner guests moved outside to view Jonah's photograph studio, Mrs. Cooper squeezed Meredith's arm. "Come along with us, dear."

Meredith trailed behind the group, headed up by Jonah, then Herbert Bloomfield, the banker, whose gait was quite enthusiastic. His wife's hand remained looped through his arm, where he'd placed it, but her back was rigidly straight. Jonah gestured and chatted, and Mrs. Cooper turned to wait for Meredith.

"Don't let that woman intimidate you," Amelia whispered. "I have every bit as much say in this town as she does."

"Let's hope Jonah can impress her," Meredith whispered.

His studio enthralled Mr. Bloomfield and held the others' attention. Jonah explained some of the chemical processes involved in dry-plate photography and showed them photographs of the waterfalls from their trip.

"These are of the logging camp. I'm going to send them to *McClure's* magazine to go along with Miss Mears's articles."

Herbert Bloomfield adjusted his glasses. "They are quite good."

"I would love to take a photograph of the two of you." Jonah included the banker's beautiful wife in his gaze. "You could frame it to hang in the bank."

"Oh. I wouldn't want to be so prideful," Beatrice Bloomfield said.

"Not at all. If anything, it adds an air of respectability to an establishment."

"Really?" she asked. She released her husband's arm and moved closer to Jonah. "And where would you take this photograph?"

Jonah shrugged. "Anywhere you like."

"That does give us something to think about, doesn't it, Herbert?"

"And Meredith could write a caption to put beneath the photograph. Couldn't you?"

"It would be my pleasure," Meredith said with an appreciative smile.

"It's settled then," Mrs. Cooper declared.

Chapter 9

I see you and Mrs. Cooper are on a first-name basis now," Jonah said.

"I was wrong about Amelia," Meredith said. She hovered over Jonah's shoulder as he coated albumen paper with a silver solution.

"I'm just glad to see the two of you getting along."

"Me, too. Those are great, Jonah."

"They could be better. See the shadows there? I'm still experimenting with the lens to get the lighting the way I want it."

"I've never seen you use flash powder."

He shook his head. "Don't like it." Meredith browsed around the studio. "You working on a problem?" he asked.

"Hmm?"

"Usually, when you get that expression, you're sorting out a problem."

"I guess I am. Maybe you can help. I need you to take a special photograph."

He looked up from his work. "That shouldn't be a problem. What do you need?"

"I need a photograph of Thatcher Talbot."

Jonah grinned. "Lovesick, are you?"

"Of course not. This is strictly business."

"Seriously, Storm, you know I promised him I wouldn't take his photograph. I gave my word."

"He'll never know." Meredith leaned her elbow on the studio worktable, close to Jonah. "Listen. I think our Mr. Talbot is a wanted man. If there's a story on him, it's worth a look."

Jonah jerked the thin paper. "I don't like it, Storm. I like Thatcher. Anyway, if he were a wanted man, he could be dangerous."

"I just want a photograph to send back to Asa. I'll let him do the investigation."

"And if he uncovers something?"

"Then I'll bring my finds to you, and we'll make the decision together."

"Even if I wanted to help you, he's too smart, too cautious. I'd never get the photograph."

"I'll distract him for you."

"How? No, wait!" His hand shot up. "Don't tell me. I don't want to know."

"Does that mean you'll help me?"

"I don't know, Storm. I'll have to think about it."

"I'm riding out to Bucker's Stand tomorrow. I'd like it if you went along." Jonah sighed, and Meredith said, "I know. You have to think about it. Take all the time you want as long as you let me know by tomorrow morning. I'll let you get back to work now."

ॐ

The next morning Meredith thanked Jonah repeatedly when he said he would accompany her, although he was careful not to make her any promises. When they reached the camp, Josiah Jones, the bull, tipped his hat at Meredith as she rode past his tent.

"You are in a fine mood today, sir," she said, after she dismounted.

"I want to thank you for your article. It boosted the morale mountain high."

"I only wrote the truth, the way I see it."

"The men will soon be in to eat. You'll see for yourself."

The loggers entered the mess tent in twos and threes, all vying for Meredith's attention.

"Won't you join us, Miss Mears?" asked one of the older lumberjacks. "You, too, Jonah."

"Don't mind if I do." Meredith tried to ignore the stench of working bodies as she and Jonah joined him at a long table. The loggers shoveled in food as if their innards were empty, yet they managed to keep up a conversation.

"Here to write another one of your stories?" The older man asked.

"I'd like to add a bit to the last one, if I could get your help," she gestured to all of those seated about her. She could tell by their grunts, grins, and nods that they would help if they could.

"If I were to ask why you do it, why you jeopardize your life by working at such a dangerous occupation, what would you say?"

"So's a pretty reporter women can ask us questions," one quickly replied.

She smiled.

Another piped up, "Don't know how to do nothing else."

Meredith grabbed her portfolio and fumbled for a paper and pencil. She wrote while the responses flowed without pause.

"Once you see these trees, you can't never leave them."

"There's glory in these trees."

One younger man, who reminded her a lot of her stepbrother, Charles, said, "Got a mother who needs the money."

"Got a wife and kids," another said.

"Working the trees chases the demons out of you," offered a fierce-looking man.

"It's the smell of the woods," Silas said.

"Came west looking for gold. Ended up here instead."

"Wanted to see the West." The phrase was familiar, as was the voice, and Meredith looked up at Thatcher Talbot. She swallowed when Jonah reached down for his camera and slipped away from the table.

"And is the West better than the East?"

"It's different," he replied.

Meredith tried not to concentrate on his handsome features. She pressed hard on her pencil until the lead broke. "Oh no."

"Here, let me." Talbot's hand brushed against hers and sent a flurry of sparks through her arm. With expertise, he withdrew a small knife from his belt and began to whittle the writing tool.

A guilty stab pierced Meredith, but she squelched it. "Thank you." She retrieved the pencil from Talbot, with a small gasp, for there was another jolt of physical awareness. She hadn't distracted him long, but Jonah gave her a nod.

A bell rang, and the loggers stampeded out of the mess hall. Meredith stuffed her supplies into her portfolio and smoothed out her riding skirt.

Thatcher Talbot had moved away, and now he leaned against the doorway, his arms crossed against his chest, waiting for her.

She gave him a weak smile.

"On behalf of the camp, thanks for that article."

"It was just the truth."

"The truth sounds lovely, coming from you."

"What a nice compliment."

His eyes were soft like suede; his hair hung in boyish waves across his forehead. "I'll bet you get plenty of those."

"Whatever happened to that rude man I once knew?"

He chuckled as they left the mess hall together. "'I'd rather be hung from a rope and dragged by my heels through these here woods than be escorted by the likes of you.'"

"You'll do."

He slapped his thigh with his hat as, together, they burst into laughter.

Meredith experienced a sense of wonder at Talbot's personality transformation and felt as if she were falling under a spell of charm. Such magical eyes.

"I have to go out to the field. Are you coming?"

"Hmm? Not today." She patted her portfolio and gave him a final smile. "I have what I came for."

He nodded. "Another time, then." She watched him walk away, sorry that he was such an enigma, sorry she was pressed to investigate him, worried over what she would find.

"Ready to go?" Jonah asked.

⁂

Back at his studio, Meredith helped Jonah process the photographs he had taken at the camp. Once they were hung to dry, she inspected them.

"Here, Storm. This one of you with all the loggers would be a good one to show your grandchildren some day. Want to buy it?"

"It's a moment I'll never forget." She sighed. "It was like being the belle of the ball."

His eyes twinkled with a mixture of pride and amusement. "You brought some light into their lives."

Meredith's tiny hand brushed away tears. "And they to mine."

Jonah said softly, "I was only teasing. You may have it."

"Thank you."

"Don't cry, missy."

"I'm not." She sniffled as she turned to the next photograph. It was the one of Thatcher. "It's good."

"Should give you the information you are after."

"Do you think I should send it to Asa?"

"Maybe you need to set your mind at ease about him so you can. . ." His voice trailed off.

"Can what?"

"Like him."

"Oh."

〰

Once the photographs dried, Meredith needed to make her decision. Jonah was right. She must know. With decisive movements, she prepared the photograph and package she would mail to Asa, along with a note:

> *See what you can find out about this man. His name is Thatcher*
> *Talbot. He got on the train in Chicago. He may be a wanted man.*

All she could do, Meredith determined, was wait to hear from Asa. In the meantime, she should put Thatcher Talbot from her mind.

Chapter 10

That night Meredith slept poorly and dreamed of Talbot just before she awoke. She dressed and went straight to her typewriter. When her wastebasket spilled over with crumpled wads of paper, she sighed and pushed away from her desk. Maybe if she went for a walk, the morning air would clear her head. She found herself strolling up the town's main street.

It was a pleasant morning with blue sky and fluffy clouds, a melodious string of birds roosted on the cobbler's hitching post, and a smattering of town residents went about their daily rounds. One, Beatrice Bloomfield, bustled out of the bank's main entrance, her head bent over an armful of packages. When she recognized Meredith, she gave a start, then a terse greeting before she swooshed away in her chic day dress.

At least it wasn't a total snub. I'm making progress.

Meredith crossed the street, drawn to her favorite store, the dress shop and milliner. The little yellow hat with the green ostrich feather still beckoned from its window display.

✍

Across the street, Thatcher Talbot strode toward the bank, his mind occupied with the news he had received at the camp: One of his old acquaintances was in town. However, his thoughts shifted when he spotted the fascinating reporter, slightly bent and peering intently at something inside a store window. Thatcher lingered over the delightful vision, his back against a hitching post and his arms and legs casually crossed, until she entered the shop.

✍

Meredith positioned the little yellow hat with the green ostrich feather on her head while the dressmaker secured it with pins.

"Take a look in that mirror. You look pretty in it."

Meredith moved to the cheval mirror. "It's exquisite."

"Would you like to see the matching gown?"

"I have a gown from New York that matches perfectly." Meredith dallied over her reflection until, with a final sigh, she removed the hatpins.

"Actually, I'll need to sell a few more stories before I can afford this hat. But if someone doesn't beat me to it, I'll be back for it. It caught my eye the very first day I came to town."

"That's how it goes, my dear. Once something strikes your fancy, you must have it. I hope it's here when you are ready to purchase it."

"Yes, so do I. Thank you."

Meredith exited the dressmaker's and made a quick assessment of the street only to catch a glimpse of a man who resembled Talbot. *What would he be doing in town on a weekday?* Unconsciously, she found herself trailing after the man across the street. Still unsure of the man's identity, she watched him enter the bank. She loitered, window shopping, and waited for him to reappear. The owner of the general store happened to be sweeping in front of his store, so she engaged him in conversation, where she could keep a watchful eye on the bank.

After a time, the man came out of the bank. *It is Talbot. And he's with another man.* She was surprised to see both men attired in Eastern suits of clothing. Her curiosity intensified; a small voice inside her chirped, *I told you he was suspicious.*

The two men engaged in conversation until they turned a corner and vanished down an unfamiliar side street. Meredith curtailed her conversation with the general store owner and skipped across the street toward the intersection where Mr. Talbot had disappeared. She rounded the corner in haste and, to her horror, ran smack into Mr. Talbot's broad side. With a shriek of surprise, she allowed a strong hand to steady her.

"In a hurry, Miss Mears?" Thatcher Talbot cast her a look of censure. The only establishments on this street were a men's haberdashery, a saloon, and a blacksmith shop.

Meredith saw the irony. "Excuse me, Mr. Talbot." She released herself from his grip. "I was just out for some exercise. I'd never been this way before, and. . ."

"It might not be the best proximity for a lady. The main streets would be safer."

"Yes. I'll remember that." Her eyes darted to his companion.

"May I introduce you?"

Meredith gave the brim of her hat a push so she could better see the stranger's face.

"Mr. William Boon of Chicago, may I present Miss Meredith S. Mears." Meredith felt the heat rise to her cheeks as Talbot overplayed her middle initial. "William is an old friend of mine, and Miss Mears is a reporter from New York City."

Meredith detected a glint of humor in William Boon's eyes and had the distinct impression they were making sport of her. Nevertheless, she couldn't miss this opportunity to snoop.

"Are you travelling on business, then?"

"No ma'am. It's personal."

Mr. Boon had a fair rectangular face, covered with freckles, and Meredith wondered what a few hours in the California sun would do to it.

"I'm surprised you could get the day off at the camp, Mr. Talbot."

"It wasn't that hard. I just don't get paid."

"Which reminds me, I should get back to my work."

"Have a nice walk, Miss Mears."

"A pleasure meeting you."

"Gentlemen."

Meredith's feet could not get her away fast enough. *Of all the embarrassing things! What could that impossible man be up to? Was his city friend an accomplice?*

Once Meredith was out of sight, the two men chuckled. "You were right about her," William said. "She was following you."

"Nosy little thing, always probing." Thatcher tried to put her out of his mind. "Let's go have that breakfast."

Inside the café, the men ordered and received their meals. They fell into a comfortable conversation, and William caught Thatcher up on the news from the East.

"After Colleen left, I moped around for several months. One day it hit me. I want her back, and I'm willing to fight for her. I was a lousy husband, but I'll change if I can get her back."

Thatcher sympathized with his longtime friend whose wife had left him. When Thatcher had left Chicago, both he and his friend's lives had been amuck.

"I hope you can find her and forgive her."

"I've already forgiven her. Here. . ." William reached into his vest pocket and withdrew a small photograph of his wife. "I'd like you to have this. Perhaps it will help to locate her. Ask around whenever you get the chance. And here," he said as he pulled out another small slip of paper. "This is my lawyer's address. You can reach me through him."

Thatcher took the photograph and slip of paper. "She's always been very beautiful."

"I wish I'd realized what I had before I ruined things between us."

"I'll keep you in my prayers. You'll find her."

William pushed back his empty plate. "What about you? How long are you going to keep running?"

"Until I can get the courage to go back and face Father."

"He'll probably never change his business manners without your influence. He's only gotten worse with you gone."

"I just can't handle his unethical, greedy, vindictive. . ." Thatcher's voice trailed off into silence.

"He has one weakness in that mean façade."

"It's not a façade."

"He loves you. He's falling apart without you. He rationalizes all his actions. He's meaner than ever since you've left, but there's such an emptiness, a sadness about him."

"I don't think he could love anybody."

"He has offered a reward for any information of your whereabouts."

"He what?" Thatcher leaned forward and his chair scraped the floor. "How?"

"His lawyer sent out letters, inquiries. The word's out."

"I can't believe it. Father owns everything else in Chicago, I guess he thinks he can buy me, too."

"Maybe you should go back and get it straightened out."

"I can't. Are you forgetting Adaline? She's a female version of Father, and he demands that I marry her."

"Hmm. I did forget about her. I guess I was too caught up in my own problems when you left."

"Father pressed for a marriage. He even spoke to Adaline's father. Mother arranged events to throw us together." Thatcher shook his head. "There is no way that I will marry her."

"So you're going to hide out until she marries someone else?"

Thatcher chuckled. "No one else will have her."

William rapped the table with his fist. "We've gotten ourselves into some real messes, haven't we?"

"I'll pray for you, if you'll pray for me."

"Sounds like a good place to start."

Chapter 11

Several days passed. One morning, Meredith started off for Bucker's Stand clad in her comfortable men's trousers.

Just before Meredith reached the camp, her horse stumbled on a rock and began to limp. The rooftops of the bunkhouse and mess hall were visible, not more than a mile up the road, so she dismounted and led her horse the remainder of the way.

As she approached camp, she could tell that things were in an upheaval. Men scurried, shouting orders. With concern, she tethered her horse to a post and went in search of the bull, whom she found meting out instructions with a stern voice.

As soon as there was a lull, she asked, "What's going on?"

"Accident. Don't have time." The bull hurried past her.

"Where?" She started after him, but he paid her no heed. Then she spotted Talbot in the crowd and ran up to him. "Mr. Talbot! Where's the accident?"

"You don't want to see it."

"But I do."

"No."

They glared at each other until the bull interrupted, "Talbot, go after the doctor."

Talbot nodded, gave Meredith a final cutting look, then left for his horse.

The bull gave her a calculating look. "So you finally got your accident."

"It's not my fault, and you know it. I only write the facts."

"Go on, then," he motioned. "Go watch a man die."

Mr. Talbot approached on his horse. The bull called out after them, "Give her a ride, Talbot."

Talbot stopped his horse and looked down at her. "Where's your horse?"

"He's picked up a stone."

He reached down his hand and said curtly, "Come up, then."

"No. I won't ride with you. . . ." Her words choked off as she reminded herself, *It's for the story.* His face was unreadable, but he still offered his hand, so reluctantly she took it.

He hoisted her up behind him and nudged his horse. The animal jerked into motion, and Meredith grasped Talbot's shirt with two hands. *Men!* Even though she resented Talbot's and the bull's attitudes, she couldn't help but notice how good it felt to hold on to Mr. Talbot's solid back.

✑

Meanwhile, Talbot was disgusted with his own awareness of the feminine body pressed up against his. Protective feelings surged up. *Why must she insist on seeing the accident? Why is she so stubborn? Couldn't she just act like a woman?* He cut his thoughts short when they rounded the next bend.

"This is it," he said, reining in his horse. He reached back to help her dismount, but she slipped to the ground and landed hard on her bottom.

She got up and dusted off her pants. "Thank you."

Talbot nodded then made haste for the town's doctor.

✑

Meredith watched him go for a moment, then followed after the loggers. Once they had reached the accident, Meredith gasped ragged breaths from the exertion and hung back to recuperate.

Finally, she edged forward. It was a very young man. The one she remembered from her interviews, who reminded her of Charles. The boy had told her he worked at the camp to support his mother. The young man was pinned beneath a log that was too heavy to move with man-power. The loggers had already moved the donkey steam engine and were frantically fastening the log to its cables. She watched the scene before her, wondering how the young man could even have survived. His legs must surely be crushed.

Finally, the cable was secured. "Hang on, boy, we'll have you free in a minute. A doctor's on the way. You're gonna be just fine now."

Words of encouragement rallied around the boy. His eyes remained closed. Meredith turned away, too anxious and nauseated to watch. She went behind the nearest tree and dropped to her knees to pray. There was a giant crashing sound, and she knew that the log had been moved. Still, she waited.

"He's gone."

Meredith knelt behind the tree for a long time, listening to the fragments of conversation.

"Too late."

"Could've never saved his legs."

"Better this way."

"Just a boy."

"He was a good lad."

After a time, Meredith wiped her eyes with her sleeves and, never looking back, stumbled out of the woods and onto the road. She would never forget him lying there. Once she wandered back to the camp, she remembered her horse and led him to the stables. The groom gave him a careful inspection. "He'll be fine, but you can't ride him back tonight."

"Can I borrow a horse?"

"I'll check with the bull and be right back."

Meredith waited, her mind reliving the scene of the accident until the groom returned and found her a mount.

On the ride back to town, the sound of approaching riders reached her, and she looked up to see a dust cloud advancing toward her. The riders pulled up beside her. It was Talbot and the doctor.

Talbot looked at her with concern. "The boy?"

"He didn't make it."

Talbot let out a sigh of regret, and the doctor said, "I'm sorry."

"Me, too," Meredith shivered.

"You going to be all right?" Talbot asked. "I can ride back to town with you."

"No. I'll be fine. I'd rather be alone right now."

Talbot hesitated, and the doctor said, "I'll go on out to the camp, anyway."

They separated, and Meredith continued on into town, stabled her horse, and even though it was still daylight, went straight home to bed.

✍

The mother of the deceased young man lived in town. Meredith went to visit her the next afternoon. The small woman appeared strong in spite of her grief.

"I knew when I saw the bull, something had happened to my boy." She wrung her handkerchief. "He was such a good boy. Ever since his pa died, he took good care of me."

"I met him once. He was a special young man."

"Did you?"

"Yes. He talked about you that day."

"I remember," The older woman nodded. "You put it in the paper." She looked at Meredith with dewy eyes. "Will you write something good about my boy?"

"Yes. I will."

ॐ

After that call, Meredith visited Francine Wiley, the woman who had birthed twin sons. Their conversation turned out to be as special as the one with the mother of the young logger who was killed. The visit with Mrs. Wiley cheered Meredith enough that she could write up two articles. The first told of the twins' progress, and the second was a touching obituary, which included how the loggers had rallied together to try to save the young man's life. Meredith delivered her stories to the newspaper editor and mailed a copy of the obituary to Asa.

Once she returned home, she thought about the three sons, and her own father came to mind. Then, his words: *If only you'd been a boy.*

Chapter 12

Meredith attended the logger's funeral. It was her first time inside the Buckman's Pride small, steepled church. Though it was a sad occasion, a sense of peace washed over her, and she wished she had attended the congregation's weekly services.

Church, as a child, had been one of the few places her father had allowed her to sit up tight against him. Her father's silent strength, along with the churchgoers' loving smiles, had made it a special haven. When she became a young adult, she had accepted Christ as her Savior.

Today, as the people gathered to bid the deceased boy good-bye, death brought the loggers and town leaders together. Everyone gave a kind word to the boy's mother. After the brief service, Meredith sidled into the crowd that shuffled outside to wait for the loggers who carried the casket of the young man on his last earthbound journey.

The town cemetery was located behind the church. Meredith gave Jonah a thankful smile when he appeared next to her and offered his arm for support. The preacher said a few more words. There was a prayer, and then it was over except for a lunch hosted by Mr. and Mrs. Washington, owners of the sawmill.

Emotional exhaustion wearied Meredith, but she felt obligated to attend the lunch. The townswomen had prepared dishes that were arranged on makeshift tables outside the sawmill. The sound of the Mad River's rushing waters could be heard in the background.

Meredith felt a pat on her shoulder and whirled. "Come sit with me, dear, won't you?"

"Oh yes, Amelia. I'd love to."

"What a nice story you wrote about that poor boy."

"It was a hard one to write."

"I'm sure it was."

"Mrs. Cooper, may I ask you a question?"

"Of course."

"You are one of the town's most affluent and well-respected women. Why do you take in boarders?"

"Because I get bored, and I enjoy cooking. Since my husband died,

I've been lonely. The first boarder I took in was a favor to someone. I enjoyed myself and decided to keep on doing it."

"I thought it was something like that."

Folks began to settle around Meredith and Mrs. Cooper. Mrs. Bloomfield took a nearby seat, and Mrs. Washington settled in next to her. Their husbands stood with a group of men across the way.

When Meredith caught a few words of the women's conversation, her fork stopped in midair.

"Journalism in this town."

Not wanting to be conspicuous, Meredith finished her bite, but strained her ears.

"She got herself a story at that poor young man's expense."

"Give the people back East something to read about. As if they care."

"Heard she rode out alone again."

"And she lamed her horse."

Meredith felt a squeeze on her arm and sneaked a look at Mrs. Cooper. The woman's pale face held a taut smile of reassurance. *Should I get up and leave or defend myself?* Meredith wondered. She had to do neither for someone rescued her.

"I don't think you ladies need to worry yourselves over Miss Mears's welfare or her horse's." There was a collected gasp as Mr. Talbot eased into a chair beside Beatrice Bloomfield and charmed her with a smile. "I happened to be there the day the boy had his accident. Miss Mears's horse will be fine, and Miss Mears conducted herself most properly. I think I speak for all the loggers when I say that her articles have lifted the morale of the camp. And Miss Mears was sent west because she is one of the best."

Beatrice smiled up at Talbot. "Well, if you say so, my dear, then of course it must be true. We do value your opinion." She leaned close. "But you must admit, she does seem a bit unladylike."

"Au contraire. I find her most lady. . .is that berry pie you have there, Mrs. Washington?"

"Why, yes it is."

"I must have some of that. You ladies are the best cooks. Please, excuse me."

The table became eerily quiet until Meredith politely excused herself. She looked around the crowd for Mr. Talbot. He was leaning against a post, staring out toward the river.

"I must thank you for championing me."

He turned with an expression of pleasure. "Join me?"

"Perhaps if we walked down by the river, the noise would drown out the conversations."

"They don't mean anything by it."

They started down the gradual incline toward the river. "And how would you know that?"

"I've known Beatrice for years. She's not a vicious person."

"I don't understand. You knew her back East?"

"Mm-hmm."

Talbot's clamlike evasion of the personal question did not surprise Meredith. "Why did you defend me just now?"

"I only spoke the truth." He looked down at her, admiration softening his brown eyes. "You are a good reporter."

Several feet away, the ground broke off into a bluff. Below that, the rushing waters drowned out the din of the townspeople, giving Meredith and Thatcher the illusion that they were in their own private world. "And you are very good at what you do," she replied.

"Logging?"

"No. Being mysterious and aloof. In fact, I would call you an expert."

"From a reporter, I guess that's a compliment."

"Being elusive is not always a good idea." She gave him a saucy look. "Good day, Mr. Talbot."

&

Thatcher watched Meredith's not-so-elegant departure with amusement. Her boot caught in a hole, she wobbled, straightened herself again, gave her hat a fierce tug. . . . He chuckled. If he didn't know better, he'd say she'd flirted with him just now. What had she said? *"Being elusive is not always a good idea."* Now that could be taken several ways.

&

"I'm going home," Meredith told Jonah, her voice still breathless from the short climb. "Should something important happen. . ."

"I'll get you," he finished. "Everything all right?"

"Just tired."

Jonah took her arm. "Me, too. Mind if I just tag along?"

They had gone a ways in comfortable silence, and then Meredith asked, "Do you think Mrs. Bloomfield is a malicious person?"

"No. I don't think so."

"Then why does she spread bad rumors about me? She doesn't even know me."

"Perhaps you frighten her. Maybe she's afraid of the things that a progressive woman like yourself represents."

"I'm just normal."

"You're a driven woman."

Meredith shot a startled look at Jonah. "Is that bad?"

"You ask too many questions, Storm. I'm just an old man who likes to take photographs."

She patted his dark, chemical-stained hand. "No more questions, old man. I'll just enjoy your company."

Chapter 13

Mrs. Cooper rapped on Meredith's door.
"You have a visitor."

Meredith poked at stray hairs as she followed Amelia downstairs. A somewhat familiar logger was waiting.

"Yes?"

He spoke with a European accent. "I have a message from Thatcher Talbot." He held out a folded paper. "I'm to wait for your reply."

"Oh." Meredith fumbled to unfold the paper and scan its contents.

If you'll agree to have dinner with me Saturday evening at the hotel, it'll save you a ride to the camp. You can interview me for your column. Please say yes.

She tapped her fingernail on the paper and glanced up at the patient man at the door. *Does Talbot have a story for me, or is he finally going to talk about himself? Or does he just want to have dinner with me?* It really didn't matter which of these were true. She knew what her answer had to be.

"Please, tell Mr. Talbot I said yes."

"Yes ma'am." The man grinned.

After he left, Meredith dashed up the steps to her room. She leaned against the closed door with a smile. She wouldn't have to ride out to the camp this week, and she was dining with the mysterious Mr. Talbot.

❧

Meredith hummed as she made her way down Main Street, more to bolster her courage than anything else, a nervous habit she had picked up as a little girl. Whenever she faced troublesome chores, she always hummed.

When she reached the bank, she clutched her portfolio, and entered the building. Jonah had told her that the Bloomfield's always spent late mornings together.

A teller pushed at the bridge of his glasses and asked, "May I assist you?"

Meredith cleared her throat again. "May I see Mrs. Bloomfield?" She leaned close. "It's a personal matter."

He raised his brows. "I'll see if she's available." He motioned. "Please make yourself comfortable."

Comfortable, right, she mused, situating herself on a low wooden bench at the far end of the room.

Presently, the teller returned. "Mrs. Bloomfield will be right with you."

Meredith nodded and continued to wait.

With brisk steps Beatrice Bloomfield entered from a side door.

"You asked to see me?"

Meredith hastened forward. "I stopped in to see the photograph that Jonah took of you and your husband."

"Oh?" Mrs. Bloomfield pointed. "But, it's right behind you, Miss Mears."

Meredith felt a stab of embarrassment and whirled. She gave it a thorough perusal. "It's very good." Her compliment was from the heart. "It adds such a touch of dignity."

"We like it." Mrs. Bloomfield's hand fluttered at her bosom. "I. . ."

"I've brought you something to go with it." Meredith pulled a paper from her portfolio and handed it to the other woman.

Mrs. Bloomfield hesitated then accepted the paper, her finger slowly tracing the professional print as a look of wonder stole across her face. "Isn't this clever? The name of our bank, date founded, and our own names as proprietors. That's very kind of you, Miss Mears."

"You can frame it to hang with your photograph."

"I don't know what to say." Mrs. Bloomfield said.

Meredith felt awkward. "It's just a small thing." Not knowing what else to say, she eased the conversation to a close and left the bank. Outside, she smiled, quite pleased with herself.

♄

When Meredith reached home, Amelia called from the kitchen. "A package arrived for you. It's at the foot of the stairs."

"Thank you." Meredith stooped to retrieve the round box, which felt featherlight. *I wonder what this could be.*

Behind the closed door of her room, she laid the package on her bed and hastened to unwrap it. Inside the wrappings was a hatbox. *How strange.*

She removed the lid and carefully peeled back the thin paper. It was the smart yellow hat with the green ostrich feather! *How? Who? A note.*

It read: *"Looking forward to dinner. Thatcher."*

Meredith gaped at it for several long minutes before she removed it from the box. She modeled it in front of her mirror. She felt giddy. *How sweet. I adore it. But, of course, I can't keep this. How did he know? What a puzzling man he is.*

✦

Thatcher Talbot appeared on Meredith's doorstep dressed in his tan leather vest. His hair shone, and his face did, too, with the masculine confidence Meredith so admired in a man. Following an effort to greet him as nonchalantly as she could manage, she allowed him to hold her hand in the crook of his arm all the way to the hotel, where they were seated for dinner.

"I'm glad that you accepted my invitation."

"How could I not? You promised a story, didn't you?"

"Before we get to that, I'd like to tell you that you look very lovely, tonight."

"Thank you, and I must tell you that I cannot accept your lovely gift."

"Why not?"

"It wouldn't be proper, Mr. Talbot. We hardly know each other."

Thatcher laughed out loud. "First, please call me Thatcher. And second, when were you ever known as proper?"

Meredith couldn't help but smile. "You do have a point."

His voice dropped low, almost a whisper. "Please, keep the hat. I'd like to see you in it sometime."

"But how did you know I wanted it?"

He leaned close. "I saw you trying it on through the store window."

Before she could reply or protest any further, the waitress appeared to take their order. By the time she left their table, the moment was gone, and the discussion of the hat dropped. Instead, they enjoyed small talk until their red snapper arrived.

"Now about that story?" Meredith reminded him.

"I didn't have anything special in mind." He shrugged. "But I know you can come up with something to ask me."

She cocked her head. "The real reason that I came to Buckman's Pride was to investigate the issue of timber conservation."

"I don't think there's any urgency in the issue. Do you?"

"That's what the eastern loggers said. They waited too long."

"I was offered a job this week that might interest you."

"What kind of job?"

"Bucker's Stand is sending a crew inland to start work on a logging railroad."

"What's that?"

"A track used exclusively for hauling timber. Soon the area by the river will be exhausted."

"Do you know when they plan to move the camp?"

"No. But preparations are being made."

"Do you think the owners of the logging companies would employ conservation methods if they were informed?"

"I imagine each company might respond differently." He sipped on a second cup of coffee.

"Thanks, Thatcher. You've given me something to think about."

They finished their dinner, further discussing the issue of conservation. Meredith enjoyed the evening so much she was sorry to have it end. When Thatcher escorted her home, he hesitated outside the door.

"I probably shouldn't invite you in. Mrs. Cooper was very specific about men callers."

"I understand," he said, although he made no move to leave.

Meredith said the foremost thing on her mind. "I still know practically nothing about you."

"I wouldn't say that. You've seen me work."

She looked skeptical. "I don't think. . ." But she was unable to complete her sentence, for Thatcher had pulled her close against him. Meredith's breath quickened, and she looked up at his face. His eyes were soft, irresistible. She knew she must step away from him, but she didn't want to. He bent down and kissed her.

Thatcher drew away first and gave her a smug smile. "You'll do. I think I'll marry you."

His arrogant attitude brought her up cold. "Of all the impertinent things. I shall never marry you!"

He chuckled. "We'll see, Miss Meredith S. Mears." He chuckled again. "We shall not see! Good night, Mr. Talbot!"

⁂

Inside her room, Meredith pressed her fingers to her burning lips. For all she knew, Talbot was a wanted man. She tried to steady herself as she fumbled with the light. The first thing she saw when the room was lit was the yellow hat with a green ostrich feather. Meredith moaned. *Oh, I should have returned you.*

⟨⟩

Thatcher continued to chuckle long after the door slammed in his face. He shouldn't have teased her, but he liked her spunk. It seemed natural to admit to her what he had just discovered for himself: He wanted to marry Meredith, even if it meant his own undoing.

Chapter 14

Meredith's fingers pounded out fragmented thoughts and facts until she came to a point where she left her desk to search through her bags. She needed the article that had first pricked her attention on the conservation problem, John Muir's "The American Forests." His bold words would make a good quote:

> *"Any fool can destroy trees. They cannot run away; and if they could, they would still be destroyed—chased and hunted down as long as fun or a dollar could be got out of their bark hides, branching horns, or magnificent bole backbones."*

Meredith tapped her cheek with her finger. *A bit too strong?* How would the townspeople react? She wanted to get their attention, and this would. She would leave it.

❦

The residents of Buckman's Pride received Meredith's newspaper article much like a hard blow to the stomach. Stunned people turned angry, even ugly. The uproar spread throughout the town until it reached Meredith early the following morning in the form of handwritten notes, delivered by a tight-faced Amelia.

Warily reluctant, Meredith read: *"Something is rotten in the woodlands. You!"*

Another read: *"If you know what's good for you, you'll write a retraction."*

Finally: *"Come to the newsroom so we can talk about this mess. Charlie."*

Meredith's face felt hot. Amelia's features resembled the sharp eyes of a vulture.

"I can just imagine what those say."

The reporter crumpled the papers. "I take it you don't approve of the article either?"

"It was a bit insensitive to imply that our sawmill is wasteful."

"I only said many around the country were."

"Humph! Same thing."

"I got their attention, didn't I?"

"You can't rip folks' hearts open and expect them to listen to you."

"They'll listen, and if they don't, someone else will."

"You're making it hard for yourself in this town."

There was a long silence, and finally Meredith said. "You'll still be my friend, won't you, Amelia?"

Meredith heard a soft sigh just before Amelia said, "I'm your friend. Just take my advice as a mother's."

"I never had a mother," Meredith said.

Amelia's arms opened in invitation. "Come here, dear."

❧

"Sit down, Miss Mears." The newspaper owner's face twitched. "We've a problem with your last article. It's too direct."

"Caused a stir?" She gave him a ghost of a smile.

"I think every citizen of Buckman's Pride's marched through this door in the last twenty-four hours."

"That's great! We've got their attention. Now we can. . ."

"Write a retraction."

"What!" Meredith sprang to her feet like a lioness protecting her cub. "Never! It's a valid issue, and Buckman's Pride's got to wake up to the facts."

His eyes snapped. "I realize that."

"You do?"

"I let you publish the article, didn't I? Now we need to back off a bit. Let things settle. Feed them some more of the fluff you wrote before."

"News isn't always pleasant to the ear."

His smile faded. "The logging industry is what this town survives on. You've attacked their jugular vein."

Meredith reseated herself. She clenched and unclenched her hands. "I don't know if I can do a retraction. I'm not saying I won't. I will if it's necessary. It's just that I have another angle in mind. I need some time. Can the retraction at least wait until the regular weekly column?"

She presented an interesting prospect.

"Yours can. I'll do one from the newspaper today."

"Fair enough." The newspaper office's door jingled beneath her departing touch. She paused and turned back to ask, "Did you get any personal threats?"

His voice held a hint of humor. "I guess you could call them that."

"Me, too."

Her hand rested on the doorknob. There seemed to be something more on his mind. "As an outsider, you can write things I can't. But you might get run out of town."

"That's part of being a good journalist, knowing when to pack up and run."

⌒

Meredith pursued her other angles at once. She eased down onto the stiff chair Clement Washington offered her. Meredith remembered that this man did not relish wasted time. As soon as her portfolio hit the floor, rousing a puff of dust, she began to recite her memorized spiel.

"I came to apologize for my recent newspaper article. My accusations referred to sawmills across the country, but in your defense, the town has taken them quite personally."

A righteous anger bloated Washington's cheeks. "Given your occupation, you are neither naïve nor stupid. Your article's intent was quite clear."

"But, it was not personal."

"Then why are you here?"

Meredith held back her own rising emotions and spoke in a calm tone. "Wasting timber is a serious issue."

"I agree."

"Then you apply methods of conservation?"

"Let's take a walk." He didn't expect an answer. His chair scraped against the floor, and a few papers fluttered up to resettle on his quivering desk.

Meredith grabbed her portfolio and scrambled after him, his words hurling back at her. "Wood is a much-needed resource. Where do you think your paper comes from?"

She panted, working up a sweat to keep up with the man's cantankerous strides. "I agree. Timber should be used. Foresters only offer suggestions to keep these resources from running out one day."

Washington stopped so abruptly that Meredith had to retrace her steps. Her chest heaved as she looked where he pointed. He shouted above the buzzing saws, his finger still thrust forward.

"See what he's doing?"

Meredith gave a half shrug.

"He's sweeping. I keep a clean mill. It cuts down on the chance of fire."

It was one of the methods of conservation she had read about. "That's a fine thing," she shouted back.

They watched the mill workers as Washington pointed out to Meredith the many ways that the mill already minimized waste. They utilized the entire tree as it passed through, from logs to shingles. When she had seen enough, they left.

"Mr. Washington, I'm favorably impressed, and I do apologize for the trouble I've caused you."

"I accept your apology."

"Even so, I'll feel negligent if I don't share something else with you."

"By all means," he gestured with outstretched palms, "don't hold back now."

She smiled. "President McKinley has appointed Gifford Pinchot as chief of the Division of Forestry. Heard of Pinchot?"

"I've heard of him. Why?"

"His division offers free advice to mill owners. Would you be willing to take a look at such materials?"

He shrugged. "I don't see why not."

"Then I thank you for your time. I'll get you the information and put some good words about your mill in my next article."

"I'd appreciate that. In your magazine article, too?"

"You're neither naïve nor stupid," she said with a grin. "Yes, my magazine article also."

They shook hands, and she turned to go, then stopped. "Can Jonah take some photographs of your mill?"

"Already has."

"Some particular shots of how you keep the mill clean?"

"Sure. He'd be mighty welcome."

Since Mr. Washington's mercurial attitude had turned obliging, Meredith couldn't resist satisfying her own curiosity. "You don't seem like a man who would threaten a woman."

"What do you mean?"

"I received some nasty messages."

"Rest assured, they weren't from me." He looked sincere.

"I believe you."

"I wouldn't do anything to hurt my friend's wife. Amelia's taken a liking to you."

"I'm glad we had this talk."

"Me, too."

Meredith chuckled at him as she left. For all his explosiveness, she rather liked the southerner. She was glad he was open to conservation. Meredith hurried home to put her thoughts in black and white.

Yet the dawn of a new day in forestry is breaking. Emerson says that things refuse to be mismanaged long. She hoped her next confrontation, with the bull at Bucker's Stand, would only go as well.

Chapter 15

A sudden dread filled Meredith. The rumbling of distant thunder filled the air and the shadowing dark clouds rolled overhead like a fast-moving locomotive breathing down the back of her neck. The unfrequented forest that stretched across either side of the road with its ghoulish-shaped trees and dense underbrush appeared dark and forbidding—an uninviting place with wild animals more fearsome than the inevitable storm. She bent low, hugged her knees against her mount, and pressed him forward.

"C'mon, boy," she coaxed. "Think stable." She might reach Bucker's Stand before the cloudburst.

There was a loud crack overhead, and Meredith's horse faltered but recovered his stride. At first the rain fell hit-and-miss, but shortly following that, stinging drops pelted Meredith and her horse.

"Almost there," Meredith urged. "Ugh," she moaned when the sky burst open just as they rode into camp.

Meredith's soggy pants clung to her legs as she swung one over her saddle to dismount. On the ground, her boots slipped on the slick mud, and she slid, her horse sidestepping from the pull of the reins.

"Whoa, boy." She grappled with gloved hands to bring the skittish beast under control. "That a boy."

By the time the horse quit dancing in circles, a groom had appeared to relieve Meredith. "Take good care of him."

"Don't worry, ma'am. We made fast friends the last time he was here." Then he turned toward the animal. "Here you go, pretty boy."

Meredith's body shivered until her teeth rattled. She clenched her jacket to her torso and ran in a careful slip-sliding gait toward the bull's tent. From beneath the sagging brim of her hat, she saw a small lake surrounding the tent. There was no way but to slosh through it. When she threw open the flap, a stream of water poured down her neck and face.

The bull's mouth gaped open. "Land sakes, woman, come in."

"What a mess."

The bull got up from his desk and disappeared into the back room of his tent. He returned with a wool blanket. "Take off your coat and wrap in this."

Meredith shivered. "Thanks."

After she was salvaged with the comforts of chair, blanket, and a warm cup of his coffee, she murmured, "I feel a bit foolish."

He nodded. "You look foolish."

"Know why I'm here?"

"Either to lambaste me or apologize."

"I already did the first. I came to apologize."

"What a relief," he mocked and stretched out his legs.

Meredith grimaced as she swallowed down the strong drink. "The town's in an uproar."

"They'll get over it."

"Why are you being so nice?"

He gave a half shrug. "Hard to yell at a drowned rat."

It was impossible to appear professional after that remark, but she tried. "Ever heard of selective logging?"

"Sure."

She removed her hat and a puddle of water ran down the brim. She wrung it out and placed it back on her head, to the obvious amusement of the bull. She threatened him with a cocked eyebrow.

"Do you use it?" she asked.

"You've seen our operation."

"I think you could do better."

"I don't strip the land clean. We only cut what we intend to use." He shrugged. "But I suppose you're right."

"Have you investigated conservation methods?"

"Nope. I've left that up to you."

"Would you, given the chance?"

"What chance?"

She took another swallow of coffee in hopes her teeth would quit clattering enough to finish the business at hand. "I have information. If you would read it, there might be some things you could apply to Bucker's."

"I'll look at it. But just so you know, I don't make all the rules. I'm not the owner of this logging organization."

"That's good enough for me."

"You're shivering again." The black-haired bull cast a worried glance past Meredith, then heaved himself up to look outside. "We need to find you a place to spend the night. You won't be going back to town in this."

Meredith's helpless gaze watched the relentless downpour.

"Maybe one of the married men can take you home." He rubbed his chin and turned back toward her. "Course you aren't the most popular reporter around here anymore."

"I..." Meredith stopped midsentence when the bull jerked the tent flap open to admit an excited logger.

"Got a minor accident."

Seeming to forget his castaway, the bull hunched his shoulders and tramped into the rainstorm behind the logger.

Meredith clambered to her feet and sloughed off the blanket as if it were a chain and ball. She had just enough good sense to grab her drenched coat and drape it over her head before she raced after him.

Through the fog and sheets of rain, she saw two injured persons being helped into the bunkhouse. She caught up to them with a gasp.

One of the injured men looked like Thatcher. As Meredith let her coat slip to the ground, her world suddenly shrank to the size of a bunkhouse, a blur of damp canvas, rivulets crossing a mud floor, rows of cots, and an injured man who meant everything to her.

The bull ordered, "Go get Curly." He was the closest thing to a camp doctor.

Meredith pushed through the haze. "Let me see Thatcher."

"You can't come in here."

She gave the bull a look that was mostly a flash of raw fear and hastened to Thatcher's side. A blood-soaked arm lay draped across his chest, where a large, jagged piece of wood skewered his coat sleeve to his arm. When Meredith saw the problem, she almost fainted.

"We've got to get his coat off and get the blood stopped." The room quieted under her words.

Her gaze swept over the other injured man, whose arms hugged the shoulders of two able-bodied loggers. "Help him to a cot."

Thatcher groaned. The bull winced when Meredith yanked her blouse out from her trousers. The silence in the room thickened, as the men watched her rip a strip from the bottom of her blouse.

The bull lay his hand on Thatcher's shoulder. "Be still," he said in his most gentle authoritative voice.

Meredith gave him an appreciative glance. Thatcher's eyes closed, his face pale and his lips parted. "Let's get his jacket off first. Do you have a knife?" Meredith asked.

The bull helped Thatcher sit forward so Meredith could remove the garment. Then he lay back. They used a knife to cut the material away from the arm. Next they cut his shirt away, and Meredith tied the strip of cloth tight around his upper arm.

"I can see to him if you want to get the other injured man's foot propped up."

The bull nodded.

Meredith leaned over Thatcher and whispered, "The bleeding has stopped some. Try not to move your arm."

His eyes flickered open. "I feel dizzy."

"Just rest if you can."

At that moment, Curly burst into the bunkhouse. He strode past everyone to a cot, from beneath which he removed the camp's leather bag filled with medical supplies. He leaned over Thatcher and said to Meredith as he probed the injured area, "You've done just right, Miss Mears."

Meredith stepped back from the cot, and the room gave an odd spin. She rubbed her arms and began to tremble. One of the loggers explained to Curly how the accident happened.

"They fell off a stand. Ran that limb right through his arm. Looks to me like the other broke his leg."

A rush of nausea swept over Meredith, and she fumbled around, looking for her coat. But something else caught her eye. From where it lay, it must have fallen out of Thatcher's pocket. She stooped to pick it up. As dizzy as she felt, she had to concentrate her focus.

It was the picture of a woman, a lovely woman. A steel band of dread constricted her chest. She cast an apprehensive glance at Thatcher and turned the photograph over. The back contained an inscription: *To my husband, with all my love, Colleen.* When the full meaning hit, the elegant handwriting scorched her palm.

Another quick glance showed Curly pouring some whiskey down

Thatcher's throat. Thatcher choked, coughed, then lay back.

Thatcher's married?

Curly poured some of the whiskey over a knife and lowered it to Thatcher's arm. Meredith averted her eyes.

The bull looked at her oddly. "Miss Mears. You've done enough here. Let's get you to a fire."

Dazed, she nodded. Her foot hit Thatcher's discarded coat. She looked at the bloody heap and tried to remember its import. Her stomach lurched. Then she remembered.

The photograph.

She stooped on unsteady legs and slipped the photograph inside a pocket; then she reached for her own coat and stood up. The room swirled, and everything went black.

⌒

Meredith awoke to a crackling fire. Her body sought its warmth, and a strong grip on both her upper arms lifted her to a sitting position.

"Easy, now." The bull kept a wary eye on Meredith as she looked about the room.

"I'm glad you came around. Had me worried."

"Where am I?"

"Mess hall. You still look rather green." The bull shouted, "Cook! Can you keep an eye on Miss Mears?"

"Sure." The cook narrowed his eyes at her, then returned to his work.

I guess Cook reads, Meredith mused as she eased herself closer to the fire.

"Dry out here until I come back for you," The bull said and started to leave, but turned back. "You'll stay put, won't you?"

"I'll stay." She shuddered.

The cook peeled potatoes and ignored her. Time passed, and a sense of normalcy returned to Meredith, so she tried to start up a conversation with him.

"Do the men always work in the rain?" she asked.

Cook gave her a hard look, then said, "Ya. They'll probably get the lung fever, but they wouldn't want to miss a day of pleasure, killing trees."

Ooh. He bites, too, she said to herself.

She turned her attention back to the fire. *The photograph.* Thatcher's kiss came to mind, his claim that he would marry her. *But he can't be married.* She thought about the puzzle. *Maybe he's a widower.*

Before she could sort it out, the bull returned with a tall blond man who didn't glare at her like the potato peeler.

"The Swede lives nearby. You can stay at his house."

Meredith assessed him. "Even if he's gentle as a doe, I'm not staying with him."

The blond logger's lips twitched. "I have a wife. She'd be grateful for your company."

Meredith shrugged. "Sorry. I'm too miserable to think. Much obliged."

∽

A thin, rosy-cheeked woman stood in the open cabin door. "I saw you coming through the woods. Hurry inside. My, it's nasty."

"This is Miss Mears, the reporter from town. She's feeling poorly and needs shelter for the night."

"Glad to have ya," The young Swedish woman said. "You're welcome to what we have."

Meredith surveyed the room. There was a bed at one end and a table and two mismatched chairs at the other. A fire burned in a black box stove, the only cheery fixture.

"Will you be staying at the camp then?" The woman asked her husband.

"Ya. I've got to go back right away."

Meredith went to the stove to warm up and give them some privacy. When the woman returned, she was alone. "I'll get you some dry clothes."

"I hate to put you out."

"It's no bother. It'll be nice to talk to someone from town. Don't get in much."

Meredith felt grateful for the woman's kindness. It would be good to get her point of view regarding logging and living in the woods.

As the woman went after the clothes, Meredith wondered, *Is this what it would be like to be married to Thatcher? A hut in the woods?* She shuddered, and her thoughts ran rampant. *Maybe Thatcher is already married. If so, what was he running from that even took him away from a loving wife? And how could he kiss me and speak of marriage? I shall never* marry you, Thatcher Talbot, if indeed you are not already married. Then a more poignant pain, *Will Thatcher be all right? His wound could be quite serious if it became infected.*

"Here you go, Miss Mears. You look a mite green. Let's get you to bed."

Chapter 16

The next morning, Meredith woke to the sound of rain and a rooster crowing.

"Morning." The greeting came from the cheery woman bent over a pot on the black stove.

"Morning." Meredith threw her legs over the side of the bed and looked out the one tiny window.

"Your clothes are dry. They're at the foot of the bed."

Meredith knew she could never stay cooped up in the small, dreary cabin, regardless of the rain. As she fastened her pants, her stomach rumbled.

The woman smiled. "You must be hungry. Slept like a log."

Meredith pulled out one of the mismatched chairs. "There was an accident in camp, a friend of mine. It made me sick. That was after I got soaked from the storm. Thanks for letting me stay over, but I feel fine now. If you'll just point me in the right direction, I'll go on back to camp."

The woman's eyes widened. "An accident? My husband didn't say anything about an accident."

Meredith waved her hand. "Minor injuries. I've just a weak stomach is all."

"Oh." The woman didn't look convinced. She placed a plate of eggs in front of her guest. "You sure you want to walk to camp in the rain? Through those woods?"

"How far is it? I know we came by horse, but it didn't seem so far yesterday."

The woman swept a worried glance over Meredith. "Two miles. There's a path worn 'twixt us and the camp."

"See then. There's nothing to worry about. I'll easily find my way."

"I hoped you might stay a spell. We could visit."

Meredith hated to crush the woman's hopes. "Well, maybe I will. Just a spell." The woman instantly brightened, and Meredith tasted the eggs. "Mm. This is delicious."

The woman joined Meredith at the table. "Are you really a reporter from the city?"

Meredith answered her questions. After a while, she asked, "You have a privy?"

The woman giggled. "Out back."

Once Meredith returned to the cabin, she said, "Now that I'm already wet, I really should head back to the camp. The rain is a mere drizzle."

"I thought you'd come back with that in your head. It's been real nice talking with ya."

"My pleasure. Thanks for everything." Meredith felt awkward. She hesitated, then gave the slight woman a hug. "Maybe, I'll see you in town."

The woman nodded. "I hope so. Take care, now."

By the time Meredith took her leave, the rain was a mere mist, and the path was easy to follow, though eerily remote. Meredith kept a brisk pace, eager to leave the shadows of the deep woods and reach camp.

When she reached the bull's tent, he asked, "You're riding back to town in this?"

"I'll go slow. I can't sit around here for days."

"I suppose I could loan you a slicker."

"I'd much appreciate that. How's Mr. Talbot doing?"

"He's got a fever. If you're going to Buckman's Pride, would you mind sending the town doctor back? I was going to send someone in."

"I'll go right away."

The bull nodded, went to the back room of his tent, and returned with a slicker. "A mite big, but it'll keep you drier."

"It's perfect. Thanks." He helped her slip into it before she left.

Meredith got her horse from the stable and checked to make sure her portfolio was still safe in her saddlebags. Then with words of encouragement, she eased the beast out into the drizzle. "Let's go home, boy."

Three hours later, Amelia Cooper bustled Meredith into the shelter of her warm kitchen, shaking her head. "I was worried about you, child."

"No need. I spent the night with a logger's wife."

"I hoped as much."

"This morning I had to get the doctor. Mr. Talbot got a nasty puncture wound in his arm, and another man broke his leg."

"How awful."

"Did you know they work in the rain?"

"Yeah." She looked out the window at the drizzle. "My husband used to do the same."

Meredith followed Amelia's gaze and sneezed. "I see Jonah is in his studio."

"Yes." Amelia looked at her with concern. "Would you like to take a hot bath before you change into dry clothes?"

Meredith sneezed again. "That would feel good."

By the time Meredith's bath was over, her body had succumbed to the start of a cold and fever. Earlier, she had hoped to do some writing, but now all she yearned for was her own bed.

♨

Late that afternoon, Meredith awakened to a knock on her bedroom door. She raised up on one elbow and pulled the blankets tight. Her ears buzzed, and she could hardly breathe.

"Come in."

The door opened, and Jonah's bald head popped in. "Mrs. Cooper gave me permission to check on you."

"Come on in."

Jonah entered, balancing a tray of hot soup, which he placed on her desk. "How are you?"

"Ugh. Stuffed up. Got caught in the storm yesterday."

"I was worried about you."

"Got a good story." She eased herself into a sitting position. "And a job for you."

Jonah straddled a chair and listened to her explain how she would like some photographs of the mill and logging camp, shots that showed the implementation of conservation methods.

Jonah liked the idea. "As soon as this rain is over, I'll do it. But for now, you'd better eat this soup. We're invited to a dinner party in a few days, and you'll need your strength."

"Whose?"

"Mrs. Bloomfield's."

"Ugh." Meredith sank down into the bed sheets. "Maybe I'll take my time recuperating."

Jonah chuckled. "Get back up here and eat this."

Meredith ate a few bites and then begged him to leave. After that, she slept until the next morning. Amelia served her breakfast in bed, and Meredith fell back asleep. But by afternoon, she rose and dressed. It continued to rain, so she pulled a cozy blanket off the bed and wrapped it around her while she worked at her desk.

⚜

The next day, the sun finally shone. Meredith mailed her stories off to *McClure's* and stopped by the newspaper office.

"Here's your retraction. I think you'll like it."

Charlie looked over the article that praised the local mill and logging camp for their high standards and told how they rose above the normal tides in lumbering.

"This is perfect. Though it's not exactly a retraction, I believe it will please the townsfolk, especially the part about their fierce and commendable loyalty to the local lumbermen."

"I'm not doing this just to make the town happy."

"Why are you?"

"It's just the truth," she smiled. "And I was pleased to discover it."

"It makes me proud of our town."

"Here are two more articles. One's entitled, 'Bad Weather Doesn't Stop Loggers,' and the other, 'Tribute to a Logger's Wife.'"

"Looks like we've got enough to do your column for a few weeks," he said with approval. "That's good, because I'm going to be traveling for a couple weeks."

"Oh? Where?"

"San Francisco. My sister's getting married. Frederick will be in charge of the office." He leaned close. "I know you two don't get along very well, so this is perfect. You won't even have to come around until I get back."

Meredith felt hurt. "Have a good trip."

⚜

When Meredith returned to her room, she started another article for *McClure's* and wrote another letter questioning Asa about Thatcher Talbot. Even with her work, she could not get the man off her mind. She knew that she should not get emotionally involved with a man who could be a criminal, could be married, and even if neither of these were true, could provide nothing more than a tiny cabin in the woods for the woman he married.

But she could not deny the attraction she felt toward him. She worried over his injury. She thought about his smile, his brown eyes,

89

handsome face, dark wavy hair, and mustache.

No, she told herself. *I must forget about him. He is not right for me. I am a city girl. He is a. . . What are you, Thatcher Talbot?*

☙

The next day, Meredith still brooded over Thatcher. If she rode back out to the camp to check on him, it would be too obvious. If she asked the town doctor about Thatcher, he might question her motives.

I'm a reporter. That's my motivation.

Within the hour, she was outside the doctor's office. The door swung open easily, and she looked about. The front room was empty, but she heard some noises in the room beyond. He might be with a patient, she reasoned, so she found a chair to wait.

"Miss Mears. I'm sorry. Didn't know I had a patient."

Meredith rose. "I just came to check up on the loggers. How are they?"

"The one had a broken leg. He's laid up and only time will tell if it heals properly."

"I didn't know it was that serious. That's too bad."

Meredith waited. The doctor was absorbed in private thought. Finally, she prodded, "And the other man?"

"Oh. His arm will be fine as long as it doesn't get infected."

He certainly wasn't telling her anything she didn't already know. "But it's not infected? He had a fever the last I heard."

"No. Both men's fevers are gone. They're on the mend, barring complications."

"Good."

"You're an enigma to me, Miss Mears."

"How is that, Doctor?"

"You act as though you care for the loggers, yet your stories of late contradict your actions."

"You haven't read my latest article."

"Change of heart?"

"Conservation of timber is a very serious issue, but I believe that your loggers do a commendable job and that the men running the operations are honest, caring men. It's my intention to make them an example to the entire logging industry."

"That's good to hear."

"Good day, Doctor."

Chapter 17

One morning, Meredith visited Jonah's studio. When she entered the small shed, Jonah was putting the backing on his most recent photographs. "May I see them?"

"Help yourself."

Meredith browsed through the photographs, taking special care with the unmounted ones. "These are perfect for my articles." She turned to him with satisfaction. "We're doing it, Jonah, getting Asa some great material."

"He's got to be pleased."

"When you were at the camp, did you happen to see Thatcher and the other injured logger?"

"Yes. They're both doing well."

Meredith exhaled a sigh of relief. "I'm so glad."

Jonah chuckled. "But they're bored. Eager to get back to work."

The way Jonah talked about the camp, it was obvious he was fitting in with the loggers, with all the townsfolk.

"You're going to stay here, aren't you?" Meredith asked.

Jonah paused from his work and turned toward her. "I haven't decided yet. I like it here."

"I'll probably go home before winter." Her voice was distant.

"Something bothering you, Storm?"

"It's been so up and down for me."

He nodded. "The townspeople liked your last article. You should be up again."

"That reminds me, are you going to Mrs. Bloomfield's dinner party?"

"Of course. Mrs. Bloomfield loves me," he said.

Meredith rolled her eyes. "I'm still amazed I even got invited."

"I hope you can behave yourself."

"Mm-hmm. So do I."

✍

The evening of the dinner party, Meredith gave particular attention to her attire. She put on her new yellow hat with the green ostrich feather and her matching gown from New York. It was high necked with rows of horizontal tucks on the bodice and around the hem. She smoothed down the skirt, did a little twist, and watched the hemline swirl just right.

Jonah escorted Meredith and Amelia Cooper. Mr. and Mrs. Bloomfield met them at the door.

"Do come in. It's so good of you to come."

"I am so pleased to be invited," Meredith said.

"I have a few more guests to greet, please go into the sitting room and make yourselves comfortable."

Meredith wondered who the other guests would be. When they entered the room, Meredith hesitated and Jonah slammed into her.

"Sorry," he whispered. "Go on."

She took a hesitant step, then pasted on a smile and entered the room. Thatcher Talbot stood, as did the other men.

Why did I have to wear this wretched hat? Meredith thought. She moved forward to greet him. "I am surprised to see you here," she said.

She saw his gaze settle on the hat.

"The Bloomfields are my friends. Remember? I told you at the funeral."

"Yes, of course," she said, determined to ignore his smile. "But your injury."

His arm was in a sling. "It's almost good as new."

"You certainly are looking better."

"Please, have a seat."

Meredith took a nearby chair after she greeted everyone.

When conversations picked up again, Thatcher said to Meredith, "You were my angel of mercy that day."

Meredith smiled in spite of herself. "When I saw all that blood and that stick in your arm, I was scared to death."

The woman's photograph came to Meredith's mind, and she grew quiet. She wondered if he had discovered that it was moved, or if she replaced it in such a way that he didn't notice.

He lowered his voice. "Your articles have been the talk of the camp."

"I can well imagine," she said. She looked about the room, then leaned close. "I'd rather not talk about my articles tonight."

He smiled. "I understand." His voice perked up. "We could talk about how lovely you look in that hat."

She whispered, "I don't want to talk about that either."

"Hmm, that doesn't leave us much to talk about."

Mercifully, Meredith was saved from answering as they were invited in to dinner.

About halfway through the main course, Meredith's hostess asked, "Miss Mears, your articles have caused quite a stir, haven't they? Are you used to that sort of thing?"

"No. I'm not. Before I came here, I was doing some routine things. This has been challenging."

Mrs. Bloomfield's eyes squinted. "Why do you do it?"

"It's personal. Just something I have to do." She concentrated on her food. "I must compliment you on this dinner."

"Thank you. I was a bit nervous inviting you here."

"Why?"

"I think everyone in Buckman's Pride is just a bit worried over your opinions. . .fearing they might find themselves in print."

"The townspeople are uncomfortable around me?"

Beatrice Bloomfield intercepted a look of censure from her husband and shrugged. "I'm sorry if I've offended you."

"Not at all. It is I who must apologize."

Beatrice changed the topic, and the rest of the dinner was pleasant.

Perhaps Jonah was right when he said people feared change, and maybe Meredith was a different kind of woman than they were used to. She could prove herself, if given the time, but she wasn't sure she would be in this town long enough to do so, or if she even wanted to be.

After the meal, Thatcher singled Meredith out in the sitting room. "I can't let this evening end without pursuing our conversation. Now what were we talking about before dinner?"

"I believe we were talking about what we cannot talk about and how that doesn't leave us. . ."

"Much to talk about," he finished.

They both chuckled.

"I think we can do better than that. Tell me about your life back in New York City."

Meredith would rather they discuss his life, but thought if she cooperated a bit, he might open up in turn.

"As you know, I work for *McClure's* magazine. My editor is an older

DIANNE CHRISTNER

man and has been like a father to me, helping me get started in the world of journalism. He didn't want to let me come on this assignment. He was worried about me."

"I'm glad you have someone like that to care for you. What about your parents?"

"My mother died when I was born. My father has thrown it in my face every day of my life. He wanted a son. I've tried all of my life to be one. Never could."

"Did you move away from home?"

"Yes. After many years of keeping house for him, trying to please him, and only receiving set downs."

"I'm sorry. You sound hurt and bitter. Not that I blame you. Have you kept in touch?"

"I called on him before I left. He called me a fool." She shrugged. "We argued."

Thatcher shook his head. "You and I have much in common."

Meredith's curiosity mounted. Was he going to talk at last? "How's that?"

"I'm not good enough for my father either."

"Where is your home?"

"Chicago. My father wants me to help him run his business. He's very wealthy."

"That doesn't sound so bad."

"He's a cruel, hardhearted man. His business methods are unscrupulous. I'm a Christian, and I cannot do things the way he wants."

"So you walked out on all that wealth to travel?" she asked in amazement, thinking of the horrible accommodations at the camp. She remembered her own disappointment that it was not the kind of life she could ever share with a man. These thoughts circled back to the realization that he might already be married.

"Like I said, we're not so different. You walked out to travel, didn't you?" he asked.

"In a sense. I see your point. Can I ask you a personal question?"

"I thought we were talking personally," he said.

"Are you married?"

"Of course not. If I were married, I would not be here alone."

"Have you ever been married?" Meredith saw that her line of

questioning puzzled, yet amused him.

"No. Are you remembering what I said after I kissed you?"

Meredith felt as if her face were on fire. How embarrassing for him to bring up that kiss. Perhaps, he was more like his father than he knew, unscrupulous. Then she remembered his rudeness on their first encounters.

She settled on ignoring his question and asking one of her own. "You were very rude to me when we first met. Why have you changed?"

"If you're fishing for a compliment, I'd be glad to oblige. In fact," he leaned close and said very low, "I'd be pleased to walk you home."

She shook her head at him. "You are impertinent."

"You haven't answered my question."

"No, you may not. Jonah and Mrs. Cooper will accompany me."

"Furthermore, I certainly was not fishing for a compliment, and I still find you a very evasive person."

"I was rude to you, Meredith, because you are a reporter. I didn't want to talk about my life." His eyes darkened. "Do you understand?"

"Yes. I think I would be wise to remain wary of you."

Thatcher laughed out loud at that.

Several people in the room looked his way.

Thatcher leaned close again. "You need never be wary of me. I'm harmless, and anyway, I'm very fond of you. See how I'm confiding in you."

She studied him, but did not reply. If only she could read his mind.

He gave another irritating smile. "You don't need to try so hard to make it in a man's world, you know. Just be yourself."

Her lips quivered. "I am myself. And, I believe it is time to remove myself."

She rose from her chair and moved toward Amelia with a fake yawn. "My. I've grown so tired. Will you be ready to go home anytime soon?"

"Oh, yes dear. I was thinking the same thing."

Jonah saw his cue. "Are you ladies growing weary?"

"Yes," Mrs. Cooper said. "It's been such a lovely dinner party. But I don't want us to overstay our welcome."

"I'm only so glad you could come," Mrs. Bloomfield said.

Jonah accompanied the women to the door.

Across the way, Meredith could feel the pull of Thatcher's eyes, but she did not turn around. If he could be so contrary, then she would be likewise. The wretched man.

Chapter 18

Meredith carried in her hand the long-overdue envelope from Asa. Her staccato heartbeat was only matched by the fast pitter-pat of her boots as she hurried home to seek the privacy of her room. She leaned against the door. Her hands tingled as she opened the envelope. There was a letter and a check.

> *Dear Storm,*
>
> *Good work. Keep the articles coming. The description of the logging community is fascinating and the human-interest stories gripping. I look forward to more information on the conservation issue. Jonah's photographs are going to add a special touch. I'm glad I sent you both. Add a personal note next time and let me know how you are doing and when you plan to return. We're publishing a series of your articles. Will send you a copy of the first. Thought you could use an advance. Buy a new hat. Nothing's turned up on that man you asked about, Thatcher Talbot. Sorry. Miss you. Come home before winter sets in.*
>
> *Asa*

Meredith read it over two more times, then looked over the check. *A hat?* What sort of opinion did these men have of her anyway? *This money will go to Amelia.* She rose and went to the window. Jonah was in his studio. He would be pleased to know that they had heard from Asa.

After Jonah and Meredith had discussed the letter from their editor, they discussed their future articles, which would finish off the series. Their plans included a trip to the camp the following day.

The next day was sunny and perfect for riding out to the logging camp. At breakfast, however, Jonah threw a kink into their plans.

"I heard late last night that there's a schooner expected in the harbor this morning. I'd like to see if I can arrange for some supplies from San Francisco."

"For your studio?" Meredith asked.

"Yes. If you want to start out without me, maybe I'll catch up with you. At any rate, I'll be right behind."

"I'm disappointed, but that will be fine."

"Good," Jonah said. "I'll try to make arrangements with someone else so I don't actually have to wait on the ship."

✍

Meredith took her time. Wildflowers and ferns trimmed the edge of the road like lace and embroidery on the hem of a gown. Beyond the trimmings, thick tangled shrubs, sprawling berry branches, and trees that reached to the sky made a high wall at either side of her. Even though she had traveled this road several times, the scenery always humbled her, for she was touched by its beauty and frightened by its unknowns.

Asa was right. She should return to New York before winter set in, which meant that she needed to gather as much information as she could in the next couple of trips. She wished she could talk Jonah into accompanying her when she left California and stopping at some other logging camps along the way. But Jonah might not be returning; he seemed to have found his place in Buckman's Pride.

The quiver of horseflesh against Meredith's leg brought her out of the intellectual world and back into the physical one—of horse, road, trees, and *bear*!

"Steady, boy. Steady, boy."

Her voice wavered, and she tightened her grip on the reins, but her horse didn't steady. He let out a snort and balked in the road. Then he kicked his forelegs high into the air and brought them down to stomp the ground. Meredith fought to control him; he backed a few paces, hoofed the ground, then tossed his head and forelegs up again.

Meredith clung to the reins in terror as she saw the bear approach. The beast swung his body from side to side and snarled. Meredith's horse suddenly lurched and bucked Meredith hard.

She felt her body slide sideways. The reins slipped loose. For a moment she thought she was going to be dragged upside down, but then her boot released from the stirrup, and she landed with a large thud off the side of the road. Her head smarted and her vision momentarily blurred.

In an instant she knew that her horse was gone. But what about the bear? She rolled onto her side so she could see. The bear stood in the middle of the road, still swinging his body from side to side and staring after the horse until his eyes discovered Meredith.

She heard a groan coming from deep inside her, and then she heard herself say *Run*.

The bear went down on all fours and started moving again, this time toward her. Meredith scrambled to her feet and ran for all she was worth. Through the trees she ran, never looking back. The bushes tore at her trousers but she kept on going.

I can't hear him. Wouldn't I hear the bear if he were chasing me? But I can't stop. Finally, she looked over her shoulder. She couldn't see anything but forest. She slowed and looked back again. She didn't see the bear or the hole in front of her, and her foot slipped into it.

Down she went. Meredith gasped. A pain shot up her leg. She tried to get up again, but her leg gave out. She crawled onto her stomach and turned herself around. Her heart beat wildly; she could feel it in her throat. She listened, and her eyes gave a frantic search over the woods for the black monster. She thought she heard some cracking twigs in the distance.

The bear is still there.

She gave a panicked glance for a place to hide. There was a fallen log and a large redwood. She chose the living tree and crawled toward it. When she reached the trunk, she sat behind it and peeked around to see if the bear was coming. Surely it would smell her. What could she do?

She heard cracking twigs again and leaned up tight against the tree, its bark against her cheek. Tears made the bark a blur. The animal was taking its time, probably tracking her. A squirrel started scolding, and she cringed.

Oh, please be quiet. Dear God, she prayed. *Protect me. Hide me. O God.*

The noise grew closer. She swallowed hard and leaned toward the edge of the tree trunk. A little more, and she could see. She jerked still.

Oh.

She sobbed with relief. It was three deer. If they could graze so peacefully, the bear must not be near.

She watched the deer and sobbed, deep sobs from within. Their heads shot up, and their ears stiffened. They felt her presence. One turned and began to traipse away. Another anguished sob escaped Meredith, and the deer bounded away. Within moments, all three were out of sight, and Meredith was alone.

Don't go.

She pulled her knees up and leaned against the tree until her chest quit heaving. Her foot throbbed. With the back of her hand, she swiped at her face. Her finger caught in her hair. The pins had fallen out, and it was tangled. She must have lost her hat with her horse. She tried to stop hiccuping.

What should I do?

As far as she looked, there were trees. The road was somewhere behind her, but so was the bear. Should she crawl back in that direction? Could she stand the pain if she did?

⌘

Jonah arrived in Bucker's Stand and wondered what the commotion was about. Seemed there was always something going on. He was surprised that Meredith was not in the midst of it, getting the story. As he drew his horse up, he saw what the men were crowding around. It was Meredith's horse.

The bull rushed toward him. "Is she with you?"

"You mean Storm?"

"I'm talking about Miss Mears, the reporter. Her horse came in without her."

Jonah dismounted and ran his hand over the horse's neck.

"He's been running. Must have thrown her. But I should have seen her. She would have waved me down."

"Unless she's knocked out."

"Still, I should have seen her."

One of the men in the group was a stern-faced Thatcher. "I'll go search for her." He stalked away.

"I'm coming, too," Jonah said, swinging back onto his mount.

Thatcher nodded, and Jonah waited for him to return with his own mount.

By noon, the two men had ridden nearly back to town, and they still hadn't found any sign of Meredith.

"Why don't you go on to town?" Thatcher said. "Maybe she walked back. I'll double back the way we came, slower this time. If I don't find anything by the time I get to camp, I'll form a search party. If you find her, send word right away."

Jonah nodded. "Good luck. She's a feisty thing, but I'd sure hate for her to have to spend the night alone in these woods."

"Pray," Thatcher said.

He turned his mount and started back. He kept the pace slow and studied the sides of the road for any indication of Meredith.

Thatcher swallowed back the bile that pushed its way into his throat. If she was there, he would find her. He kept on with his diligent search until he was about halfway between town and the logging camp. Then he saw it. The tracks ran off the main road, probably why he'd missed them before.

"Whoa."

He dismounted, led his horse by the reins, and investigated the area. It didn't take him long to figure out what had happened. Meredith's horse had stomped the ground, then veered off the road into the thickets. He found where Meredith hit the ground. But where was she? He tied his horse up to a tree and gave a thorough search of the area, calling out her name.

"Meredith!"

He'd make a circle and let his eyes search the woods, then down the road and beyond. He asked himself, *What made the horse buck?* If it were a wild animal, he might have noticed it from a distance. He walked back to the road, covering it for a short distance. There it was. Bear tracks! No wonder Meredith wasn't there. She must have run from the bear.

Thatcher hurried back to the place where Meredith had fallen from her horse. He'd follow her tracks. Panic rushed over him. By the tracks, he soon discovered that the bear had two cubs. A bear protecting her cubs was a dangerous thing, even for an armed man, let alone a woman without any means of protection. He and his horse scrambled through the woods as fast as he could go without losing the trail.

Just when he thought the bears' tracks were not going to cross Meredith's, he saw them. The bears were following her. His mind went numb with fright, but his body pushed forward. And then he stopped, a wave of relief washing over him. From the looks of things, the bears gave up the chase and ambled off in another direction.

He looked toward the road. It was several miles back by now. Presumably, Meredith was lost in the woods, probably in hysterics. He had to find her before nightfall. He made a vow to himself that he would.

Thatcher pressed on, following Meredith's trail of broken twigs and indentations from trodden rocks. The area was plush, which made the tracking tedious. Once he lost her trail, but found it again. At one point, when Thatcher thought he recognized a fallen log, he worried that he was going in circles.

Then he heard the sobs.

"Meredith?"

Chapter 19

Meredith couldn't crawl out because it hurt too much. Dark shadows and creepy sounds pressed all around. Someone called her name. She cried out weakly, "Jonah?"

"Where are you?"

"Here! Over here behind a tree!"

She crawled toward the sound of her rescuer's voice. Her head peeked around from the trunk of a huge tree. Her face was dirty and tear streaked; her hair hung wild over her shoulders.

"Thank God. Meredith! Are you hurt?"

"Thatcher," she gasped with relief. "Yes. My ankle."

"Hold still."

She nodded, and his heart lurched with sympathy. As he reached the tree, he slowly knelt down until they were face to face. "It'll be all right now."

She nodded again and hiccuped.

Ever so gently, he moved toward her, mildly surprised when she threw herself into his arms, best as she could with her hurt ankle. Meredith clutched tight onto the back of his shirt. Her sobs became convulsive, and he pulled her close.

"You're safe now. Everything will be all right."

After what seemed like a very long time, she started to speak. Her words tumbled out in spurts.

"Bear. A bear. Big bear."

He set her at arm's length and looked into her swollen eyes. "I know. I saw her tracks. But she's gone. You're safe."

A sigh of relief escaped her, and she pulled away from his hold. "I was so frightened. I stepped in a hole, and then I was helpless."

"Can I have a look at your ankle? Lean against the tree and get comfortable," he instructed.

Meredith leaned her back against the trunk of the tree and stretched both legs out in front of her.

"Which one?" he asked.

"This one." She pulled her pant leg up past her ankle, but her boot covered the injured area.

"This boot will have to come off." He began to unlace it and gave it a gentle tug. Meredith released a small moan.

"It might hurt some," Thatcher said.

She nodded and closed her eyes.

He saw her pinched lips and the way her back pushed hard against the tree as he worked the tiny foot free from the boot.

She released a sigh.

Thatcher probed the injured area. "Does this hurt? This?" After a careful examination, he said, "I'm no expert. I can't say if it's broken or just bruised or sprained. But it's swollen. You won't be walking on it."

She glanced at his horse.

"You can ride out, but not tonight," he said.

"What do you mean not tonight?" Her words sounded frantic. "I can't stay in these woods."

"Meredith. It's getting dark. We've gotten turned around. I'll need the sun to guide us out of these woods. It's best we camp here tonight and ride out in the morning."

~

Meredith listened to Thatcher as he prepared camp and started a fire. He still favored his injured arm.

"I wish I'd thought to bring more provisions," Thatcher said. "But I have a few things in my saddlebags so we won't starve." He pulled out a canteen, tin cup, small tin pot, and coffee. He also had some dried meat. "First time you camped out?" he asked.

"No. We camped out between San Francisco and Buckman's Pride."

"That's right. Silas said he brought you over."

"After you refused."

"Like I said the other night, you are a reporter."

When the coffee was ready, Thatcher gave her the tin cup first. "Try this."

"Mm. Good." She watched him and wondered what secrets he harbored. Finally, she said, "So I don't trust you, and you don't trust me. A fine pair we make, except you have the advantage. I'm injured."

He gave her a look of reproof. "You have no reason not to trust me. I would never harm you."

"Nor lie to me?"

"No, I wouldn't. But I suppose every man has things he doesn't want to talk about."

"Like that picture you carry?"

His face looked puzzled.

"The one that you carry in your pocket."

"I'm sorry, I don't know what you're talking about."

"The one of the beautiful woman? Colleen."

"Oh, that." He sloughed it off. "I forgot all about that. How did you know about her?" His voice sounded defensive.

"It fell out of your coat the day you hurt your arm."

It took a moment for that to settle. "You're jealous. Aren't you?"

"How absurd. Of course, I am not. It just goes to show why I cannot trust you or the things you say. I don't believe any man could forget that he carried a picture of his wife."

"She's not my wife. The woman is nothing to me. She's my friend's wife."

Meredith rolled her eyes and shivered.

"You're cold. Let's see if we can move you closer to the fire." He rose and reached for her arm.

Meredith raised her arms to fend him off. "I can manage." She handed him the empty tin cup, then hobbled closer to the fire.

Thatcher made a seat of small timber and leaves for her to sit on by a stump. "Better?" he asked.

Meredith did not reply, choosing to sulk.

Thatcher prepared the small amount of food that was available. Soon he offered her some jerky. "This will help."

With a loaded look, she accepted the peace offering. It tasted good.

As the night grew darker and the sounds of animals and forest creatures grew louder, Meredith dropped her prejudices against Thatcher.

"Do you have any weapons on you?" she asked.

Thatcher pulled out a knife from a pouch he wore on his belt. "Just this." Meredith frowned.

"And the fire of course. It will keep the wild animals away."

Thatcher rose and went to his horse. He returned with a woolen blanket. "It's strange that it can be cold this time of the year," he said.

"Amelia says it's because we're so close to the ocean."

"Autumn's just around the corner. We'll stay warm if we share this."

Meredith looked at the blanket draped over his arm and nodded. She already wore his jacket. It would be selfish to take his blanket, too.

He added more wood to the fire, then sat next to her and placed the blanket over them, their shoulders touching.

"Nice," he said.

"Don't get any ideas."

His lips pinched together, and his face looked pained. He remained silent, and they watched the flames of the fire.

After a long while, Thatcher said, "I meant what I said."

"About what?"

"Wanting to marry you."

"I don't want to talk about that."

"Why not? Don't you like me, Meredith?"

She wanted to shout no, for her heart knew that she could not love a man whom she could not trust. There was still the issue of the photograph. But she did like him—too much. She changed the topic.

"How did you find me?"

"Followed your trail."

"No. I mean why you? Where's Jonah?"

"Jonah arrived at camp about the time we found your horse. He and I went looking for you together. I sent him back into town."

"Did the bull send you after me?"

"I came because I was worried about you. Is it so hard to believe that I care about you?"

"But. . ."

Meredith's face warmed, and she felt him leaning closer. His arm slipped around her back. She pushed him away.

"This is not proper. We cannot talk about this now, here alone."

His voice was low. "You didn't answer me. Don't you like me?"

"I don't know."

"You're right. Some other time. Let's try to get some sleep." He leaned back against the large stump and closed his eyes.

Meredith felt abandoned. But she knew that it was best this way. She closed her eyes and told herself that she was fortunate he had found her, fortunate she wasn't alone in the cold and in the dark. She poked Thatcher.

"Humph?"

"Do you think we should sleep?"

"Of course."

"Shouldn't one of us keep watch or something?"

He sighed. "You sleep. I'll keep watch."

"Promise?"

"Mm-hmm."

Chapter 20

Meredith burrowed her face into her pillow. Unconsciously, she shifted her leg in an attempt to alleviate some obscure pain. Slowly, as if coming out of a deep hibernation, her senses returned, her surroundings, the distressing events of the past twenty-four hours, the pain in her ankle. She had spent the night in the woods.

Her eyes started open. It was no pillow she was intimately nuzzling, but Thatcher Talbot's broad shoulder! With a jerk so severe that a jolt shot from her injured foot up through the tips of her hair, she pulled herself upright.

"Ouch." She sucked in her breath.

Her brown hair clung to Thatcher's shoulder. She passed her hand through the wisps to clear the sizzling air between them.

With startled amusement, Thatcher said, "At last the princess awakes. My turn to sleep now?"

A pang of guilt gripped Meredith. He had been on watch all night while she slept. She squirmed into position. "Just hand me that knife of yours, and you may sleep as long as you like."

He chuckled. "That won't be necessary."

To Meredith's humiliation, Thatcher rose and tucked the blanket over her, before going to the fire. He jabbed the coals, and sparks shot into the air.

He must have replaced the wood throughout the night.

"I can't believe that I actually slept," she said.

"I can. You were exhausted."

He fiddled with a canteen and coffee preparations.

Meredith felt a growing alarm. "I need to find a private spot."

Thatcher swiveled around on his haunches, gave their surroundings a sweeping gaze, and strode over.

He scooped her into his arms. "Up you go."

"You don't need to carry me."

"No trouble. Here you go." He set her down behind a cover of trees, then cleared his throat. "I'll go back to the fire. Holler, when you're ready."

She pinched her eyes shut from embarrassment. *This cannot be happening to me.*

When she opened them again, he was gone from sight. She finished with her toilet, and an idea flashed across her mind to see if she could hop back to camp. But she discarded it. Any method she used would be equally belittling.

"Ready," she called.

His impersonal manner led her to wonder if he was going to throw her, sack style, over his horse. Rather, he lowered and released her, and with a nothing-out-of-the-ordinary tone, said, "Coffee should be ready."

The hot tin felt good in Meredith's hands. "Thanks."

"You're mighty welcome."

"For everything. For finding me. You don't understand how hard this has been for me."

"Don't try so hard, Meredith."

She gripped the cup. "Excuse me?"

"It's my pleasure to help. You're a likable person. Just because you have a cruel father doesn't mean others don't accept you."

Her chin jutted upward. "I try hard because I want to succeed."

"Maybe." He studied her. "You are a good reporter. Do things because you want to, not to please others."

"Is that what you do?"

"I guess, maybe I do."

Meredith watched him kick dirt to douse the fire.

"I didn't mean any offense," he said.

"None taken," she said.

"Ready to go home?"

"Mmm, yes."

✍

Thatcher finished packing his gear, then carried Meredith to his horse. "You ride. I'll walk. If we keep the sun to our backs, we should find the road again."

Meredith certainly didn't know which direction would lead them out of the deep woods.

"Oh. . ." He took something from his saddlebags. "You might want this."

"My hat."

He shrugged. "Found it along the trail." He gave his saddlebags a pat. "Got your boot in here, too, for safekeeping."

She gave him a grateful smile.

℘

An hour passed.

"It shouldn't be long now," Thatcher said.

By midmorning, they intercepted the road.

Meredith gave a joyful cry. "This road never looked so good."

"How's your ankle doing?"

"It hurts, but I'm getting used to it. How about your arm?"

"It doesn't bother me much. But if you don't care, I wouldn't mind joining you up there."

She did mind, but how could she refuse him? She shrugged. "I just want to get home."

He effortlessly swung into the saddle behind her, then gave his horse a gentle nudge. "Let me know if the pace is too hard on you."

Her ankle ached at the increased jostling, but Meredith didn't tell Thatcher. She only wanted to get home, off this horse, and away from this man whose arms wrapped around her. She appreciated his rescuing her, of course, but their close proximity only hindered her resolve to stay emotionally detached.

They reached Buckman's Pride before noon. Thatcher slid off the horse and led her through town, which bustled with its usual activities.

Please don't let Mrs. Bloomfield see me like this, thought Meredith.

Only her eyes moved, assessing their progress and hoping against all hope that they would remain anonymous—parading, as it seemed to her, through town.

Thatcher looked tense as he returned nods and greetings.

Meredith chose to ignore them, her lips pressed over gritted teeth. She gave her hat a tug to shield her face, but it did nothing to conceal her wild, matted hair, and she wondered what kind of nasty notes she would receive this time.

As they neared the bank, she sucked in her breath and sat statue still. A heat of humiliation crept over her. Silent spurts of defense rushed through her mind—much like one whose life passed before them in a time of danger: *All part of the job. Couldn't help it that bear came out. . .Jonah was supposed to come. . . .*

109

Then to her most nightmarish dread, she heard the bank's door creak open. Meredith dipped her head, and tears soaked her shirt. She felt the horse stop and swiped a hand across her eyes.

Thatcher reached up, and she fell into his arms. She felt his breath against her face. "It's going to be all right now."

He carried her to the doctor's office and paused just outside the door to wipe away her tears.

"Ready?"

She nodded.

Thatcher shouldered the door open.

"What have we here?" The doctor asked with concern.

"Horse threw her. Hurt her ankle."

"Lay her here." The doctor carefully examined Meredith's ankle.

Thatcher backed away. "I'll go tell Jonah and Mrs. Cooper you're safe."

"Yes, please," Meredith called softly. "Thank you."

"Now then, let's see what you've done to yourself," The doctor said. Meredith flinched as his hand probed the injured area.

❧

Meredith's ankle was only sprained. The doctor wrapped it, gave her something to drink, then delivered her home. Mrs. Cooper and Jonah heard them approach and ran outside. Jonah carried Meredith into the house, where she caught a glimpse of Thatcher's face and anxious eyes.

Up in her room, Amelia cleaned Meredith enough to slip her between the sheets.

"You just rest a bit, and when you're up to it, I'll fix you a hot bath. We can talk later."

"I'm so tired."

"Probably something the doctor gave you. Rest easy, now."

Meredith gave a feeble wave of her hand. "Amelia, give Mr. Talbot my thanks."

"I will indeed, and that's not all. I'm going to fix him a big meal before he rides back. I'm mighty grateful he found you and brought you back to us safe."

"Me, too," Meredith murmured, just before she dozed.

Chapter 21

For the next couple of days Meredith did little except mope around the house and receive visitors. There was Mr. and Mrs. Washington from the mill. Francine Wiley brought over her pudgy-cheeked twin boys to cheer Meredith. Even Mr. and Mrs. Bloomfield came calling.

The latter confided, "I heard you were missing, and then when I saw you ride past the bank looking so pathetic. . . . I do hope the experience wasn't too horrifying."

"It was. I was never so frightened in my life."

"Tell me everything that happened."

Meredith did not know why Mrs. Bloomfield was suddenly so concerned. Was she as caring as her honeyed tone implied? Meredith saw the raw anticipation in Mrs. Bloomfield's eyes, and Thatcher's advice came to mind.

Just because you have a cruel father doesn't mean that others don't accept you. Do things because you want to, not to impress or please others.

"I'll tell you everything, but you won't faint on me, will you?"

Mrs. Bloomfield leaned forward, a gloved hand fluttering at her lips. "I should hope not! Please, go on."

"I was riding without a care, knowing full well that Jonah was to follow me, of course. All of a sudden, my horse reared up. And then I saw it. A bear. . ."

Mrs. Bloomfield gasped. "I would have died on the spot. What did you do?"

"Well, I had no choice. . . ." Meredith went on to detail the entire episode.

When Mrs. Bloomfield left, she pecked Meredith on the cheek. "Please call me Beatrice, won't you?"

Even Amelia gave Meredith a nod of approval from across the room. Most likely, Beatrice would let the townspeople know she had the entire delicious story straight from the source. It was a thing too good to keep. Being a reporter, Meredith knew the thrill of a good story.

✒

After Mrs. Bloomfield's departure, Jonah helped Meredith up the steps to her room.

When he had left her alone, Meredith did some soul searching. Thatcher's observations had given her some new insights.

Her father verbally abused her and discredited her talents and skills. Yet she sought his approval through accomplishments, the type a son might pursue, not the daughter he never wanted. Could she face the fact that she would never win her father's acceptance, that she should quit trying?

Having never known a mother's love, Meredith craved women's approvals as well. Oftentimes, her progressive behavior offended women. Jonah said she frightened them. But when she'd allowed herself to be vulnerable with Amelia, the woman had wholeheartedly accepted her, and now she had risked the same with Beatrice.

She sat at her desk, stared out the window, and thought about Thatcher's alternative. If she didn't have to prove anything, would she still be writing stories for *McClure's*? A still, small voice—one she had not listened to for quite some time—broke into her thoughts.

"Don't live for others, but don't live for yourself either. Live for Me."

It was true, she had left God out of things when He should have been the center. She buried her head in her folded arms.

God, forgive me for my selfish groping. Forgive me for my hatred, my anger, my. . .vanity.

She let God convict and heal all the soreness. Afterwards, she lifted her head.

✒

On Sunday, Thatcher visited Meredith with Mrs. Cooper's approval. They sat in the parlor.

"I've thought about what you said, that I need to do things because I want to, not to impress others," Meredith said.

"And?"

"The statement has some merit, but doesn't it sound selfish?"

Thatcher's brow burrowed in thought.

"Let me put it this way," Meredith said. "I know you are a Christian, but are you working in California because you're doing what you want or you're doing what God wants?"

"You ask some tough questions."

The room grew silent.

Finally, he said, "Both, I think."

She lifted her injured foot to illustrate her point. "I've had plenty of time to do some serious soul searching. What I'm trying to say is I was seeking the praise of others. I don't want to do that anymore. But neither do I want to indulge my own selfish desires. I need to live for God."

"That's admirable," Thatcher said.

"Do you think so? You're serious about your faith?"

"Of course I am. Your question about selfish motives gives me something to think about."

They smiled and gazed at each other, neither quite knowing what to say. It was one of those moments when souls mesh.

"Maybe we can help each other," he said.

She cocked her head. "What do you mean?"

"As Christians."

"Oh."

Thatcher fiddled with his hat, which lay across his knee. "I've been thinking I should go to church. I miss it."

"Me, too."

"See there. We've helped each other already."

Meredith wondered if she should ask him again about the photograph of the woman. Would he tell her why he didn't want Jonah to take his photograph? If only she could trust him. She didn't want to ruin the special moment. Instead, she asked, "Do you think you'll ever go back to Chicago?"

"Perhaps someday. I'd have to be ready to make things right with Father."

"When I go home, I'll apologize to my father." She sighed. "Not that it will do any good. I'll put aside my expectations."

"Do you have plans to return?"

"Asa, my editor, wants me to return before winter."

Thatcher grew pensive.

⚘

That evening after Thatcher was gone, Amelia brought a sealed envelope to Meredith's room. "A message boy brought this."

"Thanks." Hesitant, not knowing what to expect, Meredith opened it and read: *"Stories circulate around town. We think you're a tramp. Go back to New York where you belong."*

Meredith gasped, and Amelia, who had waited by the door, stepped into her room with concern. "What is it, dear? Bad news?"

Disappointed and hurt, Meredith handed Amelia the paper. The older woman's eyes quickly scanned the contents.

"This is outrageous! Whoever wrote such a thing is the one that needs to leave town. Don't you worry yourself about this demented person, whoever he is."

"He?" Meredith murmured.

Amelia calmed. "That's the bad thing about someone who does things backhandedly. It makes you crazy trying to guess who did it. But we shouldn't accuse anyone. It's probably not at all who we think it might be."

Meredith nodded. Journalism demanded evidence. "Could you look in that bag for my Bible?"

"Surely I can." Amelia's hips swayed determinedly as she crossed the room. Her lips pinched, she searched for the book. "Here you go, dear." She hovered over Meredith. "I'll run along, but I'll check on you before I go to bed."

Meredith clung to her Bible and nodded.

Amelia tiptoed from the room as if she treaded on holy ground.

Chapter 22

The following Saturday evening, Thatcher rode into Buckman's Pride, got a room at the hotel, and ordered a bath. After he shaved, he wrestled back his wavy hair, donned his best tan leather vest, brown pants, and boots. The hotel provided him with a hot, tasty dinner of clam chowder and fried chicken. Once his stomach was full, he started out for Mrs. Cooper's.

Meredith's plans to leave California before winter pressed him with an urgency to do some serious courting. After that, he would propose, only properly this time. He chuckled over the memory of his last one, feeble as it was. She sure was pretty when she got mad. He would start his new courting campaign with an invitation to attend church with him tomorrow.

As he walked, the setting sun provided enough light for Thatcher to admire a carefully landscaped yard, which included a flower garden. Overcome with a sudden romantic urge, he plucked a handful of flowers. He would do things properly tonight.

◈

Mrs. Cooper answered the door, took one look at the bouquet, and gave Thatcher a conspiratorial smile.

"Mr. Talbot. What a pleasant surprise. Come in."

"Is Miss Mears at home?"

"Yes, she is. She's in the sitting room. Go on in."

With his bouquet of flowers held just so, Thatcher went to the parlor. He entered with a confident step. He opened his mouth to greet Meredith, but quickly snapped it closed.

On the sofa sat a prettily posed Meredith, a man pressed up against her. Thatcher clenched his fists and felt the flower stems snap.

Meredith stared at him, her eyes going from his face to the sagging bouquet and back to his face.

Finally she said, "Mr. Talbot."

Thatcher did not miss the use of his formal name nor the uncertainty in her tone of voice. He couldn't even reply.

Meredith stumbled to her feet. The man beside her lurched forward, offering Meredith his arm. They stood there, staring at him, she with her vulnerable expression, the man with his hand supporting Meredith's elbow.

"Thatcher, I'd like you to meet Charles."

A quiver flicked Thatcher's cheek. He bumbled forward, awkwardly sticking out his hand. The man introduced as Charles looked at the flowers thrust out at him. Thatcher snatched his hand back and offered the other one. "How do."

"Pleased to meet you," Charles said.

Is he going to give me the flowers or not? I've never seen Thatcher act so strange. This is beginning to get awkward.

"Let's all sit down," she said with stilted friendliness.

"No. I have to go." Thatcher gave a small nod, turned on his boot heels, and fled from the room.

Meredith took a few steps after him, her mouth agape.

The outer door banged.

"What was that all about?" Charles asked.

"I'm not sure," Meredith said. She turned back to Charles. "I think you scared him off. He's either very jealous or very mad about now."

"Why didn't you tell him I was your brother?"

Meredith's hand clasped over her mouth. "I bumbled that, didn't I?"

"Do you want me to go after him?" her stepbrother asked.

"No. It's better this way."

The two settled back onto the sofa. "Want to tell me about him?"

"I think I'm falling in love," she said.

"Mm." Charles's eyes narrowed. "Father was right to be worried about you."

"I still cannot believe that Father cares anything about me."

"He does. I know he doesn't show it. But when you left, it crushed him. He said it was like losing your mother all over again. He broke down and cried, begged me to come after you."

"I'm frightened. It's what I've always wanted, but now I'm afraid to face him."

"It will take time and patience."

"Do you think he'll get angry when he finds out I'm not coming right home with you?"

Charles shrugged thoughtfully. "I don't know."

"I have to finish this story."

He patted her hand. "Do what you have to do, sister."

✍

Back in his hotel room, Thatcher plopped on the bed, his arms behind his head, and glared at the ceiling. What a coldhearted woman. How dare she question him about the picture in his pocket when all of the time she had a gentleman friend in New York City?

What a fool he had made of himself. If it was the last thing he ever accomplished, he would wipe the memory of that traitorous woman from his mind. He had come to town to attend church services. Maybe God was stopping him from making a terrible mistake.

✍

Meredith dressed carefully for her first church service. She would wear the yellow hat. It was by far her favorite, and if by chance Thatcher showed, maybe it would encourage him. She hadn't meant to embarrass or hurt him. If only she could get a chance to explain about her stepbrother and clear up the misunderstanding.

When Meredith arrived at church, heads nearly jerked off necks, twisting to get a better look at her and the stranger. She couldn't help but wonder if anyone seated in the pews had sent her that nasty message. But she quickly cast the thought aside, for God's house was certainly not the place to harbor grudges. When she let it go, a peace settled over her.

Mrs. Bloomfield turned from the pew in front of Meredith. "Good morning, Miss Mears."

"Good morning." Meredith leaned forward with a smile. "Mrs. Bloomfield, this is my stepbrother, visiting from New York. His name is Charles Mears."

"Welcome to our church, Mr. Mears. It is good to have you." She gave Meredith a flashing smile and turned back.

After the service, the congregation disassembled, and Meredith noticed Thatcher fidgeting. He was blocked in the pew, wearing the expression of a frightened bird. If she hurried, she might be able to reach him before he flew the coop. She tugged Charles's coat sleeve.

"Come along."

Meredith felt her stepbrother's hesitation, but gave another tug. This time he followed.

117

When he saw where they were headed, he whispered, "Don't do it, Meredith."

She turned to Charles with frustration. "I just want to explain. It isn't right to leave Thatcher thinking. . .you know."

"But you told me you have suspicions about him," Charles whispered. "I can't let my sister throw herself at someone who isn't worthy."

"Nonsense." She released his arm and turned away. But when she did, the pew where Thatcher had been standing was empty. She shot an angry glance back at Charles and hurried down the aisle toward the door.

"Miss Mears," Mrs. Bloomfield said, "everyone is waiting for you to introduce your stepbrother."

Meredith's spirits sagged. "Of course." She waited for Charles to join her, and by the time they exited the church, Thatcher Talbot was nowhere in sight.

Chapter 23

Meredith met Jonah in the upstairs hallway. "Oh Jonah. I need to talk to you."

"I was going down to breakfast. You?"

"Yes, I was. But I wanted to speak with you privately."

Jonah leaned against the wall. "What's on your mind, Storm?"

"I'm making plans to return to New York in September. I hope to visit one or two other logging camps during the time I have left. Are you returning with me, or do you have your own plans?"

Jonah's boot drew involuntary circles on the floor. "I'd like to stay through the winter at least, maybe longer." He looked up at her. "But don't you worry. We'll find someone to travel with you. I won't let you down."

"That's just it. Charles has offered to come back for me. I need to give him my answer by tomorrow."

Jonah's face lit. "That'll work out fine, then, won't it?"

"I'll miss you."

He gave her a brotherly hug. "This whole town'll miss you."

"Let's go get breakfast."

During the meal, Meredith discussed travel plans with her stepbrother. They would spend a couple of weeks visiting other camps, then take the train from San Francisco to the East. She had a month to finish her business in Buckman's Pride.

⚘

The following day, Meredith saw her brother off, then went to the newspaper office. Her ankle felt completely healed, and the sun made the walk pleasant. She hoped the editor would be back in town. She had not heard anything of him since her accident.

Ralston bristled at her entrance.

"Is Charlie back yet?"

"Nope."

"When do you expect him?"

"Don't know."

"Really?" She placed her hands on her hips, knowing full well that

Ralston would not have been left in charge of the newspaper without knowing when Charlie was returning or without knowing Charlie's tentative plans.

Before she could utter a reply, however, the newsroom's front door flew open, and the bell clanged as the door hit the wall. Meredith jumped and turned.

There stood Thatcher Talbot, his eyes furious. "I'd have a word with you," he said.

She squared her shoulders. "If you can wait one moment." She turned back to Ralston.

Thatcher, however, ignored her request and covered the few steps between them. "Why did you lie to me?"

"I did no such thing." By this time, the reporter across the room was on the edge of his seat.

"Why didn't you tell me he was your stepbrother? You led me to believe he was a suitor!"

"You did not give me a chance to explain." She looked back at Ralston, who had a smile plastered across his frail face. "Mr. Talbot, may we please go someplace private to continue this discussion?"

"You want to take it on the street?"

She glared at him. "May we use the back room, Ralston?"

"By all means. Don't break anything," The reporter said.

Meredith stomped past him and into the back room. Thatcher followed and closed the door. "You should have told me he was your brother," he repeated.

"I'm sorry. When I saw you there with those flowers, I was so stunned that I made an awkward introduction. If you'd stayed around, I would have explained."

He splayed his arms. "How could I know?"

Meredith heaved a great sigh. "I tried to reach you in church, Sunday, to explain, but you rushed out." She earnestly appealed. "I'm really sorry."

He shook his head. "You have no idea how humiliated, how furious I have been at you."

"Charles is my father's first wife's son. My father adopted him. Just so you know all, Charles is returning for me in September."

This news doused him like a canteen of icy water from the Mad River, and Thatcher instantly softened. "I'm only thankful that Beatrice told me when she did. Otherwise, I might have wasted these last few weeks. I'm sorry for embarrassing you in front of that reporter out there."

At the thought of the gloating reporter in the other room, Meredith said, "We'd better go if you feel things are settled now."

Thatcher opened the door. It was an awkward moment.

Meredith made stiff strides across the newsroom, Thatcher right behind her. At the door she turned back.

"Let me know when the editor returns to town."

Ralston saluted her.

Outside, Thatcher gently took her arm. "I've got to get back to the camp. I was doing some banking for the bull. That's how I found out."

"I understand."

"May I call on Saturday night?"

"Oh Thatcher, I don't know."

"Please."

"Do as you think best."

"Saturday night then." With a big reckless grin that melted her heart, he tipped his hat.

⟳

Back at the newspaper office, Ralston was having a glorious time, typing furiously. This spoof would catch the town's attention. *"Town reporter caught in lie. Hero duped by stepbrother, wishes he had left reporter for bear meat."*

⟳

A few days later, a storm flew into the same newspaper office. The door clanged, and the bell vibrated.

Meredith halted.

"You're back! High time!" She slapped a copy of the newspaper down on the editor-in-chief's desk. "Can you tell me the meaning of this?"

"I was just discussing this with Frederick." Ralston only looked amused, rather like a cat savoring a mouse.

Meredith's lower lip trembled with indignation. "Is this how you allow your reporters to be treated? Haven't I experienced enough humiliation in this town without getting stabbed in the back by this paper?"

The editor-in-chief looked at Ralston. "What have you to say to that?"

He shrugged his shoulders. "It was a spoof. Everyone knows that.

Can't you take a joke, Miss Mears?"

"You made me out to be a liar. You know what that can do to the credibility of a journalist. I want a retraction."

"And you'll get one," The editor soothed.

Cold steely eyes bored into him from the other desk.

Meredith walked over to Ralston. "You'd better make it sweet, if you know what's good for you."

"Is that a threat, Miss Mears?"

The editor-in-chief pushed back his chair. "That will be enough. I'm sick of this childishness." He cast angry eyes on the male reporter. "You've work to do," and then back on Meredith, "I'll see you another day, when you've cooled down."

Meredith stalked out of the office. Her head stooped, she marched down Main Street.

"Miss Mears!" A feminine voice beckoned from across the street. "Please, wait."

Meredith stopped. *Not now!* The adrenaline still boiled her blood. It was Beatrice Bloomfield. Meredith swallowed hard, then turned to wait. She concentrated on giving a calm, steady greeting.

"I am so sorry for the trouble I've caused," Beatrice said with all earnestness. "I never meant to harm you, dear. Please. Come over for some tea. Let me explain."

"That isn't necessary."

"But my dear friend, I must."

The "dear friend" drew Meredith, and she nodded.

The other woman took Meredith's arm and led her back across the street and into the house that was situated just around the corner from the bank.

They entered the parlor where Beatrice had received her guests the night of her dinner party. Meredith took a seat on one of the mahogany chairs and stared down at the floral rug while she struggled for composure. Beatrice prepared their tea.

When Beatrice returned to the room, she said, "Thatcher Talbot is a dear friend of our family. I probably shouldn't tell you this, but he's quite taken with you. He was the one who helped me to understand you and. . .well, I wasn't very kind to you at first." Her eyes became pools of regret.

"He did?"

"Yes. After that, I discovered for myself you are a fine person. It was my own fears that gave me such a bad start with you. Will you forgive me?"

Meredith set aside her cup and gave Beatrice a sincere smile. "Of course I shall. It was my fault, too. I'm much too forceful, and too vain, and..."

"Do stop. There's more. I've messed things up badly. I mentioned your stepbrother to Thatcher. By the way he stormed out of the bank, I know I got you in trouble."

Meredith giggled. "I am glad he didn't have an axe in his hand that day."

Beatrice smiled. "I think Mr. Ralston must have it in for you."

"His male pride, my female pride. I'm so ashamed. I just came from the newsroom where I blasted all of them."

"Oh my."

"Yes. I think I need to go home and pray."

"As do we all."

By evening, Meredith felt much recovered. After supper, Meredith and Jonah lingered companionably at the table with their coffee. Amelia wiped her hands on her apron, gave a nervous smile, and then went to the cupboard.

When she returned, she mumbled sorrowfully, "Another message," and snapped it on the table, where they all stared at it as if it were some evil thing.

Meredith's good spirits wilted. "You read it, Jonah."

His eyes scanned the note. "It's most unpleasant." He shook his head. "I can't do it, Storm."

"Please. Go on."

His baritone held distaste: "'A tramp and a liar. What other traits may we look forward to? You're a disgrace to Buckman's Pride. Move on.' Don't pay any attention to this," Jonah urged.

"I think it's time that we find out who this troublemaker is," Amelia said.

"How?" Jonah asked.

"It was the same delivery boy. He wouldn't talk to me, just ran off. But if we confront him in front of his mama, the lad might speak."

"I'll go tomorrow," Jonah said.

"I know his mama. I'll go along."

"We'll all go. You're such good friends." Meredith said. "I think I'll go to my room."

"Good night, dear." Amelia gave an effort at cheerfulness.

In the privacy of her room, Meredith took out her Bible. She was learning that God could sustain her through hard times.

Chapter 24

I nside the mess hall at Bucker's Stand, Thatcher bent over his meal, chewing but not tasting, as the conversation around the table grew more and more annoying.

"We saw what was happening between you and that reporter."

"Be blind not to."

"Not that we blame you. Never saw a prettier girl."

"I want to know what you was thinking, cozyin' up to a reporter."

"Maybe he wanted to make the news."

"Sure way to do it, courting a reporter."

"It might be worth a night in the woods alone."

"This the only tree you men can climb?" Silas growled.

"She's got a spell cast over you, too."

"Her spell is over all of you, if you'd only admit it," he replied back.

Thatcher didn't mind so much that he was the camp's joke, nor care much if anyone came to his defense or not. What worried him was what Ralston's spoof would do to his and Meredith's relationship. Would she pack up her bags and leave? What if she left town without a word to him?

He was glad tomorrow was Saturday. Otherwise, he'd forget about work and ride into town today. But one more day shouldn't matter that much. If she was gone, then. . .then maybe it was meant to be. He took another mouthful and chewed.

"She's said some decent things about us, right enough."

❧

Meredith straightened her hat. She stood outside the Browns' home. Jonah knocked. A light-haired woman in a dark blouse and skirt cracked the door. "Yes?"

Mrs. Cooper stepped forward, "May we come in?"

The woman's eyes warily rested on Meredith. The door creaked open. They followed Mrs. Brown to a couch and two chairs. After they were seated, the woman cast an anxious glance at Mrs. Cooper. "Is there a problem?"

"We hoped you could help us solve one."

The woman folded her hands in her lap.

"Is your son at home?" Amelia asked.

"No. He's working with his pa. I don't understand."

Jonah leaned forward, his elbows propped on his knees. "Your son has been a message courier for someone who has been sending offensive letters to Miss Mears. We are trying to find out who the writer is."

The woman's hand went to her breast. "My son has delivered these?"

"Yes. No fault lies at his door, but it's important that we find out who's behind this mischief and get it stopped."

"But of course. I won't see him until tonight." She stood up and began to pace. "But rest assured, I shall find out. I'll send word as soon as I do."

"Thank you, ma'am," Jonah said.

"I'm sorry to have troubled you, Mrs. Brown," Mrs. Cooper said. "Please, don't worry about this. Like we said, it's not the boy's fault. But I knew you would want to help."

"I do," Mrs. Brown nodded vigorously.

Mrs. Cooper rose, and the others followed suit. "We'll run along, then, and wait to hear from you."

✑

Saturday evening, Mr. Brown and his son brought the news. The father cleared his lean throat and straightened his very tall frame. "We came to tell you that we know where the letters came from. They were from Frederick Ralston." He nudged his boy. "Right, son?"

Meredith flinched.

The boy nodded and kept his eyes to the floor. The father placed his arm on his son's shoulder and gave it a squeeze.

"My boy didn't mean you no harm, Miss Mears."

"I understand. Thank you for telling me."

The boy looked up. "He made me promise not to tell who they was from."

"Don't worry," Mr. Brown said to his son. "After I speak with him, he won't harm you none."

"We do appreciate your coming here. May I get you both something to eat, to drink?" Mrs. Cooper asked.

"No. Thank you. His ma's rather anxious about this whole thing. We'll run along now. Sorry for our part in this."

Meredith smiled kindly at the lad and nodded.

When they had gone, Meredith eased into a chair. "I don't understand why that man is so hateful." Jonah handed Meredith his handkerchief.

"There was plenty of room for both of us, but I won't write another article for that paper."

"We'll speak with him and the editor," Jonah said. "I'll go with you on Monday."

Meredith nodded, and there was a knock at the door. "That must be Mr. Talbot."

"I'll go answer it, dear," Amelia said.

"No. I want to get it."

"I'm off to my room," Jonah said.

"And I'll be in the kitchen if you need me," Amelia called on her way out.

Meredith dabbed her eyes with the handkerchief and made her way to the door. "Come in."

Thatcher followed Meredith wordlessly to the parlor and took the chair that was next to hers. "I've come at a bad time, haven't I?"

"Yes. But I was expecting you."

"Do you want to talk about it?"

She looked up at him from beneath dark wet lashes.

"Is it about the article?" He leaned forward and touched her arm. "That is entirely my fault. How can I ever say how sorry I am that I burst into the newspaper office and said all of those horrible things? I'm so sorry. Can you forgive me?"

"I just found out it was him."

Thatcher gave her an odd look. "Who else could it be?"

"No." She shook her head. "I mean he wrote those horrible letters I've been getting. They're threatening and ugly."

Thatcher withdrew his hand. "He wrote threatening letters to you?"

She twisted the handkerchief in her lap. "The boy who delivered them finally confessed that it was Frederick Ralston. He's done everything in his power to turn this town against me. It's time that I go. There's no need to wait another month."

"Please. Don't make any rash decisions."

"It's best."

"But what about us?"

Meredith was too overwrought to think clearly. "Us? You carry that wretched picture of your wife in your pocket and talk about us? What kind of man are you?"

127

"Are you still worrying about that picture? I told you she's nothing to me."

"'To my husband, with all my love, Colleen,'" Meredith recited.

Thatcher's face paled. "Have you been mulling this over all this time? She's not my wife. I had no idea that you still thought such a thing."

"She's really not your wife?"

"Of course not. She's my best friend's wife. But she left him. He's the fellow I introduced you to the day I saw you trying on the hat."

Meredith mentally backtracked to that day. "Go on."

"His wife left him because he treated her badly. Now he's sorry, and he's trying to locate her. He passed through town and gave me this photograph in hopes that I might run across someone who had some information about her. I've been so busy at the camp and thinking about you that I haven't given it much thought. I thought you were jealous, that's all. I didn't think it would hurt anything."

The strain of the past several days weighed heavily on Meredith, and in a moment of sudden anger, with little regard to possible consequences, she jumped to her feet and shook her handkerchief at him.

"You fool! You had the audacity to barge into that newsroom and accuse me of all kinds of things because I didn't properly introduce my stepbrother to you, and yet you deliberately misled me to think you had an attachment or a wife. All this time I have thought. . .I have had it with you and this town!"

The word "fool" brought Thatcher to his feet. "Then I shall accommodate you, ma'am." With his stubborn reply, he picked up his hat and strode furiously toward the door to leave and lick his wounds. But first, he turned and smirked.

"Storm. The name suits you perfectly!"

Then he was gone.

His words hit her like a slap in the face. At last, she had driven him away. When she heard the door slam, she ran from the room and to the stairway. Partway up the steps, her weak ankle turned, and she collapsed on the staircase. Her hands flew out and grasped at the steps. The whole commotion brought Amelia from the kitchen and Jonah from his room.

She lay sprawled on the steps.

"Storm!"

Chapter 25

Jonah helped Meredith to her feet. "Are you hurt?"

"Yes, but it doesn't matter," she whimpered.

With all of Meredith's weight shifted onto himself, Jonah asked, "Is it your ankle again?"

"He hates me. Everyone hates me."

"Oh no, that's not true," Amelia said. "We love you."

"He doesn't! I've made such a mess of my life."

"Of course you haven't, Storm," Jonah said, easing her up into his arms and heading toward her room. "You've just had too much excitement for one evening."

"It'll all look better in the morning," Amelia said. "But let's take a look at that ankle. Perhaps we'll need the doctor."

Meredith groaned and lay back on her bed. "And how did he know my name?"

✍

They did not call the doctor, for the sprain was not bad, but Meredith didn't go to church the following day. Instead, she sought the seclusion of her room and lay abed. She felt like packing up and going back to New York, but there was still the business of her unfinished story.

She considered her father, waiting to make amends, considered Asa, who trusted her to deliver. In the end, she opted to stick it out, square things with Ralston, and forget about Thatcher. It was just as well to end it this way.

That afternoon, Mrs. Bloomfield called on Meredith.

"At church today I heard about your fall. I'm so sorry you're not feeling well. Perhaps these will cheer you up."

The bouquet that Mrs. Bloomfield placed in one of Amelia's vases resembled Thatcher's droopy ones.

"Thank you," Meredith murmured.

"Oh dear. You are blue today, aren't you?" Her friend seated herself on a nearby chair. "Is it more than just the ankle?"

Meredith gave a dismal nod and gazed off into space.

"Is it Thatcher again? What has he done this time?"

"It's me. I railed at him. He hates me now."

"I'm sure he doesn't. Perhaps his feelings are just hurt or something."

"I don't think there's much hope left between us. It's better this way. But it's so hard."

"I understand. We won't talk about it anymore, then."

"Perhaps it's time for me to return to New York City."

"Oh, but you can't go now. You must at least stay until after Pride Day."

"Did you say Pride Day?"

Beatrice nodded enthusiastically.

Meredith moaned, "I have enough trouble with pride, and you celebrate it?"

Mrs. Bloomfield tilted her head. "It's the day we clean up the town. We replace floors and sidewalks that the loggers tear up. Everyone chips in, and we clean up the whole town."

"That is the most amazing thing I've ever heard. You're absolutely right. I wouldn't want to miss a thing like that. It'll make a wonderful story."

❧

Monday morning, things looked clearer to Meredith. Her ankle felt tender but strong enough to carry her weight. Jonah insisted that they take care of things at the newspaper office so Meredith could get her life back in order. He brought a wagon around from the stables.

The bell announced their arrival, and Meredith limped into the newsroom with a great deal of grace.

"I've come to settle some matters." She coveted the closest chair to her. "May I sit?"

The editor-in-chief motioned toward the chair with a nod and glanced at Jonah, who hovered over Meredith. "Is there a problem?"

Meredith pulled several wrinkled pieces of paper from her portfolio and thrust them in the air. "These are threatening letters written to me. The boy who delivered them said that they came from you." Her eyes settled on Mr. Ralston.

His face turned hateful. "Can't take the truth, Miss Mears?"

"Let me see those." The editor snapped the letters off the floor and leafed through them. When he was finished, he turned a condemning gaze on his male reporter. "This is the lowest thing I have ever seen. You're fired."

130

"No!" Meredith's hand shot up in the air. "He stays. I quit. I'm leaving soon anyway."

She turned toward Ralston. "But I want to set the record straight. I was never after your job. This has only been a temporary assignment. You knew that from the start. The logging camp was an assignment for *McClure's* magazine. I don't know why you hate me so, but I didn't come to get you fired. I just came to tell you that I know you wrote those letters. You can quit writing them. You can have your job, and you'll get your way soon enough. I'm leaving in September."

She rose from her chair and faced the editor. "I'm through here, but I thank you for the work you've given me."

"Wait a minute," The editor said. "I'm not finished. Ralston, you're still fired. That was the most ungentlemanly thing to do. I don't need your kind representing this paper."

The pale reporter glared at Meredith and at the editor. "I don't need this cheap operation. And I surely don't need a woman bossing me around. I quit." He threw a few things together and started to leave; at the door he turned back, a wicked smirk on his face. "But you're still a tramp and a liar, Miss Uppity."

Jonah lunged toward the door.

"Jonah. Let it be," Meredith said.

The reporter gave the photographer a parting hateful look and fled.

Jonah chased after him and returned within moments. "He's gone."

Meredith slumped back into the chair and dipped her head in her hands.

"I'm ashamed for the trouble he's caused you, ma'am. I'll get you something to drink. You look pale." The editor left them to fetch the drink.

Jonah knelt beside Meredith's chair and grinned up at her. "You were beautiful."

She smiled. "So were you."

The editor returned with a drink of water, and Meredith accepted it gratefully. He apologized again and said, "The job is yours, you know. On behalf of this town, we'd love for you to stay."

She shook her head. "I don't think so."

"No." The editor's hand shot up. "Don't answer me today. You're too distressed. Take your time and think about it."

✍

Meredith slept on it and the next day returned to the editor's office.

"I appreciate your offer. I feel terrible to have cost you a valuable reporter, especially since I'm only staying until September. But in the meantime, I'd be glad to fill in if I can also work on my articles for *McClure's*."

"The facilities are at your disposal."

"I won't be going to the logging camp anymore," Meredith said. "But I'll be doing some research by mail and continuing the story. I plan to stop at a few camps on the trip home."

"Sounds good to me."

"So what's my first assignment?"

"I thought we should do a blurb, 'Reporter Leaves Town.' Nothing too informative, unless it's too painful."

"I'll get right on it, boss."

✍

Meredith worked hard at the newspaper. She did not ride back to the logging camp and did not run into Mr. Talbot, so things settled down for her in town.

Chapter 26

Two Saturdays passed from the time that Thatcher walked out of Meredith's life. She had not seen him since. Each Saturday a tiny hope rose within her that maybe he would show up on her doorstep. But it never happened. It was Saturday again, and Meredith felt restless. She decided Jonah's studio would provide a proper diversion.

It was raining, so she donned a jacket, but Amelia intercepted her by the door. "And where do you think you're going in this rain?"

"Just to the studio to chat with Jonah. Want to come?"

"Oh. Well. . ." Amelia gazed longingly toward the studio, but her practical disposition won out in the end. "No. One foolish woman in this household is enough. You'll need someone to nurse you again."

Meredith giggled. "You're probably right. But it's not like I'm going far."

"But it's pouring."

"And I'll hurry," Meredith said, before bursting outside.

"Watch your ankle!" Amelia shouted after her.

Meredith chuckled as she ran, but wisely kept her eyes downcast and watched her step, then danced up and down in the rain, waiting for Jonah to answer her knock.

"Come in," he yelled.

She pushed open the door, and a gust of wind blew her in.

"Storm?" He could not stop his particular task without harming his photographs, but his eyes flashed concern. "What are you doing out in the rain?"

"Visiting you."

He caught her playful mood. "I can see that. You're dripping all over my floor."

"So what are you working on?"

"Photographs of the dock. The ocean is a wonderful backdrop."

"Mm-hmm. That schooner looks majestic sitting on top of that wave."

"Unique, isn't it?"

"So, Jonah." She leisurely milled about the studio, fingering different things and looking at his finished works. "You've done a wonderful job with this studio. But where are you going to live after I leave?"

"Pardon?" His head bobbed up and down as he dipped paper in and out of a solution.

"It wouldn't look proper for you to live here alone with Amelia."

He frowned. "I've given it some thought, but haven't come up with a solution yet."

"I have one," she ventured. "Why don't you marry her?"

The paper slipped from his hands and down into the pan of solution. "Now look what you've gone and done."

She moved closer and leaned over his shoulder as he removed it. "Is it ruined?"

"Fortunately for you, it's not."

"So?"

"I guess that would be one possible solution."

"Have you considered it?"

"I have."

She giggled. "And?"

He smiled. "I rather like the idea."

"You sly old fox, you." She sidled up to him.

"Watch it. Stay back."

"Well?" she pressed.

"A few weeks does not give a man enough time to court, propose, and marry, does it now?"

She laughed with delight and grabbed his arm. "Congratulations, old man."

"Watch it now, Storm. Be careful there."

"Maybe she'd let you stay at the mill. But you'd better start making your intentions known if you expect such a favor."

His hands stopped midair, and his eyes lit with hope. "That's a great idea. There's plenty of room there. Surely there would be someplace. . .and Amelia does have the connections." He grinned appreciatively at her. "Thanks, Storm."

"You're welcome." She hugged his stiff body, for he held his soupy hands out away from her. "I just want you to be happy."

"I am. I love it here."

"Good. Well, I'd better get back to the house. Talking with you has given me the lift I needed."

She ran back to the house, and Amelia appeared almost as soon as the door opened. "See how wet you got! What's a body to do?" she scolded.

Meredith gave her a sly smile. "Let's sit by the fire, shall we? So I can dry off."

The next day, a steady rain continued. Jonah dressed in a slicker and went to the stables around the corner. He returned with Amelia's horse and carriage. Bundled up in summer coats, Meredith and Amelia scurried into the protection of the carriage. All the way to church, Amelia chatted on and on about how poor Jonah would be drenched.

"He'll be fine. He's dressed appropriately. Anyway, it makes him feel chivalrous to do this for us," Meredith said.

"You think so?"

"I know Jonah. I'm sure of it."

With that, Amelia seemed appeased.

At the small church, they scurried inside, allowing Jonah to take care of the horses and carriage. Spirits weren't gloomy in spite of the weather; folks smiled and greeted each other as normal. When Meredith pulled her hooded cape back away from her face, she saw something that gave her a start. Across the entryway stood a dripping but handsome Thatcher Talbot.

Thatcher saw Meredith enter. Her rosy cheeks and sparkling eyes almost took his breath away. Now he knew he had been a fool to come. He should have waited until she had gone back to New York. God would have understood. When her hands faltered and her gaze rested upon him, he looked away and engaged the nearest person in a conversation about the weather.

Meredith's cheeks burned at Thatcher's snub. She tried to look away, to enter into the conversation of the nearby circle of women. Her smile was weak, and her hands felt icy. She couldn't tell how much time passed until they all shuffled into the sanctuary, and she tried to ignore Thatcher, but nevertheless, she noticed him sitting a few pews back on the opposite side.

Good. Out of sight. Now if I can only keep the back of my neck from turning red.

The sermon was on forgiveness and was most compelling. Meredith lost herself in the Word of God. The preacher explained no sin was too large to forgive. She would have to think about that. He explained that a person is saved by grace and since one sin is as bad as another, all can be forgiven by God and should be forgiven by man.

All too soon for Meredith, the service ended. Just as she knew they would, her rebellious eyes sought out Thatcher Talbot. It almost looked as though he were purposely waiting for her. Or was he waiting for the rain to slow? Her heart gave a foolish flutter, and before she could do a thing about it, her legs propelled her forward, down the center aisle.

Please someone stop me. Oh, where is Beatrice Bloomfield when I need her?

"Hello, Meredith."

If he was so bold as to use her first name after what had passed between them, then she would be just as brave.

"Hello, Thatcher."

He looked toward the window. "Quite the cloudburst."

Thatcher looked so forlorn, so vulnerable. Meredith heard herself say, "Given the preacher's sermon on forgiveness, I feel the fool standing here talking to you."

He looked at his boots then up again. "Meredith. . ."

"I'm sorry for getting so angry," she said.

"Me, too."

There was a lengthy silence, and then she said, "Something's been plaguing me since our last meeting."

He arched his brows, leaned forward, and whispered, "Knowing us and our past experiences, I'm not sure this is a safe place to start another serious discussion."

Her hand shot out and touched his arm briefly, and he quieted.

"Ask," he said.

Her hand slipped back down to her side. She leaned close and whispered, "How did you know my name?"

"That bothered you, did it?"

She gave him an earnest nod. "It hurt, but I deserved it."

"The day your horse appeared in camp without you, Jonah came riding up to the group of men gathered there. The bull asked him if he knew where you were. Jonah said, 'You mean Storm?' No one else caught it, but I'd always wondered what that middle initial stood for. The instant he said it, I knew."

"I should have known. He calls me that all the time. It's what I go by back home. But I told him I didn't want people here to know. You might as well stamp volatile across my face in big red letters."

Thatcher laughed. It grew quiet between them again for a while, and then he turned pensive. "I had to think of my father during the preacher's sermon."

"Me, too." She waited and when he didn't say anything more, she added, "When Charles was here," she gave him a tentative glance, "he told me that my father is sorry for our argument. He actually sent Charles to see how I fared." She shook her head. "It's almost more than I can hope that things might improve with Father."

He touched her arm. "Why, that's wonderful news. You must believe."

"I've been praying about it."

"Then it must be God at work."

"What about you? Will you ever return to your father to try and make amends?"

"You don't know my father. But I have thought about it. I know I will someday. I just want the time to be right."

"You're praying about it then?"

"Yes, I am."

Amelia interrupted them. "Jonah has our carriage. Are you ready, Meredith?"

"Yes. I'll be right there."

Meredith turned back to Thatcher. "I'm glad we had this talk."

"I wish I could see you home. But all I have is a horse."

"I'm leaving for New York very soon. It's probably just as well."

Thatcher watched her walk away, then hurry through the rain and climb into Mrs. Cooper's carriage. He watched it slosh away, disappointed Meredith hadn't invited him over for the afternoon.

Chapter 27

Thatcher ate his lunch at a table in the hotel's dining room and gazed out the window. The street was deserted except for an occasional carriage or intrepid horseback rider. He didn't relish riding back to camp in the rain; the ride from the church to the hotel had been bad enough.

"We have berry pie for dessert."

Thatcher looked away from the steamy window just long enough to answer the waitress.

"Pie sounds good."

The pie was just an excuse to put off the inevitable decision. Would he go see Meredith? At the church, she had said it was better if they didn't pursue their relationship. *But,* he wondered, *did she really mean it?*

The waitress returned with his pie just as an unexpected patch of sun broke through the sky, and by the time he had eaten the last bite, the rain had ceased entirely. He paid for his meal and strode outside.

The air was rain scented with musty forest and wet soil odors. The eastern sky shone hopefully bright; he could probably make it to camp. To the west, the Cooper house lay beyond his vision, the sky dark and threatening.

He would return to camp.

⌘

The whole next week, Meredith wavered between wishing she had invited Thatcher over on Sunday to feeling confident that she had been right to discourage him.

Regardless, she kept busy. She sent Jonah to the logging camp with the conservation suggestions she had promised the bull and hand-delivered the same information to the mill. Her correspondence research was going well, her work at the newspaper, time consuming. The most interesting business at hand was also the talk of the town, Pride Day.

Finally, Saturday, the long-awaited and highly praised Pride Day arrived. The mill prepared and donated wagonloads of special materials for repairs. The mill owner drafted a blueprint of the areas needing repair and posted it on a sign in front of the general store on Main Street.

Main Street, the hub of activity, was one of the major areas that needed work. Jonah set up a tripod for his camera on the far side of the street. The mahogany camera was shined to a high gloss, and its brass hardware twinkled in the sunlight.

Meredith positioned her station of refreshments nearby. She kept the water barrel full and food tables of sandwiches and cookies ready for the working men. Meredith purposely wore a large-pocketed apron to stash writing supplies so she could jot down notes throughout the day.

Men ripped up damaged sidewalk boards with wicked-looking crowbars and threw them into the streets, where others picked them up and tossed them onto a wagon. When the wagon was full, it was taken to the mill. Nails would later be removed so the scraps could be given out as free firewood. The rest would go in the big stoves at the mill.

Meredith marveled and wrote notes about the small amount of waste. Pride Day would make a fitting conclusion to Meredith's articles, using Buckman's Pride and Bucker's Stand to demonstrate good conservation methods to the entire West Coast.

"Doing two jobs at once, I see."

"Good morning, Beatrice. One keeps my mind busy and the other my hands."

"There's plenty today for both. I love this day and the way the town pulls together." The banker's wife wore an old dark skirt and white blouse. She balanced several pans of freshly baked cookies.

"Are you here to help serve?"

"Oh, no. I'm washing windows."

"You don't say? Well that's a noble thing to do."

"All I know, I've done it every year since I've lived here, and every year I'm so weary by the end of the day that I vow I'll never do it again. But, here I am."

Meredith giggled. "Amelia Cooper says that every year she gets a kink in her neck from knocking cobwebs out of the rafters. I feel guilty doing such an easy job."

"Toting those water buckets isn't easy. Wait till the end of the day. That's when you can tell how hard you've worked."

Meredith thought about the saddle blisters and other hardships she had endured on this assignment. She doubted if anyone understood how hard she worked. The satisfaction that came with a job well done was pay enough. She bade Beatrice good-bye and turned her attention to the various other activities taking place around her.

"Hello," a shy voice said.

Meredith looked up. It was the Swedish woman from the lumber camp. "Well, hello."

"It's all so exciting, isn't it? Can you use some help?"

"Yes, it is exciting, and I would love some help."

The young blond moved behind the table. Then the two women fell into a companionable time of conversing and working together.

Meredith saw Thatcher. She had secretly been watching for him all morning. Thatcher's sleeves were rolled up, and his lower arms bulged with muscles acquired from his weeks at the logging camp. He hoisted several pieces of lumber up over his shoulder. She watched him shoulder his load with seeming ease, every muscle a fluid motion. He dropped the load onto another stack of lumber and turned. Their eyes met, and Thatcher gave her a large smile.

He knew that whole time that I was watching him, Meredith thought with shame. She gave him a small nod, then fussed at the table. *What an irritating man.* She rearranged and tidied things, trying to work with a semblance of normalcy.

She knew that every hardworking man eventually helped himself from the water and food at her table. Still, when Thatcher appeared it felt awkward, and her hand shook uncontrollably. She placed it behind her back. The Swedish woman dipped out his drink. She and Thatcher were acquainted from the camp.

"Saw you working over here," Thatcher said to Meredith, his eyes suspiciously merry.

"I saw you working over there," Meredith returned. "Trying not to miss a thing. It's all going to make a great story, what the loggers are doing for the town." He dipped out his second glass of water himself. "It's not just the loggers, everyone pitches in, even pretty reporters."

"Help yourself to some sandwiches and cookies," The Swedish woman interrupted, then discreetly found something with which to occupy herself.

He studied her a moment. "Meredith, I'm dining at my friends, the Bloomfields. May I call on you afterwards?"

"I don't know. I . . ."

"Please, Meredith." His eyes were dark, soulful, imploring her to yield. Finally, she nodded.

With a newfound boldness, he said, "I shall be able to get twice as much done, now, with such a reward awaiting me at the end of the day."

When he had left, she said to herself, *And I shall get nothing done if I keep watching you.*

"I think he has his eyes on you," Meredith's Swedish friend said. Meredith spun around. She gave a weak wave. "Him?"

"Ya, him."

Meredith just shrugged, relieved when a group of loggers approached their table. This time, she leaned forward to be the one to help.

Chapter 28

The sterling silver brush made long, even strokes through Meredith's clean brown hair. She wanted to look her best for Thatcher. Regardless, if they were meant to be together or not, she wanted to make this evening special, one they could always remember. She would allow him to make his move, if he intended to make one.

There was such little time left until she returned to New York. She knew she loved him. It was true that she did not want to make the necessary sacrifices of becoming a logger's wife, but maybe it was not his intention to be a logger the rest of his life. She only hoped that he had some wonderful plan to sweep her off her feet.

Her fingers nimbly went to work arranging her hair in a long style, swept up from the face, but hanging loose in the back. She slipped into her gown and shoes and went to the window that overlooked Amelia's backyard. There was a light on in Jonah's studio.

Jonah had taken several photographs of Pride Day that would complement her story. It would be a good one, she knew. Even if she never stepped foot inside a camp that needed to hear about conservation or saw with her own eyes the devastation that she had read about, her stories would make a difference. It would be hard to leave this place. The people had grown dear to her.

Especially Thatcher. She had tried her hardest to keep him from slipping into her heart, but looking back, she believed he had done so that very first time she had laid eyes on him on the train from Chicago. She drew away from the window and started toward her bedroom door.

What lay in store for her hopeful heart tonight? Would Thatcher make the declarations she wanted to hear?

❧

Meanwhile, Thatcher had just finished helping Beatrice with the dishes. His spirits were high. His friends had entertained him hospitably with simple fare, since everyone felt fatigued from the day's hard work.

Thatcher's mind was on Meredith. There was such little time to profess his love and win hers before she went back to the elegance of New York City.

He unrolled his shirtsleeves. "Beatrice, this has been a most enjoyable time. The meal was delicious."

"You've already thanked me a dozen times, Thatcher," she said.

"Don't spoil her. I have to live with her," Herbert said.

"I have a confession to make," Thatcher said.

"So that's it. Well, have a seat and tell all," Beatrice said.

Thatcher seated himself and looked sheepishly from his hostess to his host, although he knew they would understand when he told them of his plans to call on Meredith.

"I. . ." He stopped. Someone had knocked at the door.

"Excuse me," Herbert said.

Beatrice shrugged, and she and Thatcher both eyed the hall, waiting to find out who the caller was.

"William Boon! What a surprise. Do come in."

Thatcher jerked. William was back? In moments, the two men entered the room. It was Thatcher's old friend from Chicago. They greeted each other all around.

"What timing! To find you here as well, Thatcher. For I haven't much time. In fact, I thought I might not see you at all. I'm moving on tomorrow."

"What's the rush?" Thatcher asked.

"Father's ill."

William's face looked worried, deeply lined. Thatcher thought he looked travel worn, not the city gentleman he had seen only weeks earlier.

"You know how long it takes for word to reach you when you're always on the move. I've no time to waste. And then there's the family business. Mother will need my help."

"Any word of Colleen?" Thatcher asked.

"That's the worst of it." Thatcher's friend looked broken, as if he might weep at any moment, but he continued in a weary voice. "I was so close. I found out that she is alone and pregnant with our child."

"Are you sure you should turn back?"

"I don't know if I'm doing the right thing or not. But even if I found her, she might not return with me. Now that I know where she is, I'll hire someone to go after her. I feel I must return to Father first."

Thatcher wanted to insist, *But she's with child, your child.* But it wouldn't do any good to argue with a decision already made. He would

143

have to support his friend and pray for God to protect Colleen and their unborn child.

Beatrice served leftover cookies from Meredith's food table. "You must be starved," she said to William.

Thatcher suddenly realized how much time had passed and that he was supposed to be calling upon Meredith. A sinking feeling pulled him. He knew it was too late to call now. The time had slipped away. His friend needed him. He tried to push the consequences of what this would do to his relationship with Meredith out of his mind as he politely took the offered cookies.

⊘

At the Cooper residence, Meredith waited patiently at first, chatting with Amelia. As time passed, however, and her friend's gaze became more sympathetic, Meredith paced the room.

Finally, she said, "He isn't coming. I suppose it's just as well."

"I'm sure he has a good explanation."

"I suppose he just forgot."

"No, Mr. Talbot would never forget. Don't think the worst, my dear. Trust that something came up. You'll probably get the whole explanation tomorrow."

"Tomorrow?"

Meredith could not remember a time she had ever gotten stood up by a gentleman, except her father, of course. She hadn't had that many callers because her father had wanted to keep her at home to care for the house. When she went to work at the magazine and found her own place to live, there had been some men interested in her, and they had never left her waiting in the lurch.

"I think I'll go to bed now. It's been an exhausting day."

⊘

The next day, Meredith opened her eyes with dread. Church. Thatcher might be there. She didn't want to listen to his excuses or see his infuriating smirk. If she stayed at home, however, he would think she was pining over him. That wouldn't do. Reluctantly, she dragged herself out of the security of her bed and began to dress.

The moment Meredith entered the church house, Thatcher and Beatrice Bloomfield bore down upon her. *So he brings a buffer.* Meredith's face twitched unnaturally as the pair drew closer.

"My dear Meredith," Beatrice said, extending her hand, "I have come to plead for Thatcher." Her other hand was set securely in the crook of his arm. "Last night an old friend dropped in just as he was preparing to call upon you. Thatcher was in the very act of making his apologies, of getting ready to leave. Our visitor from Chicago was only going to be in town that night, and he was so beset with personal problems. The time slipped away."

Meredith felt amused. Thatcher was turning red. "I see," she said.

Beatrice released her grip on Thatcher's arm and turned to him. "Forgive me, Thatcher, for interfering so," she said then turned back to Meredith. "I only wanted to help. Please, hear him out. He speaks the truth. There was nothing we could do."

Meredith watched Beatrice depart.

Thatcher started where Mrs. Bloomfield left off. "His arrival was so abrupt, so unexpected that by the time I could have sent you word, it was too late. I'm so sorry. I had truly looked forward to seeing you all day yesterday. You can't imagine how much it meant to me."

He looked sincere.

"Where is your friend now?" Meredith gazed about the room for this invisible scapegoat.

"He had to leave early this morning. His father is ill, perhaps dying. He has many troubles. You do believe me, don't you?"

"Of course," she said. To her irritation, her face twitched again.

He leaned close. "Beatrice felt so bad that she made us a picnic lunch. Please, say you'll share it with me."

"I don't know. I'll have to think about it. I'm going to find a seat now."

Meredith could feel Thatcher's pleading eyes burn her back as she walked away.

The sermon seemed long and, as always, convicting. As Meredith turned her eyes upon God and felt His grace and forgiveness anew, she realized that she must forgive Thatcher one more time and allow him the opportunity to speak his mind.

The service was barely over when Thatcher appeared at her side. "Will you come with me?"

"Yes. For if I don't, I know that I'll receive Mrs. Bloomfield's wrath."

"I'll accept any reason you give me. I want to be with you."

Meredith felt her walls tumbling down again as she allowed Thatcher to make the final arrangements and whisk her away in the banker's carriage. They stopped by the river.

"This place is wonderful. How did you find it?"

"The Bloomfields told me about it."

"Seems they're matchmaking."

Thatcher chuckled. "You should know by now that I need all the help I can get." He artfully arranged their blanket and food, talking as he worked. "I've done nothing but bumble our relationship from the start."

Meredith settled in beside him, setting her gaze on the river, wishing he could convince her of his loyalty. They enjoyed the picnic, and Thatcher continued to woo her throughout, making it one of the happiest moments of her life.

"Thank you for bringing me here," she said softly.

"I feel so helpless," he said.

"Why?"

"I care so much about you, and I feel you slipping away. Our time is so short. I don't have the finesse to do this right. Can you forgive me for all my clumsiness?" He reached out a finger and traced her cheek, her chin.

She leaned into his touch. "It's not been all your fault. We have wasted time, haven't we?"

"Oh yes," he said.

She wanted to ask him, *What now?*

His soft suede eyes drew close, and he tipped her chin. She felt his sweet breath before his lips tenderly kissed her. And then she knew that she could never go on in life without him. Her hand went up to touch his face. When they parted, he searched her face and murmured those words she longed to hear.

"I love you, Storm."

Chapter 29

Meredith floated through breakfast and later floated over the town's new boardwalks. She was in love with the most wonderful man in the world. She had no idea love could be so wonderful. They had not made any plans, but Thatcher promised to call midweek. He said he would follow her to the East Coast if that's what it took to prove his love sincere.

She stopped humming long enough to open the door to the general store, where the post office was located. The owner knew her quite well by now. "Good morning, to you," he said. As he nodded, his glasses worked forward on his nose, and a quick swipe of his hands set them back in place.

"Anything for me?"

"You must be expecting something good. You sure look happy this morning." He handed her an envelope, and the door swung open again.

"Thank you," she said, leaving him to help the next person. As she moved back outside and her boots hit the taut wooden sidewalk, she was reminded of the recent repairs and let her eyes fall across the walkway.

A shadow fell across her path. The sun had moved behind a cloud. She glanced up. *Hope it doesn't rain. Nothing could ruin this day.* And she even had a letter from Asa.

She slit it open with her fingernail and pulled it out to read as she made her way to the newspaper office. She blinked. Her steps faltered. Unconsciously, she reached out for a nearby post. She leaned her shoulder into it and blinked back tears as she let each word sink into her mind.

Storm,

I've received news on Mr. Talbot. Sorry it is so slow in coming. But you were right, he does have a reward out on him, only not by the law. The reward, strangely enough, is being offered by his own father. Seems he left his father short-handed in the business and ran out on some woman besides. His father is hoping to find his whereabouts and bring him home to face up to his responsibilities. So I guess it's a family scandal of some sort. Hope that helps. Looking forward to seeing you again. Keep up the excellent work.

Asa

Family scandal, ran out on a woman.

Instantly, the photograph came to Meredith's mind. He had told her about his father, but what if he weren't telling the entire story, but only the parts he wanted to tell. What if he had run out on a wife? What other explanation was there if his own father was searching for him? It was not the woman who had run off, it was Thatcher. And, it was not his friend's problem, it was Thatcher's. Of course, this explained everything.

Why had he turned against his own wife? Did he truly love Meredith? It mattered not. He was married. He had many responsibilities.

✍

Somehow, Meredith floundered through the remainder of the day. And the next day, with a desperate resolve, she threw herself into her work to wrap up all loose ends. If only Charles would arrive early. She wanted to leave today, now. But it was impossible.

Thatcher would call on her midweek. He would break her heart again. In the days that followed, she nursed her hurts and rehearsed what she would say to Thatcher.

✍

Midweek finally rolled around. Meredith was working in the newsroom. Her editor walked into the room with an intense expression on his face.

"Something wrong?" she asked.

"I figured out what Ralston had against you," Charlie said.

Meredith turned full around in her chair. "Oh?"

"Seems he had a bad record with his past employers." Charlie gave a sheepish look. "When he arrived, I was so hard up for help that I didn't check his references. I was curious after he left and made some inquiries."

"I don't understand."

"He's been fired before, and I think he was just plain worried about keeping his job."

Meredith shook her head. "I feel sorry for him."

"I don't. You ready to quit for the day? I've got a banking errand here for you, if you are."

"Sure."

Meredith left the newsroom, glad to be able to put the mystery of Ralston behind her, but troubled over the impending situation with Thatcher. She stopped in at the bank to make the deposit for her employer, her mind mulling over her problem.

"You look preoccupied," Herbert Bloomfield said. "Working on a problem?"

"That's what Jonah always says to me. I must be a mirror."

"Most women are. Speaking of," his head motioned in the direction of his home, "the wife has some news she wants to share with you. I know that she would love it if you stopped in."

Meredith needed to stay busy. She certainly wouldn't need any time to primp tonight. She wasn't even going to change her clothes. And if Thatcher had to wait on her, all the better.

"I'll stop in now. Thank you."

She made her way past the few buildings down to the end of the street and turned the corner where the Bloomfields lived, ill prepared for what she saw: Thatcher's horse. Should she retreat? She felt adrenaline pulse through her veins; her anger surfaced.

She would get this over with, once and for all. She marched forward with purposeful steps and tapped on the door. Beatrice greeted her with a hug.

"I wanted to see you. Sit down. I have something special to tell you."

She gripped the back of the chair instead. "Is Thatcher here?"

"Well, yes."

"In there?" She nodded toward the back parlor.

"Yes, but. . ."

"I'll just be a moment, if you don't mind." Meredith tossed her head and started toward the sitting room.

Beatrice followed close behind.

What Meredith saw caused her to halt. A wave of nausea swept over her. Thatcher and the woman of the photograph were wrapped in each

149

DIANNE CHRISTNER

other's arms. Her mouth flew open to spew out hateful accusations, and then she remembered that this was Thatcher's wife. She snapped her mouth closed and turned, running headlong into Beatrice.

Thatcher looked up and released Colleen, as if she were live coals. Instantly, he moved toward Meredith.

"Storm."

"Stay away from me!"

His arms extended toward her.

"And keep those filthy hands to yourself."

"Meredith, wait. It isn't what it seems."

"It seems," she spat, "that you're going to be a daddy. Congratulations."

With that she pushed past Beatrice and fled out the door. She heard him call out her name again. "She's my friend's wife. Listen to me."

Meredith kept walking.

"I have to leave for a while. I'm taking her to San Francisco. But I'll be back for you. I'll find you if I have to search New York City every day for the rest of my life."

"Let her go," Beatrice said. "Meredith won't listen now. She's too angry. Maybe I can explain later. Come back in, Thatcher."

Thatcher knew Beatrice was right and returned with reluctance. Colleen needed him. Meredith hated him.

Meredith broke into a run and burst into the Cooper home in a flood of tears.

"Whatever's wrong?" Amelia asked.

"Leave me alone!" Meredith pushed past Amelia and ran up the steps to her room. The door slammed.

"What's wrong with her?" Amelia asked. "She's acted so strange all week."

Jonah frowned. "I would imagine it has something to do with Mr. Talbot. I knew the moment I laid eyes on him that he and Meredith would have a hard time of it. They fell for each other from the start."

"Lover's quarrel?"

"Probably." He made his way toward Amelia and laid his hand upon her shoulder. "Speaking of love. I think it's time we had a talk of our own."

Mrs. Cooper's eyes flew open, and Jonah led her toward the nearest chair.

"Amelia. I have a great admiration for you. Would you allow me to court you?"

The older woman swallowed then lowered her eyes. "I believe I would."

"I only hope we don't have as much trouble as that pair." His eyes looked toward the stairway.

"I don't expect we shall," she replied.

Chapter 30

Meredith threw herself on her bed and cried out to God. "Help me. O God, help me."

She continued her tantrum for a few minutes more, but as the supplication kept pouring from her lips, a peace flooded over her. Meredith recognized it as God's love. He loved her now, when she needed Him most.

"Forgive me, Lord," she prayed. "You are the one I've been searching for. It is You whom I need."

His love enveloped her, and it was as if new pages of Meredith's mind were turned, and all of this understanding floated off the pages and into her heart. Every part of her knew that she had been going about everything the wrong way, making all the decisions, pushing, pushing, pushing. She'd been trying to control her father, trying to make love happen or not happen.

"I've not kept my eyes on You, Jesus. Forgive me. Your peace and love are better than any earthly person's. You are all I need. Thank You for showing Yourself to me."

She would survive. Her God would never forsake her, though she turned back and forth to Him like an old toy. In an ongoing prayer of praise and confession, Meredith finally dropped off into an exhausted sleep.

When she awoke, God's name remained on her lips. "You are still here. Live in me. Then I can live," she prayed.

⬦

At noon, Meredith felt doubly blessed. Her brother arrived early. She threw herself into his arms with a wild abandonment. "I'm so glad you arrived early. I want to go."

"Do I have time to rest up?"

Her expression turned serious. "Of course. How much time?" Then she recalled that the Prince of Peace resided in her, and she didn't need to push. "Take all the time you need. I'm just excited, is all."

"We'll leave in the morning."

Jonah pushed away from the table where they had been sharing a lunch. "I'd best be packing my things also."

Meredith realized what her leaving meant for Jonah. He would have to leave this house.

"But where will you go?"

He grinned at her. "The mill. Don't worry. Amelia and I have all the details worked out, don't we, dear?"

Amelia blushed, and Meredith covered her hand with her mouth. "You mean. . . ?"

"Yes, dear," Amelia replied.

"I'm so happy for you," Meredith said.

"Seems as if you've come a long way since last night," Amelia said.

Meredith turned serious again. "I apologize for my rudeness. I'm going to be all right now. I'm letting God rule my life. All of it."

Meredith saw her friend's face soften and wondered what her brother thought of her declaration. But it didn't matter. A deep, abiding peace flowed through her. In fact, she was so full of God's love that the thought even went through her mind, *If all that has happened to me with Thatcher, with my father, happened only so that I could truly find God, then it was all worth it. And whatever lies ahead would all be worth it even if I only had this one day of God's love to experience. But I don't. I have a lifetime. God is so good.*

"I'd best go pack," she said.

"Let me know if you need help," Amelia called.

First Meredith arranged all of her writing in a neat stack and placed it in the bottom of one of her travelling bags. She took a look around to decide what would go in next when a light tap sounded on her bedroom door.

"Come in."

It was Mrs. Bloomfield. "Amelia just told me you're leaving."

Meredith pulled out the chair from her desk and offered, "Please, sit down."

As her friend sat, Meredith cleared a spot on the bed and sat also. "I wish to apologize for last night. I was rude and thoughtless."

The woman's hand sliced through the air. "Nonsense." She looked about the uprooted room. "I wish you didn't have to go and that I had your pluck and courage."

"Don't wish it. I've learned a better way." She rubbed her palms against her skirt. "I've given everything over to God, and I feel so much better." Then she waved her hand. "I'm through being a progressive woman. Now I'm..." She tilted her head, looking for the right word. "Just God's."

"I can see there's a new peace about you. You were so angry last night."

Meredith chose not to think about Thatcher and asked instead, "Your husband said you had some news, a surprise. What were you trying to tell me?"

Beatrice smiled deeply and even turned a little red. "We're going to have a baby."

The words hit Meredith with such impact that she flew to her feet and rushed to kneel before her friend. "I'm so happy for you. How wonderful."

"I'm so happy." Beatrice sighed. "But my happiness would be complete if only you and Thatcher could make amends."

Meredith rose, backed up a few steps. "How can you say that when you know that he's married?"

"Thatcher isn't married."

"He has you fooled, too. The woman that he was with. He carries her photograph. It is signed from his loving wife." She saw Beatrice's look of shock. "Perhaps you don't know. There's some sort of scandal with his family. His father has a reward out on him. He ran off on that woman. His wife."

"No, no." Beatrice shook her head. "I know all about it, but you've got it wrong. Thatcher is not married. That is his friend's wife. The one who ruined your plans the other night. Our friend was searching for her, but then his father got sick. When Colleen appeared and needed help, Thatcher agreed to help her get home. She's pregnant."

Meredith plopped back onto the bed. "I saw." The pieces fell into place. "You're sure?"

"Of course, I'm sure. Thatcher is the most upstanding man. Even all his father's money could not corrupt him after he became a Christian. When we heard what was happening in Chicago, we encouraged Thatcher to come to Buckman's Pride and visit us. The idea of working at the logging camp intrigued him from the moment we suggested it. You can trust Thatcher, Meredith."

She shook her head regretfully. "If he is all that, then he surely doesn't deserve me."

"Nonsense. He loves you."

Meredith remembered Thatcher's declaration of love. "It's too late. My brother's here. It's time to go."

"Please, don't leave with things like this."

"God is in control now. Thatcher knows where to find me if he wants to. I hate to leave you and all my friends, but I must go."

"I'll write to you."

"Come visit me."

"Perhaps I shall."

❧

That afternoon Meredith went by the newsroom to pick up her things and say farewell to the editor. She glanced sadly at the sign in his window. REPORTER WANTED. She stopped by the mill and left a letter at the post office for the bull at Bucker's Stand. This town would always hold a special place in her heart.

The following morning, she unashamedly let the tears flow as she hugged Amelia and Jonah good-bye. She gave them both her blessings, and then Meredith and her brother rode out of town.

❧

That evening, around a campfire, memories flooded Meredith. She remembered Silas, who had guided her and Jonah through these woods, and the campfires she had faced with them. But most of all, she remembered the night she was lost in the woods with Thatcher.

She had treated Thatcher shabbily from the start. He was an honest man, and she had probed into his painful personal life and harbored accusations against him from the start. He had loved her, and she had spurned him at every turn.

She let out a deep regretful sigh.

"Are you sure you want to leave?" Charles asked.

"It's only that I learned too late."

"Learned what too late?"

"To trust God. To trust the man I loved."

"I think it's time you told me the whole story. We've got all night. What's going on in your life, Storm?"

Meredith told her brother the whole thing, every ugly detail.

Chapter 31

Thatcher rode into Buckman's Pride weary and downcast. His friend's pregnant wife was on a train, where he had paid an attendant to give her the best of care. He could only imagine what joy William would experience when his wife returned to him. Colleen mourned her actions of leaving her husband and rejoiced when Thatcher explained the changes William had made—how he longed for nothing more than to be reconciled and to be able to prove his love to Colleen. Thatcher knew there would be a happy reunion and prayed that all would go well with her trip. He prayed for William and the things he was facing at home with his father's illness.

If only Thatcher's own romance had turned out so well. Thatcher felt that he had ruined things between him and Meredith for good. It seemed that the harder he had tried, from the beginning, the more he had hurt her. He wasn't sure how it kept happening or why. But he knew he loved her, and he would hunt her down if it took every breath he had. He would never let her go until she understood how much he cared for her. But right now, he was only so tired.

He tied up his horse outside the Bloomfields' and knocked on the door. His friends received him warmly and showed him to a soft bed, where he slept the rest of the day and that night through.

At daylight, he started out for the logging camp.

The Bloomfields had told him that he had just missed Meredith. What a wonder he hadn't met her on the trail somewhere. He had arrived the same day Meredith had left. He didn't know her plans, what other logging camps she intended to visit along the way. He wanted to give her time to cool off before he showed up in New York City.

One thing he knew for sure. His logging days were over. He would give his resignation to the bull and pack up his belongings. He would stay the night and say farewell to his friends.

The bull took the news of Thatcher's resignation with little emotion. Thatcher headed for the bunkhouse. It was empty. He packed his things, then sat on his bed, wondering what his next move would be. He prayed, "Lord, You know the desires of my heart. Please, help me."

"Thatcher?" The words sounded soft, hesitant, familiar. But, it couldn't be. His head jerked around. It was! He jumped to his feet.

"Meredith. It is you." His voice held reverence.

Hers quivered in return, but picked up force. "I shall not let my vanity ruin my life. I came back for you, Thatcher."

He didn't know whether to laugh, cry, or throw himself into her arms.

"My sweet. I was going to come for you."

"We've wasted enough time, haven't we?" She took a hesitant step toward him. "Can you ever forgive me?"

He closed the distance between them and pulled her to himself, saying the words against her hair. "Forgive you? I love you. I always have."

She pushed back away from him, looked up into his dark eyes. "I want you to know everything. Please, let me explain."

He nodded and dropped his arms.

"I've been so proud and controlling with my life. I'm not happy with the way I've treated you and others. God has shown me a better way. I'm yours, if you'll have me."

"Have you? Meredith, don't you know? I was going to follow you and beg, plead for you to believe me and marry me."

She reached up and touched his face. "I believe you. I always shall from this day forward."

"Marry me?"

"Yes."

He stooped to kiss her, and Meredith thought that nothing could ever be more beautiful than her life this day, with Christ's love, with Thatcher's. Her heart soared with emotion.

"Hmm-mmm." A deep clearing of the throat came from the bunkhouse doorway. They both looked up, and Meredith drew out of Thatcher's arms.

The man in the door said, "I don't believe we've been properly introduced. I'm Storm's brother."

Thatcher strode toward him. "I'm her fiancé."

Meredith smiled up at her brother. "Charles persuaded me to come back after you."

Thatcher looked at the man with surprise. "Then I know I'm going to like you a lot."

Charles chuckled. "We'll get along fine."

The wedding was held the following Sunday in Buckman's Pride with all Meredith and Thatcher's friends attending. Both Jonah and Beatrice promised to bring their spouses to visit them. Jonah, Meredith was sure, would marry Amelia soon.

After the wedding celebration, Thatcher took Meredith for a stroll along the river.

"I really like Charles," Thatcher said.

"I'm so glad. I hope when he breaks the news that father takes it well."

"From what Charles says, he's trying to change. Are you anxious to see him?"

"Yes."

"We'll visit him on our honeymoon."

"I'm not expecting miracles, though."

"You should; we're living one."

"I know."

They stopped at a high bank that looked down over the water. The sun was just starting to set. Beautiful colors made a promising display, and hope for the future filled both their hearts.

"We'll camp our way to San Francisco and have our own private celebration there," Thatcher said.

"That could be expensive."

He pulled her close. "I can afford it."

She smiled up at him.

"Then we'll go to the land office and let you pick out the camps you want to visit."

"Any that I want?" she asked, even though they had already agreed upon all this earlier.

"Any. We'll find us a little cabin. I'll work and you'll write, undercover."

"And we'll stay as long as it takes to finish my story."

"Probably as long as you can stay cooped up in a small cabin is more like it." He bent and tasted her lips. They were sweet and gave promise of a wonderful life ahead for them. He drew back. "Let's go to the hotel, shall we?"

Meredith nodded shyly.

Thatcher took her hand, then began to chuckle.

"What's so funny?" she asked.

"I was just thinking of my father. When we move to Chicago, I'm going to love the moment he meets his new daughter-in-law. You're going to be such a sweet torment to him."

"I thought you wanted to make amends."

"Oh, I do. It's just when I think how you blew into my life, I can't wait to see what happens when you storm into his."

"I've been meaning to talk to you about that. Maybe we shouldn't use my middle name at first. I'd hate to give him the wrong impression."

Thatcher laughed again.

"Stop it," she said.

Dianne Christner lives in New River, Arizona, where life sizzles in the summer when temperatures soar above 100 degrees as she writes from her air-conditioned home office. She enjoys the desert life, where her home is nestled in the mountains and she can watch quail and the occasional deer, bobcat, or roadrunner.

Dianne was raised Mennonite and works hard to bring authenticity to Mennonite fiction. She now worships at a community church. She's written over a dozen novels, most of which are historical fiction. She gets caught up in research having to set her alarm to remember to switch the laundry or start dinner. But her husband of forty-plus years is a good sport. They have two married children, Mike and Rachel, and five grandchildren, Makaila, Elijah, Vanson, Ethan, and Chloe.

She welcomes you to visit her website at http://www.diannechristner.net.

Strong as the Redwood

by Kristin Billerbeck

Enjoy Your
Bonus Story

Chapter 1

Rachel Phillips' mother gazed at her daughter lovingly. The older woman had tears welling up in her hazel eyes, and her soft voice was shaky. "I know this is frightening, but your stepfather wants what's best for you. From what I hear, Searsville is a beautiful place, and it's not that far from San Francisco. We'll be able to visit at Christmastime."

Her voice held no conviction, and Rachel was forced to question whether this move was beneficial to anyone other than her stepfather of one year, Marshall Winsome. Rachel was saddened by the thought, but also comforted knowing her mother would be well cared for by Marshall. She glanced angrily his way as the large man paced nervously along the wharf, obviously anxious to leave.

"Oh Mother." Rachel embraced Peg Winsome tightly. "I shall miss you so. I will forever be grateful for all that you've done for me. I am thankful that you are finally living the life Pa dreamed for you. He would have wanted it this way." Rachel knew the words weren't true. Her father would never have allowed Rachel to be shipped off, alone, at eighteen, to live among lawless loggers. But she also knew her mother was terribly burdened by this action of her stepfather, and Rachel had to be strong.

She watched her mother's pained expression. Rachel felt it, too, the pangs of separation. The young woman's mind filled with memories, memories of all she and her mother had endured together, of their unusual partnership that had been created out of necessity. It had been over two years now since their life had changed course, shattering their plans and forcing them to become equals in order to withstand the hardships. The young woman's mind drifted back.

✍

The 1849 wagon train rolled slowly to a stop. Rachel was only four at the time, but she could still recall her muscular father, Rodrick Phillips, jumping from their wagon to help her and her mother down, before exclaiming, "There it is, the mighty Sierra Nevada! We made it!"

Before the seemingly endless line of wagons lay the magnificent, rugged mountain range they had heard tales about for months. The magnificent, snow-capped peaks beckoned, for the weary emigrants had only to cross them to reach their final destination: California.

"Have you ever seen anything so beautiful? They sure don't have mountains like these in Missouri! This here, my darling," Rodrick scooped his little girl into his arms, "is the very handiwork of God!" Rodrick smiled broadly and reached for his wife as the young family realized their long and arduous journey was almost over.

The family's dream had been to homestead amidst the rolling hills of the new territory, building a better life for themselves. The trip to the wilderness of the West had been much more treacherous than they had expected, but they knew it had all been worthwhile at first sight of their very own property: ten acres in a golden valley.

They had purchased land in Weberville, a small town nestled in the Sierra foothills. The original plan had been to work the land and raise livestock, but Rodrick soon discovered that he, too, had gold fever. Exchanging his plow for the tools of the mining trade, he soon began working as a miner in the great California Gold Rush of 1850.

As a miner, Rodrick earned a meager income. But he was a doting husband and father who took special pride in his daughter. Rachel always felt like a princess around her Pa.

"It's a right good thing they have no kings here; I'd lose my daughter's hand in the blink of an eye," he'd say, tickling Rachel while she giggled uncontrollably. Later, as she grew older, Rodrick's tone would become more serious toward his daughter. His voice would become gentle as he fondly brushed the hair from her face. "You're the very image of my mother, Rachel. An exquisite beauty, you are. Such ivory skin and sparkling green eyes, the likes of which California has never seen. And I do declare, that shade of auburn is known only to the Phillips women."

The day her father didn't return from the mines was still clear in Rachel's memory, as if it had happened only the day before. She had just turned sixteen. She was setting the table for supper, when a family friend knocked on the door of their small cabin. When Mrs. Phillips opened the door the hardened miner had tears in his eyes. His words were few, but their meaning left the household silent with shock.

The tragedy of Rodrick's death was compounded by the fact that all his hard work had done little more than take care of the family's daily needs. Peg Phillips and her daughter were left to fend for themselves in Weberville, which had few options for poor and unattached young women. No suitable opportunities presenting themselves, Rachel and her mother acted on the advice and invitation of a traveling preacher and joined his evangelizing caravan to San Francisco.

"You'll find more civility there," The minister's wife had said. Once in San Francisco, however, it was difficult to see the civility they had heard about. The streets were violent, and vigilante justice, often more vengeful than the original crime, ruled.

They found many men willing to help them out of their lonely predicament. Marriageable women were a precious commodity in the city, and attractive women were even more valuable than gold.

Peg Phillips was no ordinary widow. Only thirty-three at the time of her husband's death, she was a comely woman, despite her many years of hard work and misfortune. Peg was blessed with an exotic dark complexion, hazel-green eyes, and an abundance of silky black hair.

Mrs. Phillips, well aware of their precarious situation in San Francisco, would drop to her knees daily in prayer, asking God for His steady guidance. Their first stop in San Francisco was at the home of Marshall Winsome, a prominent banker and owner of three hotels in the city. Rachel couldn't help but wonder what life might have been like if her mother had knocked on a different door.

Marshall's name had been given Mrs. Phillips by the traveling preacher, so that she could inquire about work. When the businessman saw the young widow, his gruff demeanor softened instantly, and two positions immediately became available.

Although Marshall was overbearing and rough in personality, he had not taken advantage of the Phillips's vulnerability. He had provided respectable housekeeping and cooking positions, as well as a decent room in one of his hotels. Additionally, he kept a close eye on the women, ensuring their safety.

Peg and Marshall's courtship had been brief, but it had also been extremely proper. Marshall made sure Peg understood that their personal relationship was completely separate from her work, and seeing him on a friendly basis was her choice.

When Rachel's mother decided to marry Marshall, Rachel had to ask if it was for love or their best interests. She certainly did not want her mother sacrificing her life to make Rachel's a little easier.

Peg's answer was slow and carefully contemplated. "I've had my once-in-a-lifetime love, dear. No one will ever take your father's place. You are the beautiful result of what we shared, but Marshall is a fine Christian man. He has been so good to me—to us. The Lord has used him to answer so many of my prayers and alleviate my fears. I am convinced it is God's will that I marry Marshall. The Lord has given me the gift of knowing a new kind of love with him, one that has grown from mutual respect and friendship."

In August of 1862, when Rachel was seventeen, Marshall Winsome became her stepfather, a role he hadn't taken lightly. Following the nuptials, the women moved immediately into Marshall's elegant and expansive home. It was a stately mansion with three floors and countless windows, which provided sweeping views of San Francisco Bay when the fog cleared.

The home boasted silver-plated doorknobs, imported French-cut glass doors, a ballroom, and parquet floors of maple, walnut, and mahogany. Rachel was most impressed with the great mahogany staircase that wound its way to the second floor from the foyer, and the servants that attended to every need.

After only a week in the courtly residence, Marshall called for a private meeting with Rachel in his darkened study. He sat pompously behind a great desk and addressed her in a very solemn tone. "You will continue your education, Miss Phillips." Marshall always addressed Rachel as "Miss," as though the use of her name might unnecessarily endear her to him.

He continued, looking over his spectacles. "You can receive your credentials for teaching within the year. As the state grows, there are many towns in need of competent instructors. This education, which I will happily finance, will provide you with the ability to earn an adequate income of your own, so that you may support yourself. Do you understand?" He stood up with finality, his butler waiting to escort her from the room.

Rachel most certainly did *not* understand. California was no place for a lady to live on her own and the mansion was large enough that they might never see each other. Didn't *he* understand? Rachel stood looking questioningly up at her stepfather, her generous mane of auburn hair falling loosely down to her lower back, her eyes wide and clear. "Am I to understand that you would like me to find accommodations elsewhere?" Rachel managed to stammer meekly.

"Miss Phillips, your mother and I plan to start a family soon. Of course, we will need help with the baby for the first year, but then you will be free to pursue your teaching career." And with that, Rachel's future was arranged. Teaching was to be her "chosen" profession, and she completed her studies in June of 1863.

That same month, Marshall and Peg welcomed George Timothy Winsome into their home. A darling, healthy baby boy with a sweet personality and a ready smile, his parents lavished him with love and attention.

Although Rachel was to help her mother for the first year of Georgie's life, Marshall soon found Rachel's presence to be a hindrance to his new family and "released" her to begin her teaching duties. Through his many connections, Marshall located an immediate opening in the small town of Searsville, a logging community, just a day's travel from San Francisco.

Rachel roused from her memories to find herself once again on a journey. She stood on a crowded pier, saying "Good-bye" To her best friend and partner in life, her mother.

Chapter 2

The port of San Francisco was a frenzy of activity. Ships of every size and description could be seen both in port and shipping out to sea. In the distance, Alcatraz, a military fort on an island of solid rock, was barely visible through the fog. The schooner *Redwood* bounced about wildly in the choppy waters of the bay.

Rachel was readying to board when her mother stroked her long chestnut curls and whispered, "Remember, Rachel, the only man for you is a believer in Christ Jesus who loves and cares for you as the Lord cares for His church. Believe that He will provide, and wait on Him."

Embarking on a new life, and for the first time making daily decisions entirely on her own, nothing could have been further from Rachel's mind than finding a husband. Her main objectives now were to *avoid* men and handle a schoolroom full of children, which she must do without the aid of her closest confidante. Rachel's mind quickly cleared of her mother's words and her own thoughts as a loud voice bellowed a final call and passengers began quickly boarding the schooner.

This is really happening, Rachel thought. *I'm actually leaving my mother, my only family, to get on this ship headed toward who knows what kind of future.* She clung to the words from her old, leather-covered Bible, *"Thou wilt shew me the path of life: in thy presence is fullness of joy; at thy right hand there are pleasures for evermore."* She couldn't remember where the verse was from, but it provided the momentary courage she needed to step onto the boat.

Overwhelmed by her emotions, Rachel was numb as she watched her mother disappear in the distance as the *Redwood* pulled away from its slip. She extended her arm as if to touch her mother one last time. Rachel's spirit that had been so strong in days past now seemed broken in the harsh reality of life alone. Rachel's forest-green eyes dampened with tears amidst the cold, foggy backdrop of the San Francisco Bay.

She was so lost in her thoughts during the trip that it seemed mere minutes before the Port of Redwood City came into view. This was to be the first stop on her journey. From here, she would board a stage in town en route to Searsville.

As the captain maneuvered the ship through the muddy slough, the excitement of the embarcadero ahead stirred a rush of conversation among the passengers. The docks bustled as men rushed to unload their cargo-laden oxen carts onto waiting schooners and sloops before the outward turning of the tide, which could transform the bay into a depressed mud flat with disabled boats bogged down helplessly in the briny muck.

Redwood was a logging port which supplied lumber to the many towns in California that had sprung up as a result of the Gold Rush. Lumber, shingles, firewood, and fence posts were piled high in stacks along the docks to help the men load quickly. Rachel briefly watched the confused scene before the boat docked and the passengers were hurried off to make room for cargo. Her trunk was dropped carelessly onto the pier before her.

Stepping onto the dock, Rachel felt her first real tinge of panic as she tried to navigate the walk and steer clear of the shoremen and their work while lugging her oversized trunk by its worn leather handle. The men that weren't behind a stack of lumber took time out to eye the beautiful stranger, and made their observations known with loud talk amongst themselves. No offer of help with her luggage came, though, and Rachel silently thanked God the men didn't bother her.

Rachel's fear mounted when she noticed that all the women from the ship had quickly disappeared with escorts, leaving her utterly alone and without aid to find her stage stop. Afraid to ask one of the shoremen for directions, she began to wander from the docks into town, hoping to find a friendly woman there.

Redwood was clearly a bachelor town. Rachel walked along the dusty path past the McLeod Shipyard and the various storehouses on the docks and soon found herself amidst a bevy of saloons, boot shops, and liveries. She spied a beautiful white building with the words AMERICAN HOUSE painted in black across its face.

Rachel sighed with relief, feeling as though she'd found an oasis. She quickly crossed the street, dodging the horse-drawn carriages and oxcarts that lined the road.

When Rachel reached the American House, she immediately realized with disappointment that this was not a hotel like her stepfather's. The entry hall was grand, with elevated ceilings, red wallpaper, and dark mahogany furniture. Upstairs, however, Rachel spotted an open door to the sleeping quarters. The large room was bare, its white walls free of decor. Cots and bunks lined the edge of the room dormitory style, and men could be seen lying upon them. Rachel, disturbed by unwillingly invading their privacy, turned to leave the lobby before she was spotted.

"May I be of service to ya, my dear?" A cheery-looking, older man presented himself behind the ornate wooden counter.

"Yes. I'm looking for the stage. The one that goes to Searsville. I–I'm the new teacher for the loggers' children," she blurted carelessly, trying to conceal her uneasiness.

"Teaching. Now, that's a right important job, I'd say. And for someone so young." He paused, looking dubious. "Ah, but I'm sure you'd know that," he added quickly.

The man's face was warm and his voice seemed to offer genuine concern for the lost young woman. "The stop you want is on Bridge Street. That's the small bridge in front of this hotel; do you know the one I mean? Well, no matter, it's only half a block out front, so you really can't miss it."

"That's where I got off the ship, but I didn't see a stage." Rachel looked out the door to see how she'd missed the stop.

"The mail stage to Searsville leaves at one o'clock, so you've got a little time to spend in our fair city. We keep a right good table, if you're hungry," The man said. "The men'll be through loading soon, so it's just as well you stay inside."

"Now that you mention it, I *am* hungry." Rachel hadn't thought about her stomach all morning, and up until now, her nerves had been too tightly strung for her to eat anything.

"Go ahead. The dining room is right through those doors and the missus will make sure nobody bothers you." The man pointed to double doors that opened to a room with about fifteen tables covered with sturdy red cloths. "Joseph Williams is the name if you need anything."

"Thank you, Mr. Williams. I'm Rachel Phillips." They shook hands warmly. "And I'm obliged to you for all your information and kindness."

Mrs. Williams offered a sweet smile. She sat Rachel at a table in the corner by the kitchen and quickly helped her to a meal of chicken and biscuits. It was a delicious, satisfying meal. Afterwards, Rachel thought a walk around town might do her good.

Rachel silently praised God for using these good people to comfort her in her state of agitation. She expressed her appreciation, left her trunk behind, and headed out to stroll the streets of Redwood until her stage arrived at one o'clock.

Rachel turned right outside the hotel and strolled along Main Street beside the waterfront. Her steps echoed along the wood-plank walkway. The first place of business Rachel passed was a saloon and billiard parlor called The Bowling Alley. Rachel could hear poorly tuned piano music playing inside as she neared the swinging double doors that marked its entrance. She also caught the agitated shouts of men embroiled in some type of disagreement.

"I'll teach ya!" a burly man yelled right before a fist landed upon his cheek.

"We'll see!" shouted the other as he took the next punch.

Before Rachel had time to discern any danger in the situation, the two men were locked in battle, the momentum of their brawl carrying them straight toward her. Never letting go of one another, the men continued to throw punches with complete disregard for their surroundings. Horses in the street reared and onlookers cleared the boardwalk quickly.

Rachel was so stunned, she stood motionless as the men, lost in their struggle, came tumbling closer. Bracing for the impact, Rachel suddenly felt herself pulled from their path and into the solid arms of a man. Rachel looked up and found herself staring into the most fascinating eyes she had ever seen. They were brilliant, partly blue, partly green, and the pattern captivating, seemingly drawing her in closer. The fight continued to rage, but Rachel was a hundred miles away in the arms of a dashing stranger.

When Rachel regained her composure, she consciously averted her gaze from the man's bluish-green eyes. Once she did, she was caught up in his clean-shaven face and freshly cut dark hair. These features were in sharp contrast to the men she had seen on the docks.

Rachel was at a loss for words as she studied the handsome man, standing tall in a dark shirt with light suspenders. Without warning, he suddenly gripped her shoulders and shouted, "You could have been hurt! Where is your husband?"

Rachel's mouth opened but no words came out as she took the barrage of questions like a beating. "Well, where is he? In the saloon?" The man roared.

"No. He's, I mean. . .there is no 'he.' I'm not married." With this statement, Rachel's temper flared. Who did this man think he was, anyway? He had no right to question her. She had a perfect right to walk on a public street in the middle of the afternoon.

She was ready to let this stranger have a little piece of her mind. She shook free from his grip and continued, "I beg your pardon, but if I had a husband, his whereabouts would remain none of your business. Now, I appreciate your rescuing me from those childish men, but I assure you I am perfectly capable of taking care of myself." Rachel's tone was attracting attention and people began to cross the street to watch the action unfold. Fist fights were a common occurrence, but a lady in a conflict was something new.

The tall stranger stepped back in surprise at Rachel's outburst, letting his eyes take in a full view. He eyed her inquisitively.

"I beg your pardon, ma'am, but this here's a logging town, with the loading done for the day. These men are ready to play, and that makes this no place for a woman alone. Certainly not one as pretty as you. Now, where are you going? I will escort you personally." He resolutely reached for her arm.

"Hmmph." Rachel's eyes had fire in them now as she shook free of his hold. "I am quite capable of finding my own way, and I certainly do not need any more help from you. Now please excuse me."

The onlookers, sensing the nature of the argument, were beginning to snicker. One of them called out, "Hey Dylan, little lady more'n you can handle? Maybe you need some help."

Rachel's face became hot with embarrassment. When she looked around her she noticed that everyone was staring and that she was the sole focus of their attention. Unable to conceal her anger and frustration, she walked briskly back to the American House to wait for her stage.

Mr. Williams stood behind the elaborate counter, smiling as Rachel entered the hotel. "Ah, Miss Phillips. What a pleasure to see you again so soon." Mr. Williams' amiable style softened Rachel immediately.

"Mr. Williams, it seems I stepped into a bit of trouble during my walk. Would it be all right with you if I waited here for a few minutes until the stage arrives?" Rachel asked, her voice flustered. She plopped herself forcefully into a high-backed chair, exasperated.

"Of course, my dear. We'd love to have such a pretty ornament grace our lobby. Dresses the place up a bit, don't you think, Mrs. Williams?"

Mrs. Williams stood in the doorway of the kitchen, her face wrinkled in concern. "Was there a problem, Miss Phillips?" Before Rachel answered, the stranger from the street entered the lobby. She stood immediately.

"There you are," The man said with relief. "Are you all right?"

"She's fine, Chase," Mr. Williams said. Rachel's head shot around abruptly to the amiable Mr. Williams.

"You know this man?" Rachel asked.

"Sure do. Allow me to introduce you to Chase Dylan. Chase is our resident peacekeeper. He owns a large sawmill up yonder in Portola Valley and comes down during the loading. Oversees his men; keeps them out of mischief. Chase, this here is Miss Rachel Phillips, the new Searsville schoolteacher."

"A pleasure to meet you, Miss Phillips. I'm sorry if I startled you." The eyes that had fascinated her just moments before once again held her complete attention, much to her dismay. "This is a coincidence. Perhaps I can give you a ride into town; I go right through Searsville on my way to Portola Valley. In fact, you'll be teaching a few of my men's children. My buggy's right next door at the Ostrum Livery, and I'd be honored to ride into town with the new schoolteacher," Chase said, a pleasant smile crossing his face, a challenge rising in his brows.

"I don't think so, Mr. Dylan. I'll be taking the stage into Searsville," Rachel answered curtly, astonished by the man's audacity.

"Chase knows the roads well, Miss Phillips. You'd probably be more comfortable with him than on the mail stage," Mr. Williams interjected.

Rachel felt betrayed. Surely her merry Mr. Williams couldn't think highly of this arrogant man, yet it *seemed* he did. "Thank you both for your concern, but my passage is planned on the stage. People are expecting me and I don't believe I should make any changes to my scheduled arrival, for their sake. Now if you'll excuse me, I'd better be on my way." Rachel lifted up her floor-length, blue muslin skirt and walked briskly

173

out of the American House. Her long, bouncing curls swung in her defiance.

Chase Dylan and Mr. Williams looked at one another and grinned. "I guess she told me, huh, Joseph?" Chase asked.

"By the look in your eye, I'd say you won't let her get away that easily," Mr. Williams added. Both men laughed merrily and watched Rachel stride confidently toward the stage, dragging her trunk along behind her.

Chapter 3

After nearly three hours, the dust from the stage was becoming unbearable. The ride had been fraught with rough spots along the steep grade, pauses for every slow-moving, redwood-hauling oxen wagon, and numerous mail stops.

Rachel, the coach's only passenger, felt as though she hadn't bathed in days and was not looking forward to meeting her new employer in her condition. *I'm sure they've seen many a dusty passenger arrive on this stage,* Rachel thought hopefully but without conviction. She lurched forward and the stage came to a final abrupt halt.

Her first view of Searsville brought only melancholy; the sight was nothing like she'd imagined. There were no beautiful redwoods shadowing the land, only a dry, dusty valley scattered with whitewashed buildings and a few oak trees. Rachel stepped down from the coach, her disappointment evident. The town certainly wasn't much.

The stage had stopped in front of the primitive Searsville Exchange and Post Office. Not far to the right was Eikerenkotter's Hotel, a simple two-story building. On the porch several men stood speaking with a questionable woman.

A young man dressed in a black suit approached Rachel, a welcoming grin on his face. "Miss Phillips?" he inquired.

"Yes. Mr. Lathrop, is it?" Rachel replied, surprised at the man's youth. As the patron of Searsville's school, she was expecting a much older man.

"It is. Robert Lathrop, the local blacksmith and benefactor of our new school. Welcome to our humble Searsville." Mr. Lathrop's arm made a sweeping motion to introduce the town. "Your trunk will be taken over to the hotel where you'll stay until you find a boardinghouse that suits you."

Rachel looked to the hotel and uneasiness gripped her. "Don't worry, Miss Phillips. You'll be well taken care of, August Eikerenkotter runs a respectable business."

Rachel watched her dusty brown trunk being pulled roughly off the stage and shook her head in disbelief.

"What is it, Miss Phillips? You'll be safe at the hotel," The blacksmith reassured her.

"Oh, I'm sure I will, Mr. Lathrop. I was just thinking of all the colorful dresses my stepfather purchased for me before my trip. Obviously, he's never been here or he would have only let me buy brown." Rachel's smile told Robert Lathrop that she knew how to make the best of a situation.

Mr. Lathrop's voice turned falsely serious in mock lecture. "Brown's a very popular color around here, and rightly so, I might add." The lighthearted conversation warmed Rachel to her new home and she decided she would reserve final judgment until after she'd had a bath.

"By the way, the schoolhouse is straight up the main road a spell." Mr. Lathrop pointed north, then continued. "My blacksmith shop is to the right there and my home is on the left. The schoolhouse is just beyond my ranch." Rachel looked in the direction of the schoolhouse, but it was not in her line of sight.

Mr. Lathrop spoke again, his voice low. "Miss Phillips, I need to be frank with you. You were selected for this position because of your faith. Your stepfather assured us you had come to know the Lord at a very young age. Maria, my wife, and I are believers and we want His light to shine through our school."

Rachel nodded, but Mr. Lathrop continued on. "Being from the gold country, I'm sure you're aware of the so-called recreation that goes on after work: the gambling, the fighting, the gun play, and especially the drinking. Well, I'm afraid sawyers are no different. In fact, most of them are *from* the mining camps. Many of their children have never seen the inside of a church, and as patrons of the school, it is very important to Maria and myself that these children learn the road to heaven. I don't want to put a lot of undue pressure on you before you begin your duties, but I'd like you to do your best to teach them about Jesus."

Rachel couldn't believe her ears. "Mr. Lathrop, I promise I will do my very best to teach the children about Jesus. Nothing would make me happier." Rachel had heard stories from the Bible since she was a tiny girl; no lesson plan for the children would give her more pleasure.

"Come along, let's get you situated so you can rest. Introductions can wait until tomorrow. Since tomorrow is Sunday, I'm hoping you'd like to join my family for the service." He picked up her trunk gently with a strong hand.

"Thank you, Mr. Lathrop. I'd enjoy that very much."

"Good. Maria and I will pick you up at 9:30. The church is a little bit of a hike, so wear your walking shoes. Actually, if you own any other kind, you can get rid of them now." Mr. Lathrop laughed, and his young companion, now in good spirits, joined him.

Rachel allowed her trunk to be dropped off at the hotel but headed south on the road to the schoolhouse, eager to see where she would perform her teaching duties. She strolled down Searsville's main road, pleased to see the town offered all of life's necessities, including a general store, where she could order books.

At the end of the main route, Rachel was thrilled to see a lovely fresh-water lake bordering the village. She passed the schoolhouse by to gaze into its placid waters for a while. The water looked so inviting that Rachel wanted to jump right into it. She bent down, cupped her hand, and splashed her face with the cool, clean liquid. Feeling at once restored, she exhaled deeply and walked at a leisurely pace back toward the school.

The schoolhouse looked surprisingly like a church, and had probably been created by the same plans. Where there would have been a church steeple, a white tower housed the large cast-iron school bell. Rachel was tempted to ring the bell, but refrained. Giggling at the notion, she stepped inside the classroom. Her eyes became big and her mouth dropped; everything was just as she'd imagined. The room was in perfect order, and someone had scrubbed the walls and polished the windows until they gleamed.

The desktops were expertly crafted from oak and securely fastened to wrought iron bases. An elegantly carved, larger desk stood at the front of the room, and the new blackboard had WELCOME MISS PHILLIPS written upon it.

Rachel traced the words with her finger, and her stomach churned with excitement as she thought aloud, "I am a teacher and this is my classroom." Rachel couldn't help momentarily crediting Marshall for his choice of careers for his stepdaughter.

"Miss Phillips?" Rachel turned to see a flamboyantly dressed woman with jet black hair and dark, piercing eyes standing in the doorway. The sweet tone of her voice simply did not coincide with the woman's looks.

Her dress was violet with a very tight fit and she wore a matching hat that had a single purple plume rising from its side. The ensemble was strangely out of place in this small logging town.

Rachel tried not to appear surprised by the woman's appearance, and answered, "Yes, I'm Rachel Phillips."

"Welcome to Searsville, Miss Phillips. I'm Mrs. Gretchen Steele and this is my son, Henry." Mrs. Steele turned to find her son missing from her side, and called sharply, "Henry!"

Henry soon appeared in the doorway, his head bent forward contritely and his big brown eyes peering shyly up at Rachel. "Say good day to Miss Phillips, Henry," prodded Mrs. Steele.

"Good day, Miss Phillips," sung the tiny boy sweetly.

"Henry will be one of your students. However, that's not why I'm here. I've come to invite you to our women's sewing circle. It meets on Tuesday evening at a different member's house each week. Obviously, since you have no home, you would be excused from being a hostess. This week we're meeting at my house, which is at the end of the main road, near the lake on A Street, second house on the left. I'm certain I'll see you there. I'm anxious to know all about you." Mrs. Steele then grabbed Henry by the shoulder and left.

Rachel stood in a daze, unable to discern if the invitation was genuine. Too thrilled about her classroom to care at the moment, Rachel turned her attention to sorting through the supplies and preparing her desk for the upcoming school year.

✑

The tinny music from the saloon below made sleeping a difficult task in Eikerenkotter's Hotel. Rachel decided locating a boardinghouse would be the day's priority. She rose early and opted to skip breakfast in lieu of strolling through town once again before attending church. The beauty of the morning surprised Rachel. The sun was glorious, coos from doves atop the hotel filled the air, and the golden hills with their majestic oaks reminded Rachel of her first home in Weberville, California.

Finding herself once again at the lake, Rachel finally viewed in the near distance the famed redwoods that provided the area's industry. She inhaled deeply, smelling their fresh scent, and suddenly the charm of Searsville became apparent. These trees were truly incredible; they were overwhelming in stature. Rachel's mouth gaped in awe as she looked up to the magnificent giants. She was reminded of her father's first words upon seeing the Sierra, and she realized she truly was witnessing the very handiwork of God.

As Rachel stood in wonderment, her thoughts were interrupted by the voice of an older woman, "Good morning, Miss Phillips. They're quite a sight, are they not?"

Rachel turned to see a woman with graying hair, dressed in her Sunday best: a long, dark plaid skirt topped by a crisp white shirt and a blue jacket. "I've never seen anything like them," she answered.

"Well, I've lived here for ten years now and I still don't tire of looking at them. I hope the mills will leave a few for our enjoyment. By the way, I'm Thelma Hopper. Since I've already addressed you as Miss Phillips and was not corrected, I'll assume you are the new schoolteacher." The older woman extended her hand and Rachel gently reached for it.

"Forgive me, Mrs. Hopper. I was a little preoccupied. Yes, I am Rachel Phillips."

"Ah, no matter. These trees are like seeing the ocean for the first time, wouldn't you say?"

"A good comparison, Mrs. Hopper."

"Well, I wanted to catch you today, Miss Phillips. I own the white house at the end of the street there." Mrs. Hopper pointed to a charming two-story house that graced the end of town near the lake. "I live by myself most of the year while my husband is off running our mill in Bear Gulch."

"Bear Gulch?" Rachel questioned the strange name.

"Miss Phillips, hasn't anyone filled you in on our local folklore yet? Ah, my dear, I will have such fun informing you of our little corner of the world." Mrs. Hopper tossed her hand. "Bear Gulch, for instance, got its name when a man and a bear stopped for a drink of water in the same place at the same time. Most unfortunate." Mrs. Hopper shook her head, clicking her tongue. "The man was pretty badly mauled, but he escaped with his life, minus half an ear. Said he owed it to good luck, a presence of mind, and a little surgery with a sailor's needle. If you want my take, though, I'd say someone upstairs was watching over the old boy."

Rachel grimaced in disgust as the older woman continued. "Oh darling, don't worry, you'll get over that soft stomach quickly enough here in logging territory. But enough of my coarse talk, I'm scaring you off before you've even started your work. My point is that I'm looking for a little company to share my home. Obviously, I have a flare for conversation and I'm missing the listening half."

Rachel laughed. She liked Mrs. Hopper and felt this offer must be from the Lord. Again she silently praised God, this time for a new home. "Mrs. Hopper, I would love to be your listening half. Thank you for thinking of me. . . Truth be told, I'm quite anxious to leave the hotel," she added.

The women finalized the details of Rachel's move and decided that in order to leave the hotel and saloon quickly, she would bring a few items this very evening and have the remainder of her things brought the following day. Both women were equally excited about their new living arrangements and went about their morning with renewed enthusiasm.

It was nearly ten, and Rachel rushed back to the hotel to meet Mr. Lathrop and his family. They had already arrived, and Rachel apologized profusely for her tardiness, proffering her encouraging news as an excuse.

Mr. Lathrop introduced his wife, Maria, and their young son, Seth. Maria appeared to be near Rachel's age and was of Mexican descent. Her long, dark hair and tanned complexion reminded Rachel of her own mother when she was younger. She felt a tinge of homesickness before realizing there really was no other home for her now; Searsville would have to do.

Maria had a warm smile and took Rachel's hand in both of hers as she spoke. "Miss Phillips, I am so happy to have you in Searsville. You will always be welcome in our home should you need anything, even if it's just a friend." Maria's Spanish accent was so captivating, Rachel could have listened to her speak for hours. Rachel discerned a genuine sincerity in the young woman's face and knew she'd found a friend.

When Seth saw his mother reach for Rachel's hand, he clumsily ran and embraced the young teacher, disappearing in the folds of her full skirt. As he shyly peeked up through the fabric, Rachel's heart melted.

"How old is he?" Rachel asked.

"He'll be two in three months." The sandy blond-haired boy smiled flirtatiously at Rachel, emphasizing his rosy, apple cheeks and a mouthful of tiny white teeth.

"Seth's also a very good judge of character, Miss Phillips," Mr. Lathrop added. "He's taken to you quickly enough."

"He just knows a pretty face when he sees one," Maria said, laughing at her charming little boy. "Now, we'd better be on our way or we'll be late for service."

The chapel bell was ringing furiously as they approached the small white, clapboard structure. There were relatively few people entering the church and Rachel wondered if it was due to the work of the season or simply a lack of interest.

Rachel recognized Mrs. Steele, who was wearing an elaborate, emerald-colored gown. It was infinitely more appropriate than the dress Rachel had seen her wear the evening before, but still surprisingly immodest for a church service. Mrs. Steele's son Henry waved wildly as he saw his new schoolteacher, and Rachel smiled graciously at the boy.

"Well, I see men of all ages recognize your charm." The voice was low and familiar and Rachel prayed it wasn't *him*. She turned quickly, as though she had imagined it, but there stood the arrogant man from Redwood. Rachel wanted to appear offended by his presence, but found herself taken captive once again by his pleasing face.

Unfazed by her apparent coolness, the handsome mill owner continued. "Welcome to Searsville, Miss Phillips. Chase Dylan, remember? We met in Redwood City." The tall sawyer lowered his chin in friendly greeting, but kept his disarming blue eyes aimed directly at Rachel.

"Chase, where have you been keeping yourself?" Mrs. Steele was suddenly standing at Rachel's side. She walked past Rachel, taking Chase's muscular arm in the process.

"I've been in Redwood, overseeing the shipment," Chase answered, dismissing her interruption and looking back longingly toward Rachel.

"Well, Henry and I have missed you. Now come, Pastor Swayles is about to start." Mrs. Steele led him reluctantly away into the chapel. Henry followed closely behind. Rachel let out an audible sigh of relief and commented under her breath, "That couple seems perfectly suited for one another," but somewhere inside, she felt a spark of jealousy.

The interior of the church was plain. Two sets of wooden benches lined a narrow center aisle. Rachel breathed the pine scent deeply, and looked toward the altar, a single table covered with a white lace cloth. A silver-plated communion chalice provided the centerpiece.

Rachel could sense Chase staring at her, and confirmed her suspicions from the corner of her eye as she made her way down the aisle. Mrs. Steele also noticed Chase's glances and tried repeatedly to engage him in conversation to divert his attention. Her attempts ultimately failed and the service began with Chase's concentration elsewhere.

Chapter 4

Rachel's move into Mrs. Hopper's home was an easy transition. Mrs. Hopper—Thelma, as she liked to be called—had an easygoing air about her that made Rachel feel relaxed and welcome. The home was well designed and carefully, yet practically, decorated. The furniture selected was mostly pine and oak, rather than the darker woods preferred in San Francisco's homes.

"My husband thought of everything when he built this home," Mrs. Hopper said enthusiastically. "This room here is the sitting parlor and it faces west, so we receive the afternoon light. That way, we never have to use a lamp during the summer months. I just can't abide the smell of kerosene."

"Your husband sounds like a very intelligent man," Rachel offered.

"Intelligent *and* frugal," Mrs. Hopper joked, tossing her hand.

Across the hallway from the parlor, also facing west, was a large bedroom. A four-post bed stood under an oversized window, and along the wall was a matching dresser of natural pine. The curtains were a deep cranberry red, overlaid with a soft, cream lace. On the bed was a handmade quilt in coordinating fabrics. "This is our room," Mrs. Hopper said proudly.

"Oh Thelma, it's lovely." Mrs. Hopper took the compliment to heart, smiling broadly at her creation. The two women admired the room for a few minutes before continuing their tour.

"Down the hall here at the back of the house is the kitchen." The kitchen was colorless, with everything, save the stove, painted a crisp white. The lace curtains over the exceptionally large windows were also white. "As you can see, we have a beautiful view of the lake here, and we get the early morning light for breakfast."

Mrs. Hopper turned back to the hallway and grasped the oak banister. "If you'll follow me upstairs, I'll show you to your room."

Upstairs were two bedrooms. Rachel's was decorated in a soft periwinkle blue and white. The other bedroom, which Mr. Hopper used as an office when he was home, was a dark, masculine green. Thelma looked longingly into the room, as though hoping for a glimpse of Mr. Hopper.

Tuesday evening arrived all too quickly. Rachel and Thelma prepared to walk next door for the weekly quilting circle at the Steele home. Rachel had been both surprised and relieved to hear that Mrs. Steele was a widow. This new information brought the woman's flirtatious manner and garish clothing into perspective.

Rachel found her large home decorated much like the homes of San Francisco, just as she had expected. The woods were all dark mahogany, and the fabrics a rich burgundy velvet. Too much furniture overcrowded the room, and the lacy curtains were excessively frilly for the cozy logging village. In the center of the room stood Mrs. Steele's quilting frame, ready for the evening's activities.

Thelma and Rachel arrived early and found Mrs. Steele dressed in her usual extravagant attire, with Henry standing properly at her side. When prompted, the boy addressed his mother's visitors: "Good evenin' Mrs. Hopper, good evenin' Miss Phillips." Rachel could see she was going to have a problem not playing favorites with Henry in her class.

"Very well, Henry. Go into the drawing room and wait for Mr. Dylan," Mrs. Steele said sternly.

"Mr. Dylan?" Rachel tried to stop the words, but they were already out. *Why am I so nervous about running into Chase Dylan? Apparently, it is going to be an unavoidable nuisance in this small town.*

"Yes. Mr. Dylan was a good friend of my husband's, God rest his soul. He comes by once or twice a week to spend time with Henry. Says he's like his own son." The latter was said with a tinge of spite, intimating there was definitely something more to Mrs. Steele and Chase's relationship. Rachel couldn't help but think Mrs. Steele's insinuations were wasted on her. *Handsome or not, I wouldn't want that man if he were the last one on earth!* Rachel thought. As if on cue, there came a brisk knock at the door.

The door opened and Chase Dylan's imposing figure stood on the porch, his focus fixed on Rachel. "Good evening, ladies. I'm sorry I'm late, Gretchen, but it was busy at the mill. Promoted Jeremiah to lead faller today, and I wanted to oversee his first day on the ridge."

Mrs. Steele's voice became intensely sweet as she replied, "No matter, Chase. We're always happy to have you when you have time for us. Would you like to come in for some coffee?"

Rachel shifted uncomfortably in Chase's presence and prayed fervently he wouldn't take Mrs. Steele up on her offer. She intended to work hard to gain a reputation as a teacher, and she certainly didn't want the victim image from Redwood to follow her here. She hoped Chase Dylan would keep their run-in to himself.

"No thank you, Gretchen. I've got big plans for Henry and me tonight, and we've got a lot to do before sundown. Let's go, pard'ner, we're going to do a little evening fishing in the lake." Henry remained in his drawing room chair until his mother gave him a signal to get up, then he bolted across the room and jumped boldly into Chase's arms.

Seeing Chase with Henry caused Rachel to question whether she had been too hard on the man, but her pride ruled quickly that she had not.

With Henry and Chase out the door, the women began arriving for their social event of the week. There were six women altogether. Mrs. Irving, Mrs. Thorne, and Mrs. Davenport were all introduced to Rachel, and all expressed pleasure over her new role in the township.

The women gathered in the drawing room, and Mrs. Steele brought out the quilt the group had just finished the week before. It was an artistic masterpiece, and Rachel admired the colorful array of fabric sincerely. She was now enthusiastic about coming to the weekly meetings and being a part of a similar creation in the future. The women took their places and the sewing and talking began.

Rachel's ears perked up in astonishment as she discovered the conversation centered on townswomen and was often malicious in nature. She looked around the room to see if anyone else was shocked by the openly spiteful talk, but she seemed to be the only one that noticed. In all the years of attending her mother's sewing circles, she had never heard talk such as this. Perhaps logging country was different from gold country after all. Since she was unfamiliar with the objects of the rumors, she paid little heed to the talk, until. . .

"I heard Maria Lathrop is pregnant again," Mrs. Thorne said, her head shaking in contempt.

"You know how those Californios are, one baby after the other. I can't believe our Mr. Lathrop was taken in by her kind," Mrs. Irving added, her head shaking in disbelief. Rachel's hands involuntarily stilled.

"When he has eighteen mouths to feed, he won't be so deceived,"

Mrs. Steele said, and the women cackled with laughter.

"Seriously, what can he possibly see in her? She's so dark, so completely unattractive, if you ask me," Mrs. Thorne said.

"The spices she uses give her the most unappealing scent. Have you ever noticed?" Chimed in Mrs. Davenport, sniffing for effect.

"Lucky for Seth he takes after his father," Mrs. Irving snorted, referring to Seth's light coloring.

Rachel felt ill over the conversation and tried to blink away the tears as she heard Maria being spoken of in such evil tones. *What rubbish! Maria is lovely, just like my mother! And how many men whistled at her! I hugged Maria myself and I distinctly smelled lavender, not any peculiar spice.* Rachel thought to herself how untrue each of the statements had been.

Enthusiasm for the next patchwork quilt in Searsville was instantly replaced by the desire to leave the present gathering. She found herself inventing excuses, her mind searching for something that was not obvious. She wanted to confront the women, but worried about how it might appear.

As the gossip continued, Rachel looked at Mrs. Hopper for moral support. Rachel was saddened that although Thelma had not participated in the mean-spiritedness of the evening, she had done nothing to stop it. In fact, she seemed to be relishing the vicious lies.

It was at least an hour before Rachel could invent a reason to pardon herself. She finally came up with the mundane excuse of a headache, making apologies as she headed for the door. Once outside, she burst into tears and fled home to Mrs. Hopper's. She put the kettle on with plans for tea and sat down to have her first gushing cry since leaving her mother.

⟡

Outside Mrs. Hopper's home on the shore of the village lake sat Chase Dylan and his small companion.

"I thought you were supposed to fish in the morning," Henry stated innocently.

"What do you think, the fish leave the lake after noon?" Chase asked, a sparkle in his eye.

"Then why does everybody fish in the morning? Are the fish sleeping?"

"If they are, it should be that much easier to catch 'em." Chase laughed and Henry joined in, thrilled to be fishing at any time of day with Mr. Dylan.

"I heard you tell Mama Jeremiah got 'moted to faller. What's that?" Henry asked.

"*Promoted*. Jeremiah got promoted, which means he moved up to a better job with more responsibility. The lead faller is a very important job that takes lots of skill. He's the man that yells, *TIM-BERRR* before the tree comes down. But first he must decide exactly where the tree should fall and plan for it. Once he knows where the tree will lie, he prepares a 'bed' for it. That usually means leveling the ground so the trunk won't break in two. We lose valuable lumber that way."

"I want to be the lead faller when I grow up, Mr. Dylan," Henry declared.

"Well now, I thought for sure you'd want to be an engineer on the new railroad in town," Chase teased, while painfully recalling Henry's father's death at the mercy of a poor faller.

"Have you seen the new train? Is it as big as they say? Is it loud? Can I ride it someday?" Henry's eagerness would have produced forty more questions had Chase not curtailed it.

"The train begins running through Redwood in October. I'll work it out with your mother so that you can come with me to town and see the big steam engine. But, only if you behave properly in school."

"Oh, I will, Mr. Dylan, I promise. I want Miss Phillips to like me. I like her, she's real pretty."

"Yes, she is, Henry." Chase sighed and began threading a flipping worm onto Henry's hook. With a mighty thrust, Henry's hook was hurled toward the center of the lake, and the two sat watching their lines in the stillness of the water with satisfaction. The crickets chirped and the air began to cool pleasantly as the sun started its descent. Chase and Henry fished in silence for quite a while before Chase brought up the lesson in tonight's fishing trip. "Do you know why we're fishing tonight, Henry?"

"To catch a fish?" The boy's eyes looked up questioningly at his companion.

"Well, of course that's part of it, but it's in our Bible lesson for tonight. Did you know that Jesus knew quite a few fishermen?"

"They fished back then?"

"That's right. A long time ago Jesus walked by the Sea of Galilee, and He came across two fishermen. One was named Simon, who was also called Peter, and the other was Andrew, his brother. They were casting their fishing net into the sea. You see, they used to fish with big nets instead of a pole." Chase's hands moved to demonstrate the size of the net, and he continued.

"Jesus told them, 'Follow me, and I will make you fishers of men,' and they left their nets to follow Him. Then Jesus saw two more brothers, their names were James and John, and they were *also* fisherman. Jesus found them on an anchored ship with their father as they were mending their nets. Jesus called for them, too, and they immediately left their ship and their father to follow Him. Do you know why these fishermen left their jobs and their tools to follow Jesus?"

"Because He asked them to?"

"Yes, because He asked them, but also because He was the Lord and they left everything, including their livelihood and their families, to put Him first. That's what God asks of us, that we put Him first. He called these fishermen 'disciples' and told them they would now be fishers of men, spreading the Word of God."

"Do I have to leave my mom to follow Jesus, Mr. Dylan?" Henry's face was fraught with worry. Chase hadn't anticipated this; he had to remember when he prepared these lessons that Henry took everything quite literally.

"No, pard'ner. Your mom is here to take care of you, until you're big enough to do it alone. James and John were all grown up when they met Jesus."

"How come we always talk about Jesus, Mr. Dylan?"

"Don't you like to talk about the Lord, Henry?"

"Yes. . .I always tell Mama what I learned when we talk."

"And what does she say?"

"She says, 'That's nice, Henry.'"

"Well, Henry, your father loved Jesus very much. That's how we know your daddy's in heaven with the Lord right now. It was very important to your daddy that you learn about Jesus, and since he's not here, he asked me to make sure you were taught." Chase hoped he'd found the right words, but this promise had been harder to keep than he'd imagined.

Chase wanted to do everything correctly around Henry to help ensure that the boy's father would get to see him again, in heaven. Although he knew Henry's salvation was ultimately in the Lord's hands, he felt he must do everything within his power to help the process along.

"I'm glad my daddy's in heaven, Chase."

"Me, too, Henry." Chase smiled down at the boy and they turned their attention to the tranquillity of the calm lake, each lost in his own thoughts.

The quilting circle came to a close and Mrs. Hopper returned to a darkened house. She climbed the steep staircase with a candle and knocked softly on Rachel's bedroom door. "Rachel honey, are you all right? May I come in?"

"Sure, Thelma. Come on in." Rachel was glad for the darkness that would shelter her puffy eyes from the older woman. She relinquished the pillow she'd been clutching.

Mrs. Hopper set a tray of tea and cookies before her. "Oh my dear, I was so worried about you. How is your headache?" Thelma set the tray on the dresser and rested her hand upon Rachel's forehead.

"I'm fine, Thelma. Thank you. I guess I just needed a little rest. Preparing for the school year ahead has perhaps been too much for me." Rachel hadn't decided how she would broach the gossip subject, but she did know now was not the time. She was still far too emotional about the issue.

"I brought home a few cookies for you. I don't know a headache yet that can't be remedied with a little tea and cookies." Mrs. Hopper had a tender smile that made Rachel forget about the offensive events of the evening and enjoy her present company.

"I've been meaning to ask: What do you think of your room?" Mrs. Hopper looked around the room with pleasure.

Rachel's bedroom was decorated entirely in various shades of blue and white. There were gingham curtains on the window and a lovely star-patterned quilt on the bed. All of the furniture was of the highest quality carved oak, and even the wash basin atop the dresser was embellished with hand-painted, coordinating blue flowers.

Rachel had never had a room of her own like this one. In Weberville she slept in the main room of the cabin, and in San Francisco her quarters in Marshall's mansion never really felt like home. The simplicity of the furnishings here pleased Rachel immensely.

"Thelma, I love this room. It's so feminine and it makes me feel as though I decorated it myself," Rachel answered truthfully. Mrs. Hopper had a look of satisfaction as her eyes surveyed her handiwork.

"That's just how I wanted our guests to feel…at home." Mrs. Hopper's comment suddenly made Rachel think of her mother. That was all this home was missing, her mother and little brother. Suddenly, she longed to speak to her mother, to have one of their special discussions, even if it were only on paper.

"Speaking of home, I should get started on a letter to my mother. I haven't written my family yet; they don't even know where I'm staying." Rachel's voice was agitated as she remembered her neglect.

Mrs. Hopper sensed Rachel's dismay and announced, "Far be it from me to keep a daughter from writing home. You know, Mr. Hopper and I were never blessed with children, but I know I'd expect a letter nearly every day if my own daughter moved away." With that statement Thelma quietly exited the room, leaving Rachel to her writing.

✍

"Mama, Mama. I'm going to be a fisher of men!" Henry rushed into his mother's arms and excitedly began to tell her of his night's lesson. In the doorway, Chase Dylan stood with a set of fishing poles, a bucket, and a smile on his face.

"That's nice, son," Gretchen said, her attention on Chase. "Now go on up to bed, sweetheart, it's late."

"Well, we didn't catch anything, but I'd say the evening was quite a success," Chase's deep voice announced.

"Chase, I just can't thank you enough for taking Henry off my hands tonight." Her voice was exceptionally sweet as she started toward the door with her arms outstretched. "Won't you come in for coffee?"

"I think not, Gretchen. I've got an early morning and I want to find my way back to the mill before it gets too dark."

Chase had always avoided such invitations. It was important the town not get the wrong idea about his intentions, but it was equally important that civility between them continue, for Henry's sake. It was a delicate balance Chase often found difficult to maintain. "I best be off. Thank you for sharing your son with me. He reminds me so of his father. Good night, Gretchen," he said absently.

Chase exited, shutting the door quietly behind him. Gretchen Steele stared at the back of the closed door, punching her hands to her hips in frustration. "I never get anywhere with that man. When is he going to wake up and see he needs a wife?"

"Pardon me, ma'am?" The maid appeared from the kitchen.

"Oh, nothing. I was only talking to myself. See to the dishes, will you?" she barked.

❧

Rachel rubbed her puffy eyes and started her letter.

> *Dear Mother,*
>
> *I hope this letter finds you all well. I miss you and my darling Georgie so very much. How is my little man? I miss his gorgeous smiles and his stubby little toes.*
>
> *My trip was pleasant and I find that Searsville is a unique place, with what Father would call "quite a collection of folks."*
>
> *I'm living with the wife of a mill owner whose husband spends most of his time in a place called Bear Gulch. (Don't ask!) Mrs. Thelma Hopper is her name, and she has taught me a great deal about the local industry.*
>
> *For instance, I have learned that the head bullmaster is the most respected position, and apparently he is paid as much as the mill owner himself. Bullmasters control as many as ten oxen, using only their voice as a tool. I tell you, Mother, it is a sight to behold when they come down the road through town. The oxen are frightening because of their size, and to see a man command authority over them is really unnerving. Apparently, the townspeople have complete faith in the bullmasters, for they don't even flinch as the team comes through the village. I've also discovered, the hard way I'm afraid, that the lumbering wagons have the right of way on the road! When you come to visit, prepare for a bumpy ride.*
>
> *I met a wonderful couple in Redwood while I waited for my stage, a Mr. and Mrs. Williams. They were truly kind to me and, after traveling alone, their friendly faces were a welcome sight. They own a hotel called the American House; you'll have to ask Marshall if he's acquainted with them.*
>
> *I'm so excited that the railroad will be coming into Redwood before Christmas. That means you, Georgie, and even Marshall, if he can get away, can come visit often. It will be such a quick trip, we'll be like neighbors. By the way, I've seen my classroom, and it's just*

191

perfect. I can't wait to show it to you. Write to me soon, Mother, now that you know where I am staying.

In His Love,
Rachel

Rachel had tried her best to keep the letter lighthearted, but what she really wanted to tell her mother was that life without her seemed empty. And that the thought of Georgie growing up without his big sister around made her stomach feel ill. It was almost too much to bear, but Rachel knew her mother was living the life that Peg Phillips deserved, in a beautiful home with a man who loved her. Rachel smiled serenely at the thought of her mother being comfortable and turned out her lamp to go to bed.

Chapter 5

Rachel had spent her last week before school preparing her classroom and readying supplies for the upcoming school year. Sunday morning came quickly, and Rachel dressed for the church service. She flounced the apricot-colored gown that Marshall had specially created for her. Rachel wanted to leave her hair down under her floral bonnet, it contrasted so well against the light fabric, but she knew that would be inappropriate for a schoolteacher.

Mrs. Hopper's familiar voice announced that Mr. and Mrs. Lathrop were outside, waiting to walk to the sanctuary. Rachel hurried to finish pinning up her long, chestnut curls and rushed breathlessly down the stairs.

Mr. and Mrs. Lathrop's friendly faces were a welcome sight and, just as Rachel remembered, warm and open. Little Seth had a big, toothy grin and was waving his hands and saying "Bye-bye" over and over.

"Seth hasn't quite mastered 'Good morning,' so I'm afraid 'Bye-bye' is his only greeting," Mr. Lathrop said while patting his son's head.

"Well, with a face like that, I think I can forgive him." Rachel smiled good-naturedly, squeezing Seth's cheeks.

"Miss Phillips, I certainly hope you can join us for Sunday supper after church. Seth might never forgive us if you say no." Mrs. Lathrop's beautiful accent made the invitation impossible to decline. Rachel was excited to spend more time with Maria and learn of her exotic background on the *rancho* Mrs. Hopper had told her about.

"I would love to. Thank you for the invitation, Maria." Rachel was truly moved by the offer. Maria's anxious expression melted into a happy smile.

"Mrs. Hopper, what about you? Could you be talked into a hearty, home-cooked meal without the work?" Mr. Lathrop asked.

"Thank you, Robert…but I'm afraid I have other plans." Mrs. Hopper's voice seemed to search for a better excuse, but none came. Rachel looked to Maria to see if she had noticed the slight, and it was apparent she had, but she was gracious in her response. Rachel ached for her new friend.

"Well, perhaps another time, Mrs. Hopper," Maria said sincerely. The church bell clanged and Mr. Lathrop led the group toward the chapel. Rachel was pleasantly surprised at how many people remembered her and welcomed her to church this morning. She had met so many people over the week, it was impossible to know everyone's name, but Maria casually whispered well-wishers' names as they passed.

Pastor Swayles was his usual animated self. He delivered a powerful message about trusting in the Lord, asking the congregation to reflect on whom they trusted in: themselves or the Lord. He finished his sermon quoting a passage from Psalm 91: "'He that dwelleth in the secret place of the most High shall abide under the shadow of the Almighty. I will say of the Lord, 'He is my refuge and my fortress: my God; in him will I trust.'"

Rachel left unmoved, thinking it was a nice message, but taking pride in the fact that it didn't necessarily apply to her. After all, she had trusted in the Lord since she was a child.

"Miss Phillips, what did you think of Reverend Swayles's message?" a deep voice asked of Rachel. She turned to see Chase Dylan following behind her, obviously trying to begin a conversation.

"I liked it just fine, thank you," Rachel stated, while twisting her body back around in an exaggerated movement to let him know their discussion was over.

"Miss Phillips, I'd like to—"

Chase was cut off in mid-sentence as Rachel turned abruptly and announced, "Look, Mr. Dylan, I don't know what your fascination with taunting me is, but I can assure you I have had enough." Chase looked astonished by the remonstration, and for a moment, Rachel thought he might even have appeared hurt. But it was done now, and Rachel felt quite satisfied with her firmness.

Rachel hurried to reach the Lathrops, who had left right at the close of the service. When she finally caught up with them, her face was flushed.

Mr. Lathrop turned around, a wide grin coming over his face. Rachel noticed he looked beyond her, toward the mill owner. "Chase, we wondered what happened to you, but we knew you'd find the way. You always do." Rachel exhaled deeply. Her desperate attempt to flee Chase Dylan obviously was futile; he, too, apparently had been invited to the Lathrops for supper.

"Chase joins us every Sunday, if he's able." Mrs. Lathrop's warm tone told Rachel she, too, thought highly of the pesky mill owner. Rachel remained dumbfounded over what people saw in this man, apart from his obvious external attributes.

"I'm not one to turn down a free meal, especially if it's made by Maria Lathrop." Chase winked at Robert Lathrop and freed Seth from his mother's hold, sweeping him onto his wide shoulders for the remainder of the walk. Seth squealed in delight and kicked his legs in jubilation. As the assembly reached the front door of the small adobe home, the smell of roasted chicken issued from inside.

Dinner was a fairly quiet affair. Seth had already gone down for a nap. After the plates were filled with sumptuous food, the blessing was followed by complete silence, the Lathrops' guests had nothing to say to one another. Rachel knew her hosts were desperate to warm the chilly atmosphere, which perplexed them, but she still felt too angry to speak.

"So, Robert, what did you think of the message this morning? Did it hold any special meaning for you?" Maria appealed, while her eyes begged her husband for a rambling answer.

"Maria, I'm so glad you asked." Robert smiled knowingly. "Pastor Swayles's sermon on trusting in the Lord spoke directly to me. I thought about the time when we were courting and I didn't know if we would ever be allowed to marry." Mr. Lathrop's answer roused Rachel's interest, and she inquired about how the two had met.

Maria was delighted to tell the story, and continued for her husband. "As you know, my father owned a large rancho in the valley, and Robert came to work as a *vaquero*." Robert gave his wife a sideways glance, and Maria corrected herself with the English version: "Robert came to break a horse that belonged to my father. My papa was an excellent horseman, but news of Robert's talent with the horses had passed from rancher to rancher and Papa wanted only the best. When Roberto, Robert, came to *Rancho de Estrella*, I loved him from the first moment I saw him." Maria paused and gazed lovingly at her husband. Rachel found herself feeling slightly embarrassed for intruding upon the moment.

"What I didn't know was if he was a Christian, and that was very important to Papa and me. One evening, after a long day, Papa invited him for dinner, and Robert offered to say the prayer. It was so heart-felt and beautiful, I rejoiced in the knowledge that this man knew the Lord. And I prayed that very night that God would allow me to marry him. And He did, so how could I ask for more?" The couple exchanged looks, and Rachel momentarily felt a twinge of envy. She caught herself glancing Chase's way, and he smiled warmly. Rachel felt herself blush and quickly looked toward Robert for safety.

Robert finished his wife's story. "It wasn't quite as easy as all that; you make it sound like a fairy tale, my dear. I was a traveling horseman and I made a right good living doing it, but when I saw Maria I knew I was in the market for different work; blacksmithing just seemed the natural choice. I went away for two years, apprenticing under one of the best blacksmiths in the territory, until I learned the job completely. Only then did I return and ask Maria to be my wife. We did a lot of praying in those two years."

The whole table enjoyed the romantic tale, but when it was over, the quiet resumed. Robert looked at Maria's pleading eyes and continued. "If that blacksmith could see how much time I spend with horses, he'd laugh heartily."

"What do you mean?" Rachel questioned.

"I'm afraid there's not that much work for horses here in logging country. I spend most of my time shoeing oxen, an animal as large as it is dumb. We have to hoist 'em up in a special harness because they're not bright enough to bend their legs for the shoe."

Robert shook his head in apparent disgust. "I'm not complaining though. I'd shoe oxen for the rest of my life to be with Maria." He glanced at his wife, who turned pink at the compliment.

Rachel found herself fearful she would again search for Chase's face, so she rose quickly to help with the dishes.

"Rachel, please sit down. You are our guest," Maria said sweetly, and Rachel sat down nervously.

"Perhaps, Rachel," Maria began uncertainly, "you might help me with the dessert."

"Of course, Maria, I'd be delighted." Rachel jumped at the chance to leave the room and followed Maria quickly into the kitchen.

"I'm very sorry I didn't tell you Chase would be here for supper. He's here just about every Sunday, unless he's out of town, so I never thought to mention it. He appears to make you uncomfortable. Do you mind if I ask why? Chase usually gets along so well with people. . .especially women." Maria added the last casually.

"Let's just say we got off to a bad start." Rachel decided to keep her comments brief; there was no sense in rehashing the whole ugly scene in Redwood.

"Well, I hope you'll come to an understanding soon and forget about the past, that's what God would have us do." Even though offered kindly, Maria's words stung Rachel. *I have been acting so childish.* She had allowed her feelings of hostility to fester to the boiling point, and she had never given her emotions up to God. Certainly Mr. Dylan had been arrogant, but for the first time Rachel realized *she* had, too.

The sermon! It was for me, Rachel whispered to herself in realization. *Oh, I have indeed been proud, completely relying upon myself.*

"Rachel?" Maria questioned Rachel's quiet self-recrimination.

"Oh Maria, would you mind if I skipped dessert and walked to the redwoods this afternoon? I need some time alone, and I've been dying to see the giants up close." Rachel turned and walked in a daze toward the door.

"Rachel, why don't you let Chase and Robert go with you? It's not always safe out there..." Maria's warning was unheard by the preoccupied young teacher.

❦

"What on earth did you do to that poor woman?" Robert Lathrop asked of his friend as they stood on the porch watching Rachel walk away toward the forest.

"I saved her from a saloon brawl." The brevity of Chase's explanation left his companion vastly unenlightened.

"Yep. That'll do it every time." The two men laughed at the incompleteness of the answer.

Something told Chase that Robert's ignorance of the rift was best, for Rachel's sake. "It seems I spend a fair amount of time watching Miss Phillips' backside." Chase referred to Rachel's huffy exits, but Robert seemed to misunderstand.

"It seems to me you're enjoying the view."

❦

The light from the day was beginning to dwindle. It was only three in the afternoon, but the mighty redwoods drained the sun's rays from the sky and below. Rachel was a bit spooked by the phenomenon as the eerie darkness enveloped her. Being in the forest surrounded by these giant wonders, Rachel questioned how anyone could fell them, and yet she knew her own livelihood depended upon the industry. Finding a soft spot, padded with moist needles from the trees, Rachel knelt down to pray.

"Dear heavenly Father, I have been so proud lately. I have allowed angry feelings toward my stepfather, and now this Chase Dylan, to take over. Heavenly Father, I feel so ugly at the thoughts I've had about Marshall. Mother told me it was Your will that she marry him. Who am I to question that, Lord? I know You must have me in Searsville for a reason, and I pray I am worthy of Your calling. Please forgive me for my arrogance and help me. Help me to lose this animosity toward Marshall and Chase and the women of the sewing circle. Help me to remember that Marshall secured this position for me, that Chase prevented me from being hurt in Redwood, and that the women of Searsville have tried to include me in their socials, while I only passed judgment upon them. Lord, be with me tomorrow as I start teaching. I pray that Your Holy Spirit would be present in my classroom and that my words would be guided by You."

It was a short prayer, but it took its toll on the young woman. Her dark green eyes were lost behind the tears, and her body was void of energy.

A sudden crackle alerted Rachel that she was not alone, and her body stiffened. The words she hadn't really heard Maria utter now echoed in her mind, *"It's not always safe out there."* Rachel's head swam with the possibilities: A bear? A hermit? Loggers? *Oh Lord, what?*

Scruffy and dirty, a man with a tattered beard and unkempt hair emerged from behind a tree. His clothes were filthy, hanging loosely from his scrawny frame, and an evil grin shone with intent. Rachel was frozen with fear and tried to speak, but found her voice was gone.

Just then another man, equally disheveled and wild-looking, approached her from the opposite side; Rachel was trapped. She tried to scream, but once again found she was without speech. Soon another crackling came from behind her, and Rachel knew there was nowhere to run.

The men laughed, enjoying the anxiety and dread they saw upon their prey. "This must be Chris'mas. She's sure pretty," one of them announced before spitting to his side.

"She'll make a right fine wife if she can cook," The other snickered, but Rachel knew holy matrimony was not their intention.

They were closing in and Rachel saw no escape. She instinctively prayed, *Father, help me. In Jesus' holy name, I ask You to clear a path for me.*

A sudden gun shot peeled through the air and Rachel fell to the ground in fear. "This is private property. Can you give me a good reason why I shouldn't shoot you for trespassing?" Rachel turned to see Chase's towering, muscular form looming with threatening strength, gripping the smoking rifle. She sighed heavily with relief before dropping limply further into the ground.

The two men cowered as they reeled off excuses. "We didn't mean no harm," offered one.

"We thought she was lost," piped in the other. The defenses continued until Chase spoke sternly once again.

Chase lifted his rifle and aimed between the men. "If I catch you on this property again, I won't be asking any more questions. Is that clear?" The two men nodded in agreement, waited for Chase's signal, and contorted their bodies in clumsy confusion to hasten their getaway.

Chase dropped his intimidating stance and walked tentatively toward Rachel. He put his hands tenderly under her arms, lifted her from the ground, and looked deeply into her forest-green eyes. "Are you all right, Rachel?" In answer, her shivering frame sought refuge in his powerful arms, and she seemed to melt into his chest. The use of her Christian name provided an instant peace, an impassioned feeling of security.

"I. . .I'm fine." After finding her voice had returned, Rachel began to sob. The emotions from the incident were overwhelming. Chase pulled her closer and let her cry.

"It's okay, Rachel. I'm here now. I won't let anyone hurt you." Rachel felt his grasp tighten and she allowed herself to be held, relishing his shelter and clinging tightly to his wide shoulders.

Rachel looked up and was lost in the cool depths of his eyes. He came closer, and she soon felt his lips brush hers. His touch sent a wave of emotion throughout her body, and her awareness returned abruptly, forcing her to pull away. "I'm so sorry, Mr. Dylan. That was completely inappropriate; my emotions got the best of me." She wiped the tears roughly from her face and sniffled.

Reluctantly, he let her go. "It's quite all right, Miss Phillips. I understand."

"How did you know where to find me?" She looked up, her eyes still glistening with tears. Rachel now knew she had been wrong; Chase

Dylan was a man she could trust.

"When I heard where you went, I followed at a distance. I didn't think you'd want my company." Rachel closed her eyes, stung by the comment, yet she knew he was right. She would never have let him accompany her, her foolish pride would have seen to that. How thankful she now was that Chase had not allowed her silly haughtiness to bring her harm.

"I thought your property was farther south, in Portola," Rachel commented, referring to his threat to the men.

"It is, but this is *somebody's* private property, after all." Chase grinned and quickly changed the subject. "We should get back. Maria's waiting dessert for us."

Rachel shyly took the arm offered to her, and the two walked silently back to Searsville, each content with the mere company of one another.

Chapter 6

The weather for the first day of school was splendid. Rachel awoke to the bright sunshine enveloping her room in a brilliant golden glow. She breathed deeply with excitement at the sun's warm rays and the realization that today she was "Miss Phillips, teacher." Rachel opened her Bible to pray and prepare for her day. She took special care to dress appropriately for her first day: a long, navy blue skirt and a pressed white shirt with a smart blue ribbon tied at the neck. When the outfit was complete, the young woman went downstairs for a bite to eat and found Mrs. Hopper already busy in the kitchen.

"Well, good morning. What lovely weather for your first day of work."

"Isn't it though? What are all these baskets, Thelma?"

"They're for your students. I've been told many of the children don't have proper lunches during the day. I've packed five baskets full of food. Should you see someone without a meal, you can hand the child a basket in confidence."

Rachel marveled at her thoughtfulness. "Oh Mrs. Hopper, thank you. I would never have known, and how helpless I would have felt if I didn't have anything to give."

"Think nothing of it, Rachel. I will be happy to refill the baskets daily. If you find you need more than I've provided, please let me know."

"I had better get going. It wouldn't look very good to have the new teacher late on the first day." Rachel picked up the baskets and headed for the back door. The walk to the schoolhouse was short and pleasant. On the way, she looked over the roster Mr. Lathrop had given her; it stated she would have forty-two students.

Forty-two students. How will I ever handle such a number, especially with the older boys? I promised myself I would never use a ruler for anything other than measuring, but with those numbers, I hope I'll be able to keep order.

Little Henry Steele was one of the first students to arrive. "Good morning, Miss Phillips. Can I help you?"

"Well, Henry, yes you *may*. Would you like to ring the bell?"

"Yes ma'am!" Henry shouted with enthusiasm.

"Very well, the cord is right over there." Rachel pointed to the vestibule of the schoolroom. Soon, the school bell was clanging away and children of every size flooded the room. She looked at the clean-scrubbed faces, all gazing expectantly at their new teacher.

"Children, my name is Miss Phillips, and I'd like you to take a seat anywhere. I will assign desks as soon as we get settled." Once all the children had taken their chairs, Rachel counted only thirty-four heads. She began to take roll, and asked if anyone knew the missing students.

An older girl raised her hand. "Miss Phillips, it's because the weather is so nice. The older boys won't come to school until the rain starts."

"Very well, thank you. . ." Rachel paused waiting for the girl's name.

"Veronica. Veronica Thorne."

"Thank you, Veronica. I believe I met your mother at last week's sewing circle." It was going to take an effort not to judge Veronica harshly because of her mother, and Rachel was determined to be fair.

Rachel began the school day by asking each student to stand and state their name, age, where they lived, and their favorite pastime. Rachel was surprised at a few of the answers to the last question, including "shootin' 'coons" and "watching the races."

When Rachel questioned the children further, she learned that raccoon hunting was a local sport because the animals ate food destined for the livestock. She also discovered that a popular Sunday activity in Searsville was horse racing, complete with wagering. Whether teacher or student received a better education this first day of school remained in question at the end of the day.

&

The men stood at attention. The giant could go at any time, and everyone now prepared for the fall. The chopping continued for a good ten minutes until the first snapping sounds were heard high above. *"TIM-BERRR!"* Several cracks like the pop of a rifle were heard until the slow thunder of the branches roared through the forest, followed by a ground-shaking blast as the tree hit the forest floor; then silence.

"It never ceases to amaze me." Chase shook his head in awe.

"Peelers, let's get to work!" Jeremiah yelled. A group of young men standing by with sharp iron tools ran, mounted the giant, and began stripping away the bark.

"A few of the men saw you walking into town with the new school-teacher," Jeremiah remarked.

"Miss Phillips got into a little trouble in the forest. I'd really appreciate it if you didn't mention it, I think it would embarrass her." Chase tried to keep his voice level, but the mere mention of her name sent his heart racing.

"Well, a word of warning: The whole town is talking, even here in Portola."

With all the wild happenings of the area, Chase couldn't imagine why the town would take such an interest in so minute an event. Then again, women like Rachel Phillips were not a common occurrence, and her actions were certain to be monitored.

"I appreciate the information, Jeremiah. Thanks. If you've got everything under control here, I'm going to head back to the mill." Chase turned and walked away, his head hanging low in thought as he processed this piece of information. He hoped the incident wouldn't start any trouble for Miss Phillips.

"Sure thing, Chase." Jeremiah set back to work.

The new schoolteacher was much more relaxed on her second day of school. She had managed the children well on her first day, and it had granted her confidence. Rachel still wondered how she would learn all thirty-four names, but hoped it would happen before the other eight students returned for the remainder of the school year.

Rachel had seated the children by a combination of age and alphabetical order, and she studied her chart intensely while the group read to themselves. Although she had been warned, the young teacher was surprised by how much planning each day would demand and how short the attention span of the younger children was.

She had been up well past dark, with the aid of her kerosene lamp, preparing for the day's lessons, and by the end of the day her eyelids were beginning to droop. The children were excused, and Rachel closed her eyes and sighed heavily at the thought of preparing for the next day.

"Miss Phillips?" Veronica Thorne stood before her teacher.

"Yes, Veronica, what is it?"

"Miss Phillips, I would like to ask a favor of you."

"I'll do what I'm able."

"I'm sixteen years old now, nearly seventeen actually, and I'm to be married. My fiancé, Jeremiah Smith, has just been promoted to lead faller in Portola Valley. And, well, only a bullmaster makes more. So, he's ready to take a bride. And. . .well, as a faller's wife, I hardly think I need more educatin'."

Rachel looked at the young girl in disbelief. After a brief pause she answered, "What is it you'd like from me, Veronica?"

"I'd like you to talk to my ma. You're friends and all, and I thought you could tell her I don't need more schoolin'."

"I'm sorry, Veronica, but I can't tell your mother such a thing in good conscience."

"Why ever not?"

"Veronica, how many years have you been in school?"

"Over four!" Veronica answered powerfully, four slender fingers rising up.

"Veronica, I don't mean to be insensitive, but I think you need to hear this. Think about how many widows live *alone* in Searsville. Not just the widows, think of the women who live alone for nine months of the year while their husbands are working at the mills. A woman alone must know her sums and read well to manage on her own. Are you prepared to do this alone?" Rachel studied the young woman's face, hoping she had made her point.

"But Miss Phillips, I wouldn't live alone. Jeremiah works for Chase Dylan in Portola, so he'd be home every evening." The girl's own words made her blush, and her eyes darted from her teacher.

"I'm very happy to hear that, Veronica. However, what if God should have different plans for you?" Rachel searched for Veronica's eyes, but the girl refused to meet her gaze.

"Whatever do you mean? I'm to be married, I already told ya." Veronica tossed her long, loose hair, twirling a piece carelessly around her pinkie.

Rachel lowered her voice. "Veronica, I did not plan to become a teacher, I truly feel God's hand made the choice for me. Now I am so glad He did. You have the chance to become educated, so please don't miss the opportunity. Just think how pleased Jeremiah will be, knowing he has a wife who can care for him and his home." Rachel inadvertently brushed her fingers across her teaching certificate, displayed proudly upon her desk.

Veronica let the words sink in. "I don't see a benefit to another year, but I can see you're not willin' to help me."

"Miss Phillips?" Rachel was startled by the familiar voice of Chase Dylan, who bent to fit through the doorway of the small schoolhouse. She was surprised at how happy his appearance made her. She stood up quickly, straightening her skirt; she hoped he didn't notice the redness in her cheeks.

"Mr. Dylan, do come in," Rachel said with enthusiasm.

"I'm on my way to pick up Henry for our evening out; I just wanted to stop by and let you know there's a letter for you at the post." Rachel was oddly disappointed that he had only come to deliver a message.

"A letter?" she asked. She realized distractedly again how handsome he was in a gallant yet rugged sort of way.

"I believe it's from San Francisco." Chase gave a smile, nodded, and left.

"Excuse me, Veronica." Rachel rushed out the door and hurried up Main Street, toward the post office.

～

Veronica ran out of the schoolhouse behind Rachel and followed Chase. "Mr. Dylan...oh, Mr. Dylan!" she yelled louder.

Chase turned and smiled. "Hello, Veronica. How are you this fine afternoon?"

"I'm fine, thank you, Mr. Dylan. I was wondrin' if you might help me with sumthin'."

"If I can, I certainly will."

Veronica shifted the toe of her shoe in the dirt. "I don't know if Jeremiah's had a chance ta tell you, but we're plannin' ta be married."

"Yes, Jeremiah's told me, and I'm very happy for both of you. A summer wedding, I suppose?"

"That's what I wanted to talk to you about. I will make a good wife, Mr. Dylan. I know how ta cook and keep a nice house. I even know how to grow a garden."

"That's wonderful, Veronica." Chase still thought of Veronica as a little girl. It was disconcerting to realize she was a woman now. He was himself only twenty-eight, but this was making him feel ancient.

"So do you think you might tell my ma that I don't need more schoolin'? I mean, you could tell her how much money Jeremiah makes and then she'd have to let me quit."

"Have you spoken with Jeremiah about this?" Chase's question unnerved the girl and she fidgeted before answering.

"Jeremiah said he's ready to get married and so am I. So why should I have to sit in some schoolroom with a bunch of children for another year?" she whined.

"Veronica, this is really not an issue for me to decide."

"Mr. Dylan, I'm not an old maid like Miss Phillips; what do I need school fer?"

Chase clenched his teeth and kept himself from speaking his mind to this spoiled young girl. He wanted to tell her how obviously she needed more education, but he took a few seconds and calmed down before adding, "Veronica, what Jeremiah makes for his living is his business. If he chooses to share that information with your mother, that's fine, but it's really not my place."

Veronica's face was red with frustration, "So you won't help us either?"

"I'm afraid I cannot," Chase stated calmly.

Veronica stormed off in the direction of Eikerenkotter's Hotel, and Chase, in a quandary, watched her before continuing on his way.

❦

There was a line at the post office when Rachel arrived. Sawyers in their work clothes were anxious to see if there were any letters for them. Rachel's toe was tapping nervously as she waited behind the loggers. Finally, it was her turn. The clerk knowingly reached for a letter from a series of wooden boxes behind the counter and handed it to the town's teacher with a smile. "Welcome to Searsville, Miss Phillips."

"Thank you. Oh, thank you!" Rachel beamed with happiness as she held the letter. She ripped it open anxiously and cried as she saw a little purple footprint at the base of the letter. Rachel's mother must have dipped Georgie's foot in berries and stamped the stationery.

"That must be quite a letter. From a beau, perhaps?" Mrs. Steele's sweet voice lacked sincerity, but Rachel was determined not to make an enemy of the widow. She did not want to be the topic of this week's sewing circle.

"It's from my mother. See here?" Rachel thrust the letter in front of Mrs. Steele. "This is my baby brother's footprint. Have you ever seen anything so precious?" Rachel's voice broke.

"No, I most certainly haven't," Mrs. Steele droned.

Mrs. Steele's sarcasm was intolerable. Rachel pocketed her letter and decided she would wait until she was home to read it. She wanted to relish every word, and Mrs. Steele's presence would make that impossible.

"Good day, Mrs. Steele," Rachel said with a forced smile.

"Oh Miss Phillips, will we see you tonight at the quilting meeting?"

"That's right, it's Tuesday. I'm afraid not, I have lessons to prepare," she concluded with finality.

"What a *pity*." Mrs. Steele's tone indicated that Rachel would not be asked back to the weekly quilting parties.

What a relief, she thought. Rachel picked up her skirt and rushed home, anxious to devour her mother's handwritten words.

⟁

"What a day," Chase sighed to himself as he was approaching the Steele residence to pick up Henry for their evening together. First, Jeremiah had let him know he'd caused a small scandal by walking with Rachel from the woods, then he was accosted by Veronica. And now he was on his way to deal with Gretchen Steele.

There had been a brief moment when the day seemed like it might redeem itself; Rachel had seemed happy to see him. However, after his own meeting with Veronica, he suspected she was just relieved to have been interrupted. Henry caught sight of Chase through the window and came running.

"Mr. Dylan, Mr. Dylan!" Henry flew over the steps from the porch.

"Well, that sure improves my day. How's my boy?" Chase asked, while patting him on the back.

"I'm fine. I started school, and I'm learning my sums good."

"You're learning them *well*, Henry."

"Yeah, I'm learning them well. How did you know, did Miss Phillips tell ya?"

Chase laughed at the misunderstanding. "No, but I'm sure she would have if I'd asked her. You keep up the good work; a train engineer needs to know his sums."

"Mama's not home yet, she went to the post office. Milly's in the house making dinner. What are we gonna do tonight?"

"We're going to plant redwood trees." Henry looked up in wonder. "You'll see, it will be fun," Chase promised.

Rachel arrived home to find a note from Mrs. Hopper. A neighbor woman had taken ill and Mrs. Hopper was attending to the family's dinner before going to the evening sewing circle. Grateful for the quiet house, Rachel made herself some tea and sat down at the kitchen to savor her mother's letter.

August 30, 1863

Dear Rachel,

You've only been gone a few days, but it seems like years. I never knew how much I would miss you. I can't believe my daughter is a schoolteacher; it makes me so proud. How many children are in your class? What are the people of Searsville like? You'll have to give me all the details.

Life here remains the same. Georgie has started to sleep through the night, so that's one nice change. I think he misses you. He looks around when he's eating his breakfast and I tell him, "We'll see your big sister at Christmastime." Georgie signed this letter with his breakfast—blackberry preserves. I think he's an artist, don't you?

Marshall hired a nurse to help with Georgie. I can't say I'm very fond of the idea, but it is helpful when I'm hosting a luncheon for the wives of Marshall's business associates. My life has become so different, I must really work to make time for God. It seems so funny, I should have more time than ever, but praying comes much harder.

Marshall is certainly busy. Between the politics of the railroad and housing the continuous flow of businessmen headed to the Comstock Lode in Nevada, we barely see him. In addition to work, he's become very vocal lately in regard to the Civil War. He's been to a few Union rallies and has even hosted a fund-raiser for the Sanitation Committee, which provides assistance for victims of the war. If it weren't for the rallies and the occasional volunteer in uniform, you'd never know there was a war on at all! I guess where you are, you probably don't hear anything about it. How I envy you.

There's so much building going on here constantly. I have no fear for your job because I see the lumber coming in a steady stream through the city. Whenever I see a lumber wagon, I think that wood

*might have passed right by my daughter. My darling, I will have
to write more later, Marshall is bringing men home for dinner, so
I need to get cleaned up. I love you and miss you. Please take care of
yourself.*

Serving Him with you,
Mother

Rachel was saddened by the letter; something seemed amiss with the woman she knew so well. Her mother's life had changed so much, Rachel wondered if she would know her when they met again. It was a silly thought. In her head, she knew that, but her emotions overruled her reason as she longed to embrace her family.

Chapter 7

Chase sat comfortably on the love seat of the Steele home, waiting for Henry, who was in the kitchen packing a supper with Milly. "Chase, what a pleasure to see you," Gretchen Steele cooed as she entered the home.

"Gretchen, you act like you weren't expecting me." Her games were beginning to wear on the sawyer. He rose from his chair and called for Henry to hurry up.

"Oh Chase, really. You're such fun," Gretchen said, dismissing the comment. "What are you handsome men up to this evening?"

"We're going to plant redwood trees above the lake."

"What fun. Now, what's this little rumor I hear about you and our new schoolteacher?" She had asked the question casually, yet Chase recognized the desperation in her voice.

"I wish there was something to tell," Chase answered, hoping to put an end to the town talk. His choice of words could not have proven more careless.

Gretchen Steele's eyes flashed with jealously, and she blatantly ignored the comment. "Henry darling, Mr. Dylan is ready to leave," Gretchen managed to say as she quickly hustled the pair out of the house. "I haven't waited around this one-horse town all these years for nothing, Chase Dylan, and I'm certainly not going to let any bright-eyed schoolteacher take you away." The comment was spoken to the back of the door. "I have a plan."

❧

"Rachel dear, are you all right?" Thelma entered the kitchen from the back door, her face drawn and weary.

"Yes, I'm fine, Thelma. I've just had a letter from Mother, so I'm a little homesick."

"You're home now, you must remember that. Think how proud your mama must be to know you're supporting yourself and teaching all those children." Thelma gently rubbed Rachel's back. Rachel smiled. The thought was little comfort, but the touch helped a great deal.

"Thelma, I've been meaning to tell you, God must have put you to work planning those lunch baskets. There were exactly five children without meals. It has been such a blessing to have food for them."

"Well, we wouldn't be Christians if we didn't take care of the wee ones, now would we? Speaking of which, I'll be home late tonight from sewing and off early in the morning to help Mrs. Kramer with her children while she's ill. So if you need anything before then, leave a note on the kitchen table."

"Mrs. Hopper, truly, you're going to wear yourself out."

"Maybe, my dear, but if I'm going to wear myself out, I might as well accomplish something in the process." Thelma's hand rested on Rachel's shoulder. "I'm exhausted. I'll be resting a bit before the quilting circle."

⟋⟍

Chase carried a leather satchel containing his Bible and four redwood saplings wrapped in cloth. He sat alongside Henry by the peaceful evening lake and began his lesson. "I'm going to read from the Bible, Henry."

Chase opened his black leather Bible. "I'll be reading from the Gospel according to Saint Matthew, chapter 13, beginning with verse 3: 'Behold a sower went forth to sow; and when he sowed, some seeds fell by the way side, and the fowls came and devoured them up: Some fell upon stony places, where they had not much earth: and forthwith they sprung up, because they had no deepness of earth; and when the sun was up, they withered away. And some fell among thorns; and the thorns sprung up, and choked them. But others fell into good ground, and brought forth fruit, some an hundredfold, some sixtyfold, some thirtyfold.'" Chase's arms exploded wildly with expression as he read.

"Do you understand this story that Jesus told, Henry?"

"No sir." Henry's head dropped.

Sensing his frustration, Chase said, "Henry, I didn't understand it the first time I read it either. That's why we're here, to learn together." Henry lit up, and Chase went on. "The seed is the Message of Jesus Christ. We'll use these redwood saplings as our seeds. The first one fell by the way side." Chase put the sapling on top of the packed earth of the path around the lake. "You see, if we leave this here on the path, it would never sprout. Someone would come along and step on it and it would be carried away, not allowed to grow. When someone hears the message of God and doesn't understand it, the wicked one will come and snatch it away. Do you understand?"

The six-year-old nodded positively. "Mr. Dylan, we have to get the baby tree or someone will take it," Henry said fearfully.

"We'll get it soon, Henry. Let's talk about the second set of seeds. Jesus said that these seeds fell on stony soil." Chase laid the second sapling under the stones of the rocky shore of the lake. "Will this tree grow here?" Chase's hand pointed toward the sapling.

"No. There's no dirt; the roots couldn't sink in."

"That's right, Henry! In the Bible, the soil is people's hearts. This is the person who hears the message of God and it brings him joy, but it lasts only a short time, and he falls away from the Lord because his heart did not accept the Word."

"Oh yeah!" said Henry, happily understanding.

"Now, what about the third seed? Jesus said it fell among thorns." Chase put the third sapling in a nearby bush. "This is a hard one. Why won't the tree grow here?"

"Because there's no dirt again."

"That's right, but there's also a lot of things surrounding the tree, isn't there? This is the man who hears the message but is too caught up in the things of this world to care."

"The things of this world?" Henry inquired.

"The things of this world could be anything that you put before God. For some people that means nice things like furniture or gold pieces. For others, it could be knowledge or travel. All those things *choke* the Word, like the third sapling. Do you understand?" Henry nodded once again.

Chase took the final sapling and a shovel to a soft spot in a clearing. He dug a hole and dropped the sapling in, covering its roots with the loose soil.

"This one will grow, Mr. Dylan!" shouted Henry excitedly.

"That's right, Henry. This is the man who hears the Word of God, embraces it, and lives to spread the Word, through good works and by telling others about Jesus."

Henry clapped wildly and Chase felt as though he had just finished a one-act play. *This time with Henry is so special,* Chase thought. *I have learned so much about my heavenly Father by sharing it with this child.*

❧

The quilting circle had gathered at Mrs. Thorne's house, and the evening was off to a rough start: Mrs. Thorne complained she had just listened to an hour of her daughter's whining; she was still trying to convince her mother that she should be allowed to marry. Mrs. Hopper was exhausted from serving Mrs. Kramer all day. Gretchen's grumpy mood remained a mystery. Had the women seen Chase Dylan leaving her home with Henry, the women probably would have made a good guess. Mrs. Irving and Mrs. Davenport were the only women who arrived anxious to begin quilting.

"You were right about Maria Lathrop last week, she's starting to show," Mrs. Hopper said, her hands sewing rapidly.

"I told you, those Californios don't waste any time," Mrs. Thorne added, a hint of disgust in her voice.

"We better see to it that she stays away from our pretty young school-teacher. All that pretty little thing needs is a husband, and that's the end of Searsville education for a while," Mrs. Irving offered.

Gretchen was very interested in the conversation, dropping her sewing to concentrate fully upon it. Suddenly she blurted, "I've heard it said that our Miss Phillips has a checkered past." Gretchen's eyes were transfixed on her resumed sewing, her gaze never meeting any of the intrigued women's.

"Oh, really now, Gretchen. Miss Phillips is far too young to have such a past," Mrs. Irving said, her tone begging for more details. Mrs. Hopper looked on in intrigued terror as they discussed her boarder.

"Well, if you don't believe *me*, I suggest one of you ask her about her baby *brother*. I think you'll find there's more to the story." The women gasped, and Gretchen took apparent satisfaction in their reaction.

The rest of the evening was quiet at the sewing circle. The group was ruminating over such a juicy tidbit, thinking about who they would tell first and the reactions sure to be had. Thelma Hopper had a different reaction altogether; she appeared agitated and speculated aloud how best to evict her young friend who was no longer a suitable boarder. The women silently sympathized, but no one offered a suggestion.

Rachel woke feeling spry, although she had once again been up late into the night preparing for the day's lessons. A new teaching method had her anxious to get to school, and she selected a bright green dress with matching bonnet to match her mood.

Walking up Main Street, Rachel felt the townspeople's eyes boring through her. *Perhaps this dress is too much.* The young teacher was tempted to turn around to change her clothes, but reasoned by the town's reaction that might only be worse. Once inside the classroom, everything seemed normal. All of the children were happily playing outside, and Rachel sought refuge behind her large desk. *I'll just remain at my desk today, and tomorrow I'll wear my usual dark skirt and white shirt.*

Miss Phillips called to Henry to come and ring the bell. The students were soon in their desks, with the exception of Veronica Thorne.

"Does anyone know where Miss Thorne is this morning?" All heads shook. "Very well, let's get started, shall we?"

"Miss Phillips, I'd like to have a word with you." Mrs. Thorne stood in the doorway, her voice echoing loudly throughout the room.

"Very well, Mrs. Thorne." Rachel was upset to have her lesson interrupted, but knew Mrs. Thorne would never impose unless it was important. "Children, please take out today's reading assignments and begin reading quietly to yourselves." Rachel followed Mrs. Thorne outside, irritated that her selection of dress was probably to blame.

"Mrs. Thorne, if this is about my gown. . . ."

"Miss Phillips, you know perfectly well this is *not* about your gown. I don't know how you thought you could keep such a secret, but it's out now. I cannot think of anything you have left to teach my daughter. I have decided to let her quit school and marry Jeremiah at once. He will provide a decent and respectable life for her, which is more than she will learn from you."

"Mrs. Thorne, I beg your pardon, but I don't know what you're talking about." Rachel was shocked by the intensity of the insinuations, and her hands went up in questioning protest.

"Look, Miss Phillips, save your excuses for someone else. The men in this town don't care what you've done; most of them are runaways from somewhere, anyway. You can find yourself a husband easily enough in one of them sawyers, so why don't you do so and quit this teaching business. Apparently, most of the mothers don't care about your past. That's why you have a schoolroom full of children. But my husband and I are decent folk and we will not have our daughter taught by such a. . .such a. . . No, I will not say it; I will do the Christian thing and rise above it." Mrs. Thorne stormed away in a huff.

The young woman stood bewildered. *What on earth was that all about?* Rachel was upset, but not angry. Mrs. Thorne obviously had been led astray about something and Rachel actually felt sorry for her. *What could I have done that would cause Mrs. Thorne to allow her daughter marry at sixteen without finishing her education?* Rachel shrugged her shoulders and reentered her classroom, determined to clear up the situation after school. She was thrown by the encounter, and decided to save her special lesson plans for another time.

"Class, please take out your slates. We're going to work on our numbers."

Chapter 8

The overpowering smell of smoke from the fire forced Chase and Robert to hold their conversation outside the blacksmith shop. Robert had been shoeing a team of oxen before hearing the awful rumor, courtesy of a visit by Gretchen Steele. He had sent word to Chase immediately.

"A baby. That's ridiculous. Rachel couldn't be but eighteen, with a teaching certificate," Chase replied indignantly.

"I know it, Chase. But that's what's going around town. They're saying her baby brother is not her brother at all, but her *own child*." Mr. Lathrop's tone was serious.

"That's what's wrong with this town, Robert. They desperately need someone to teach them arithmetic, and then they run her out of town when she comes. You have a copy of her teaching papers, right?"

"Of course. She graduated in June of this year in San Francisco," Mr. Lathrop announced. "I've got a copy of the credentials back at the house."

"Well, according to Rachel, her baby brother is almost four months old, and if we count backward, then that puts his birthdate at about the same time, correct?"

"Correct." Robert was smiling now, liking where Chase was headed.

"Then I'd say our Miss Phillips is more talented than we've given her credit for, Mr. Lathrop. She was able to finish her studies, graduate from teaching school, and have a child all in the same month. What a woman! We shouldn't be stoning her, we should be applauding her!" Chase's face was red with exasperation.

"Well, Chase. We do have a serious problem. The town's perception is more important than the truth right now, and I don't know if Rachel will ever get her good name back."

"Does she know?" Chase asked.

"No. Apparently she had a run-in this morning with Mrs. Thorne, but she's ignorant of the reason." Robert's chin dropped as he thought of the young schoolteacher.

"Do you want me to tell her?" Chase's voice was soft. How he wanted to hold her in his arms again and make her troubles disappear.

"No, Chase. I think that would only embarrass her further. Maria and I are going to sit down with her tonight. We thought it best that she get through the day."

"Please let me know if there's anything I can do." Chase knew what he wanted to do. He wanted to protect her from these awful words. He wanted to let her remain unaware of them forever.

"I will, Chase, and thank you." Robert walked slowly back to the blacksmith shop.

⟨✦⟩

"Miss Phillips, I think it would be best if you were to find other living arrangements. What a pity you weren't honest with me from the beginning; we might have worked something out." Thelma's head shook back and forth. Gone was the grandmotherly concern she had always shown toward Rachel.

Things were beginning to get out of hand and Rachel was losing her patience. "Thelma, what is going on around here? All day I've been a leper, and now, with no notice, you're asking me to move out? What have I done? No one will say a word. Won't you at least tell me what I've done?"

"I'm sorry, my dear. You cannot deny your past any more. You must know I have no choice but to ask you to leave. I've worked long and hard to fix my reputation in Searsville and it just wouldn't be proper for you to remain here. I live here most of the year by myself, and I can't afford to lose my friends."

Rachel, still stunned by the cryptic answer, finally accepted the eviction. "I'll be out by morning, Mrs. Hopper. Thank you for your hospitality." The words were said with sincerity, and Thelma appeared momentarily wounded.

Rachel walked slowly up the wooden stairs and made her way to her beloved blue room. She would no longer wake up to the sun's reflection from the lake or sleep under the handmade, star-patterned quilt. *Moving again,* Rachel thought, *and this time I truly have nowhere to go. Oh heavenly Father! What are You trying to teach me in all this?* Rachel dropped to the bed and let her head sink deeply into her pillow.

⟨✦⟩

The Davenport General Store buzzed with "customers" late Wednesday afternoon.

"Mrs. Steele, have you heard? Jeremiah and I are to be married next month. I've already ordered my wedding dress from the catalogue. The dress will be like nothing Searsville has ever seen, not even on you, Mrs. Steele."

"Married?" Gretchen managed to reply, ignoring the remark. "You can't be serious. Surely your mother wouldn't let you *marry* over this simple scandal."

"My mother says that woman has nothing left to teach me, so she said Jeremiah and I could be married right away. Have you ever heard anything more romantic?" Veronica asked.

The general store continued to hum around them with the latest developments, including rumors of twins and the severe financial burden placed upon Rachel's mother, left to care for the abandoned children.

"Pardon me, Veronica. I'm not feeling very well." Gretchen excused herself.

"Hello, Gretchen. What brings you out this afternoon?" She was stopped by Chase's entrance. He eyed her wearily.

"Chase, I needed. . .you know, I. . .I needed some flour, but it seems Mr. and Mrs. Davenport are unusually busy today, so I'll just come back tomorrow." Mrs. Steele ran into a large barrel displayed near the doorway as she tried to make a hasty exit. Chase looked back at the young widow before walking to the rear of the store. As he made his way to the counter, the buzzing conversation abruptly died down. He glanced about the room suspiciously.

"I've never seen Mrs. Steele quite so agitated. Do you think she's ill?" Chase inquired of Mrs. Davenport, who was displaying a new set of gold earrings in the glass case.

"I'm sure she's very well. She's just upset by the news. You know, her son is a student of Miss Phillips." Mrs. Davenport whispered the last statement as though her comment should be understood perfectly.

"I'm sure I don't know what you mean, Mrs. Davenport. I've heard Miss Phillips is an excellent teacher, sent with the highest qualifications and the best of recommendations." Chase had increased his volume purposely. It was time the women of this town came clean.

"Of course, Mr. Dylan, of course. I was only. . ." Mrs. Davenport stammered the words. "But you know, it is up to us as a community to ensure decency."

"Here's my list, Mrs. Davenport. I'll be back tomorrow to get my supplies." Chase thrust the list into Mrs. Davenport's waiting hands; his patience had worn thin, and he needed to pray.

✑

"Rachel, do you understand what we're trying to tell you?" Maria's voice was gentle and quiet. She rose from her pine kitchen table and placed her arm around Rachel.

"They think I had a child?" Rachel's meek voice was incredulous.

"Rachel, we know it's impossible to believe, but somehow. . .somewhere your little brother became your son." Robert tried to explain.

"So, we'll just explain that he's *not* my son."

"Oh Rachel, I wish it were that simple. Searsville's sewing circles. . . Let's just say truth is subjective and, quite frankly, unimportant," Robert said. "As we speak, I'm sure a committee has been formed to demand your expulsion from the school."

"Well, I'm *not* leaving. It's that simple. I am committed to teaching school through next June, and I intend to fulfill my agreement, all of it."

Maria's gentle voice was low and concerned. "Rachel, we'd like nothing better and we admire your fortitude, but I think it's only fair to warn you just how cruel the rumor mill can be. You will probably not notice any change in the way the men treat you. However, the women will be brutal. Believe me, I know firsthand. And, unfortunately, I don't think I would have any positive influence over their behavior. If you decide to stay, we will support you completely, but we want you to know what you're up against."

Rachel was pained by Maria's words, but with them came a full understanding. *Maria knows how the town's women persecute her and she's preparing me for the same fate.* Rachel remembered the words she had heard regarding Maria; they were hateful, ugly lies, and yet the town regarded them as truth. *Will I be able to withstand the same fate?*

"We shall form an alliance, Maria. I will not let them win." Rachel was insolent; she was determined to show the women of Searsville who was stronger.

"Come what may, the Lord will be here for us." Maria's words were said as much for herself as for the schoolteacher.

At the time, Rachel didn't think about the Lord or praying; she only thought about how she had survived alone thus far.

Chase's pace was heavy along the quiet country path as he left Davenport General Store and walked north toward the Lathrop's ranch. The store had been teaming with gossips, each relishing the latest dirt about his Rachel. *His* Rachel, that's how he felt about her, and yet there was nothing he could do to keep her from this pain.

Chase prayed silently. It wasn't his usual type of prayer; it was angry and questioning. *Lord, I just don't understand. Why would You bring Rachel to Searsville, only to have her tormented by gossip? She's done nothing to deserve this, and she's just not strong enough. What can I do to protect her, Lord? Being a man, anything I say or do will only make her cause worse! What would You have me do? I think I love her.*

Chase stood in front of the Lathrop's one-story adobe home, wondering why he had come. What could he possibly say to Rachel to make things better? Looking down at his black trousers and fidgeting with his suspenders, he pondered what to do next. The Lord had been quiet, and Chase's path remained obscure.

"Rachel." Chase was surprised to see her walking from the Lathrop's garden, looking lovely in a bright green dress, and without a hint of tears. He had expected to find her shattered by the news of the rumor. Instead, she had a fresh blush on her cheeks and her hair was casually knotted down her back.

Rachel's eyes brightened at the sight of him, and Chase noticed with delight that her animosity toward him had disappeared. "Chase, what a pleasure to see you. Are you in town to pick up Henry? He's one of my favorites, you know, and I'm so glad you spend time with him." Rachel wiped her hands on the apron she wore.

"No, that was yesterday. I was at the Davenports' store dropping off a list. How are you?" His last words were soft and said tentatively.

"I'm fine, thank you." There was no sadness in the voice, and Chase was left to wonder if Maria and Robert had had a chance to speak with her about the rumor. Perhaps he would have to tell her after all. "It's a shame to waste this beautiful evening," she said. "Would you care to go for a walk?"

Chase was taken aback by the suddenly talkative Rachel, but loved it, and extended his arm quickly before she changed her mind.

Rachel unconsciously felt her hair. "My hair's down. Would you mind waiting just a minute?" Chase wanted to tell her he'd wait forever, but he simply nodded. She slipped back inside the Lathrop home.

Moments later, Rachel dashed out the door, telling Maria about her walk. Robert and Maria jumped up from the dinner table and followed her to the porch. "Perhaps a chaperone would be in order. Maria and I can follow behind you with Seth," Robert offered.

"Robert, I will not have these vicious lies rule my conduct. Mr. Dylan and I will be strolling along the most populated path in all of Searsville, our innocent intentions abundantly evident," Rachel answered vehemently.

Rachel stepped off the porch, and Chase pressed his large hand gently against the small of her back to lead the way. He felt her small frame shiver at his touch, and they looked at one another in acknowledgment. They had indeed developed stronger feelings.

Rachel tossed her head back carelessly. "We'll be near the lake if you need us."

The Lathrops silently rejoiced at seeing the feud they had witnessed for weeks end, but Maria nevertheless looked worried about the two of them being seen together.

"We'll be home before supper," Chase announced.

"Oh my goodness, *home*. I have nowhere to live," Rachel exclaimed to the astonishment of everyone.

"What?" Robert asked.

"Mrs. Hopper has asked me to leave her home," Rachel now said meekly, looking shyly up at Chase, mortified that he might believe the rumor.

"Why, that traitor!"

"Chase Dylan!" The reprimand came from Maria. Rachel covered her mouth, giggling happily at the comment. "And Rachel Phillips! You're no better." Maria again tried to maintain decorum, wagging her finger at her friends, but soon the entire foursome was laughing.

"Rachel, go for your walk and then we'll see you both for dinner. We'll find you a place to live by morning," Robert reassured her.

"Thank you, *all* of you, for your support." Rachel's voice trembled, her throat too tight to say more. She took Chase's arm and they strolled in harmony toward the lake.

"So, we're going to the lake?" Chase asked, his heavy, work-hardened build dwarfing the petite woman by his side.

"I like the lake. It calms me. And quite frankly, I could use a little tranquillity right about now."

"Rachel, do you mind if I ask what you plan to do?" Chase was too polite to mention any details.

Her answer was enough for Chase to know she now trusted him. "I plan to do nothing about it." Her voice was defiant, and her dark green eyes stared directly at Chase's own. "And if you don't mind, I'd just as soon drop the subject. Why don't you tell me what you do every day, out in the woods?" She was so close, he felt her warmth through his soft sleeve.

"I guess it depends on the day, but most days I work at the mill."

"And what happens at the mill?" Rachel's tone was cheeky.

"You know, Rachel, I was wrong to say what I did about Mrs. Hopper," Chase said.

"Yes, I know, Chase. And please forgive me for taking pleasure in your remark. I just felt so betrayed by Thelma asking me to leave. It meant she believed the filthy lies when all she had to do was ask me. She didn't even give me the chance to explain."

"Rachel, if it makes you feel any better, I don't think she believes the rumor. I think she's just worried about her status in the community."

"That's almost worse."

"Yes, I know." Chase patted Rachel's hand sympathetically. Their eyes met, and they both turned away instantly, afraid of where the look might lead.

"That's enough of such depressing talk. Tell me what it is you do at the mill," Rachel urged earnestly.

"It just depends on what needs to be done. I have two steam saws at my mill. Most of my day is spent ensuring that those saws are running continuously. Often, that means I'm fixing them or the boiler they depend upon. Sometimes I'm out on the ridge making sure a downed tree has been cut into manageable pieces and that the oxen will have it to the mill on time."

"Whenever I see those oxen coming down Main Street, I run for cover," Rachel said.

"They are intimidating, but I have an excellent bullmaster, and he keeps them in line. Soon, I plan to run as many as ten saws. I've met with a man in Redwood who can make it happen."

"Oh Chase, that *would* be exciting." The young couple had arrived at the lake just as the large, red sun was setting behind the forested mountain, creating a tapestry of pink and blue in the sky. Caught up in the pleasure of the natural beauty around them, the conversation stopped, and Chase turned toward Rachel.

Gazing into her exquisite forest-green eyes, Chase was lost in his feelings for her. "Rachel." He closed his eyes and drew her close. Rachel cuddled against his strong chest and seemed to forget her troubles. "I hope that I might save enough money to build a small cabin right here. It shouldn't cost too much. After all, I know somebody in the lumber business." Rachel smiled flirtatiously at the mill owner.

"Miss Phillips?" A small voice caused the couple to immediately separate.

"Henry. Does your mother know you're out here alone?" Rachel obviously was flustered, but her voice remained calm.

"He's not alone." Gretchen Steele's eyes squinted with bitterness as she sidled up to the couple. "We were out for a pleasant walk along the lake," she said, her voice dripping with sarcasm. "I guess we weren't the only ones with such an idea."

"Gretchen, I think. . ." Chase started to explain.

"Chase, I don't need an explanation from you. You're a grown man; you may do what you please. But as our schoolteacher, Miss Phillips," Mrs. Steele scrutinized the young woman, pointing her manicured finger, "I should think you would be concerned for your reputation. What's left of it, anyway."

"That's enough, Gretchen!" Chase shouted, his face red with anger. Locking his arm around Rachel, he led her back toward the Lathrops' home. She was distraught, and her tears were flowing easily now. Chase turned his head, directing one final comment at the angry widow. "I will deal with you later, Mrs. Steele."

Such formal address by Chase was a rarity, Gretchen knew. "I'll never dig my way out of this. He'll never forgive me." Gretchen dropped her head into her hands.

"Do you mean Mr. Dylan, Mama?" Gretchen had forgotten all about the presence of her son.

"Yes, honey. It seems I've made him angry."

"He'll forgive you, Mama. I know, because that's what Jesus would do and Chase wants to be like Jesus." His face shone up at her like a full moon. He placed his hands on her belly. "Just ask him."

"Yes, dear. Let's go home." The woman somberly led her son from the lake.

Chapter 9

Robert sighed in frustration. "Maria, it's much worse than I thought. I've been to every summer widow's home in town. No one will take her in. I've never seen them band together this tightly. They're impenetrable. I'm watching it happen again, and I'm powerless to stop it!"

"Robert, please calm down. Rachel and Chase are coming up the walk; they'll hear you. Rachel will just have to stay here in Seth's room until we can find something more suitable for her."

"But with the baby coming. . ."

"The baby won't be here for six more months. We'll certainly have found her a place by then."

"If she isn't stoned first." Seeing the doorknob rotate, Robert changed his tone instantly. "How was your walk?"

Rachel's eyes were red and it was obvious she'd been crying. "I think I'll go freshen up before dinner. Do you mind, Maria?"

"By all means, Rachel. Use our room; there's clean water and a towel on the dresser."

With Rachel out of the room, Robert addressed Chase angrily. "What have you done now?"

Chase lifted his hands. "I assure you, Robert, this time I'm innocent. Mrs. Steele is behind this." As soon as he said the words, he knew they were not entirely true. He'd had no right to embrace Rachel. He had made no profession of his feelings, no suggestion of commitment toward her.

Rachel would be the talk of the town again, and this time it would be *his* fault. "I really must be going. Please tell Rachel I said good-bye." Chase decided it best to plead Rachel's case to Mrs. Steele.

❧

Rachel sat on the Lathrop's bed and wept, using the towel to drown her sobs. She felt an arm around her, and Maria's head came to rest upon her shoulder. "It's all right; let it out."

"Maria, why? Why would God let this happen?"

"I don't know, Rachel. That's not really for us to question. God always

225

knows what's best for His children. We must remember that evil is at work in Searsville right now. We must pray, pray for the women who torment us."

"Why would I want to pray for them, Maria? I don't care if they—"

"Rachel, don't say such things! It is precisely because you don't want to pray for these women that we must."

Rachel knew Maria's words were true. She had heard her mother telling her to pray for those who persecute since before she knew what the word meant. But now, as the enemy became so real, it was a much more difficult task.

"Maria, you wouldn't pray for them if you knew what they said about *you*." Rachel spat out the words like a child.

"You mean, that I'm always barefoot and pregnant or that I smell like Mexican spice?" Maria laughed while Rachel's mouth gaped.

"You know what they say?"

"You know, the funny thing is, most of them have more children than I do. That's why I can't let it bother me, Rachel. God's truth is eternal. Theirs lasts until the next rumor proves otherwise."

"Maria, I'm afraid it isn't all lies."

"What do you mean?"

"During our walk, I allowed Chase to embrace me."

"Has he declared his feelings toward you?"

"No."

"I see." Maria paused to word her next question carefully. "And do you think you were seen together?"

"Yes, I know we were. By Mrs. Steele and Henry." Maria closed her eyes and Rachel understood her frustration.

"Let's not worry about it now. I've got dinner on the table. We'll pray about it and decide what to do after dinner. By the way, Robert and I think it best if you stay here for a while." The words brought instant comfort, and Rachel relaxed about finding a new home.

✍

Chase knocked briskly three times. He would have to contain his anger if he was to speak rationally to Gretchen about the events of this evening.

"Chase. What a delight to see you. I want to make it clear, I'm not upset with you. But certainly you must take my advice on how it looks for you to be seen with the likes of that schoolteacher."

"Gretchen, I think we need to talk." His tone was firm.

"Of course, Chase. Please come in and make yourself at home. I've got coffee brewing; I was expecting you."

Chase took a seat in the parlor on the burgundy chair near the window. Gretchen followed him closely and sat upon the footrest adjacent to the chair, rather than the sofa across the room. Uncomfortable with her proximity, Chase slid back in his seat, arranging his long legs so that his right ankle rested on his left knee.

"Gretchen, I need to speak with you about Miss Phillips... Where is Henry, by the way?"

"Don't worry, Henry's in bed. Chase, what more can I tell you? If you want to salvage your reputation, you need to forget about her." She continued without giving him a chance to answer. "It's obvious you've let yourself be blinded by her beauty. You must know what kind of woman they say she is."

"She is a very sweet and naive young woman who has been sorely misjudged by this town."

"Not according to what I just witnessed by the lake," she sniffed.

"I allowed myself to comfort Rachel in an inappropriate fashion, and I will apologize to her for that, but I would appreciate it if word of this did not spread."

"Chase, you know *I* would never say anything, but this did happen at the lake. Who knows who might have been peering out their window as you *touched* her? You know, Chase, I have to think about my son. It's bad enough that he must be taught by her, but if you're going to continue embracing the young women in town, perhaps Henry shouldn't spend any more time with you either."

"Gretchen, you're making more of this than is necessary. I will explain everything to Henry."

"I don't want you explaining your immoral behavior to my son."

"Gretchen, you're being unreasonable."

"Why, because I don't want my son learning scandalous conduct?" They sat eye to eye, locked in battle, Chase witnessing her true character for the first time. He would have to relent; he must think of Henry.

"Very well, Gretchen. I can see we're not getting anywhere. I hope we'll be able to discuss this later. Good night." Chase rose to leave, and Gretchen was visibly upset.

"Chase, please don't go. I'm sorry," Gretchen said, tugging on his plaid shirt. His demeanor softened.

"Gretchen, what I did was not right. I have admitted that and now I think a little forgiveness is in order. You know perfectly well that I would never do anything to harm my relationship with Henry."

"Yes, I know, Chase." Gretchen reached for Chase's hands and held them firmly.

"Now, I'm asking you as longtime friends..." Chase's blue eyes pierced her own. "Will you please let this go?"

"Yes, Chase. Consider it forgotten." And for the moment, it was.

"Thank you, Gretchen." Chase gripped the widow's hands briefly and turned to exit.

"Chase, the coffee should be ready," she mentioned quickly.

"I can't stay, but thank you."

"Will we see you Tuesday? For Henry?"

"Of course," Chase answered kindly.

∽

"Rachel, where have you been? I was beginning to worry; it's well past dark." Mrs. Hopper was waiting in her sitting parlor, staring out the large window.

"I've been looking for a room, Mrs. Hopper," Rachel responded without emotion.

"Did you find one, honey? I'm sorry I didn't provide more notice, but you do understand, dear," Thelma replied guiltily.

"Yes, thank you. I will be living at the Lathrops, starting tomorrow."

"The Lathrops? But, my dear, they have a child, with another on the way. And she's a Calif—"

"Yes, I know. I'm afraid I have very little choice in the matter, but to impose upon them. I'll be helping with some of the household responsibilities." As she said the words, she was reminded of her stepfather's words, *"Of course, we'll need help with the baby for the first year, but then you'll be free to pursue your teaching career."* Would the Lathrops feel the same way? Would she be in the way there, too?

"Miss Phillips, are you all right?" Rachel found it interesting that Thelma was now addressing her formally, just as her stepfather had always done. Rachel felt as though she'd come full circle.

"I'm fine. I'll be turning in now."

"Good night, Miss Phillips," Thelma called after her.

Rachel walked upstairs and sat on her bed. She would miss the fine furniture and surroundings at Mrs. Hopper's. She had never even met Mr. Hopper, and yet she had lived in his home for nearly a month. If only Thelma had given Rachel the benefit of the doubt. She rested her head on her pillow and thought warmly of Chase Dylan and his handsome face; it was a pleasant diversion that sent her dreamily to sleep.

✍

The next morning Rachel awoke for the last time in her cheery, sunlit room. She began the morning by packing her dresses and few personal items in her trunk. She placed her leather Bible on top and closed the heavy lid. She sat on the trunk and gazed one last time at the lovely view. A mallard duck and his mate floated lazily across the tranquil waters, enjoying the bright morning sunshine and its blinding reflection.

"Miss Phillips!" Mrs. Hopper shouted from downstairs, causing Rachel to start from her peaceful reverie.

Wearing only a thin cotton nightgown, Rachel cracked the door. Peering out, she answered, "Yes, Mrs. Hopper."

"Chase Dylan is here for your things."

"Thank you." Rachel tried to sound calm. "If you'll give him a cup of coffee, I'll be right down." Rachel hurried to wash her face and dress. She brushed her hair, quickly pinning it rather sloppily, and ran down the stairs.

"I'm sorry, Rachel. I should have let you know I was coming. I saw Robert in town this morning, he was on his way to get your things, and I took his place." Rachel breathed quickly with excitement.

"Wonderful. I should have packed last night, but I was overly tired." They exchanged a harrowed look. "My trunk is upstairs. I'll help you bring it down."

"That's okay, I'm sure I can handle it." Rachel felt her unkempt hair and was suddenly self-conscious. She excused herself and ran upstairs to fix her hair. When she returned, she was rewarded by the most sincere smile she had seen on a man since her father died two years earlier.

"Rachel, would you mind if I had a word with you outside before you leave for the schoolhouse?" Chase opened the door at the bottom of the stairs and looked to Rachel expectantly. Mrs. Hopper watched with meddlesome interest.

"Certainly, Chase." He extended his arm for her to pass.

Rachel walked down the steps and behind the house so that she could see the lake.

"What is it?" Rachel didn't care what his words were. This morning she was happy just seeing his bluish-green eyes and his freshly shaven jaw line. His clean scent floated near her, and she instantly remembered the warm embrace they had shared.

"Rachel, I've had a very long night. I've been praying for most of it and I've come to a conclusion."

His words caused her stomach to churn. *Is he going to declare himself?* she found herself thinking, her heart racing in anticipation.

"Rachel. . ." he looked into her eyes solemnly, "first, let me apologize for yesterday. I shouldn't have held you, in a public place or otherwise. Secondly, I think it's best if we're not seen together for awhile." The words were a stunning blow, and Rachel stiffened with coldness.

She looked at the dusty path, blinking quickly to keep the tears from falling. She would not give him the satisfaction of knowing he'd hurt her. If he wanted to abandon her, just as much of the Searsville population did, that was fine, but she would never let him know she cared.

"Of course. I think that's best." Rachel said the words in strict business fashion, the way she'd heard Marshall say them a dozen times. "I must go; I'll be late for school." Lifting her skirt, she dashed toward the schoolhouse without so much as a cup of tea for breakfast.

Chase remained in place, a look of confusion coming over his face. He had thought they had reached an understanding the previous night. Perhaps he had only caught her during a moment of weakness and had taken advantage of her situation. *Still, she must agree this is best for now. The whole town is talking. We'll be able to see each other as soon as the gossip dies down.*

Chapter 10

I tell you I saw them by the lake, in each other's arms." Gretchen Steele was telling the story with relish, her inflection greatly exaggerated.

"No!" Mrs. Davenport gasped. Just then Mrs. Irving and Mrs. Thorne entered the general store and the story was repeated again with evil delight.

"I knew I was right about her from the very beginning. I'm so glad my daughter will not be attending school any longer," Mrs. Thorne bragged.

"You're so lucky your son's too young to understand any of this, Gretchen," Mrs. Irving said.

"Well, my son was witness to it though. His poor innocent eyes. Afterwards, Henry asked me if they were to be married. Ha! I told him directly that men like Chase do not marry women like her."

"Good for you, Gretchen," Mrs. Davenport affirmed, her head nodding.

"I plan to talk to Mr. Lathrop today about finding a new schoolteacher. We may live in the woods, but that doesn't mean we don't have common decency," Mrs. Irving clucked.

"Amen!" Mrs. Davenport agreed.

The women had banded together in a tight circle near the large wooden barrels. Their tones, which started out hushed, became louder until Mr. Davenport entered from the back room. The conversation was redirected immediately.

"Veronica's wedding is four weeks from Saturday. She's so excited, she's simply impossible to have around," Mrs. Thorne said. The women parted and began milling around the emporium, fingering the latest goods. Mr. Davenport eyed them all suspiciously, but went about his work pricing the latest inventory.

"You're so lucky to have her married off to a fine gentleman like Jeremiah. I hope there's such a man when my April is old enough to wed," Mrs. Davenport commented. Mr. Davenport shook his head at his wife and reentered the back room.

Mrs. Davenport dashed to the back doorway to ensure her husband was safely out of earshot and the circle resumed until Chase Dylan arrived.

Chase was extremely wary, his eyes narrowing in suspicion when he saw the gathering of familiar women in the shop. He looked directly at Gretchen Steele, whose guilt forced her to avert her eyes. Once again, the women separated.

"Mighty popular place you've got today, Mrs. Davenport."

"Yes, Chase. Thursday, you know. Quite a big day for supplies. Speaking of which, I've got yours right here." She lifted a paper-wrapped bundle onto the counter. "That will be $4.10."

Chase paid his bill and collected his goods. As he strolled out the door, he looked back knowingly; he had been deceived by Gretchen Steele. Gretchen's knowing expression and fierce hand-wringing had given her away.

✍

Rachel began to wish she had never gotten out of bed that morning. She was having a difficult time maintaining order at school following her talk with Chase. The children were especially wild this day and seemed to question the schoolteacher's authority continuously. When she had finally had enough, she decided to make an example of the rebellious leader. "Michael Hansen," she said sternly.

"Yes, Miss Phillips," a boy of twelve answered sarcastically, rising from his seat; he stood a full head taller than his teacher.

"Michael, do you see the chalk line I've drawn in the rear corner?" Rachel pointed and Michael turned to look to the back of the classroom.

"Yes, Miss Phillips." His crooked smile remained.

"I'd like you to stand there, facing the corner, for exactly half an hour. I will tell you when your time is up. The rest of you may go outside for recess." The boy stared in defiance and Rachel's eyes met his own in challenge. Sauntering slowly, the boy walked to the rear of the classroom and Rachel exhaled deeply with relief. She had won, this battle, anyway.

The children walked out one by one, each snickering as he or she passed the disconcerted Michael. Rachel hated to make the boy a laughingstock, but it was important she not lose her control in the classroom, especially now. The students' parents might openly discuss her personal life, but she would give them no reason to question her professional capabilities.

"Miss Phillips?" Veronica Thorne had entered the schoolroom and now leaned over the young teacher's desk.

"Veronica, how are you?" Rachel was deeply concerned for the young woman and the seriousness of her tone told the girl so. "Your mother told me you wouldn't be attending class any longer. I must say, I am disappointed. You were one of my most promising students."

Veronica brightened at the unexpected compliment. "Thank you, Miss Phillips. I'm busy planning my weddin', so I don't miss it too much. The weddin's gonna be a potluck at the church, four weeks from Saturday. You will come, won't you?"

Rachel knew Mrs. Thorne would be livid if she knew that her daughter had extended the invitation, but she had every intention of attending Veronica's wedding. Feeling somewhat responsible for the match, she would certainly be there to celebrate the bond.

"I wouldn't miss it, Veronica." Rachel looked at the young woman standing before her; she was beaming with happiness. True, she had gotten her way, but for the first time Rachel felt comfortable with Veronica's decision.

Women were married at sixteen every day, and Veronica's mother had probably been preparing her for marriage from the day Veronica was born. Rachel's own mother had been married at sixteen and bore Rachel at the still-tender age of seventeen.

Veronica broke into Rachel's thoughts. "Well, the reason I came by was to give you my slate. I figure if I'm not gonna use it, you'd be able to give it to one of the older boys when they come back."

"Veronica, that's very generous of you." Rachel took the slate with misgivings. They smiled warmly at one another. No longer were they teacher and student, but friends.

"I better go." Veronica walked toward the door and stopped when she approached the silent figure of Michael Hansen. Veronica lapsed into girlhood: "What ya do, pull somebody's hair? I guess it don't matter, you probably won't do it again." Veronica winked at Rachel and laughed as she exited.

⌇⌇

Chase entered Robert's blacksmith workshop and found his friend bent over a huge black pot, mending a large hole in its base. "Robert?"

Robert put his tools down and stood. "Hello, Chase. I was just thinking about you. I had a little run-in with Gretchen this morning. She was here again to call for the immediate dismissal of our schoolteacher." Robert's teeth were clenched.

"She's been mighty busy this morning. I just saw her over at Davenport's General Store. Do you mind if I ask what you told her?"

"I told her that since I paid Miss Phillips's salary, I would need to pray about the matter. Obviously, I already have, and I'm quite comfortable with my decision to keep the school as it is. But you know how Gretchen can be. I thought it best to appease her for now."

"Thanks, Robert. I appreciate your support and I know Rachel does, too. That's actually why I'm here. I have a favor to ask of you." Chase lowered his voice. "This morning I spoke with Rachel about us not seeing one another for a while. You know, give the town a little time to get used to the idea. With the logging season coming to an end, I'm going to be spending time in Redwood helping the Williamses remodel their hotel for the train's arrival.

"I think we both know who started the rumor about Rachel. Worse still, I think I'm the reason she was targeted. Robert, I want you to watch over her while I'm gone. Protect her from a certain sewing circle until I return." Chase's eyes were pleading.

"I'll do what I can, but I think you're asking the wrong person. I can't even protect my own wife from those women." Robert's head hung in shame. "Go to Redwood, Chase. I'll do my best, but you'd be better off praying."

"Thanks, Robert. I'll be praying for all of you. Say good-bye to Rachel for me, will you?"

"I think that's something you should do yourself," Robert answered.

Chase cast his head downward, thinking hard about seeing Rachel again before leaving, and finally shook his head. "No, I don't think so. It's best for Rachel if we just wait until I get back."

"Well, you take care of yourself and we'll see you when you return." Robert waved and picked up the pot he'd been fixing.

"Tell Maria I'll be back for her home-cooked meals just as soon as I can get here." Chase felt dejected leaving for Redwood now. He wanted to be in Searsville to carry Rachel through this difficult time, but in his heart he knew it was best for her that he leave.

꧁

Rachel grabbed her study plans and left the schoolhouse early, trying to put an end to a troubling day. She was eager to unpack her things and get settled into the Lathrop home. Jaunting along the main route toward the Lathrop ranch, she neared Mrs. Steele, who was mumbling angrily to herself as she headed toward the town center. Rachel decided it was best to avoid her and took a circuitous route off the main road. When she arrived at the house, Maria had already returned from the butcher and was preparing a roast for dinner.

"This house smells divine!" Rachel exclaimed.

"It's a special occasion for the newest member of our family. Well, that and I'm desperately craving roast beef!" Maria laughed and Rachel hugged her. "What was that for?" Maria asked.

"That was for standing by me and giving me a home."

"Rachel, I told you when you came to Searsville that I would always be your friend."

"Maria, you just don't know what that means to me right now," Rachel said. "Often those words represent nothing more than a hollow gesture, but you and Robert have shown that's not true in this house. Thank you.

"Unless you need my help," she continued, "I'm going to go get unpacked. Then I'll be back to finish up dinner so you can get off your feet."

"You go right ahead. I've put Seth down for his nap in our room, so he won't be in your way."

Rachel walked down the hallway to the rear of the house and entered the right bedroom. There were two small beds with matching oak frames. One was decorated with brightly colored bedding and the other a soft rose quilt. Rachel's trunk stood at the foot of the rose-draped bed, and Rachel assumed it was hers.

Although she was thankful for the Lathrops' hospitality, she was still upset that she had been asked to move from the elegantly feminine room at the Hoppers'. She already missed her calming periwinkle-blue bedroom and her view of the lake. Now she would have to share a room with a toddler; it was just too humiliating. This was all Marshall Winsome's fault! What kind of place had her stepfather sent her to? Every town Rachel had ever been in that had a schoolhouse provided a private home for a schoolteacher.

Rachel shook her head in disgust and then decided it was time to get on with her unpacking. She opened the case and saw her Bible lying on top of her things. The sight of it brought back all of the recent events, making her instantly irate and causing her to lash out in silent fury.

Where are You now, God? Where were You when those women accused me of having a child out of wedlock or talked about Maria falsely? Where were You when I gave my heart to Chase, only to find out he was just like all the rest of the people in this godforsaken little town? It seems obvious that You've abandoned me. My family was always so committed to You, and how did You repay us? You took my father when I was only sixteen and left us all alone in the rugged gold country. But that wasn't enough for You, was it? No, You had to have my mother, too. Now she's living at the top of Knob Hill with a pompous man who won't even accept his wife's own daughter. Well, God, You may have my family, but You won't have me. I'm through with this Bible, the church, and with You!

Rachel took her Bible and flung it carelessly onto her bed.

Chase arrived in Redwood shortly before supper. He didn't remember any of the ride, he had been so caught up in worrying about leaving Rachel in Searsville. Seeing his weary horse when they arrived at the livery, he knew he must have ridden hard. Chase paid a man to water and feed his horse and walked next door to the American House.

"Chase Dylan, it's been weeks. Where ya been?" The outstretched arms of Joseph Williams came toward him.

"Chase. We were beginning to wonder if you'd hauled off and got yourself married. You haven't been around for my cooking in so long. . ." Mrs. Williams wore a gay smile, and she wiped her hands on her apron before reaching out for a hug.

"I was just trying to close things up at the mill for the winter. I wanted to be free to help you with the renovations for as long as you need me." Chase momentarily forgot all his troubles as he basked in the warmth of his old friends.

"Well, you just come over here and see what we got planned." Mr. Williams walked behind his heavy wooden counter and pulled out a tightly rolled set of building plans from behind it. He flattened the sheets and held them down with two large, polished rocks. Chase noticed there were dents in the counter where the rocks had been placed many times before. "This here is going to be the missus's new kitchen, and this here is a suite, and over here. . ." The hotelier continued to ramble, and Chase found himself pleasantly diverted from his earlier concerns.

Chapter 11

Three weeks passed and autumn began to appear in Searsville. Very little happened to mark the season's appearance. There were no brightly colored leaves or bitter chill in the air, but the sky often remained cloudy throughout the day and a few light rains soon came.

To the delight of most of Searsville's residents, but to the farmers' dismay, the heavy downpours stayed away. The ranchers met at Davenport General Store and complained about the statewide drought that was now in its second year. The plight of their crops and livestock was now of great concern, and praying for rain became a central topic of discussion.

As the seasons changed, Rachel was relieved that only four, rather than the earlier eight, older boys came to school. Two of them, John and Joseph Duncan, were completely enamored of their beautiful teacher and did their best to please her. The other two, however, were troublemakers from the very first moment they stepped into the schoolroom. They were more concerned with establishing leadership over the other students and impressing the young girls.

Aubrey Dawson was a bully who, at fourteen years of age, stood well over six feet tall. His partner in calamity was Dennis Shine, a short, stocky boy of fifteen. The two boys would typically start their day by placing some type of live critter on the chair of their once unsuspecting teacher. Their particular favorite was the banana slug.

Miss Phillips had accommodated the pranksters for a few days, but after that decided it was time to take action. After school, she asked the two boys to remain for a short discussion. The boys chuckled and smirked, whispering to their classmates that Miss Phillips wanted to declare her love for them both.

Rachel sat behind her desk primly after the other students had left. "Dennis and Aubrey, your behavior in this classroom is completely unacceptable. If I do not see a marked improvement by tomorrow, you will both be sent home for the day."

Dennis and Aubrey laughed out loud. "Our pas would only bring us back. Miss Phillips, we don't mean no harm. We get sent to school so Ma don't have to feed us and put up with us all day. We don't need no educatin'; we're sawyers. Alls we need to know is how to strip a tree of its bark, quick like. We's just trying to have a little fun," Aubrey explained confidently.

"Is that what you two want to do forever, be barkers for the rest of your lives?"

"I'm gonna be a bullmaster," Dennis stated proudly.

"Yeah, and I'm gonna own my own mill," Aubrey offered, not to be outdone.

"Very well, boys. I will see you tomorrow and we'll talk in detail about your plans." Rachel had an idea, and she was determined to prove to these boys that intelligence was a necessary and integral part of the logging business. As soon as the idea came to her, she found herself wishing she could confer with Chase about the particulars of the logging industry, but knew that would be impossible. He had made his intentions toward her obvious; going to Redwood without saying good-bye had made that clear.

✍

The door to Seth and Rachel's room remained closed for the entire evening following supper. Rachel had come home with an armload of books and paperwork and was scratching frantically upon her desk. A light knock broke her concentration.

"Yes? What is it?" Rachel asked without opening the door.

"It's Maria. I need to talk with you."

Rachel cracked the door and looked suspiciously at Maria.

"We can sit in the kitchen. I've got a lamp burning there," Maria said.

Rachel looked back at Seth to be sure his sleep hadn't been disturbed and then quietly exited, shutting the door behind her. The two women walked to the pine table where Maria had placed two cookies and a cup of coffee at Rachel's place.

"Is this going to take long? I've got quite a bit of work to do. . ." Rachel crossed her legs, swinging her foot nervously.

"That's what I wanted to talk to you about. I'm concerned you're becoming too consumed by your work. You come home from school in the dark, barely offer us a hello, and shut yourself up in that room all night. If it weren't for little Seth, we might never hear your voice. I miss my friend Rachel." Maria's eyes filled with tears, but the sight had no effect on Rachel.

"Maria, I'm sorry you feel that way, but I'm really busy with lessons. We'll have time come summer." Rachel patted her friend's hand and rose to leave.

"No, Rachel. There's more." Maria motioned for Rachel to return to her seat and Rachel did so unwillingly. "I've noticed that you put your Bible in the closet when you moved in. I haven't seen you use it since. I'm concerned what you're teaching the children from the Bible. Robert and I made it clear that we wanted His light to shine in our school and we want to make sure that's happening." Maria's gaze was intense and Rachel shifted uncomfortably in her seat. Maria had never chastened her before, and the sweetness in her voice made it hard to take.

"Maria, the children read out of the Bible every day during quiet time. What more do you want?"

"I want the children to know about Jesus in a personal way, to know that it's a relationship with their Lord and Savior that provides salvation. I thought we understood one another when you came to work for us," Maria said firmly yet sweetly.

"Fine, I'll make a lesson plan." Rachel wanted to add that she ought to be able to teach what she saw fit, but caught herself before saying it. "I'm sorry, Maria. I just have a lot on my mind right now. The older boys have returned and I really have my hands full. We'll talk about this later."

Rachel walked back to her room without touching her cookies or coffee, while Maria bowed her head in prayer.

❧

The morning roads were wet from a light rain. Rachel arrived in her classroom at the break of dawn to begin preparing for the day. The conversation she'd had with Maria was upsetting her, and she'd had a restless night's sleep. She straightened up the classroom and swept the floor before sitting at her desk to review her plans for the day.

"Miss Phillips." Gretchen Steele stood in the doorway dressed uncharacteristically in black.

"Mrs. Steele, what a surprise." Rachel tried to sound gracious, but inside she seethed at the sight of the woman.

"Henry will be missing school next week. The railroad is running in Redwood and I've promised to take him to see the engines. I'm sure it will be quite educational for him. Do you have any work you'd like him to take along to keep up with the class?" Gretchen approached the desk and let a white handkerchief drop onto its surface. Rachel saw the initials "C. D." and knew Mrs. Steele's real intentions in Redwood. She was going to see Chase. *Rachel's* Chase.

She picked up the linen and handed it back to the widow, pretending not to have noticed the show so callously performed for her. "Henry will catch up. Have a wonderful time in Redwood."

Rachel was relieved to see the children now filing into their seats. She was excited about her lessons this morning and was not going to let Mrs. Steele ruin it for her or the children. She had spent the previous evening in a detailed study of the logging industry. She was determined to show her class troublemakers that an education was important, particularly now, after the state's rapid growth from the gold rush and the railroads.

"Good morning, class," she said brightly.

"Good morning, Miss Phillips," The class sang in unison.

"Today we're going to work on our numbers." Aubrey Dawson and Dennis Shine let out a groan from the back of the classroom.

Rachel ignored the outburst and was prepared to continue, when a girl of eight with red pigtails announced, "Ouch! Miss Phillips, Aubrey pulled my hair."

"Very well, Aubrey. We shall start with you today. How many board feet can you get out of one redwood tree?"

"That's easy, 'bout a thousand."

"Now, as a mill owner—that *is* what you said you wanted to do, isn't it?"

"Yep." His bored expression left him and he unconsciously sat up in his chair. "Gonna own my own place with ten saws." The class laughed and Aubrey got out of his seat, slapping his hands violently on the desk. He peered around the room, displaying a threatening stare, and the laughing stopped instantly.

"That's wonderful, Aubrey. Please sit down. Now, let's say with those ten saws you have 25,000 board feet ready to take to Hanson & Ackerson's in Redwood. They will pay you fifty dollars for each thousand board feet; how much money will you be bringing back with you to Searsville?"

Aubrey sat stunned, his eyes wide with embarrassment. "I. . .I don't know. That's a stupid question." Aubrey fidgeted uncomfortably in his seat.

"Is it, Aubrey? I would think that if you were going to sell your red-wood, you would want to know if you were paid correctly." Rachel stared intently at the boy, who refused to meet her eye.

"Yeah, well, Hanson's an honest man; don't need to worry about him," Aubrey replied smugly.

"That's good, because if, by chance, Hanson makes a mistake, you might not have enough money to pay your sawyers. That would probably make you very unpopular with them and their families." Aubrey's face was now red with humiliation and Dennis covered his face, pointing and laughing along with the entire class at his friend.

"Dennis, I understand you're going to be a bullmaster." Rachel's gaze became fixed on Dennis, and he stiffened with dread.

"Yes Ma'am," Dennis answered politely, hoping Miss Phillips would continue her example without him.

"Dennis, as bullmaster you may be entitled to pay equal to that of the mill owner, correct?"

"That's right," Dennis replied brazenly, remembering himself.

"Dennis, you're a bullmaster dropping off the lumber in Redwood. Unfortunately, some of the redwood is of poor quality and Hanson only pays you half of what your wood is worth. He gives you $12.50. What amount should you have received for the wood?" Rachel took great plea-sure in watching the flustered boys. She had beat them at their own game and it felt good.

"It doesn't matter," Dennis answered.

"Well, it will when you must put food on the table. Let's answer the first question, shall we? Can anyone else tell me how much money a mill owner would receive for 25,000 board feet of lumber at fifty dollars per thousand board feet?"

Many hands sprang up throughout the room, and Rachel heard the scratching of slates. Aubrey and Dennis sheepishly looked around at the younger children and eyed them threateningly. The children were surpris-ingly unaffected and kept their hands raised.

Miss Phillips called on a small boy of about eleven. "One thousand two hundred fifty dollars."

"That's right, Jacob, and would you like to explain to the class how you arrived at this figure?" Jacob went on to bask in his glory and explained his multiplication. The class was ecstatic in this practical use of their knowledge and were anxious for more questions.

"Okay, now this one's a little more difficult," Rachel said as she repeated her second question. "If you are the bullmaster and your wood is of poor quality so that you only receive fifty percent of its true value, what would the true value be if the amount you received is $12.50."

"That's easy. Thirteen dollars," Dennis replied arrogantly.

"No, I'm sorry, Dennis. That is incorrect." The young schoolteacher tried to be gentle now; she had seen that the older boys were more than humiliated, and had had their share of the day's lessons.

A child of twelve raised her hand. "I know, I know. Half of anything is fifty percent, so if he got half of what he should have at $12.50, then he should have received twenty-five dollars."

"Very good, Michelle." The children were enjoying themselves immensely, having answered questions that could help their parents *and* silencing the school bullies at the same time. Rachel had prepared enough questions to keep the children actively involved until recess time. Dennis and Aubrey remained sheepishly at their desks. Rachel momentarily thought about how much Chase would have enjoyed the spirited lesson, but then remembered Mrs. Steele. Chase had probably invited her to Redwood; Rachel thought perhaps she had only been a simple diversion to the handsome mill owner before he made any commitments. If he returned, he would probably be married and a proper father for Henry. The idea pained her and she bent over her desk to lose herself, once again, in her work.

✑

Chase Dylan bent over a floorboard, hammering a nail with fury. His black trousers were white with board dust and his black hair was colored with pink redwood shavings. The heavy fall rains had never come, and the heat caused the dirt to stick to everything.

The room additions to the once "bunk style" hotel were almost complete and Chase's project was ending. Mr. Williams would arrange for professionals to do the finishing work, and Chase could return to Portola to start up his mill due to the lack of inclement weather. The dry winter would be a blessing for his men, who were used to being without work in the winter. Chase was anxious to get back before other mills hired his sawyers out from under him.

"Chase, I just made some iced tea. Would you care for some? Joseph says I need to practice my serving skills if we're going to wait on those rich folk from San Francisco." Mrs. Williams held a silver tray, filled with two crystal glasses and a large pitcher.

Chase laughed at the scene. "My dear Mrs. Williams, you have such a servant's heart, you could serve any king or queen."

"Oh my, Chase, but you always know what to say. It's a wonder you've managed to remain an eligible bachelor for so long."

Chase smiled at the compliment and his blue-green eyes sparkled with merriment.

"You're just determined to get me married off, aren't you? Well, I have news for you. I think I just may be heading in that direction. That is, if a stunning young schoolteacher in Searsville will have me."

"Why, you little schemer. You've been here for over a month and you haven't said a word." Mrs. Williams brought her hands to her hips in mock anger.

"All I can say is," Mr. Williams added, "if your intention is to marry that girl, you better get yourself back to Searsville. Ain't no telling how many sawyers might have laid claim on such a pretty little thing while you've been gone." His genial tone made light of the situation, but Chase knew there was truth in his words.

"I'm sending Mrs. Williams along behind you. I want her to stay in Searsville while the finishing work is done. She'll drive those poor carpenters to tears with her instructions." Mr. Williams smiled amiably at his wife. "That hotel still up and running?"

"If you think I'd let my Mrs. Williams stay at Eikerenkotters' Hotel, you don't know me too well," Chase said.

"Now Chase, you know I'm perfectly capable of handling myself in the midst of sawyers."

"I know Missus, but I've got a better idea. There's a dry winter widow who could use a little spiritual guidance. I think you two would get along wonderfully, and I have ulterior motives." Chase winked cryptically, and Mrs. Williams was clearly intrigued.

After her successful day of teaching loggers' math, Rachel had a bounce in her step as she approached the general store. She usually had Maria pick up her supplies because of the way Mrs. Davenport treated her, but today she felt especially confident and decided to go it alone.

The idea seemed like a good one until she spied Gretchen Steele coming out of the store. She had Henry in tow, and Mr. Davenport followed along behind her to her carriage with a large number of packages. Mrs. Davenport pursued the trio outside the store upon seeing Rachel and spoke loudly for her benefit, "Now you enjoy yourselves in Redwood. I hear it's going to be the peninsula's San Francisco during the foggy winter months. If you see Mr. Dylan at one of those balls, tell him hello for us."

"I'm sure we'll have many opportunities to do so, Elizabeth. We'll see you at the wedding when we return." Gretchen lifted her heavy black skirt into her buggy and reached for Henry when Mr. Davenport handed him up. Gretchen's hired man finished helping the store owner with the packages and then climbed aboard to take the small family to Redwood.

"Why, Miss Phillips, I didn't see you there." Mrs. Davenport had stepped in front of the doorway, blocking Rachel's entrance. "Your order hasn't arrived yet. Is there something else that you need?"

Rachel reached for Mrs. Davenport's hands and held them gently. "Why yes, I need quite a few things," Rachel replied sweetly. She knew she had flustered the woman with her touch and she took the opportunity to casually spin herself into the store.

Mrs. Davenport remained in the doorway, a look of astonishment on her lined face. Mr. Davenport gave his wife a sideways glance as he passed her, smiling at the teacher's ingenuity. "Miss Phillips, how nice to see you," he said.

"Thank you, Mr. Davenport. It's been so long since I've been here, and I needed to pick out a gift for my mother's birthday. Do you mind if I browse?"

"Of course not, make yourself at home. I'll be in the back; just call when you're ready." The proprietor disappeared into the back room and Rachel could feel Mrs. Davenport's glare boring into her back. Rachel allowed her anger to give her strength, and she walked slowly through the mercantile, eyeing each item methodically and never looking back at Mrs. Davenport.

Rachel approached the main counter and appreciatively eyed the small collection of jewelry set beneath the glass. Mrs. Davenport walked heavily into the back room and began whispering loudly at her husband. "I don't want her in here. Don't you understand? If my friends and our customers see her here, they are going to protest with their purses."

"Elizabeth, you're being ridiculous. No one believes that inane gossip."

"Well, you may play the innocent, but. . ."

Rachel lost track of the words when she noticed an order book open before her on the glass countertop. In it was a catalogue dress order for Gretchen Steele. Rachel studied the description of the gown, which was a yellow satin with a lace neckline. The thought of Mrs. Steele in attractive attire sent a wave of jealousy through Rachel. She looked up to see if the Davenports had noticed her discovery, but their argument was heated.

Rachel noted the dress size on the order and once again peered about the empty room. Quickly, she picked up the abandoned pen near the catalog and wrote a "1" before the entered size. She giggled at the mere thought of Gretchen's dress showing up big as a tent and dropped the pen as though it were on fire.

It wasn't long before Mr. Davenport returned and asked if she'd decided. Rachel's heart was pumping wildly as she managed to calmly reply, "I believe I'll take this small cameo. Will you have it sent to this address for me? I have a letter to accompany it."

"Certainly, Miss Phillips, and thank you for your business." Mr. Davenport sounded sincere, but his wife watched with crossed arms from the back room.

⬧

A soupy fog enveloped Redwood, but the building and loading on the docks proceeded as usual. Chase had spent his morning in prayer before packing his leather satchel to return home to Portola after a month away. He planned to stop at Robert's place on the way home to inquire after Rachel. The thought made his heart ache to see her.

Mrs. Williams prepared a lunch for him to eat on the way and now stood before him in the renovated hotel lobby with tears in her eyes.

"When I think of all you've done for us, Chase. . .I am forever thankful the Lord brought you into our lives. Joseph couldn't have done this work in twice the time without you. You're like a son to us, Chase. You know that, don't you, dear?"

Chase placed his large hands over the older woman's. "I know. And I also knew you'd be there if I needed *you*. Wipe your eyes, I'm going to see you in a few days. I'll send word when I have a proper place for you to stay. Then we'll begin our plan."

Joseph walked in and looked at them both warily. "I don't know what you two are up to, but I don't like the sound of it."

"The sound of what?" A familiar voice jarred Chase and he turned to see Gretchen and Henry Steele in the unfinished lobby. Her full-skirted dress of shiny fabric contrasted sharply with the still-crude skeleton of the hotel.

After the initial shock of Gretchen's appearance, Chase immediately focused on Henry. "There's my boy! Did you see the train yet?" he asked as he playfully tousled the boy's hair.

"Not yet, but I heard it from our room at Mrs. Littlejohn's, and I saw the tracks and the station and I even met a conductor."

"A real conductor?" Chase inquired.

"In a uniform and everything."

"Gretchen, this is quite a surprise. Do you remember Mr. and Mrs. Joseph Williams?" Chase asked graciously, while his mind searched for a reason she might be in Redwood. He hoped it was not him.

"Of course, I'd never forget a friend of yours, Mr. Dylan." Gretchen smiled coyly and extended her hand to the older couple. "You're not on your way out, are you?" she asked Chase. Noticing her evident disappointment, Chase knew he was indeed the reason she had come to Redwood.

"I'm afraid so. I'm going back to Portola to restart the mill."

"Would you mind if I borrowed Mr. Dylan from you for a moment?" Gretchen said to the Williamses. "Before he leaves, I must discuss some pressing business matters with him. Henry, stay here in the lobby and keep out of trouble."

"Yes, Mama."

Gretchen lead Chase to a small, sheet-covered sofa in a far corner of the lobby. She sat down first and motioned for him to follow. "I want to talk with you about Miss Phillips and my impression of her. I know you may think this out of place, but hear me out. I've noticed you developing a sort of attachment to our schoolteacher, and as your longtime friend. . . After all, you were best man at Harold's and my wedding. Due to our long and intimate history together, I feel I must warn you about this young woman's questionable character. Harold would want me to watch out for you, just as he asked you to care for Henry and me, should anything happen to him."

Chase wanted to be livid. But, upon hearing her words, he knew how alone Gretchen would feel if he married, and suddenly his heart softened toward her. There was a time when, playing the chaperone for Gretchen and Harold, the three were inseparable, taking Sunday picnics and afternoon strolls along the bay in Redwood. Looking into her dark eyes, he recalled the sparkling young girl that once held the attention of nearly every man on the peninsula. He remembered with sadness the adoration and worship she had shown to her husband, and the terrible grief when he was gone.

"Gretchen, I don't think. . ."

"I'm not asking you to make any promises, I just want you to think about what I've said." Gretchen's pleading eyes were convincing.

"Very well, Gretchen. Of course I will." Chase decided immediately that, out of respect for Gretchen's feelings, he would not go by Robert's on the way home. Rather, he would bide his time and wait for the right moment to ease the blow to his best friend's widow. She was right that they had too much history for him just to put aside her objections. He would continue to pray about the matter.

Chapter 12

R achel, are you certain you want to attend this wedding?" Maria asked with marked concern. "You know we weren't officially invited, and if you aren't comfortable..."

"Maria, the entire church body was invited. Pastor Swayles said so at service last week; you told me so yourself. Besides, Veronica invited me personally, and *I* am the reason they're getting married in the first place."

"Rachel, I think you may be going to this wedding with the wrong intentions."

"I have not been invited to even *one* social event since my first week here in Searsville, and that was a horrible sewing circle. I want to meet people, the parents of my students; I want to explore Searsville." Rachel's arms danced as she spoke. "This is the perfect opportunity, and I promise I'll be on my best behavior." Rachel smiled mischievously and walked toward her room to dress.

Undaunted, Maria followed her. "I appreciate your wanting to mix socially with our neighbors, but I am concerned about your heart. I know what you did with Mrs. Steele's dress order."

Rachel's eyes popped open wide with surprise. "But, how—"

"I walked in when you did it. I left before you saw me, and didn't tell anyone because I was afraid of what might happen if you were caught. But I've never been comfortable with my decision. Rachel, I can't continue to cover for you; my conscience won't allow me to do it any longer. Pastor Swayles often asks why you haven't been in church, and Seth is beginning to ask as well. I know you don't want to let him down. Please, Rachel, I'm begging you; pray about your feelings."

"Maria, please don't upset yourself and the baby. I'll work on it, I promise."

Maria nodded through her tears and left the room. Rachel opened her closet and began to dress for Searsville's big event.

After fastening the last button, Rachel studied her reflection in the small mirror above her dresser. She approved of what she saw. The rose-petal pink, long-sleeved gown that Marshall had purchased for her was magnificent. Coordinating fabric buttons lined the fitted bodice, and an elegant white lace collar framed Rachel's fresh complexion.

She pinned the forward portions of her hair up with a small silver pin, but left the back cascading in luxurious, auburn curls. Her ivory skin was set aglow by the soft color of the dress, and she gently bit her full lips for the ruby-colored mouth she shared with her paternal grandmother.

"Pi-tee." Seth's tiny head bobbed up and down in approval.

"Thank you, my love. Would you like to escort me to the wedding?" Again Seth's head nodded vigorously. "Well, let's be off then." Little Seth was dressed in black pants and matching suspenders. Underneath he wore a white, starched shirt that his mother had sewn just for the occasion. Rachel knelt down near the doorframe of the bedroom, fixing his collar. "Oh my, but you are very handsome. I shall be the belle of the ball with you on my arm." Rachel kissed his plump cheek and was rewarded by a gleeful hug.

Rachel hoisted Seth up on her hip, reached for his small hand, and danced cheerfully into the sunlit kitchen. Robert and Maria stopped in their tracks and stood, mouths open wide, when they saw Rachel emerge from the darkened hallway. "Oh. . .it's breathtaking!" Maria finally said.

"True, it is that. But do you think it might be a. . .well, uh. . .a little too fancy?" Robert stuttered.

"Rachel, you look lovely," Maria whispered, silencing her husband.

"I will hate to see the bride's face when I escort the two most beautiful women in Searsville to her wedding!" Robert said as he kissed his wife on the forehead. Maria wore a traditional Spanish gown of dark lace with a hint of crimson, which had been let out in order to accommodate the growing baby. "Maria, you are a vision, just like the day I married you."

⁊

The church was filled to capacity. Recent rains had slowed the work for a few days, bringing sawyers in from each of the surrounding mills. Workmen of all ages had gathered in their best clothes, and they fidgeted in the pine pews of the sanctuary. Pastor Swayles stood at the altar, welcoming the uneasy faces. Mrs. Steele entered on the arm of her young son, dressed in a modest navy skirt with coordinating jacket.

They seated themselves near the front.

A murmur arose from the crowd, and Rachel felt all eyes turn toward her as she entered the sanctuary, her quiet steps watched by all. Rachel's gown of satin rustled as she moved, and her cheeks flushed the same soft pink as her dress. A jealous rage flamed within her as she spotted Gretchen Steele, yet Rachel also felt the envy in the widow's glare. Things had not worked out well for her in Redwood, and Rachel took pleasure in seeing Gretchen and Henry alone in the pew.

Mrs. Thorne, seated in the front row of the church for her daughter's wedding, gave Gretchen a knowing look that Rachel could not help but notice.

"Ahem!" After Rachel was seated, Pastor Swayles signaled his flock with an obvious cough, and slowly, one by one, the eyes returned to the altar.

It was several more minutes before the wedding began. Guests continued to fill the sanctuary as the pastor welcomed them. Soon the groom appeared at the end of the aisle; Jeremiah nervously tapped his toe while playing with the chain from his pocket watch. The gathering stood in unison upon the pastor's signal, and the bride appeared in the foyer on her father's arm.

Rachel thought her dress was charming. Its white taffeta skirt, topped by an elegant laced neckline, was the latest style; but sadly, it was nothing compared to the exquisite gown Marshall had purchased for Rachel. Her own gown had obviously been made by a fine dressmaker, not purchased from a mail-order catalogue. Unaware of the earlier commotion, Jeremiah had eyes for only one woman. To her relief, Rachel Phillips went unnoticed by both the bride and the groom.

Veronica and Jeremiah looked lovingly into one another's eyes and completed their vows with conviction. After the nuptials, the couple was introduced as Mr. and Mrs. Smith while they beamed at their friends and family seated before them. A reception outside of the church began immediately following the ceremony. Tables overflowed with breads, pies, and special creations the townswomen had been busy preparing all week.

Feeling uneasy at the attention she'd received entering the church, Rachel patiently waited until everyone had left the building to rise from her seat. *Perhaps Maria was right; I shouldn't have come.* She had noticed the looks she got from both Mrs. Steele and the town's men, all of them looking as though they'd like to eat her for lunch. The men had eyed her lustfully, and Gretchen's eyes had fixed upon her with a deep rage. This certainly wasn't the reaction she had intended.

Seth had followed his parents out earlier, and Rachel was agonizing over how to leave the sanctuary without being the object of attention once again. Her gown was simply too much for a small town like Searsville, and as the town's teacher, she should have known better.

Just as the last person exited, Rachel rose, and her pulse raced at the sight of Chase Dylan ducking through the doorway. He was handsomely dressed in a gray pin-striped suit with a black tie, and his dark, thick hair was combed neatly to the side. Rachel's heart thundered at the sight of him, and her hand went quickly to her chest as though to keep her feelings to herself. Momentarily, she was glad for her gown choice, hoping he would take notice and feel differently.

Chase strode confidently toward Rachel and she was caught breathless as he smiled, but to her dismay, he continued walking past her row toward Pastor Swayles at the altar. Rachel's shoulders dropped with disappointment, and she remained transfixed on his back until a small voice startled her: "Bye."

"Seth, did you come to find me?" The toddler's eyes widened and he nodded. "Well, bless your heart. You certainly know how to escort a lady properly." Rachel lovingly reached for his outstretched arms to lift his little body to her hip.

"Pastor Swayles, forgive me. I know this probably isn't the best time." Chase also had been caught breathless from the striking sight of Rachel in her city gown. He had never seen anything more exquisite than Rachel in the soft pink dress, and her appearance threw him. It took every ounce of his inner strength and a quick prayer to walk past her, but he knew by the very display she was making today that a conversation between them would be powerful ammunition against her among the townspeople.

"Chase, don't be silly. My work is done here. How may I be of service?" Pastor Swayles asked. "Perhaps, you'd like to have a ceremony of your own performed?" The pastor nodded slyly toward Rachel, and Chase became flustered; his mouth opened yet he remained silent.

"Oh, come on now, Mr. Dylan. Don't tell me you didn't notice?" The pastor needled.

"Of course, Pastor Swayles. Miss Phillips is quite beautiful today, but I see she already has a date," Chase said, trying to make light of the situation by referring to Seth.

"Well, I suppose it's just as well. Never see the girl in Sunday service anyway."

The comment was a splash of cold water in his face. *Rachel hasn't been to church? Why not?* Were the women of Searsville too cruel or were there deeper, more important reasons for her to not attend service? Chase's mind was reeling with the possibilities. He tried to compose himself quickly, and remembered his reason for speaking with Pastor Swayles.

"Uh. . .Joseph and Martha Williams, friends of mine from Redwood, are in the process of remodeling their hotel, the American House. Mr. Williams has elected to stay and oversee the finishing work, but Mrs. Williams is in need of some temporary housing, and I was wondering if you thought asking Thelma Hopper might be appropriate."

"I don't see why not. Mr. Hopper is running his mill this winter since there's been no rain to speak of, so he's not likely to be back until the holidays. I'll speak with her if you like."

"That's a fine suggestion, Pastor. Perhaps I'll discuss it with Mrs. Hopper as well today at the reception." Chase walked away, thankful his plan had worked. His mind was full of Rachel and her present status in the community. *What happened while I was gone? Maybe she met someone.* He had never declared his feelings for her before he left for Redwood; perhaps that had been a mistake.

⟡

"Rachel, we're going to sit for a while under the tree. Maria is worn out from all the excitement." Robert motioned to his wife's rounded belly, and Maria smiled self-consciously. Rachel relinquished Seth's hand, and he followed his parents under the pleasant shade of a nearby oak. Rachel stood motionless, unsure if she should follow them or stay put where her path might again cross Chase Dylan's.

"Beesh, Beesh!" Seth announced ecstatically, pointing toward the lake.

"Come sit down, sweetheart." Maria hadn't understood the words,

KRISTIN BILLERBECK

but that wasn't unusual with the toddler's limited vocabulary. The little boy stamped his foot in defiance, but finally followed his parents when he saw them seated under the large tree near the lake.

Rachel walked toward the bride and groom to offer her congratulations, but was stopped by a harsh, familiar tone. "Have you not caused enough trouble today, Miss Phillips?" Gretchen Steele leered down her nose at the small woman before her. Her face was wrinkled in revulsion.

"I beg your pardon, Mrs. Steele?" Rachel's tone was sugar-sweet and peppered with mock innocence.

"Gretchen, it's so nice to see you. So sorry we were just passing in Redwood." Chase Dylan interrupted the conflict, addressing the widow as though she were the only woman present.

Rachel opened her mouth, anxious to speak with Chase, but she closed it quickly at the obvious slight.

"Chase my dear, what a pleasant surprise. Now, you haven't forgotten the *special* trip to Redwood have you?" Gretchen smirked as she looked over toward her female rival, relishing the moment of being Chase Dylan's chosen one. Chase wanted with all his heart to explain to Rachel about Henry's *independent* trip to Redwood to ride the steam engine, but he knew it would only cause more friction.

"Of course not, Gretchen. I'd be happy to discuss it with you." Chase extended his arm and led Mrs. Steele gallantly toward the lake, protecting his beloved from the widow's wrath. Rachel stood stunned, a painful expression coming over her. She looked down at her dress with disgust. *A lot of good this thing did me.*

"Good afternoon, Miss Phillips." A large, burly man with a blond mustache and beard and a plaid shirt, loomed over Rachel.

"Hello," Rachel said with an absent nod.

"The name's Jack Burbank, bullwhacker, pardon me, Ma'am, bullmaster for Dylan Mills in Portola Valley." Jack's forwardness released an endless stream of men who came to introduce themselves to the pretty schoolteacher and take their chances, but Rachel's heart was decidedly spoken for. Surrounded by loggers from every local mill, she continued to make polite conversation while she intently watched Chase romantically stroll, arm in arm, with Gretchen Steele.

I was right about him all the time. He's an arrogant, good-for-nothing, two-timing wretch, Rachel thought. But if he was all of those things, why was she so miserable watching his familiar gait along *their* path near the water with another woman?

Rachel's attention was suddenly wrenched away from the couple, and she gasped in horror. "No!" The crowd eyed her with confusion and milled about, forming into a large group.

In the distance, Rachel could see Seth's diminutive figure splashing freely at the edge of the lake near the oak where his parents had once been. She cried out, "Seth, no!" But the little boy only turned and grinned as he dodged from sight behind a large tree, splashing farther out into the lake.

Lifting her skirt, Rachel began running as rapidly as her legs would allow. "No, God! No! You can't have him! Do what you will with me, but not my Seth!" She was so angry at God right now, she spat a series of angry protests up to the Lord she once had loved. "You will not take another from me. I will fight this time! Do You hear me?"

Perhaps if she'd fought before, she might be living with her mother and brother still in a posh mansion in San Francisco. Another splash alerted Rachel, and she knew if Seth fell into the deeper part of the murky water, he might never be found. She summoned sudden new strength, and her pace quickened beyond what she thought she was capable. The noise from the reception dwindled, and once again all eyes focused on Rachel and her as yet unexplained behavior.

"Seth, Seth!" Rachel screamed as she finally reached the path near the lake. The onlookers watched as Rachel disappeared behind the great oak near the water's edge, the object of her desperate speed a complete mystery to them. Once Rachel reached the dark green pool, she could see only Seth's hands flailing wildly on the surface, his head and body submerged.

She raced into the lake and grabbed her precious little roommate, dragging him swiftly toward the water's edge, fighting her heavy skirt. She placed the small boy over her knee and began to repeatedly rub his back forcefully, sobbing, "Seth, Seth! Please, oh please, don't leave me. *You can't have him! Do You hear me?*" Rachel screamed frantically.

"Gretchen, go get Doc Winter, *NOW!*" Chase had finally understood what was happening and ran to Rachel's side, taking the boy from her and laying him carefully on the soft ground. Chase pressed the boy's stomach and the child promptly began to cough and sputter water. Soon Seth was wailing loudly. "Well, little fella, it looks like you're going to be fine," Chase chuckled, sitting back in the dirt with a sigh.

Rachel had lifted Seth's head to her shoulder and embraced the boy with all her strength, then separated from him. "Seth, you must never go in the water without Mama or Papa or Rachel, do you understand?" Rachel rested her hand upon Seth's cheek and stroked it soothingly. Seth inhaled raggedly between cries and calmed enough to nod his head.

"Beesh, beesh," Seth said in explanation.

"Seth, we catch fish with a pole, not by swimming. You are not to go in the lake again, do you understand?" Rachel's voice was stern and the little boy nodded tearfully.

"What on earth happened?" Robert's surprise at Rachel's appearance was quickly replaced by fear at the sight of his son. "Seth!" The small boy looked at his father's face and began to cry heartily once again. Robert picked up his son and held him tightly. "This is all my fault. Maria needed a rest so I took her into the church for a moment; we thought Seth was right behind us." Robert exhaled deeply.

"It's all right, Robert. He's fine. Just had a little scare, that's all." Rachel's voice was gentle and soothing. "Let's get him home with his Mama and pour him a tall glass of buttermilk; I know that will make him feel better." Rachel stood up, entangled in the dripping, muddied mess that had once been her dress. The beautiful pale pink gown was ruined, but Rachel didn't care one wink; her precious Seth was safe.

"Rachel?" Chase's familiar voice made her want to cry all over again. She looked up and tossed her head to free her face from the wet, tangled mass of ringlets that stuck to her cheek.

"What is it?" She asked, crying easily now.

"I'm so very sorry," Chase said sincerely, his bluish-green eyes gazing warmly into her own. Rachel didn't know exactly what he was sorry about, but she assumed his apology referred to Seth's accident. Rachel smiled in vague acknowledgment and followed father and son toward their ranch. She turned and glanced at the handsome sawyer, his clothes soaked from cuddling Seth. Rachel felt a loss that was overwhelming, the kind she'd felt when leaving her mother and baby brother on the pier in San Francisco. It wasn't just Seth, it was the acknowledgment that Chase Dylan didn't want her the same way that she longed for him.

"If Doc Winter comes, send him to the ranch, please," Rachel added.

"Certainly I will," Chase agreed readily. He turned to find the entire reception had migrated to the lake and probably had witnessed Rachel's wrathful outburst against God, not to mention her dripping frame. It was suddenly clear to Chase why Rachel had not been attending church. She was angry at God, angry and bitter. The very thought caused Chase to grieve for the woman he loved. *Oh Rachel, why have you forsaken God when you need Him the most?*

Chapter 13

Rachel, we're going to have a family prayer time, praising the Lord for saving our Seth. Will you join us?" Robert asked, peeking his head into the doorway of Rachel's lighted room.

"I don't think so, Robert. I'd like to get a little work done." Rachel dropped her head and continued to scratch with her quill on the paper before her.

"Rachel, let me rephrase that. We have everything to be thankful for today. Our son was spared from a dreadful, untimely death. Seth admires and loves you. Whether or not you choose to give proper credit to the Lord, that's your business alone, but tonight you will join us for Seth's sake. This house rests upon the foundation of the Lord; we thought you understood that when you moved here. You will honor that as long as you live in this house." Robert's face was red as he spoke through tightly clenched teeth.

Rachel was appalled. She had never even heard Robert get angry before, much less carry on in such a way. Robert's voice was low and steady, but unmistakably commanding. He turned, expecting her to follow. Rachel was livid at his audacity. *They are the ones that should be grateful! They can thank God all they want, but He's the one who wanted to take Seth away from them. Don't they understand? God always wants the good ones. If I hadn't seen Seth, he would have died today.* Rachel's thought pattern remained unchanged as she grimaced and followed Robert into the front parlor.

"Oh, there you are, Seth's been waiting for you. I'm so relieved you decided to join us." Maria's voice called from the kitchen.

Seth plopped himself in Rachel's lap and his parents gathered around him, thanking the Lord that He had used Rachel to save their special little boy. Rachel closed her eyes out of respect for Robert and Maria, but inside she fumed.

∽

The following Monday Rachel learned that Dennis and Aubrey had dropped out of school after learning their dreams were lost to them because they didn't know their sums. Rachel felt broken. She had become so embittered since moving to Searsville, but all the while she had taken solace in the knowledge that she was a good teacher. Rachel was starting to see how her negative attitude was taking a toll on those around her.

She wondered how she could have become so insensitive to other people's feelings, making sport of the two older boys. Normally, she would have instantly prayed about the situation, but she had given up prayer altogether. God was not listening, and praying just seemed a waste of time.

✍

The weekly quilting circle had gathered at Mrs. Davenport's home and Rachel Phillips was the main topic of discussion.

"Did you see her dress?" Mrs. Irving asked, her short fingers working diligently on the quilt piece before her.

"Disgraceful; and her the village schoolteacher!" replied Mrs. Davenport. "Soaking wet and muddied in front of the whole town; what a shame for you, my dear." Mrs. Davenport directed her comment to Mrs. Thorne, mother of the bride.

"I know, it was terrible. And the reception was going along so beautifully, too," Mrs. Thorne answered pitifully, her head shaking in self-pity, "I certainly hope Veronica and Jeremiah will soon forget the whole incident. Such a terrible blight on the beginning of their marriage. Veronica certainly got more than she bargained for when she politely invited that, that *teacher* of hers. I tried to tell her, women like that have no place in decent society. But, you know my Veronica, always thinking of others," Mrs. Thorne said in a hushed tone.

"I hardly think Miss Phillips should be faulted for overlooking her appearance to save a child from drowning," Mrs. Hopper finally injected.

"Mrs. Hopper, she's the town schoolteacher. She could have beckoned to any one of those pathetic sawyers drooling over her, getting them to jump into the lake and save the boy," Mrs. Thorne reasoned, while the other women nodded in agreement.

"Chase Dylan didn't seem to mind her appearance at all," Mrs. Hopper said, looking maliciously at Gretchen Steele. Gretchen's eyes narrowed in Thelma's direction, and her sewing instantly dropped to her lap. Thelma watched her expectantly, but Gretchen picked up her needle and returned to her sewing as though nothing had occurred.

The conversation was picked up by another. "Thelma, you needn't stand up for the woman simply because you took her into your home before you knew her character. That was the Christian thing to do." Mrs. Davenport offered her forgiveness.

The hostess's words caused Thelma to react unexpectedly. She stood abruptly, throwing her sewing project onto the chair behind her. "You all ought to be ashamed of yourselves. You sit here with smug satisfaction while you shred anything left of that poor woman's reputation! I'll tell you, Rachel was a dear friend while she lived with me, and I am ashamed of my behavior. I will no longer be a party to this pettiness."

Thelma stormed out the doorway of the formal parlor and asked Milly to get her coat. She stood in the hallway, pacing the small space until her garment arrived. The young girl helped Thelma into her wool overcoat, and she walked outside, slamming the door behind her.

"My, what a scene," Mrs. Davenport said, rocking nervously in her chair.

"Was that really necessary?" Mrs. Irving asked Gretchen Steele coolly.

"I wonder what she'll do without us," Gretchen said, and the gaggle of women looked at one another in knowing agreement and cackled heartily.

✑

"Tonight will be our last get-together for a while, Henry. I talked to your mother about another trip to Redwood, just you and me, and she doesn't think it's a good idea right now." Chase Dylan sat alongside the rocky shore of Searsville's dark green lake preparing fishing poles for himself and the young Henry Steele. His voice was filled with sadness, and he concentrated on tying his lure to avoid looking at the child.

"Chase, you're not going away are you?" Henry reached for Chase's arm, pulling him away from the task at hand.

"No, of course not, Henry, but I'll be busy until Christmastime. I'm going to start up the mill again and I probably won't make it into town as often."

"Are you mad at my mom, Chase? Is that why you're leavin'?" Henry's question was heartfelt and his eyes carried a pained expression.

"No, son, I'm not. Your mother and I just disagree on a few things and we'll discuss them later, but there's nothing for you to be concerned about. Do you understand?" Chase felt as though he were abandoning the boy at such an inopportune time, but he had promised his men work for the winter. Anyway, his presence in Searsville only seemed to make matters worse.

"My mom doesn't like Miss Phillips. Is that why you're mad at her?" Henry untied his boots as he asked the question. He dangled his feet in the murky waters of the lake before them, avoiding eye contact with Chase.

"Henry, like I said before, I'm not angry with your mother. We do disagree about Miss Phillips, but that's as far as it goes, and that has nothing to do with you."

"I heard my mom telling Mrs. Davenport you only like Miss Phillips 'cause she's got a pretty face. Is that true?"

Chase's initial reaction to the question was hostility, but he remained even-tempered as he looked at Henry's steel-gray eyes. "Do you think that's true, Henry? That I only like Miss Phillips for her looks?"

"No sir," Henry replied meekly.

"So we'll plan to ride the train after Christmas, how does that sound?" Chase felt the time was right to change the subject. He was troubled that Gretchen had chosen to speak ill of Rachel in front of Henry, but he wasn't about to do the same thing to the widow, regardless of whether or not she deserved it.

"Yippee!" Henry shouted.

"All right, then," Chase said.

"Well, another trip to Redwood. Doesn't that sound exciting?" A low evening shadow encompassed the boy and the pair turned to see Mrs. Hopper on the path, her hands clasped in enthusiasm.

"Mrs. Hopper, what a pleasure." The words from Chase were uttered with complete sincerity. Chase had heard from Jeremiah that Thelma Hopper had been officially disowned by Searsville's women's society, and in his heart he knew it had something to do with Rachel, knew that Thelma Hopper had finally taken a stand.

"Chase, I saw you from my kitchen window and I wanted to come by and thank you." Mrs. Hopper's happy spirit was genuine.

"Thank me for what?" Chase was completely in the dark.

"For finding me a new houseguest. You know how I hate to be alone. And to have found someone my own age; well, it's just more than I could have hoped for." Mrs. Hopper bent at the waist so that she could pat Chase's broad shoulder. "I simply can't wait for Mrs. Williams to arrive.

She'll be coming on Tuesday, and I've been frantic to get the house ready."

"Mrs. Hopper, I think Mrs. Williams could come in the dead of night, any night, with no warning at all, and you'd be ready with fresh flowers on the mantle and sugar cookies baking in the oven." Chase's eyes sparkled with mirth.

"Oh Chase, really. You flatter me." Mrs. Hopper tossed her hand, laughing at the ridiculous notion.

"I don't know if you know what you're getting into, Mrs. Hopper. You and Mrs. Williams together might be more housekeeping than Searsville will allow. She'll probably arrive with fresh-cut flowers and a cake or two herself." Chase flashed a sporting grin, thrilled to be responsible for Mrs. Hoppers' houseguest and the way God had worked things for the best. Mrs. Williams was of solid character, and she would definitely be a strong role model and friend to Mrs. Hopper, keeping her away from the sewing circle that seemed to brew so much trouble. He also knew that with Rachel's present state, *she* was better off at the Lathrops'.

Chapter 14

Dearest Rachel,

   How I wish you were here to see your baby brother grow.
He's such a fine eater; I dare say his appetite might soon surpass
his father's. I heard the railroad station has opened in the city of
Redwood, and Marshall, Georgie, and I will book passage on the
train December twenty-third. We will probably spend the night in
Redwood before coming to Searsville, so don't count on us until late
the twenty-fourth. It will be just like old times, my love, Christmas
together. We'll tell the story of Jesus' birth in the manger and then
sing the glorious hymns to celebrate His life. It will be Georgie's first
Christmas, and I want it to be so special; so of course, it must be
with his big sister.

   Marshall has been so involved in the railroad lately, we hardly
see him. His business associates have been laying track for the
Central Pacific Line, which will connect California with the rest of
the country. It's very exciting, but it's been a very slow process, and
he's starting to feel the stress from the situation. I'm hoping a trip to
Searsville will help him clear his mind for a while.

   I'm still so surprised at the difference in weather from
Weberville (I mean Hangtown. I just cannot get used to the fact that
our old home has become the hanging capital of the state. It just sends
shivers up my spine.) The weather is so cold here in San Francisco.
I wouldn't believe it was possible without the snow, but when the
wind comes up with the late afternoon fog, it's downright unbearable. It was never an issue before, but now we do not even allow
Georgie out of doors, so I'm anxious for the spring which is only
slightly better.

   The trip will be such a blessing for all of us. For one thing, I
hear the weather is much milder in Searsville. Won't it be grand for
Georgie to get outside while we visit? I am looking forward to our
special talks. Sometimes I feel as though the servants are my only

*friends here. Don't get me wrong, I certainly don't feel above them;
however, I just can't help but wonder, would they still be my friends
if they weren't being paid to be here? I'm sorry, my darling, the
last thing I want to do is depress you. I know you must have many
friends in Searsville, and we are anxious to meet them all.*

With Love,
Mother

Rachel read the letter in her bedroom, and a single tear fell. Her
mother's visit had been the furthest thing from her mind before the letter
arrived. If the town saw her little brother, and Rachel showing him affec-
tion, the rumor would surely be confirmed as true. And what if Marshall
were to find out that she had been evicted from Mrs. Hopper's home?
Would he allow her mother to continue corresponding with her? *And
worst of all,* Rachel's eyes shut in horror at the thought, *what if they were
to find out that the entire town had seen me in the ruins of my drenched gown
clinging tightly to me. That would certainly be reason enough for Marshall to
disown me.* Rachel knew there was only one possibility; she must tell her
mother the trip would have to be postponed.

"Kish." Seth was at her side, clearly upset by Rachel's melancholy
mood.

"I would love a kiss, my sweet," Rachel said, lifting Seth onto the
bed. He snuggled his tiny head into her neck as she planned her letter of
regret.

✍

Rachel entered the living room after supper to see Maria staring intently
into a painting on the wall. "Are you okay?"

"I'm just missing my old home. This painting was done by my
uncle. It's *Rancho de Estrella, Ranch of the Stars,* my only home before
coming to Searsville. I remember it as such a place of love, free of
gossip and the secrets that seem to shroud Searsville. There was always
so much going on with all my brothers and sisters; how difficult it has
been to get used to the deafening silence in our small home. On the
rancho, families live together for generations, and each family member has an expected role. When I moved here, with Robert at work
during the day, I was completely independent. I had to create my own
direction and duties. It was such an adjustment."

Rachel moved toward the wall and studied the picture closely. Nestled in the rich, fertile, green valley was a collection of wooden buildings surrounded by rustic fences and great oak trees. The sun radiated light off the center structure, which Maria had indicated was her home.

"It's so beautiful there. I can see why you miss it." Rachel looked into Maria's dark eyes and for the first time knew she was not alone. Maria had lost her family, too. She had a husband and child, a family to call her own, but like Rachel, she must have understood the pain of leaving her mother for an unknown place. "It's not the home you miss, is it?"

"No, but I realize now I've been very selfish to sit here moping, staring into a painting and remembering how things were."

"Selfish? I hardly see how wanting to go back where you're loved is selfish."

"The Lord has given me a new family—a husband and a beautiful child, with another on the way." Maria rubbed her belly. "This is my home now, but I've been wishing for something that doesn't exist, nor should it."

"How can you say that? You were taken away from the only family you've ever known. A new family doesn't replace a mother or a father." Rachel was enraged at her friend's seemingly blind submission.

"I *chose* to leave my parents. I fell in love with a man I wanted to spend the rest of my life with and *he* became my family. Just like the Bible says: We are to leave and cleave."

Rachel now felt Maria's and her backgrounds were not at all alike. Maria had been given a choice. For Rachel, there had been no such luxury. She had been forced to leave her mother and little brother to live in this forsaken logging village. "Well, I didn't choose *anything*, my stepfather did it for me," Rachel spat out.

"Rachel, it sounds like you were determined to be unhappy here to prove your stepfather was wrong in his actions. The gossip mill has only allowed you to justify your anger. Why didn't you ever tell me you didn't want to be here?"

"It's not the sort of thing you share with your employer," Rachel said, feeling relief that the burden of her secret had finally been lifted.

"I thought you enjoyed teaching. . . ."

"I do, but—"

Maria picked up a framed photograph that was on the table with the lamp and brought it toward Rachel. *"Abuelo, Abuela."*

"Pardon me?" Rachel looked at the photo which included a large number of men, women, and children solemnly staring into the camera in full traditional Mexican dress. Rachel had entered the parlor many times before, but she had never taken time to study its treasures.

"That means 'grandmother' and 'grandfather' in my native tongue. My parents have never met Seth. I will teach him the words Abuelo and Abuela before we travel to the rancho this summer to meet his only grandparents."

"I don't understand what this has to do with me." Rachel looked into the photograph and felt only pain for her friend who had come to Searsville and remained isolated due to her heritage.

"This is my home now." Maria held her palms open and looked around. "My family may be much smaller, but that only makes my place here more important. Marshall Winsome didn't bring you here, Rachel, God did. So you might as well make the best of it."

Rachel said goodnight to Maria and headed for her room, still visibly upset by their conversation. She reached for her Bible and a piece of writing paper and took out a pen to write a letter. She placed the sheet on her Bible and began the words she had sorted through all evening.

November 23, 1863

Dear Mother,

I have just received your letter and it is with great disappointment that I must ask you to reschedule your trip to Searsville. I am so busy preparing lessons that I rarely have any time to myself, and with the upcoming holiday, I will have extra duties. There is a Christmas production that will take a great deal of my effort, and the remainder of the older boys, who have been working in the mills, may be returning shortly. I'm sure the rains will begin soon, making the roads quite unmanageable for a carriage. So, regrettably, I think it will be much better if I plan to visit you in the summer when school is dismissed for the year. I will write again soon when I have more time.

With all my love,
Rachel

Rachel was sniffing, trying desperately to keep her tears from falling on the letter. She knew that her mother was probably aware of the statewide drought, but hoped her reasoning would not be questioned. With graceful hands, she folded the letter and placed it in a small envelope. *Mother, if only I could tell you what my life is like here. I am the source of constant gossip and I am completely alone. I've been sent away from my beautiful lakeside room to live with a couple that preaches at me day and night. God has abandoned me and the only one who cares is a tiny little boy who shares my room.* Rachel looked tenderly at the sleeping toddler lying in the bed next to her and laughed at the precious sight. He had kicked free of his quilt, his knees tucked up under his chest and his round little bottom pointing skyward.

Rachel went to his bed and smoothed his hair. "My sweet bear," she whispered.

"Rachel?" Maria's glossy dark hair glistened in the light from the lamp she carried as she stood in the doorway. Her large brown eyes softened at the sight of the schoolteacher with her son.

"He sleeps this way every night. Mouth open, rump high in the air." Rachel delighted in the growth and progress of Seth and relished the sight of his nightly sleeping position. Rachel smiled happily for the first time all evening, and laughing through her tears felt wonderful.

"Yes, I know. He's done that since he was a tiny baby." Maria's head tilted to the side.

"He said a new word today: piggy," Rachel beamed.

"Piggy? Oh yes. I showed him a picture of a pig in the portrait of my parents' rancho. He must have remembered.

"I'm sorry about our talk earlier. I hope you're not upset." Maria placed her hand on Rachel's slim shoulder. "But this is our home now. Searsville may not be as we expected, but the Lord has us here for a reason."

The gentle words immediately threw Rachel into her recent pattern of self-pity. *Here it comes*, Rachel thought. *The sermon. If I hear one more time about the Lord wanting me to be here, I'll be sick. It's Marshall Winsome who wants me here and that's as far as it goes.* Rachel crossed her long slender arms in front of her as she rolled her eyes and looked away.

"I'll prove to you He wants you here," Maria began. She bent over with effort and picked up a large black Bible that lay upon the table next to the lamp. She fumbled through the pages, tilting the book toward the light. "Here it is, Proverbs sixteen, verse nine: 'A man's heart deviseth his way: but the Lord directeth his steps.' You see, your stepfather may have brought you here, but God—"

Rachel lifted up her hand in protest; the last thing she wanted to hear was a quote from the Bible. Maria's faith seemed so blind to Rachel; for easy answers, all one had to do was just open the Bible. Rachel had seen enough. "Maria, please don't take offense, but I'm afraid I just don't believe that anymore. I'm very tired; I think I'll turn in for the night. I would love to hear more about the rancho later though," Rachel offered. She had wanted to end on a positive note, for she understood that Maria really was a friend to her.

One thing was obvious from their conversation: Maria truly cared about Rachel, and for that Rachel was truly grateful. Rachel changed into her night clothes and unconsciously fell into old habits, saying the first prayer she had uttered for over a month, *Thank You for Maria.*

Chapter 15

Christmas came quickly, and yet still the much-needed heavy rains had not come. The logging industry and its wagons, oxen, men, and recreation continued throughout the winter season as though nothing had changed, for it hadn't. The Christmas Eve air was cold and crisp, but the stars in the sky were clearly visible and they painted a glorious canvas of light. Rachel planned to attend church services with the Lathrop's at the personal request of Seth.

Rachel put the finishing touches on her hair, which was pinned up loosely under a new hat, with her auburn ringlets gently surrounding her delicate ivory face. Her hat and gown were a rich, deep green, a perfect match with her eyes. Her dress was sleek, with long, tailored sleeves, a fitted bodice, and an exaggerated, full skirt that required a multitiered hoop.

The entire collection was a gift from her mother and stepfather. The seamstress who had prepared Rachel's trousseau when she left San Francisco had kept her measurements and created the gown from a fabric Peg Winsome had personally selected to match her daughter's Irish-green eyes.

Rachel felt like the princess her father always said she was as she left her bedroom, carrying her lamp before her. As she approached the kitchen from the extended hallway, the Lathrop family beamed with happiness.

"Rachel, you look radiant. I'm so pleased you've decided to join us for worship services." Maria's protruding stomach made it impossible for her to hug Rachel, so she patted her back as she came closer and they laughed in acknowledgment.

"I think the dress is a tad fancy for Searsville's Christmas service, but I was so excited when I opened the package, I just had to try it. I can't imagine where Mother expected me to wear this gown, but I plan to enjoy every moment in it." Rachel lifted the sides of her skirt slightly, dancing from side to side to the make-believe music that played in her heart.

"Up?" Seth's chubby arms reached up toward Rachel so that he could join in her waltz.

"No, Seth. Rachel is dressed far too nicely for your dirty boots to kick her gown." Robert's voice was stern, and Rachel resisted the urge to pick up her favorite little friend. The foursome enjoyed a sumptuous supper of roasted lamb and potatoes before joining hands and walking to the church, happily singing Christmas carols.

*

Chase Dylan entered the festively decorated church on the arms of two women, Mrs. Hopper and Mrs. Williams. The repairs on the American House were still going on, but Chase had been assured that his services were no longer needed. The other sawmills hadn't stopped operating for the winter and Chase's obligation to his men made being in Portola a priority. Since no one would be working on Christmas Day, Chase decided to stop in Searsville for the service and to check on Mrs. Williams as a favor to her husband.

Chase welcomed having excuses to be in the small village, but truthfully, he was anxious to see Rachel. He had been praying for her constantly since they had been apart—praying that her faith had been restored and that the gossip had died down. It had taken all of his might to resist writing her a letter. But he knew that if Rachel were to receive a letter from Portola, the post would be abuzz of the correspondence within moments of its arrival.

Chase escorted Mrs. Hopper and Mrs. Williams to the front of the church and directed them into an empty pew. He saw them seated comfortably and went toward the altar to greet Pastor Swayles after his long absence from the church. The two men exchanged handshakes and congratulated each other on the excellent match they had made.

"Those two have been inseparable since Mrs. Williams arrived. They've attended nearly every church social on the calendar," Pastor Swayles noted. The minister was most delighted with the changes he'd seen in Mrs. Hopper. She had always been an excellent servant, but something was different now: She did everything with delight, not because it might be expected of an older woman living alone in town.

"Well, I'd say we have a gift for matchmaking." Chase's expression broke into laughter as he surveyed the women joyfully engaged in conversation.

"Look there, the town schoolteacher. Why, I haven't seen her in worship service since the Smiths got married. That gives me an idea. . ."

Pastor Swayles nodded toward the door where Rachel had just come in, looking resplendent in the dark green dress that matched her eyes. For a moment, Chase was so overwhelmed by the exquisite appearance Rachel made in her winter gown that the comment went unnoticed.

Chase's broad shoulders sank in dejection in response to the pastor's innocent remark. His prayers had not been answered after all. Rachel had not been to services since the gossip began nearly three months earlier. He watched her, holding hands with little Seth, as she approached the altar from the aisle, turned suddenly, and followed the Lathrops to their seats.

She was truly a warm sight, caring for Seth in such motherly fashion, but Chase had to snap out of his daze. He had to avoid these feelings if Rachel were not walking with the Lord. God stated plainly in the Bible that two are not to be unequally yoked, and Chase had witnessed that truth with his own oxen. The lesson had always been such an easy one until today as he gazed at the woman he loved.

Why had she allowed her faith to suffer at such a difficult time in her life? Chase prayed silently that something would speak to her. He forced himself to look away from his heart's desire and again spoke to the pastor. "I'd better let you get to work. It looks like just about everyone is here."

Chase walked up the aisle toward his female escorts and glanced toward the Lathrops on his way, laboring to wave and smile casually.

Rachel's heart skipped a beat as she saw the mill owner dressed formally in black. She had forgotten how truly handsome he was. The coal-colored suit set off his dark hair and made his eyes appear the color of a cool mountain stream. Rachel caught herself staring and blinked suddenly, lowering her eyes toward Seth.

The preacher began his sermon by speaking of trusting in the Lord on this fine Christmas Eve, and Rachel began preparing lesson plans in her mind. . .until he quoted a passage not usually connected with Christmas: "'And why beholdest thou the mote that is in thy brother's eye, but considerest not the beam that is in thine own eye?' Judge not, my friends." He stopped to look at the women gathered in the sanctuary. "As we reflect this Christmas Eve on the precious gift our Lord gave us in His Son, let us not forget to love all of His creations. This is one of the greatest commandments." Pastor Swayles looked directly at Rachel and she felt herself smile graciously at him.

After the service, Rachel watched Robert approach Chase and invite him for coffee and the family's gift opening. Rachel waited, breathless, a polite distance away for his answer.

"Thank you so much for the offer, Robert. I must say it's hard to resist." Chase gazed at Rachel. "I've promised Mrs. Hopper I'd come by this evening; Mrs. Williams is anxious to serve her Christmas cake."

"There's always tomorrow. You'll join us for Christmas dinner?"

"I wouldn't miss it for the world." Chase then leaned close to Robert and whispered something only for his ears, and Robert nodded, a sneaky smile crossing his lips.

Rachel exited the church with Seth on her hip, having forgotten Robert's earlier instructions to his son. Chase, standing tall and fine in his dark suit, tipped his hat toward Rachel. "Good evening, Miss Phillips."

His very words sent her reeling. Chase Dylan could be extremely charming. It took all of Rachel's strength to contain her rising emotions as she returned with a simple, "Good evening, Mr. Dylan."

As the Lathrop family walked home, Robert carried an odd-sized, rectangular-shaped package beneath his arm. The parcel was wrapped in a flour sack and surrounded by a ribbon of the palest pink. He smiled secretively as he brought the mysterious bundle into the house and placed it under the small sequoia that decorated their home in honor of Jesus' birth.

"You've been taunting us with that package, Robert. Who are you planning on giving it to?" Maria teased.

"Now that you ask, I'll have to be forthright," Robert said. "The present is for Rachel." Rachel eyes widened in wonder, for she could not imagine what the gift could be. She had already received the parcel from her mother and stepfather, so she guessed it must be from the Lathrops.

"Please tell me you didn't get anything for me, Robert. . .Maria." Rachel had already felt as though she had imposed so much by living in their home.

"There's a notecard, Rachel. Why don't you open it?" Robert reached under the tree and placed the package in her hands.

Rachel fumbled eagerly with the envelope, pulling the contents out with childlike excitement. In the center of the notecard were the initials "C. D." and Rachel breathed deeply at the possibility that the gift was from Chase. She gently placed her fingers on the raised letters and touched them carefully.

"Go ahead, Rachel. Open it," Maria said excitedly.

Rachel closed her eyes momentarily and quickly opened the card. She was rewarded by Chase's own large script, with his signature at the bottom of the page.

> *Dear Rachel,*
> *I came to understand just how much you enjoyed Searsville Lake the evening of our quiet walk along its shore. You must be missing the view from Mrs. Hopper's home, and I hope this will brighten your mornings while you are staying with the Lathrops.*
> *Chase*

Rachel read the name again and again. Chase? Chase Dylan had really sent her a Christmas gift. Why? Was it just his flirtatious manner or could he possibly care for her after all? Rachel dared not to hope.

"Well, who is it from?" Maria asked, knowing full well by the smile on Rachel's face.

"It's. . .it's from Chase Dylan," Rachel said incredulously.

"Open!" Seth shouted excitedly.

Rachel carefully untied the pink ribbon and unwrapped the package. She gasped with delight as she walked toward the lamp and examined the contents closely. "Oh my, it's perfect," Rachel whispered breathily.

Rachel held in her hand the most incredible likeness of Searsville Lake, as seen from Rachel's bedroom when she had stayed at Mrs. Hopper's home. The oil painting captured the morning sunlight perfectly, casting its heavenly light upon the lake.

"Chase had Mrs. Williams paint it," Robert commented.

"Mrs. Williams from Redwood?" Rachel asked with surprise, for the painting seemed done by a professional.

"Chase says she dabbles with painting," Robert said.

"I'd say that's putting it mildly," Maria laughingly added.

"Either way, I'm sure we'll hear all about it tomorrow when Chase comes for dinner. In the meantime, I think it's getting a little late for the rest of the presents. Let's get to bed and start early in the morning.

Seth doesn't understand this gift-giving part of Christmas yet, so I think we'll be okay putting off our tradition until morning." Robert handed the women lamps and they prepared for sleep.

That night Rachel lay in bed, her eyes open and staring at the ceiling in disbelief. *Why would Chase give me such a gift? It must have been expensive, even if Mrs. Williams did paint it. Of course I can't keep it. Yet I dread the thought of parting with it. I wonder if Mrs. Williams might sell it to me after I return it to Chase? But could I afford it on my meager salary?* After a long, silent discussion with herself, Rachel finally fell into a restless sleep.

Chapter 16

Rachel awoke to a bright stream of sunshine pouring through her window on Christmas morning. *I love California,* she thought. *Where else can people enjoy so much glorious sunshine in the dead of winter?* She knew they needed the rains for the state's cattle and crops, but today she was just content to revel in the sun's bright warmth.

"Coffee's ready," Maria called out from the kitchen. Rachel started as she splashed her face with cold water from the wash basin on her bureau. It felt invigorating, and Rachel was reminded that it was indeed winter.

"I'll be right out, Maria." Rachel was embarrassed to see Seth's empty bed; she must have slept right through his usual wake-up routine. It was Christmas morning of course; the family would be anxious to begin their celebration. How could she have been so careless? Rachel's eyes were drawn to her painting, and she remembered the previous evening. Sleep had been so difficult.

Rachel emerged from her room with her new painting under her arm. "Rachel, what are you planning to do with that?" Maria asked.

"I want to take it outside and see it in the natural light. Then I plan to return it to its rightful owner, Chase Dylan." Rachel spoke the words with conviction, but clutched the painting tightly, obviously reluctant to part with it for even a moment, much less forever.

"Why ever would you give it back? It was a gift, and Chase obviously thought long and hard about it or it would not have been so well suited to you." Maria's logic seemed perfectly rational, and Rachel was once again tempted to keep the painting.

"Dear, I think what Rachel decides to do with the gift is her decision," Robert said.

"You're right. I'm sorry, Rachel. It's not my affair. Let's sit down and have breakfast, shall we? Seth?" Maria raised her voice in the direction of the parlor where Seth was playing noisily with his new wooden blocks.

Rachel set down the painting in a stream of sunlight near the doorway and stared into it.

*

"What did Searsville's beautiful young schoolteacher think of her painting?" Mrs. Williams asked Chase as they strolled along the lake in the chilly morning air. "Besides that it was the best likeness she'd ever seen—that goes without saying," she added jokingly, a twinkle in her eye.

"I don't rightly know yet. I suppose I'll find out this afternoon at supper." Mrs. Williams had been trying to marry him off since they'd met, and he took pleasure in trying to frustrate her matchmaking ways.

"If she enjoys the lake as much as you say, I can't think of any reason she wouldn't like it. Besides, I think the artist is brilliant," Mrs. Williams said lightheartedly.

Chase stopped in his tracks and turned toward Mrs. Williams, a serious look crossing his face. "Mrs. Williams, I must confess the painting was originally meant as more than a gift. From what I understand, Rachel is really struggling with her faith. I had hoped her difficulties would be over by the time I returned from Redwood, but I'm afraid that isn't the case. I had hoped the painting might show her that I care for her, that I have serious intentions toward her. I had intended to wait until the gossip died down, but I'm afraid I was over anxious."

Chase's piercing blue eyes looked hopefully into the elderly woman's own, then he continued, "I've fallen in love with her. But what if her faith isn't just bottoming out because of the town gossip? What if she truly has turned against the Lord?"

"I'd say that was the Lord's problem, Chase. Not yours." Mrs. Williams's voice was gentle but firm.

"I understand that, Mrs. Williams. I'm just wondering. . .do you think the Lord would bring me this far, only to tell me she's not the woman for me?"

"Chase, have you asked the Lord about you and Rachel? Perhaps you're not really seeking His will for your *own* life." Mrs. Williams's motherly tone put it as softly as it could be said. Deep down, Chase knew she was right. He had wanted to make Rachel the woman he wished her to be in his heart: the fiery and independent spirit he'd seen in Redwood, with a heart for the Lord. He had only prayed for her renewed faith, never for God's will, be that what it may.

"I'll think about that, Mrs. Williams. Thank you." Chase and Mrs. Williams continued silently along the lakefront, both lost in their hopes and prayers for Rachel's future.

⌘

"Breakfast was wonderful, but I feel like a lumberjack," Rachel remarked.

"Maybe that's because you ate like one," Maria teased as she stretched to place the last dish into the cupboard.

"Maria Lathrop, that baby is making you feisty," Rachel said, placing her hands on her hips in mock hostility.

"I think we should all go for a walk," Robert said. "With what we ate this morning, we could all use it. Go get your coats," he directed, calling for Seth to bring his boots.

The women were chattering excitedly about their gifts as they walked through the hallway and came to the doorway, happy and expectant. The foursome bundled for the chilled morning air and emerged from the ranch house brimming with Christmas spirit.

Seth ran ahead of the group, and Robert, overly protective since the lake incident, sprinted to keep up with him. Maria seized the opportunity to speak to Rachel alone, and confronted her gently: "Have you decided what you're going to tell Chase about the painting?"

Rachel's heart seemed to overflow. "Maria, I want to tell him, 'Thank you, you couldn't have given me a more perfect gift,' but I think what I need to tell him is that the painting belongs in his home," Rachel answered.

"Are you in love with him?" Maria asked bluntly.

Rachel searched for the answer in her heart. Her instinct told her to say no, but something choked back the words, and Rachel was forced to examine her feelings more closely. She thought about all of her encounters with the dashing Chase Dylan: in Redwood; at Mrs. Steele's; in the woods; by the lake. And she thought about his character; how he had overlooked her pride to protect her in the woods; how he cared for Henry Steele; how he had commissioned the gift of the painting. She closed her eyes and saw his sharp jawline and handsome, rugged features. She sighed in happy appreciation.

"Yes," she finally answered.

"What did you say?" Maria was incredulous.

"I said, yes. I am in love with him." A huge sense of relief flooded

Rachel with the admission, yet she was stunned at the revelation, her body experiencing a mixture of confusion and excitement.

"Oh Rachel!" Maria clapped her hands and hugged her friend closely. "How happy I am to hear you say that!"

"Maria, what if he doesn't love me? What if the gift was simply Chase being the resident peacekeeper?" Rachel remembered the words spoken to her of Chase in Redwood.

"Then God has something better for you." Maria's sweet face came close and her eyes spoke truth. Rachel was struck by the sincerity she saw there and felt convicted for the first time in many months. Perhaps Maria had been right about God. Perhaps He *did* know what was best after all.

"Maria, look who I found." Robert's voice jolted Maria and Rachel from their deep discussion. Mrs. Williams and Chase, Seth happily riding upon Chase's broad shoulders, were coming toward them along the lakeshore.

Rachel flushed with hot embarrassment, feeling her expression gave her recently disclosed feelings away. She found it difficult to breathe and dared not meet his gaze. *I must thank him for the gift, but not now. I'm just not ready to meet him yet.* She concentrated wholeheartedly on Mrs. Williams and went straight toward the older woman, ignoring the tall man next to her.

"Mrs. Williams, what a pleasure to see you again. I was hoping I would get the chance to thank you for your hospitality in Redwood City. I still haven't forgotten your incredible chicken and biscuits." Rachel clasped hands with Mrs. Williams. She knew she must bring up the painting, but remained silent on the subject. She was completely ignorant of how to discuss it without her emotions failing her.

Chase watched Rachel closely. She wouldn't look up at him or even at Seth, who giggled relentlessly from above. He frowned and carried Seth off to the path for a free-flying "pony-express" ride.

"Did you like the painting?" Mrs. Williams asked.

Relieved that Mrs. Williams had waited until Chase was out of earshot, Rachel's voice became animated. "Oh Mrs. Williams, I love it. It reminds me of every breathtaking morning I spent gazing from that window. You captured the light, the tranquillity. . .well, everything is just beautiful. I had no idea you were such an artist. Those paintings over the registration desk at the American House, they must be yours." Rachel fondly remembered the detailed paintings of Redwood's wharves that hung in the hotel's lobby.

"Rachel dear, I'm glad you like my artwork, but I was really more interested in what you thought of the gift *giver*." The question was pointed, and Rachel saw no escape. She glanced at Chase and back at Mrs. Williams. She could feel the heat rising from the back of her neck.

"Mr. Dylan has been a perfect gentleman, and I constantly get the opportunity to appreciate his thoughtfulness," Rachel said cryptically, hoping her answer hadn't given too much away. Mrs. Williams had the kind of face and open personality Rachel felt she could trust, but after her recent experience with gossip, she held her tongue.

"Well, that tells me a lot of nothing. I am an old woman, Rachel Phillips. Please get to the point." Mrs. Williams amiable face creased with laughter, and Rachel joined her, amused by her friend's directness.

"Mrs. Williams, I think the gift was far too expensive for the type of casual acquaintance Mr. Dylan and I share. I plan to give the painting back to him this afternoon. I want you to understand, though, that it has nothing to do with the artwork itself. I *love* the painting, but I simply can't accept it. It wouldn't be proper."

Mrs. Williams's voice became soft, "Rachel, I think you should do what you think is right." The older woman patted the younger woman's sleek hands. "Far be it for me to interfere. But you should know, the gift was from his heart. Chase Dylan wouldn't have it any other way."

"It's just that it must have been expensive, and. . ."

"Money really isn't an issue here. In case you haven't noticed, Chase is not governed by money. He has simple tastes. Made his money during the gold rush and hasn't spent hardly a nickel of it, except to buy that mill."

"The gold rush? Chase was in gold country?" This new information both shocked and delighted the schoolteacher, knowing they shared a similar background.

"Well, not *in* gold country exactly. In Redwood, he and a friend named Littlejohn invented that there, oh now, what d'ya call it? A scale of some sort. It measured the gold; made a right fortune on it, I believe. So you see, honey, when Chase Dylan decides to splurge, he does so because he wants to."

"Thank you, Mrs. Williams. I'll keep that in mind." Once again Rachel dared to hope that Chase Dylan had stronger feelings for her. He certainly never ceased to amaze her. Besides being admirable and generous, he was also intelligent and resourceful. *An inventor,* she thought dreamily. *Pa would have loved him.*

"Rachel, it's time for Seth's nap. Are you ready to head back?" Robert called from the lakeshore.

"Certainly. Mrs. Williams, I hope we'll be able to get together soon. I'd love to hear about the hotel and the changes you and your husband have made."

Mrs. Williams nodded. "I'd enjoy that." The two said their good-byes and each headed along the shore in a separate direction. Seth parted with Chase, who said he'd be over later in the afternoon for supper.

✒

Seth was contentedly settled in bed for a nap when Maria came into the parlor, where Rachel was reading in the late afternoon sun.

"Where's Robert?" Rachel asked.

"He's out with his first love, the horses. Can't seem to shake them from his system. Says he just loves to appreciate their lines and graceful movements."

"He must have really loved you to leave his job as a vaquero," Rachel said with a marked accent, much to the delight of Maria.

"Yes, I know. And the best part is he tells me every day that it was all worth it."

"What about you, Maria? Was coming to Searsville worth leaving the only life you'd ever known?" Rachel now embraced the new relationship she shared with Maria. Their newfound closeness reminded her of the friendship she shared with her mother.

"When I first came here, I couldn't imagine what I'd done. The women treated me frightfully from the moment they saw me. I can't say I was ignorant of the reason, I'd seen the other *rancheros* treat the Indians the same way due to their skin color, and it hasn't been that long since the Mexican-American war. The battle for California certainly hasn't helped my cause. So, in answer to your question, I can't say coming to Searsville was worth it. But coming here with Robert, *that* was worth it." A wide grin crossed her face and the two began to giggle.

"Maria, you are a sight. Your tummy shakes so when you laugh." Rachel placed her hand on her friend's tummy. "Oh my, the baby's moving!" Rachel yanked her hand away abruptly.

"Someday, Rachel Phillips, you'll be as round as me, and I'll have no mercy," Maria said, wagging her finger.

Melancholy overcame Rachel, as her first thoughts were of Chase. Would she ever know a love like Maria and Robert's or her own mother and father's? Rachel desperately hoped so.

"Rachel, I'm sorry if I . . ."

Rachel inhaled at length and calmed herself. "No, no. There's nothing to be sorry about. I'm just doing a lot of thinking and remembering, and that won't do on Christmas day. It's a day for celebrating."

"I'm so sorry your family couldn't come. But there's always next Christmas, and you'll see them during the summer. Hotel owners just get busy, I suppose," Maria said.

"Maria, I have a confession to make. My mother didn't cancel their trip to Searsville. . . I did."

"Why would you do such a thing? You were looking forward to their visit. It's all you talked about."

"I'm humiliated at how my path has turned. I'm living with a happily married couple due to have another baby in three months. I've invaded their son's room and have nothing to call my own. Nothing except the elaborate dresses my mother sends me. If my stepfather were to find out about my 'scandalous behavior,' be it true or otherwise, he'd disown me immediately. I know he would."

"Rachel, I'm sorry you didn't tell me this before. This must have been hard for you to keep inside. But I think you're wrong about your stepfather. I think he loves and cares for you very much. When he interviewed Robert about the job, he was very concerned about every detail of your living arrangements," Maria said briskly.

"He interviewed Robert about my position?" Rachel asked dumbfounded.

"Absolutely. He asked Robert when he came to know Jesus as his Savior, how long we had been married, anything and everything that might affect you during your stay in town, under our supervision. That was another thing. He made sure you wouldn't be alone, that we would keep a very close eye on you. That's why you never had a home of your own. Robert was prepared to build a home for the new schoolteacher behind the schoolhouse, but Mr. Winsome didn't want you staying alone."

"I had no idea." This new information about her stepfather was incredible to Rachel. She had never seen anything remotely close to caring on his part, and to learn that he had overseen her entire placement was simply unbelievable. She thought he had merely thrown her into the first available position.

"Trust me, Rachel. He was very thorough; that's why we felt you were such a perfect match for our town school. I'm just so embarrassed at the way our village has treated you."

"I'm going to pray. I feel like praying." Rachel surprised herself by the sudden urge, but she wanted to talk to God. Possibly He could answer the many questions that filled her head.

"I'll leave you alone," Maria said.

⟡

Chase arrived for Christmas dinner carrying packages for all of the Lathrop family. He brought Maria a tortoiseshell comb for her hair, just like the one he'd seen in her *Rancho de Estrella* painting. For Robert, he had purchased a new pair of boots in Redwood's finest shop, and for Seth, a new woolen coat for winter.

Rachel marveled at the thought Chase had put into the gifts, and it made her appreciate even more the painting he had commissioned for her. The family rejoiced in their gifts and went off together into the kitchen, leaving Rachel and Chase alone in the parlor.

"How is the teaching going?" Chase asked.

"Not very well, I'm afraid. Dennis and Aubrey haven't returned to school since I ridiculed them. I didn't mean to, of course; I was trying to show them that an education would help them achieve their dreams. Instead, I told them their dreams were impossible."

"Would it help if I talked with them? I'll see them tomorrow at the mill."

"Chase, would you?" Rachel asked.

"Of course. I wouldn't want Searsville's best teacher to become discouraged because of one little incident." Rachel felt a weight begin to lift from her shoulders at the thought her students might return. She was caught off guard when Chase changed the subject. "Rachel, did you like the present I gave you?"

"Yes, Chase. I like it very much. The likeness was uncanny; I had no idea Mrs. Williams was so talented," Rachel answered, avoiding the real subject.

"Yes, her mother was an artist as well. Mrs. Williams always says her first toy was a paintbrush."

Rachel breathed deeply and prepared her rehearsed speech, "Chase. . .Mr. Dylan, I love the painting, but I'm returning it to you for your own home." Chase laughed out loud and the young woman stared in confusion.

"I don't understand. Is something funny?"

"Rachel, if you saw my home you'd know why I'm laughing. I'm afraid home decor has never been a priority in my life." Rachel's brow furrowed in thought as she visualized the home as a hermit's cave without the basic necessities of life. Chase added quickly, "Well, it's not *that* bad. It's just that fine artwork would hardly be at home in my cabin."

"I'm afraid the painting is just too perfect, I mean. . .personnel." Rachel looked out the window, flustered.

"Oh. . .well, that's not how it was intended. I'm sorry if you misunderstood or if I offended you," Chase said angrily. Rachel felt a rush of warmth rise from the base of her neck, becoming a flush of color on her cheeks. Obviously Chase had meant the gift only as a token of friendship, and she had read more into it.

"Dinner's ready," Maria called from the doorway.

"Maria, I don't think I'll be joining you for dinner." Chase's tone was pointed. "I promised Henry Steele that I'd come by. It's getting late, and. . .well, thanks anyway." Chase bolted for the door without addressing Rachel or Robert. He picked up the painting which was in the entryway and roughly shoved it under his arm.

Rachel stayed motionless by the window as she watched him walk toward Gretchen Steele's home, a jealous fury building inside her. Maria and Robert looked at one another in confusion.

Robert spoke first. "I'm going to check on the horses before dinner. I'll take Seth with me. We'll be back later." He excused himself and left Maria to deal with the fallout.

"Rachel? Do you want to talk about it?" Maria asked.

"What's there to talk about? I made a fool out of myself and now, if

Gretchen Steele has her way, the whole town will know soon enough." Rachel's pride was wounded. Not only because her feelings for Chase had been thwarted, but because her rival had seemingly won.

"Rachel, Chase would never tell anyone anything that would hurt you."

"I'm sure he finds it quite amusing that Searsville's schoolteacher is so dim that she can't discern friendship from courtship."

"What do you mean?"

"I told him I thought the gift of the painting was too personal."

"Yes, and what did he say to that?"

"He said it wasn't meant that way. Meaning, 'I was just trying to be nice, not make an offer of marriage.' Oh Maria, it was humiliating." Rachel stifled tears.

"Rachel, I'm so sorry. I had no idea. I thought he felt about you the way you do about him; otherwise, I would never have pressed you to accept the gift. Would you like to pray about it?"

"Not just yet, but thank you," she answered.

"How are things going with you and. . ." Maria's head nodded heavenward.

"We're still working on it," she answered.

"Listen. Listen closely for His answers and know that He hears you." Oddly enough, the words were very comforting to Rachel.

✍

Chase Dylan walked up Gretchen's front walk. From the foyer window, he watched her run from the parlor, stop at the mahogany-framed mirror, and pinch her cheeks vigorously to bring up their color. She opened the door before he knocked and stood posed in a scarlet Christmas gown.

Chase didn't speak when she opened the door, so she began, "Chase, what a lovely painting."

"Yeah, nice, isn't it?" Chase's answer was sarcastic, and he looked on Gretchen with disdain. "Is Henry here?" He was not in the mood for Gretchen's games today.

"He's outside near the lake, playing with his new trains. Would you like to see him?" Gretchen's voice was both optimistic and expectant, causing Chase to be aware of his rudeness.

"Gretchen, I'm sorry. I haven't wished you a happy Christmas. Have you enjoyed your holiday?"

"It's been very pleasant. Henry's been asking about you all day." Gretchen stepped down onto the porch, pulled her gown around the door, and shut it behind her. "Let's go find him, shall we?" She rustled down the front steps.

Chase took her arm and escorted her to the lake. Once on the familiar path, Gretchen began, "Chase, we've been friends for many years now, isn't that right?"

"Yes, Gretchen, we have," Chase agreed.

"We have both lived in Searsville *alone* for many years now." Apprehension hit the bachelor as he realized what she was getting at. He had worked for years to avoid this conversation, but it was finally happening. There was no turning back; Gretchen Steele was making her move.

"Gretchen, I think. . ." Chase tried to steer the conversation, hoping to avoid an embarrassing situation for the widow.

"No, no, let me finish. I've avoided this long enough. . .I feel as though you have been a father to my son. I loved Harold with all my heart, I still do, but I can't continue to hold a torch for a man who is gone. I must think of Henry. Not to mention that I'm lonely in this big house by myself. What I'm trying to say is, would you consider becoming my husband, for Henry's sake as well as mine?" Gretchen's voice trembled, and she looked downward.

Chase lifted her chin and smiled sympathetically into the widow's face. She was still a beautiful woman, but Chase knew he felt only friendship for her. He also knew he could never settle for less than love in marriage. And he had seen how Harold's death had torn Gretchen apart, leaving her a bitter woman, separated from God.

"I loved Harold, too, and you know I love Henry. I think highly of you, Gretchen, but I cannot marry you. I love someone else. Maybe nothing will ever come of that, but I can't marry you regardless. It wouldn't be right."

Gretchen left the path with a quick turn and ran toward the house with her hands shielding her disgraced face.

"Gretchen, wait!" Chase shouted. She stopped in her tracks. Tears streamed down her face and she reached for Chase, needing to be hugged, her vestige of pride apparently now gone. "Gretchen, you don't love me. I'm just all you have left of Harold," Chase pleaded.

She sniffed and nodded. "In my heart, I know you're right, but I'm just so lonely and you've always been there for us. I know I can always count on you." She continued to sob into his muscular chest as the sun went down on the crisp Christmas day.

Chapter 17

The Sunday following Christmas, Rachel glared at her Bible on the dresser. It lay open to Proverbs. She idly walked over and slammed it shut. *Once again You've abandoned me,* she thought while staring heavenward.

"Chooch." Seth's pudgy little hands reached for the book.

"Yes, honey. That's right, church. This is the Bible, the book from church." Rachel had been very careful about upholding her former beliefs in front of Seth. She respected the Lathrops' right to teach their son whatever they wished, and would help them do so. That was only proper.

"Achel, chooch." Seth nodded his head vigorously.

"Yes, today Rachel is coming to church." The little boy reached for her hand and happily skipped from the room, leading her to the front door.

The Lathrops and Rachel reached the church and the family headed for their regular pew. Rachel sat alongside the aisle, with Seth seated contentedly in her lap. She sighed quietly in boredom and gazed about the room. Gretchen Steele's eyes met her own, and they narrowed in understood competition.

Pastor Swayles was especially optimistic for his New Year's sermon and smiled blissfully as the church filled to capacity.

"Today," he shouted, to gain everyone's attention, "we will begin to celebrate the new year, 1864. It's a time to remember 1863 and praise the Lord for all of our blessings throughout the year and during our lifetimes."

Yes, yes, thought Rachel, rolling her eyes. *Let's thank God, even though He never gives us what we want. Let's blindly thank Him anyway, being the oxen we are.*

"And let us not forget," Pastor Swayles boomed, "what He gave to *all* mankind. . .He gave us His Son, an eternal gift that we've celebrated anew this past week, on Christmas Day! For those of you who have a child, I want you to think now of that child." Pastor Swayles went on, and Rachel smiled lovingly at her precious Seth, enjoying the game. He felt like her very own.

"God brought that child into your life for a reason. He made that child the perfect fit for your life, and you love that child with all your heart." The congregation mumbled in approval, and Rachel herself nodded her head in agreement, tightening her embrace around Seth.

"Now look at someone near you, someone who is not a member of your family." The congregation did as they were told, happily eyeing and smiling at different people gathered about them. Rachel's delight at Seth was replaced by scorn as she focused intently on Gretchen Steele, the widow's own beady eyes staring back.

"Would you give up your child for that person?"

The very thought caused Rachel to shudder. *Give up Seth for that woman? I wouldn't give up the ranch dog for her!* Rachel was immediately disgusted and ashamed by her own thoughts. *When did I become so hateful? Mrs. Steele doesn't know any better, she's hurt because she lost her husband, that's what Maria says, anyway. How is it that Maria was able to forgive the awful things Gretchen said about her?*

Rachel glanced at Maria and then back at Gretchen. Mrs. Steele was crying openly while holding on tightly to her son, rocking him gently back and forth as though he were a baby. *Surely a woman who loves her son like that isn't all bad.*

"Well, that's what God did for you." Pastor Swayles's thundering voice again interrupted Rachel's thoughts. "For God so loved *you*, He gave His only begotten Son. That whoever believeth in Him should not perish, but have everlasting life. Think about those words today as we reflect on our lives. God loved you so much in 1863 that He sent His only Child to die, so that you might have eternal life simply by believing in Him. And He loves you just as much today, folks."

The color drained from Rachel's face and her grip on Seth inexplicably released. He looked up questioningly at her blank face. "Achel?"

"Shhh," she whispered kindly. She looked down at the toddler, who had seemed to be her only friend during recent times. Suddenly, it all came clear to her as she thought about those simple words she had heard time and time again: *"For God so loved. . ."*

It was as though she were hearing the words for the first time. *God loves me more than I could ever love this child.* She looked into his beautiful, enormous light blue eyes. *He doesn't want to see me hurt any more than I wanted to see Seth drown in the lake that day. Is such a love possible?* Rachel needed time to think.

"Seth, go see your mommy, honey." Rachel handed the boy to his mother, stood as the sermon was ending, and dashed out the door. She didn't stop until she'd reached the familiar, ancient oak tree near the lake. She dropped to her knees without worrying about her gown, clasped her hands together, and sobbed in deep remorse, aware for the first time how empty her life had been over the last few months. Not because she was in Searsville, but because she had been living life without the Lord.

Dearest Father in heaven, You have shown me today how selfish and repulsive I have been. My thoughts about Gretchen Steele just sicken me. I'm beginning to see how You have kept me safe and among people who would take care of me. . .and all I've done is complain about them not being the right people. I've been so angry because Your will was not the same as mine. First, I was so angry at Marshall for sending me away, but I would have never known how much I love to teach if he hadn't done that. Then You sent me to live with Maria, who I thought simply a religious zealot. Now I know her for the kind-hearted, generous person she is, a woman who shares some of my background and struggles. She, too, was sent away from her only family. She was the focus of evil gossip. And yet she never left Your side. Why couldn't I see that before? You provided an example for me, a foundation for me. You have been faithful, asking only that I believe that You sent Your Son to die for me. Yet I was so proud; I thought You only wanted to hurt me. I'm sorry it's taken me so long to learn this lesson; I've been so hardened. Thank You for Pastor's message, thank You for Seth showing me the way, and thanks especially for Your Son. Please forgive me in the name of Jesus. Amen.

Rachel felt immediately at peace, knowing once again what it felt like to be reconciled to God. She knew her heart would have to continually be before the Lord in prayer, for her jealous feelings over Gretchen Steele and Chase Dylan had diminished only slightly.

❧

Chase had made a point to attend services after his Christmas Day discussion with Gretchen. Although he'd planned to stay in Portola through the winter, he didn't want Gretchen to think it was to avoid her. He was speaking with Pastor Swayles when Gretchen approached him. "Gretchen, what a pleasure to see you. Did you enjoy the sermon?" Chase bid the pastor good-bye and took the widow aside.

"Yes, Chase, I did, thank you. I appreciated it very much," Gretchen answered honestly.

"How are you feeling?" Chase asked with deep concern for his friend. He was pleased she had not avoided him.

"I'm fine, Chase. Really. I wanted to thank you for being the voice of reason for me the last time we spoke." Gretchen's voice was calm and even.

"That's what friends are for, Gretchen."

"And we are friends, aren't we? I'm very thankful for that." The peace behind her words was new to Chase, and he wondered what had happened after their confrontation. "Henry and I are having our very own New Year's Eve party tonight. We're going to ring in 1864 with style," Gretchen said happily, gesturing with her arms expressively.

"That's wonderful, Gretchen. I hope you both have a wonderful time. I'll see the two of you Tuesday when I pick up Henry."

"We're looking forward to it," she replied. Chase was intrigued by the woman standing before him. Never since Harold's death had he seen Gretchen so happy or content.

"Miss Phillips, are you okay?" Her eyes full of concern, Veronica Smith, the young bride, had interrupted Rachel's prayer alongside the lake.

"Yes, Veronica. Thank you, I'm fine." Rachel rose quickly, dusting off her skirt and sniffing away her tears.

"I've been meanin' to drop by and speak with you, but I've been a little afraid."

"Whatever do you mean, Veronica?"

"Do you remember when I told you that I wouldn't be alone because Jeremiah would be workin' for Chase Dylan?"

"Yes, of course I do. And how is Jeremiah?"

"I'm embarrassed to say it, but he's been workin' for Mr. Hopper since Chase left for Redwood, and I seldom see him." Veronica's voice sounded more mature and it seemed marriage had actually been good for the young woman. Gone was the ever-present childish whining Rachel remembered.

"I'm very sorry to hear that, Veronica." Rachel was sorry, but didn't understand why Veronica would confide such information in her.

"I'm living with my folks right now, until Chase begins running his mill next week. But I was wonderin' if you would lend me some books to bide my time."

"Books?" Rachel was caught off guard. First, her mind was thrown into a whirlwind at the mere mention of Chase being back at work in Portola. She thought of him in his dark, sturdy work pants and torn mill shirt. Second, she questioned Veronica's sudden penchant for learning. Veronica had always been bright, but rarely had any initiative for education.

"Yeah, I was thinkin' since I'm not really being a full-fledged wife, I might as well be learnin'. I was thinkin' a book on sums. . ."

Rachel regained her composure. "That's very good thinking indeed, and I think Jeremiah will be very proud of you for your efforts."

Veronica smiled at the mention of her husband. "We're savin' to buy a place of our own, and the more I know my numbers, the better we'll be able to budget."

Rachel was impressed with the new Veronica Smith. *Jeremiah must be quite a man to have such a positive affect on this young woman.* "That sounds like very mature thinking to me." Veronica grinned broadly, and the two women made arrangements to exchange the books.

New Year's Eve in Searsville was a ruckus that reminded Rachel of her days in the gold country. Gunfire was plentiful, and the whoops and hollers of drunken men kept law-abiding citizens indoors.

"I dare say this town gets crazier every year," Maria said as she anxiously knitted a small bootie.

"I wouldn't worry too much. From the sound of things, tomorrow will be a very quiet day in Searsville," Robert said, laughing. "Their problem is, it takes them a whole year to forget how much they drank the year before."

Rachel rose from her parlor seat. "Seth's asleep by now. I'm going to write a letter to my mother. Good-night." She headed for her bedroom with her lamp.

December 31, 1863

Dear Mother,

Happy New Year, 1864. I certainly hope this year will be all that you desire. My purpose in writing is to make a confession regarding my life here in Searsville. I have been less than forthright about my true position here in the village, and I think it's only

*proper that you know the truth. First, however, you must under-
stand that I am fine and now resting in the Lord's peace, so there is
nothing you can do for me. Be assured that I know He is watching
over me.*

*It seems that when I came to Searsville, I made an enemy of
a certain influential woman in town. Somewhere an ugly rumor
was begun, and I have been shunned by most of the town's citizens.
To make a long story short, I have been blaming Marshall and
others for my problems, instead of taking responsibility for being
out of God's Will with my life. I've since learned God's love is
sufficient, as strong as the redwood. Indeed, stronger, for He is not
at the mercy of man.*

*Mother, I want you to tell Marshall that I'm sorry for thinking
badly of him. I've since heard all that he did to make sure I would
be properly cared for here and that I would be with believers in
Searsville. Tell him I'm sorry, won't you mother? And please kiss my
baby Georgie.*

*With all my love,
Rachel*

Chapter 18

Rachel returned after the holidays eager to share the Lord with the children. She had been in constant prayer since Pastor Swayles's message about Christ and planned to speak to the children each and every day about their foundation in the Lord. "Today, children, we're reading from Hebrews, chapter four, verse fifteen: 'For we have not a high priest which cannot be touched with the feeling of our infirmities; but was in all points tempted like as we are, yet without sin.' This means Christ was able to bear all temptations without falling into sin. Is it possible for us to do that?"

"No," sung the class.

"It may not be possible, but with Christ that's not necessary. He will clothe our unrighteousness. Is there anyone here today who hasn't asked Christ to dwell in his heart, but would like to do so?" Rachel would repeat the offer daily after her Bible lesson, making sure her class was well versed in the road to salvation, just as she'd promised to do when she accepted her role as Searsville's teacher.

❧

Chase had a light step as he strolled along to pick up Henry for their first time together in two months. The chilled evening air was refreshing, and Chase was looking forward to his new relationship with Henry's mother. Gone would be the tension that had been present since Harold's death.

"Henry!" Chase shouted as the small boy came rushing out the doorway into his arms.

"Chase, Mama and me are movin' by the train," Henry explained enthusiastically. Chase's lightheartedness suddenly left him, and he took the news like a blow to the stomach.

"Moving?" He looked to the doorway where Gretchen stood, an approving expression upon her face. Putting Henry down, he walked tentatively toward her. "What's this about, Gretchen?"

"Henry, why don't you go see what Jackson's up to in the stable. Maybe he'll let you give Clarabel an apple," Gretchen directed, and Henry obediently did as he was told. "Why don't you come in? I've made some coffee and apple pie."

The color drained from Chase's face as he thought of his beloved Henry leaving. He wasn't certain of the boy's salvation, and Chase felt that vital matter was his responsibility. Harold had asked him personally upon his deathbed to see to it. Now, the opportunity was being snatched away before he had a chance to fulfill his promise. He loved Henry like his own son, and it pained him to think about Henry leaving.

Gretchen led Chase into the front parlor and set a silver tray of pie and coffee before him. Chase looked with apprehension at the fuss she had made and knew Henry's words had been the truth.

"Before you say anything, I think you should know Harold had always intended for us to live in town, in Redwood. When he died, I forgot all about those plans. I've been concentrating on other matters up until now." Gretchen made no attempt to hide her past plans to attract Chase's affections. "And now I think it's best for Henry. He'll still see you often enough, every time you're in Redwood, I would think."

"Gretchen, I just don't understand. There's so much Henry and I planned. We haven't even gotten to ride the railroad yet."

"Chase, there are no opportunities for us here. Harold left us very well off, but I'm just withering away in Searsville, from boredom and a lack of purpose. And, quite frankly, I don't like the person I've become here."

"Please don't take any offense at this, but what makes you think things will be any different in Redwood?" Chase asked.

"I don't know that they will. I just need to try something different. Mrs. Williams, your friend who's staying with Mrs. Hopper, has offered me a job."

"A job?" Chase said incredulously.

"Believe it or not, I'm a very capable woman. Before I married Harold, I ran a highly recommended restaurant in San Francisco," Gretchen said defensively.

"Gretchen, I never meant to imply. . .I only meant, why would you want to work when—"

"The only thing I've accomplished here is the occasional quilt and a great deal of trouble. Redwood will provide more stimulation for both

Henry and me, and, hopefully, I'll learn to keep my mouth quiet."

"Have you prayed about this?" Chase asked.

"What is it with you and Robert Lathrop and *that* question?"

"I just don't want you to make a mistake with Henry."

"The fact is, I'm human and I'm bound to make a mistake or two, but I feel the need to get out of Searsville. We're planning to move in the spring, when Mr. Williams is finished with the hotel."

"Gretchen, is there anything I can say to change your mind?"

"I don't think so," Gretchen said slowly.

⟡

It was a pleasant Saturday in February, and Rachel sat along the lakeside with her Bible open to Proverbs. It was her favorite book; she felt God must truly have had a sense of humor, encapsulating so much wisdom in such short passages. She came to chapter six and read with great interest:

"'My son, if thou be surety for thy friend, if thou has stricken thy hand with a stranger, thou art snared with the words of thy mouth. . . . Do this now, my son, and deliver thyself, when thou art come into the hand of thy friend; go, humble thyself, and make sure thy friend.'"

Rachel wasn't sure why, but she read the words as a commandment. On deeper evaluation, she felt God telling her to reconcile with Gretchen Steele. The very idea appalled her, but she knew God's gentle reminders would not go away until she'd put an end to the strife that was between her and the young widow. She must make it right, even if it was a one-sided effort.

Rachel closed her Bible and prayed for wisdom. Then she rose from the lakeside, dusted off her skirt, and began walking along the path toward the towering Steele home. As she stood on the front walk, her knees buckled at the thought of entering the house. The last time she had been in the home had been the night of the sewing circle, where she had heard the vicious lies about Maria. Rachel also knew that the following week must have been when the rumor about "her" baby had been circulated.

Rachel held her Bible close to her chest and continued to stare blankly at the front door of the home. Suddenly the door opened and Gretchen Steele appeared with a small rug in her hands. She began to beat the rug over the front porch banister before noticing Rachel's presence.

"May I help you?" The widow asked scornfully.

"Mrs. Steele, I think we need to talk."

"I can't think of anything I have to say to you, Miss Phillips," she said, while attempting to close the door.

Rachel's stomach churned with nervousness, but she clung tightly to her Bible, praying silently, and continued to move forward, pushing the door open with her hand. "Well then, maybe you might listen for a change."

"I beg your pardon," Gretchen finally managed.

"Mrs. Steele, I really think we ought to go inside. This is not a matter of public interest."

Gretchen Steele dropped the rug over the banister and motioned for Rachel to enter the house. The widow glanced about to see if anyone had witnessed the exchange and then followed the teacher into the house quickly, closing the door hastily behind her. Rachel wasn't invited in, so the two stood facing one another in the foyer.

"Miss Phillips, if this is about Chase Dylan, I can assure you I have nothing to do with the fact that he has no interest in you whatsoever," she snippily commented.

"This has absolutely nothing to do with Chase Dylan. I haven't even seen the man since the New Year's Eve service." Rachel was surprised that the attack didn't sting; in fact, it had caused the exact opposite reaction than what had been intended. Somehow, Rachel felt an over-whelming emotion of mercy. All at once she saw Mrs. Steele for the broken person that she was: a woman terrified of living in the rug-ged logging territory without the husband she had loved and unable to share those fears with anyone. No one seemed to truly care about the woman except her son. The only people who were on speaking terms with her seemed to be Chase Dylan and the small circle of quilting party members who met at the general store to gossip. Rachel was filled with sadness.

"Well, what are you doing here then, Miss Phillips? My son will not be attending your schoolroom next year, so I hardly think we have anything to discuss." Gretchen sounded incensed, and Rachel knew her presence in the woman's home must have been painful.

"Mrs. Steele, I have come because I believe I owe you an apology."

"An apology?" The other woman asked. Rachel thought she noticed guilt flash momentarily across Gretchen Steele's face.

"I think I need to sit down. Do you mind?" Gretchen led Rachel into the front room, motioning for her to sit down in a high-backed chair, upholstered in a formal burgundy red-and-white print.

"Mrs. Steele, as I was saying, I really must apologize for my reprehensible behavior toward you. In addition to changing the dress size on your catalogue order for the Thorne wedding, I have been rude in your presence. And, I'm sorry to admit, I have also spoken about you harshly behind your back. Regardless of what you may have done to or said about me, I do not have the right to speak ill of you. As a Christian, God asks me to forgive, and that's what I must do. I should have come to you long ago, before this got out of hand." Rachel stopped and waited, unsure if she should rise to leave or not.

"What did you say about being a Christian? Are you implying I'm not a Christian?"

Rachel's heart raced; she hadn't been prepared for this. She thought Mrs. Steele would just rant and rave, asking her to leave. She silently asked for God's words, and continued cautiously. "In the Gospel of Saint Matthew, Jesus says, 'That whosoever is angry with his brother without a cause shall be in danger of the judgment.' I knew when I read that and another scripture from Proverbs that I needed to apologize to you."

Gretchen stood, wringing her hands nervously, and looked at Rachel, unable to speak. Suddenly, Rachel was given an uncommon boldness. "Mrs. Steele, have you ever asked Jesus into your heart?"

"I think you should go now, Miss Phillips." Rachel got up slowly, hoping the widow might change her mind. Mrs. Steele stepped purposefully from the room and climbed the stairs, leaving Rachel to wonder what she was thinking. Disappointed and frustrated, Rachel let herself out.

Gretchen remained on the landing after the schoolteacher left and spoke aloud to herself, "Have I ever asked Jesus into my heart? Maybe not, but it's certainly no business of yours, Rachel Phillips."

❦

It was a pleasant March afternoon following church service, when Rachel, sitting in the front parlor with a book, heard voices on the porch.

"Perhaps, we should have asked if this afternoon would be a good time."

"Perhaps we should have, but we didn't, so go ahead and knock. You owe those women an apology, and it's long overdue."

Rachel opened the door and was shocked to see Mrs. Williams and Thelma Hopper standing there on the porch with smiles on their faces and two fresh lemon cakes in their hands. "Mrs. Hopper, Mrs. Williams, what a pleasant surprise. Won't you please come in." Rachel stepped back and waved the women through to the parlor. She took the cakes from them and called for the rest of the household. "Robert, Seth, we have visitors. I'm sorry, but Mrs. Lathrop is in isolation until the baby comes." The women nodded knowingly.

Seth was the first to race to the parlor, followed by his father. When everyone had gathered, the silence became apparent, and Mrs. Williams was the one who broke it.

"Miss Phillips, I hope we're not intruding. We baked these lemon cakes yesterday, and thought we might drop them by as a sort of peace offering."

"Peace offering?" Rachel inquired.

Thelma Hopper took over. "Yes, a peace offering for the injustice I've done to you and Mrs. Lathrop. Mr. Lathrop, I hope you will convey my deepest apologies to your wife for me. When she is up and around, I will be sure to do so myself." The older woman looked to her friend for support and went on. "Miss Phillips, you and Mrs. Lathrop have both been the victims of such terrible gossip. I hate to even mention it, for fear of bringing more pain to you. But I need to apologize for my part in the evil—for listening to it in the first place, and, most of all, for acting on it by shunning you both and by asking you to leave my house, Miss Phillips. I'm afraid I did you both a serious grievance."

Rachel felt tears coming on, and did her best to stifle them, but there was no stopping the emotion, and soon her tears flowed freely. She had been vindicated. Maybe it was only one member of the community, but it was an answer to prayer nonetheless, and for that she was overjoyed.

"Mrs. Hopper, thank you," Rachel said, wiping away tears. "I know this must have been very difficult for you. It isn't easy to admit when we've made a mistake." Rachel moved forward and embraced the older woman. Thelma stood stiff with surprise at first, but then warmed to the hug, returning it.

"Enough of all this, let's have some cake," Mrs. Williams said, breaking the intensity of the moment; excited chattering began. Seth raced to the kitchen at the promise of cake, and Rachel prepared coffee and the dishes for a pleasant afternoon visit.

Chapter 19

Chase Dylan eyed Searsville with pleasure. Over two months had passed since he had seen Rachel. Gretchen had sent Henry to stay with him on Sundays during the winter months, and Jeremiah had handled things in Redwood, so there had really been no reason to visit town. No reason, that is, except Rachel Phillips. And after her blatant refusal of his Christmas gift, he saw no good reason to pursue that alliance in the future. His heart plummeted at the very thought.

Chase approached Davenport General Store and was about to enter when he noticed Rachel Phillips strolling into the post office with a young man. A tall, sturdy young man. His pulse quickened and his jaw clenched in jealousy as he realized with annoyance that his desire for Rachel had not ended. He stopped abruptly at the store's entry and resolutely walked to the post office instead, determined to let Rachel Phillips know what a spectacle she was making of herself.

Once inside the post office, possessiveness surged through him as he eyed Rachel and the other man talking by the counter.

"Miss Phillips." Chase's voice was admonishing.

"Chase," Rachel said with pleasure, a captivated smile crossing her face.

Chase felt himself charmed to the core by her enchanting appearance, and his jealousy fled. She was wearing a simple calico gown of tan, but its plainness highlighted the luxurious red in her hair and the deep green of her eyes. Once again, Chase Dylan knew he was in love.

"Chase, you know Aubrey Dawson," Rachel said excitedly. Chase knew she was trying to thank him for getting the older boys to return to school.

"Certainly, works for me in the summers as a peeler, and a fine one at that," Chase said confidently, trying to conceal his shame over the jealousy that had just gotten the best of him, and over a mere boy.

"Aubrey's planning to be a mill owner just like you. He's just sent away for information on the latest saws and boilers. He's learning how much money he will need to earn to set up his own mill," Rachel said proudly, while Aubrey shyly perused the paperwork and diagrams before him.

"Aubrey, anytime you have questions about the mill, you can come to me. I'd be happy to tell you what you want to know."

"Thank you, Mr. Dylan. I'll do that." Aubrey smiled, then went back to the information he was reading.

Rachel and Chase unconsciously walked away together into a corner of the post office, longing to be alone together. Chase spoke first. "How have you been, Rachel?"

"Oh Chase, I've been wonderful. I've given my heart to the Lord again, Mrs. Hopper and I have reconciled, and my job is going very well. I've been studying the logging industry in great detail, and the children are learning at a pace I never thought possible. They are actually excited about their sums! Some of them have actually taken to teaching their parents about what they've learned; it's really quite rewarding. Have you spoken with Robert yet? Maria's almost ready to have her baby, and. . ." Rachel stopped in midsentence and gazed up at the entranced gentleman before her. "Oh my, it seems I need to come up for air," Rachel laughed.

He took delight in seeing her openness once again, and silently rejoiced that Rachel had gained God's peace since he'd seen her last. Perhaps that was the Lord's way of letting him know that she was indeed the woman for him. He silently prayed it was so.

"Oh, I have so much I want to tell you. First, I must thank you for getting the boys to come back to school. They are doing so well and I owe it all to you. They really respect you, you know." The two became lost in their own world of conversation, oblivious to the many customers that walked in and out of the post office.

"Rachel, if you would ever like to visit the mill, I'd be happy to show you around. That way, you could explain to your class how a mill is run in detail by witnessing it for yourself." Chase made the offer with ulterior motives. Of course, he could help her with her teaching, but his true motivation was to see the woman he loved at his mill.

"That's a wonderful idea. I could explain to them about each job, and they could tell me what their fathers do. They would love that!"

"Very well. You name the day." Chase was overjoyed, for he now knew he would not go another two months without seeing this woman again. He noticed that Aubrey was through studying his paperwork, and Chase said a reluctant good-bye to Rachel before heading back to Davenport General Store, a happy sparkle in his eye.

☙

"Miss Phillips, would you mind if I had a word with you?" Gretchen Steele appeared outside the post office with a worn black leather Bible in her hands.

"Certainly. Aubrey, will you please excuse us?" Although confused, Rachel had the presence of mind to pardon herself and lead Mrs. Steele to a wooden bench on the building's porch.

"This was my husband's Bible. After you left the other day, I opened it to Proverbs, the book you said told you to come and speak with me. I started reading it, and I discovered some pretty awful things about myself. This book talks about there being a right way to do things and a wrong way. I can't say I've done much right in my lifetime. Did you know God despises gossip? It's one of the seven *deadly* sins! Can you believe that? Right up there with hands that shed innocent blood! I had no idea." Gretchen's face wore a pained expression. "Anyway, I think it's me who owes *you* the apology. I have had a lying tongue and a 'heart that deviseth wicked imaginations.'"

Listening to Mrs. Steele's confession, Rachel was filled with the grace of God. She was so appreciative that the Lord had allowed Gretchen Steele to recognize her sin and that He had given her the grace to want to do something about it.

"Would you like to have God's forgiveness?" Rachel inquired softly.

Gretchen's eyes pleaded before she said, "Yes."

"Let's pray then, shall we?" The two women bowed their heads. "Dear Heavenly Father, we thank You for the opportunity to come before You and ask You for Your forgiveness, made possible by the blood shed by Your Son, Jesus." Rachel grasped Gretchen's hand and said gently, "Repeat after me, if you feel led: Dear heavenly Father, I ask for the forgiveness of my sins and that Your Son would come to dwell within me." Rachel led Gretchen in the prayer of her life, and she followed willingly and joyfully. The two of them sat for the rest of the afternoon on the bench, excitedly discussing their histories and plans for the future.

☙

Time was running out for Henry and Chase Dylan's weekly meetings together. Henry would be moving in one month. Chase had decided tonight was the night he would talk to the boy about salvation and God's plan for his life.

When he reached the Steele home, he was surprised to find Gretchen at home, quilting by herself over the large, wooden frame in the parlor. "I thought the quilting circle was at Mrs. Davenport's house tonight."

"It is, but I'm not planning to attend any more of those. I don't find them edifying, and I'm afraid they cause me to be tempted to gossip."

Chase was bewildered by the open and honest comment, and sat down to avoid falling over. He stared directly at Gretchen's face, hoping for a hint as to the change in her. *No, it couldn't be,* he thought. But still he had to ask, "Gretchen, is something different about you?"

"I believe so. I've asked Jesus to be my Savior, and I've been truly convicted over the behavior of my tongue," Gretchen admitted openly.

"Gretchen, I'm so proud that you have the courage to recognize your sin."

"Unfortunately, it's been very difficult for me. I thought asking Jesus into my heart would solve the problem, but I'm tempted constantly; it's a daily struggle. I hate to entertain this fact, but I just relish a good piece of gossip! So, I've had to avoid the situations that enable me to be a part it. That includes meeting at the general store and my beloved quilting parties."

"Gretchen, congratulations; that's a big step. You're learning that being in the will of God is a constant effort that requires staying in His Word and lots of prayer. Some days are just easier than others, but never fear, the Lord will bring you new interests." Chase stood and smiled down upon her.

"Miss Phillips is partly responsible for this, you know," Gretchen said softly.

"Rachel?"

"She's the one who confronted me about my tongue. Actually, she came to apologize to me, which was convicting in itself. I just recognized something different in her, a peace I wanted a part of. A few days later I asked her about it, and lo and behold, I ended up praying with her."

Chase was anxious to hear more of Rachel's part in Gretchen's conversion, and the two carried on in a rapid-paced discussion until Henry came into the room.

"Hi, Mr. Dylan. What are we doing tonight?"

Chase was now more eager than ever to share God's Word with Henry. He patted him gently on the back and said, "Tonight, we're going to learn about the Light of the World."

"You mean Jesus?" Henry asked confidently.

"Yes, Henry, I do. How did you know that Jesus was called the Light of the World?"

"Miss Phillips told us in school, then she asked if we wanted to ask Jesus into our hearts. I told her I knew all about Jesus from my time with you, and that I did want to ask Him in."

Chase rejoiced in the knowledge that his promise had finally been kept, but inwardly he felt a tinge of regret that it had not been him who had prayed with Henry. "My my, Miss Phillips has certainly been busy lately." Chase smiled broadly at the thought of his beloved Rachel, his beautiful, evangelizing Rachel.

Chapter 20

Spring came early to Searsville, and the season warmed in late March. The big rains had never come, and only the disappearing evening chill and afternoon fog marked the end of winter. The freshness of spring was both exhilarating and blissful for Rachel, who relished the year-round sunshine, but took special pleasure in the continuous warmth.

Rachel had offered a reading club at the schoolhouse on several Saturday afternoons, and she'd been surprised at the consistent attendance by Veronica Smith. The two had become close while discussing various books and their themes. Rachel delighted in the maturity she saw in the young woman, and the two began spending Saturday afternoons together, regardless of the club's meetings.

"Maria, I was planning to visit Jeremiah with Veronica out at Dylan Mills this afternoon. Might I take Seth with me? It would give you the chance to rest, and maybe Robert a chance to ride Bess for a bit." Rachel's voice was pleading; she had seen how simple chores exhausted her pregnant friend, now a few weeks past her expected delivery time.

Rachel tried not to sound too anxious, but secretly she was praying she'd be able to take Seth. She hadn't told Chase Dylan she'd be coming with Veronica Smith, and although she was eager that she might see him, she was also fearful of how forward it might appear. She thought back to when he had invited her to the mill for an educational tour and took solace that she might use the invitation as an excuse, should he see her there.

Maria had been so tired lately. Rachel tried as often as she could to take Seth out and give Maria a break, but it didn't seem nearly enough.

"Dylan Mills? How are you getting there?" Maria asked.

"Veronica's borrowing her mother's buggy. We'll probably be gone for three hours or so."

"That would be wonderful. I could certainly stand to rest my eyes for a few moments at least." Maria went to the entryway and fetched Seth's black wool coat. "Now, you'll be sure Seth keeps his coat on when you get into the trees? And you'll keep him away from the saws? As if I need to ask. . ."

"Absolutely." Rachel smiled, inwardly relieved Maria had allowed her to do this favor. Maria constantly gave of herself, rarely giving a thought to her own needs. At times, it made Rachel feel quite unnecessary. Although Rachel knew that thought would be just as troubling to Maria's gentle heart.

"Seth?" Maria called her son from his bedroom.

"Yes?" Seth answered, in perfect English.

"Miss Rachel is going to Portola Valley in the buggy. Would you like to go with her?" Maria awkwardly bent over her stomach to speak to her son.

"Yes, yes!" Seth jumped up and down and dashed into his mother's arms for a good-bye kiss.

"There's your answer, Rachel," Maria said, while fitting Seth into his boots.

"Wonderful, we'll have a dandy time. Seth, let's start up the path. Mrs. Smith is going to fetch us soon." Rachel grasped his hand, leading him outdoors. Once outside, the energetic boy burst into a sprint and stayed twenty feet ahead of his companion, yet never out of her sight.

Soon the slow, familiar *clip-clop, clip-clop* could be heard, becoming louder until a small black buggy came into view. Veronica pulled slightly on the reins and the graceful chestnut horse came to a stop.

"Seth is coming with us. I hope you don't mind." Rachel lifted the boy into the trap next to the young Mrs. Smith and climbed in after him.

"No, Jeremiah loves children; he'll enjoy seeing Seth." Veronica handed Seth an unattached strap of the reins and told the boy to pull. As he did so, Veronica snapped the bridle, yelling "Yaw," and the buggy started with a jolt. The sensation was exhilarating, for it had been a long time since Rachel had been in any type of carriage.

The threesome rode for about an hour before coming to the wooded canyon that was home to Chase Dylan. The mere thought that this was his home sent a chill through Rachel. Secretly, she hoped he would be here today but knew chances were good that he was in Redwood. The threesome hopped from the buggy and tied the horse to a post near the wooden building that housed the mill.

"There's Jeremiah. You just wait here and I'll come back for you in a minute." Rachel and Seth stood in a hollow, pine needle-strewn valley between two forested hills. To their right was a large, black iron boiler that bubbled and sputtered, its noise deafening as they walked closer. This was the lifeblood of the process. Rachel knew from her study of the industry that without the boiler to run the saws, the milling operation would cease. She watched the machinery inquisitively. The shouts of men could be heard over the ear-piercing shrill of the saw, and Rachel found herself wondering if Chase might be the one speaking.

To their left in the distance was a large, raised platform with a ladder leading to the huge wooden tub that stored precious water for the area. Rachel looked up at the equipment with healthy respect. The machinery made her feel so small and helpless. Above them, Veronica and Jeremiah disappeared into the mill, motioning that they would return soon. Rachel knew they probably needed their privacy and walked about the valley floor with Seth, pointing out the different birds and wildlife present in the trees.

Chase casually emerged from his upper mill, and Rachel felt a rush at the sight of him. Suddenly, an odd gurgling sound caught her attention, and she saw Chase's eyes focus on the boiler. Rachel knew the boilers were precarious machinery, often in danger of exploding. An explosion would send tons of metal shards into the air, killing anyone within their reach, and here, possibly igniting a forest fire as well. Gazing down at Seth and once again at Chase, she knew by the terror in the mill owner's expression that her fears were not unfounded. The boiler was readying to explode. Possibly she had a few minutes, but more than likely she had one at best.

Chase pointed to the ridge above the mill valley floor and yelled something. Rachel didn't wait for confirmation; she grabbed Seth and ran for the hillside. She tripped in her haste, and the two fell in a bundled heap, rolling down the grade they'd just climbed. She clawed her way to her feet again, holding her skirt in one hand and never relinquishing Seth with the other. The boiler's whistling scream became thunderously loud, and Rachel trembled as she sought refuge behind a great redwood on the ridge. Seth remained silent in fear.

The boiler sputtered and shook, and Rachel looked on in horror as

Chase cleared the mill, sending his sawyers up the shallower hillside near the buildings. She closed her eyes in prayer when he returned alone to the wooden structure. Unable to keep her eyes shut, she opened them and witnessed Chase running toward the water shed with a large ax. Panting with dread, Rachel watched as he struggled up the hillside. Once he reached the ladder at the shed's base, he expertly manipulated it with his free hand, landing on the plank that surrounded the structure. *Oh Lord, please,* Rachel prayed again.

Chase began hacking away at the wooden water shed, and soon a trickle appeared in its side. He cut away more wood and the flow increased to a wide gush. He struck three more blows before the rush threatened to bring the storage shed from its perch. Striking one last blow, he made his break for the back of the board landing, jumping feverishly for the remote hill below him. The water shed lurched and plummeted toward the ground, releasing an explosive flood of water.

Chase landed on his feet upon the grade and fell backward, his momentum carrying him down the mountainside toward the surge of rushing water. He seized a roughened redwood root and held on for dear life, his body finally coming under his own control, stopping just above his manmade stream.

"Chase!" Rachel screamed. But she knew her voice could not be heard over the thunderous noise that echoed throughout the valley.

Slowly, gingerly, Chase crawled for higher ground. Once on a flat area, he turned to watch his actions take their intended effect. Seeing he was safe, Rachel also turned toward the boiler. The water hit the boiler with a great splash, extinguishing the fire beneath it, accompanied by a powerful eruption of steam. The black beast rumbled and vibrated until a large crack appeared in its base, and water trickled from the breach. Finally, the pressure proving too great, the boiler crumbled into a pile of useless metal debris.

Rachel watched what happened with tragic recognition. Years of Chase's work building his beloved sawmill had vanished within a few minutes, but she silently thanked the Lord that the boiler had been the day's only casualty. As soon as she saw the danger was over, Rachel picked up Seth and ran breathlessly along the hillside toward Chase.

"Chase?" Rachel stood above him a muddied mess, her hair bedraggled and Seth clutching tightly to her skirt.

Rachel!" Chase jumped to his feet and took her desperately into his arms. Chase's rugged hands cupped her face, lifting it sweetly toward him. Rachel gazed up expectantly, and he kissed her passionately. He pulled away, looking again into her hopeful expression, and kissed her once again.

"Chase, I'm so sorry. . .the boiler," Rachel said, her heart broken over his damaged logging operation.

"There will be other boilers. I'm just so thankful no one was hurt, especially you and Seth. How did you know to run?"

"I can't explain it. I simply saw something in your face that warned me, and when you pointed, I just knew. Something just made me grab Seth and run."

"You were so brave, I'm so proud of you. Most women would have frozen with fear, waiting to be rescued, but you were so capable. I'm amazed by you more with each passing day." His words were an encouragement to her. "I've been such a coward, Rachel. I can't fix the moment I fell in love with you, but there was some depth to my feelings the day I spied your independent spirit in Redwood. I've harbored my feelings long enough for the sake of the town's gossips. I know now that was a mistake. Trying to protect you, I only hurt you more. Can you ever forgive me?" Not waiting for an answer, he continued. "I adore you Rachel Phillips, and I want you to be my wife as soon as I can have you."

Rachel's heart overflowed; she had longed to hear these words from Chase Dylan, yet never expected them. She closed her eyes wistfully and embraced the words carefully. She opened her eyes again, half expecting the figure before her to be a dream. Rachel stared eagerly into his eyes, unable to speak.

"Rachel, maybe I didn't make myself clear." He bent down before her on one knee, and Seth watched him questioningly. "I'm asking you to be my wife."

Rachel answered in a slow whisper, "I would like nothing more than to be your wife, Mr. Dylan." Her mind stirred in a dozen directions as she gazed into the handsome face: Whom would she tell first? How might she most quickly get word to her mother? Would she continue to teach? It was all so much to think about, but somehow, none of it really mattered.

Chase rose to his feet and once again gathered her into his arms. They held each other tightly, until Seth yanked violently on Rachel's skirt. The young boy pointed into the ravine at the line of sawyers mourning the lost boiler. Chase, holding Rachel close in his arms, happily shouted, "We'll replace it! I'm getting married!"

A roar of shouts went through the valley, but the men stood in confusion. Respect for their boss caused genuine happiness for his wedding plans, but concern for their jobs remained an issue. Chase shouted again, "Full pay until it's fixed. Now leave that mess alone until it's cooled."

The roar flared up again, and the men began eagerly kicking the smaller iron pieces, trying to reassemble order as quickly as possible. Chase picked up Seth and took Rachel's hand, leading them down the hillside toward the mill.

❧

Chase escorted Rachel, Veronica, and Seth to Searsville personally. He insisted upon it since the accident had kept them late in the forest. He dropped off Veronica first, vowing to return soon with her family's buggy. Seth slept quietly between the engaged couple, within the slow-moving trap which rounded the dusty path to the familiar lake.

"Rachel, I've been waiting for the gossip to subside so that I might court you properly. I'm sorry we never had that opportunity."

Rachel shook her head. "It doesn't matter, Chase. That's all behind us now." Chase pulled the reins on the horse and the animal stopped alongside the lake near Mrs. Hopper's home. He jumped from the rig and, after laying Seth down on the seat, helped Rachel down. His arm reached around her and Rachel cuddled into his great chest. The moon above cast a glittering blue shadow upon the water, and the moment seemed perfect.

"Do you still love the lake?" he asked.

"More than ever."

"That's good, because this is your property we're standing on." Chase smiled broadly.

"What?" Rachel asked incredulously, pulling away to look into his face.

"I bought it after hearing about your little visit with Gretchen. I knew that must be a sign from God that you were meant for me, and

310

it was time I did something about it. Since I have no mill to worry about at present, I figure my sawyers can start building our house right away."

"But Chase—"

"I figured you'd want to continue teaching, right?" Rachel nodded her head, unsure of what to think. "So we'll need a house in town, and Gretchen's is far too formal for my tastes. Jeremiah and Veronica will be letting it until they can afford to buy it from her."

Chase had taken care of everything. "I love you, Chase."

"I love you, too, Rachel."

Chapter 21

Rachel arrived home to find Maria in labor and Robert pacing frantically. "Where have you been?" His voice was angry.

"I'm sorry, Robert, it's my fault," Chase declared.

"Go get Doc Winter, right now! We're going to have a baby!"

Rachel rushed to the bedroom and found Maria biting on a pillow to silence her screams. She held the mother's hand and calmed her while they waited for the doctor to arrive. Rachel went into every detail of the long, full day, trying to help Maria concentrate on something but the pain. Doc Winter arrived in record time, and Rachel stayed throughout the entire ordeal, encouraging her friend.

After having a healthy baby girl, Maria slept throughout the rest of Saturday, and the entire morning on Sunday. Rachel stayed with her, tirelessly making sure she was comfortable and that the baby was well taken care of, while Robert spent his time looking after Seth.

When the proud mother finally awoke, Rachel was by her side. "Oh Maria, I believe she's the most beautiful girl I've ever laid eyes upon. I think it's a good thing her daddy works with tools and metals. That ought to keep those sawyers at bay. Well, for a little while anyway."

The two friends smiled at each other knowingly. They had seen so many prayers answered over the last year and took solace in the fact that God had provided for their every need. Even when it hadn't seemed that way.

"I'm still looking forward to the day when I can't see any remnant of your tiny little waist," Maria joked, her face still drawn.

"Before you go making any plans about my disappearing waist, I was hoping I might wear your wedding gown. I noticed it in your closet when I was getting your night clothes." Rachel's voice was tentative. She wasn't sure if her friend would mind sharing such a sentimental piece of her personal history.

"Oh Rachel, I would love for you to wear it! The lace was imported from Spain and my mother sewed the entire dress by hand. Nothing would give me greater pleasure than to watch you be married in it. Not until the day that my precious Elena might wear it." Maria cuddled her daughter close to her, and her cheeks streamed with tears.

☙

Late Sunday afternoon came sooner than the courage Chase Dylan would need to share his marriage plans with Gretchen Steele. His gait was purposeful and determined as he approached the forbidding home. He mumbled as he walked in the cool evening air, practicing what he would say to Gretchen and Henry Steele about his upcoming marriage plans. Although their relationship had changed a great deal within the last week, he was still concerned about how the widow would react to his happy news.

Much to his surprise, Gretchen answered the door before he knocked, and he was captured completely off guard. She wore a wide smile, and with outstretched arms came rushing toward him, hugging him tightly. "Chase, congratulations. Rachel will make an absolutely beautiful bride, not to mention a godly wife."

Chase's mouth dropped, and he was stunned speechless. Gretchen laughed at his reaction. "I'm sorry to steal your thunder, but I must inform you the whole town knows. Maria had a baby girl yesterday and told Doc Winter. I'm afraid Doc Winter's wife struggles with the same problem I do. But it was such happy news; you couldn't really expect to keep it to yourselves for too long, now could you?"

Chase laughed out loud, "No, I suppose not."

"I'm making a wedding quilt for you, started a few weeks ago. I think it's some of my best work."

Chase was truly moved by the gesture. "Wait a minute; you say you started a few weeks ago, but how could you have known?"

"Chase Dylan, I've known you for years. What do you think, I'm blind? I saw the way you looked at Rachel Phillips. It was the same way my Harold looked at me. I knew it was only a matter of time."

"Gretchen, thank you," Chase said sincerely, and Henry appeared on the staircase landing.

"I told you Miss Phillips was pretty, Mr. Dylan. Remember? A long time ago by the lake."

"Yes, I do, Henry. It seems this family is very attentive." The threesome moved into the kitchen to partake of a rhubarb pie that Gretchen had prepared. They sat in a cheerful circle happily discussing the wedding plans.

"It's not too late, if you've changed your mind about the move. Jeremiah and Veronica can make other arrangements, if need be."

"No, we leave at the end of the month," Gretchen said softly.

"But, I thought you might have worked everything out that. . ."

"Chase, the Bible says, 'Slothfulness casteth into a deep sleep; and an idle soul shall suffer hunger'; I think that's been part of my problem here in Searsville. I shall be busy in Redwood with my new job and I'll have less time to concentrate on meaningless things. I don't think it will solve my problems, but I do think it will help. I've prayed a lot about it and I feel this is God's will for our lives right now."

Chase just nodded. He knew his friend had reached a place of peace in her life and knew he needn't worry.

⁂

The following Monday morning, Rachel arrived at the schoolhouse exhausted from tending the new baby. She had been tempted to cancel class, but knew the children would have traveled far and their parents wouldn't be expecting them home for hours. Soon she would have a husband and a house to call her own, and the very thought made her giddy and gave her the energy she needed to get up for work. Before her class arrived, Rachel heard a faint knock at the closed door. She rose to open it and nearly fainted at the sight of her mother, stepfather, and baby brother.

"Mother!" Rachel gasped, flying into her mother's outstretched arms. "Mother, what are you all doing here?" She pulled away from her and opened her eyes wide, trying to make sure once again she wasn't dreaming.

"I think you have to ask your stepfather about that." Marshall Winsome handed Georgie to his big sister, and Rachel playfully lifted him into the air, enjoying the gurgling smile that spoke back to her.

"Georgie, you've gotten so big!" Rachel declared. She gazed at her stepfather in a quandary. His face was decidedly different; he looked older since she'd seen him last, although it had only been a little more than six months. And she thought his face appeared kinder, less serious.

"Rachel, it's so good to see you, my dear." Rachel cowered as he came closer, afraid his gentleness had an ulterior motive. He resisted moving forward and explained his uncivil past actions toward her. "Rachel, when you and your mother came to live with me, I thought you needed to learn how to survive in California on your own. After all, if you work

314

hard and have a bit of luck, California is a land of opportunity. I thought you needed to learn, but I realize now I was wrong about that." Rachel unwillingly fell against the wall behind her, with Georgie still cooing. "I thought by finishing your education, you would be able to live the life of your choice, but I had lost sight of the fact that you had just lost your father. I came along and, in some sense, took your mother away, too. It's not what I meant to do, you understand, but it happened just that way. I'm hoping you can find it in your heart to forgive me."

Rachel looked at the burly man standing before her. She had carried so much animosity in her mind over this man, even following the letter to her mother asking for his forgiveness, but now he seemed shattered, vulnerable, and repentant, his apology sincere. She couldn't very well hang on to her anger. His genuineness wouldn't allow for it, and when she looked into her mother's eager eyes, she knew forgiveness was the only answer.

"Of course I forgive you, Marshall. If it weren't for you, I would never have met Chase Dylan." Rachel's eyes sparkled with mischief as she mentioned the name casually, looking away from her mother, who giggled with delight.

"Sounds like you two need some time alone. I'll head back to the hotel while you get reacquainted."

"Chase Dylan, and who might that be?" her mother questioned excitedly. She took her daughter by the arm and they sat for a private conversation, Georgie happily babbling at his big sister.

Epilogue

A little to the left," Rachel directed. "Right there. That's perfect." Chase hammered the nail into the wall and placed Rachel's beloved lake painting over their newly finished mantel. He stepped back and the two admired their work together. Rachel looked lovingly into her husband's clear, bluish-green eyes. Her heart was overjoyed at the memory of sharing her wedding day with friends and family. It all appeared too wonderful to be true. But as she peered at Chase's Bible, lying open upon their new kitchen table, she knew God's goodness and faithfulness were indeed true.

Kristin Billerbeck is a bestselling, Christy-nominated author of over forty-five novels. Her work has been featured in *The New York Times* and on "The Today Show." Kristin is a fourth-generation Californian and a proud mother of four. She lives in the Silicon Valley and enjoys good handbags, hiking, and reading.

If You Liked This Book, You'll Also Like...

The Carpenter's Inheritance by Laurie Alice Eakes
You'll enjoy this gripping historical romance between an upstart female lawyer and her client, a carpenter with a questionable past. When faced with a choice, will Lucinda Bell choose career over love? Also includes a bonus story, *A Love So Tender* by Tracey V. Bateman.
Paperback / 978-1-60742-580-9 / $9.99

The House on Windridge by Tracie Peterson
Romance readers will be enthralled with this historical romance set in Kansas from bestselling author Tracie Peterson. Jessica takes her son and returns to the ranch where she was born, but alone in the world, she worries about whom she can trust. Also includes a bonus story, *Lucy's Quilt* by Joyce Livingston.
Paperback / 978-1-63409-778-9 / $9.99

Love's Betrayal by DiAnn Mills
Enjoy a riveting historical romance between a patriot and a redcoat when Delight is forced to nurse a British soldier in her home. Can she trust him when he switches sides? Also includes a bonus story, *Faithful Traitor* by Jill Stengl.
Paperback / 978-1-63409-779-6 / $9.99